Books By Rick Bentsen

The Blademaster Chronicles
The Blademaster
Willowdale
** The Age of Darkness

The Chronicles of Xarin
The Crucible

The Audra MacAllister Files
** Midnight Revenge

Gamma Strike
* Dawn of a New Age
The Dawning of a New Age

* Out of Print
** Forthcoming

THE DAWNING OF A NEW AGE

By Rick Bentsen

Steel Drake Press
Taunton

The Dawning of a New Age
Book 1: Gamma Strke

Cover image © Philcold | Dreamstime.com

First Print Edition

For information, contact the author at
rickbentsen@rickbentsen.com

www.rickbentsen.com
www.facebook.com/RickBentsenAuthor

This is a work of fiction. Names, characters, places and incidences are the product of the author's imagination. Any resemblance to actual locales or people or events is purely coincidental unless otherwise noted in the acknowledgements.

ISBN: 0692560173
ISBN-13: 978-0692560174

Foreward

September 11, 2015

What a ride it has been!

Fourteen years ago, my first novel, Dawn of a New Age, was released. It was a simple little science fiction novel. What was published was my first draft. I did not get the time I needed in order to really go through a second time and edit the book so it would be the way I wanted it to be. And for fourteen years, I just let it be.

In the meantime, I released The Blademaster and Willowdale, the first two books in my epic Blademaster Chronicles. I learned a lot about my craft by writing those two books. They helped me figure out the way to truly weave a story together.

And now, I am getting the chance to redo my first book.

Last month, we pulled the original version of Dawn of a New Age. It's out of print. That was a bittersweet moment for me. You see, it was my first book. My baby. And I had been telling myself that it wasn't good enough and needed to be redone. For years, I have wanted to rerelease the book, but I wasn't sure how to go about doing it.

Now I have the opportunity to bring Gamma Strike home to my press where the rest of my books are. And in doing so, I am getting the opportunity to redo the book.

So what you are holding in your hand, wheter the print version or the Kindle version, is a full retelling of the story that launched my writing career fourteen years ago. The story is the same story as it was in the original book, but there are a lot of additions. I've made a lot of much needed changes. And I think that the story is a lot better for it.

I've also included not one, but two whole brand new short stories, The Wedding and Blitzkrieg. These stories fill in a little bit of the back story. But only a little bit. There will be other stories that tell more of the back story, I am sure. But I hope you enjoy this little look behind the curtain.

[v]

I want to thank each of you for being on this wild ride with me. I could not do it without any of you. Here's too many more years of great books!

Next year, I hope to finally release the sequel to this novel. That book, called THE WINDS OF CHANGE, has been percolating in my mind for fourteen years, and while I don't know for sure that it will come out in 2016, I am hopeful. Keep an eye on my Facebook page for more information on THE WINDS OF CHANGE when such information becomes available.

Also, in 2016, the Star League Defense Force will launch. The SLDF is a fan organization for fans of the Gamma Strike books. Membership will be free. When information is available on the launching of the SLDF, that information will be released on my Facebook page as well.

Keep the faith!
Rick Bentsen

Rick Bentsen

Acknowledgements

I can hear it now. "Oh, goodness me, the author is about to blather on and on about who did what to help him... Do we really have to read this?" First of all, I love the word blather and I now firmly promise to use the word far more often.

Second, no, you don't have to read this. But I would be remiss if I did not include my thanks. So, yes. Feel free to skip this section, but I shall now blather (told you I would use the word more often) on about Team Rick Bentsen and all they've done.

First of all, thanks to God for the gifts that make the writing possible. A little bit of imagination goes a long way, it would seem.

To my parents, who have been arranging many in person appearances for me to sign and sell my books. It has been a very interesting journey over the past several months, but I have enjoyed every bit of it.

To my brother who gave me a great deal of constructive criticism on *Dawn of a New Age* and gave it to me again when I was finally ready to hear it.

To my continuity expert and editor, Joanna, for everything she does.

To my readers, because without you, there would be no point to doing this. I love each and every one of you.

Finally to K'Alan, K'Itea, Mario, and the rest of the crazy cast of characters in Gamma Strike. Fourteen years ago, I first tried to tell your story. And I didn't do it right. But you gave me another chance and have stuck with me. Thank you for letting me tell your story to the world.

The Dawning of a New Age

.

Rick Bentsen

For my parents and my brother
for believing in me when I needed
it the most. And when I didn't always
quite believe in myself.

The Dawning of a New Age

Rick Bentsen

THE DAWNING OF A NEW AGE

A GAMMA STRIKE NOVEL

Chapters

The Dawning of a New Age

CHRONOLOGY

A brief timeline of events leading up to the events of *The Dawning of a New Age:*

2003-2010: World War III on Earth. After a series of terrorist attacks, the United States of America declares war on Iraq and Afghanistan. By 2003, most of the world has joined the conflict on one side or the other. Over the next 7 years, both sides would use devastating biological, chemical and nuclear weapons causing vast casualties and destruction. Although the side led by the United States would end up the victorious side, the death toll on both sides was far too high for either side to truly celebrate a victory.

2010: Founding of New United Nations on Earth. In an effort to keep the mistakes that led to the devastating World War III from happening again, the New United Nations is founded. Over the next two years, every country on the Earth would sign on giving the people of the Earth their very first planetary government.

2011: First long distance space mission by Duterius Prime.

2014: Duterians visit Earth. After receiving a transmission from Earth, a small contingent of Duterians land on Earth to introduce themselves to the Terran people. This first contact with another planet goes peacefully for the Terrans.

2015: First long distance space mission by Earth. With help from their Duterian friends, Terrans build a ship capable of long distance space travel.

2018: First long distance space mission by Jarada V.

2030: A ship from Jarada V encounters the Brentax Empire for the first time. This contact was not a peaceful contact, and the Brentax Empire is logged as a race to avoid in the future.

2036: The Duterians and the Terrans formalize their friendship into an alliance, forming the Star League. The headquarters for this new organization is located just outside of Falls Church, VA in what used to be the United States on Earth. The Star League is tasked with trying to keep the peace in this part of the galaxy. The Star League Defense Force is founded a year later.

2042: Jarada V joins the Star League becoming the third of the six core races of the Star League.

2047: Angelia joins the Star League becoming the fourth of the six core races of the Star League.

2054: Selvius joins the Star League becoming the fifth of the six core races of the Star League.

2059: Sandaria joins the Star League becoming the final core race to join the Star League.

2087: A small colony ship crewed by Jaradans lands on the third planet in the Khrinnus System. A small, but hardy, colony is founded. The colony grows and thrives over the next 20 years.

2096: The Brentax Empire lands a small colony ship on the other side of Khrinnus III as the Jaradan colony. Not knowing that the planet is already inhabited, the Brentax colonists form a colony of their own.

2106: A survey team from the Brentax colony encounters the Jaradan colony on the other side of the planet. A conflict quickly ensues over ownership of the planet. Not long after, the Brentax Empire declares war on the Star League over the Khrinnus System.

The Dawning of a New Age

⟨ PROLOGUE ⟩

THE alarm woke him with a start.

The man had not meant to fall asleep while watching events on the monitor, but he had. It was an inexcusable lapse in concentration for the man, especially since he would have yelled at any of the others if they had committed such a lapse.

Now fully alert, he immediately turned his attention back to the monitor he was sitting in front of. Looking at the data that was scrolling across the screen, he smiled. He nodded once, knowing that what he was seeing was what they had been waiting for, and shut the monitor down.

He left his quarters and went in search of the others. He knew that, based on what he'd just seen, the events that they had long been waiting for were upon them.

There were twelve of them. They had been watching and waiting for over a hundred years, ever since the Eldest One had told them of what was to come. The Eldest One had spoken of a great war to come. The twelve of them were not enough to turn the tide of the war. But the Watchers were never supposed to be the ones fighting the war according to the Eldest One.

They simply had to find the ones that were supposed to and direct them.

As he walked down the hallway to where he would find his wife, he ran into the Watchers' engineer.

"Is the holosphere working, Martin?" he asked the engineer.

"Aye, Alan. It should be working now," the other man nodded.

"Good," the one called Alan smiled. "Assemble the others in the Central Chamber."

"Is it time?"

"Indeed," Alan nodded. "Our long watch is, at last, coming to an end."

The Central Chamber was dimly lit. The only light came from the soft glow given off by the large holosphere floating in the center of the room. The holosphere was not actively broadcasting but it was ready to broadcast at any time. The glow from the holosphere, however, was not nearly bright enough to fully penetrate the darkness shrouding the chamber. For years, the Central Chamber had been home to the Watchers' Council, allowing them to watch for the coming of the those prophesied by the Eldest One.

A soft bell sounded throughout the complex. Footfalls and the quiet rustling of velvet against velvet broke the tranquility of the Central Chamber. Two by two, a ring of twelve white lights winked on overhead, shining down in a circle around the softly glowing holosphere. Each light illuminated a figure wearing dark grey robes. Each figure wore a dark grey crushed velvet hood which obscured their faces and made it difficult to distinguish one from another. Indeed, it was even difficult to distinguish whether the individual figures were male or female.

"Are we all here?" one of the figures asked in a soft yet strong male voice. He was easily distinguishable from the others as he wore an ornate golden medallion about his neck. Quiet murmurs of assent from the rest of the figures answered him. "Then let us begin."

The first figure gestured to the person to his right, indicating that she should speak.

"My friends," the indicated woman began as she pulled her hood back. Long curly red hair bounced lightly as it was freed from being under the hood. "The time we have long been waiting for has finally arrived."

"How can you be so sure, Samantha?" another of the figures asked as he too lowered his hood. His hair was close cropped and graying slightly at the temples. He had hawk-like features that were dominated by his hazel eyes. "We've thought that before."

"Events have begun to follow those prophesied by Argus when we began this journey," Samantha retorted, crossing her arms across her chest as she did so.

"Samantha is correct," the first figure said, his soft voice cracking like a whip and silencing the others. "The ones we have been waiting for are about to enter play."

"They are not ready, Alan," the hawk-faced man protested, frowning. The frown only served to sharpen his features even more. His gruff and gravelly voice seemed out of place in the tranquility the Central Chamber seemed to always offer.

"They will be, John," the one called Alan assured the other. "They are, after all, the key to our success."

"So you keep telling us, Alan," another female in the circle grunted. Unlike Samantha and John, she kept her hood up, keeping her face hidden from the others. "Only time will tell if these are the ones we are looking for."

"Yes," Alan nodded, a soft rustling sound coming from the velvet of his robes. "Time will tell. Martin, start the holosphere so we can watch what is to happen."

One of the figures waved his hand in front of the holosphere. The soft glow turned into a gray haze. After a few moments, the haze cleared and the twelve Watchers observed in silence as a new scene unfolded before them in the holosphere...

The Dawning of a New Age

⟨CHAPTER 1⟩

1.30.2136
0813
Gamma Epsilon Station
Soran's Bar

COMMANDER K'Alan Ilan Bryce leaned back in his chair and took a sip of his Duterian Sunmist. He chuckled softly as he looked over to the person who shared his table.

"You know, Mario," K'Alan started. He gently put his glass on the table. He leaned forward again as he continued. "I keep telling myself I'm never going to come back to this place. And yet every time I get transferred, this is where I end up. Here at this table, you and I end up having a drink and playing cards while I wait to go aboard my new ship. Every time."

"I know," Mario laughed. He knocked back a long gulp of his drink. "I think Soran saves this table just for us. Lord knows we've been here often enough."

K'Alan picked his drink back up and took another sip. He looked around the bar. The walls were dark with small

[23]

twinkling lights designed to appear as if the view from the windows extended around the entire room. Small square tables were scattered about the room. Each table was illuminated from inside by either a soft blue or red light. Along one wall, a long polished oak bar stretched the entire length of the room. Soran, the bartender and owner of the bar, stood behind the bar chatting amicably with a woman in a Star League uniform. Her back was to him, so K'Alan had no idea who she was, although the long green hair hinted that she was likely a Jaradan.

"You know, this place hasn't changed much since we first came through here fifteen years ago," K'Alan noted as he returned his glance to his companion.

"And if we live another fifteen years, Soran's Bar still won't have changed," Mario grinned. He raised his glass in a salute of agreement.

K'Alan tipped his own glass back in a salute. He reached over to a pocket on his left sleeve and pulled out a deck of round playing cards. Mario's grin broadened slightly when he saw the cards.

"So, since we usually play cards while we wait to go aboard our new ships, how about a quick game of poker?" K'Alan asked as he started shuffling the cards.

"Yeah," Mario chuckled. "I was wondering if you had a deck on you."

"Mario, when don't I have a deck with me?" K'Alan asked as he offered the deck to Mario for a cut.

"Good point," Mario chuckled again as he cut the deck. "Deal the cards, Kal." He watched as K'Alan dealt out five cards to each of them. He picked up his cards and looked them over, frowning slightly. "So, what have you heard about our new commanding officer?"

"Little bits here and there," K'Alan said as he looked at his own cards. He tossed three of his cards into the center of the table. "I've heard that she's tough as nails and cold as ice."

"Well, hold your tongue, 'cause here she comes," Mario whispered, inclining his head slightly to indicate the

[24]

direction the captain was coming from. He tossed in four of his own cards, and K'Alan replaced the cards they'd both discarded before looking where Mario was indicating.

When he saw who it was that was coming their way, he almost dropped his cards. It was the Jaradan woman he'd seen talking to Soran, but what really surprised him was that he recognized her. He hadn't recognized her name when he'd received his new orders, but now that he saw her face, he knew he should have. Her long dark green hair was combed back and worn just past her shoulders. Her eyes were emeralds and her smooth skin was olive in complexion. She wore a standard Star League duty uniform consisting of black pants, tunic and boots. Like the uniforms that K'Alan and Mario were wearing, her uniform had teal colored piping running down the middle of the front of the tunic and in four stripes running diagonally from about where her belly button would be to her left shoulder. The teal colored stripes designated her as a command officer. As expected, her rank insignia identified her as a captain.

Although he was surprised to see her, he managed to cover his surprise before she noticed. He was pretty sure however, that Mario had noticed. The slight wry smile on Mario's face confirmed it. He knew that in time he'd have to tell Mario that he knew the Captain from the Academy, but he really didn't want to deal with that just yet.

"Commander,' Captain Thala Ker'sal said as she reached the table where the two friends were sitting. Her voice fairly dripped ice. "It's so nice to see you again."

"The pleasure's all mine," K'Alan said, his voice cracking slightly. He forced a smile as he looked at his new commanding officer.

"I'm sure," Thala snorted. She gave him another harsh glare before turning her attention to Mario. "Colonel Bonetti, I understand you wanted to speak to me?"

"Yes, Captain," Mario nodded, sighing softly. He put his glass on the table and laid his cards face down next to it, knowing he'd need his full concentration for the task at

[25]

hand. He always hated when he had to go up the chain of command to get what he needed, but it was sometimes necessary. This was one of those times. "See, I'm having some problems with your security chief, and I was hoping that if I spoke with you, we could clear up this problem quickly and quietly."

"And what is the nature of this problem, Mr. Bonetti?" Thala asked. She crossed her arms and glared at Mario through have closed eyes. She made a point of completely ignoring K'Alan, something not lost on the Duterian officer.

"Well," Mario said after a moment's hesitation. "She won't let my personal weapons collection on board."

Thala raised an eyebrow, in surprise, clearly not expecting that from Mario. "And why in the name of the Lords of Jarada would a morale officer need to bring a personal weapons collection on board my ship?"

"Well," Mario said, idly swirling his drink in its glass. "I've been collecting these weapons for over twenty years, and I'm an expert in each one of them. I used to teach their use to the ground forces in each of my assignments. I've also been known to go on a ground mission or two, and my weapons have saved more than a few lives in the past. Besides. I wouldn't exactly feel comfortable on this assignment without them. And if the morale officer ain't comfy..." He trailed off, letting that last statement hang in midair. He knew it would have the intended affect.

"Very well," Thala sighed, rolling her eyes dramatically. "You have my permission to bring your weapons collection on board. If Masha gives you any further problems, have her come see me."

"Thank you, Captain," Mario smiled and saluted. He took another sip of his drink and picked up his cards.

"Commander Bryce, my office in one hour," Thala said as she turned to look directly at K'Alan.

"Yes, ma'am," K'Alan barked out, fighting the urge to gulp in desperation.

Thala turned on her heel after giving K'Alan one last glare. She strode over to talk to a young woman in another

[26]

part of the bar. Mario whistled and shook his head as he watched her go then looked over at his friend.

"You are so screwed," Mario grinned as he tossed his hand in the center of the table. "What's the deal with you and the Ice Bitch over there?"

"Oh, just don't ask. Just don't go there, Mario. All I know is that this is going to be one very long and strange tour of duty." He picked up the cards from the table and pocketed them again. "And just what did you mean by used to teach? You stopped? Such a shame."

"Kal, you should have been on my last assignment," Mario shook his head. He drained the last of his drink and waved the waiter over for a refill. "The captain didn't believe in his troops learning what he considered primitive weaponry."

"So what happened?" K'Alan took a sup of his drink and leaned forward in rapt fascination.

"A whole platoon of ground troops got sent down to this one planet. Something in the atmosphere wreaked havoc with the plasma rifles. So, since the platoon didn't have any backup weapons, not one member of the platoon had a working weapon. They fought bravely, but the whole platoon got slaughtered. The captain, who'd insisted on going down on the planet with the platoon was captured. I ended up going in with my "primitive weaponry" and saving his butt. That's when they gave me my gold bars," Mario explained, proudly fingering his new rank insignia.

"Yeah," K'Alan nodded. "I noticed you got promoted. Congrats, by the way."

"Thanks," Mario grinned.

"So," K'Alan continued after taking another sip of his drink. "What happened to the Captain?"

"Court-martialed for stupidity and losing a whole platoon of troops as a result of said stupidity," Mario laughed. The waiter came back with the refill of Mario's drink. Mario smiled and took a sip before asking the burning question he'd been wanting to ask all morning. "Heard anything from Kit lately?

[27]

K'Alan took a long sip from his drink and sighed deeply before answering. "I haven't talked to her in over two months. We'd been on silent running for a long time before my transfer to the White Knight. And with the transfer, I've just been running ragged. I'm going to call her before we leave."

"Don't forget to say hi for me," Mario said, tossing off another of his famous grins.

"Sure enough," K'Alan laughed. "Except she doesn't much like you."

"Everyone loves me!" Mario said, sounding wounded. "I'm just that kind of loveable guy, you know?"

"Yeah. Sure you are," K'Alan grinned, nodding with his friend. "And you don't have an ego problem either, right?"

Mario laughed long and hard. Yes, it was definitely going to be good serving on the same ship as his friend again.

"Hey," Mario started suddenly, a thought occurring to him out of nowhere. "Stop by my quarters later. I have something for you."

"I hope it's a stiff drink," K'Alan muttered tapping his glass idly. "I have a feeling I'm going to need one after I talk to the Captain. Listen, I've got a couple things I need to do before I go see her, so I'll see you later, buddy."

K'Alan gulped back the last of his drink and stood. He smiled at Mario, clapped him on the shoulder, gave him a wink and strode out of the bar.

"I don't believe it!" Mario groaned as he watched K'Alan go. "He stiffed me with the bill again!"

1.30.2136
0847
Gamma Epsilon Station
Another Part of Soran's Bar

Three girls sat at a table in a corner of the bar. Each of the three girls were nursing a root beer and they were all watching their friend who was making her way towards their table.

"About time you showed up, Sarah," Kim Chellman grumped as Sarah arrived at the table. She crossed her arms and looked up at her friend. "I thought we agreed to meet here at 8 this morning."

"Sorry," Sarah shrugged as she sat down. The waiter came over and placed a root beer in front of her. "But guess what?"

"What?" Kim asked, uncrossing her arms and taking another sip of her root beer.

"I just talked to Captain Ker'sal. That's why I'm so late," the very excited Sarah grinned. She took a swallow of her root beer before continuing. "Mmm. Great root beer as always! Anyway, Captain Ker'sal told me that I was just assigned to the SLS White Knight as the Chief Engineer."

"Like, shyeah, right," another one of the girls at the table spat out the mouthful of root beer that she'd just sipped. "And I'm the next person to be named a squad leader. Sarah, get real."

"You haven't even been through the Academy," the third girl snorted, shaking her head in disbelief. "And you're too young to serve in the Defense Force anyway. So how do you expect us to take you seriously?"

"Besides, how could you get such a cushy job anyway. You're a hermit!" Kim teased. She took another sip of her root beer and sneered at Sarah.

"I designed the ship," Sarah said, matter of factly. She lifted her chin in a proudly defiant manner.

"SHYEAH!" all three of the girls said in perfect unison. They all looked at Sarah with complete disbelief, and Kim, the spokesman of the group, continued with a note of scorn in her voice. "Like that would ever happen."

"I'm serious, guys!" Sarah pouted. She tossed a datapad on the table and slid it across to Kim. Kim picked it up and looked at it with a raised eyebrow. "You remember that ship I was designing last year? Well, they built it, and they want me on board as the Chief Engineer since I know the ship better than anyone else."

Before any of the girls could respond, Mario made his way over to the girls table. He looked at the four girls with an appraising look and tossed off one of his famous winning smiles.

"Would one of you lovely ladies be a young woman by the name of Sarah Hodge?" he asked as he turned a chair around and straddled it.

"That would be me, sir," Sarah smiled. She waved to the Colonel.

"There's no need to sir me, Ensign," Mario chuckled. He extended his hand in a friendly greeting. "I'm not an officer and I don't much stand on formality anyway. Nice to meet you."

"Pleasure's all mine, Colonel," Sara grinned, taking his hand in a surprisingly firm handshake.

"I understand you're our new Chief Engineer," Mario said conversationally as he took his hand back. He tapped his finger against his glass thoughtfully.

"Aye, Colonel," Sarah nodded. "I was just informed of that."

"Well, it'll be a pleasure to serve with you." Mario took a sip of his drink. "Make sure you're on the White Knight before she leaves in just under six hours. I'd hate to see such a pretty young thing as you left behind just because you weren't on board on time."

"I'll be at my station in four hours, Colonel," Sarah assured Mario. Her smile broadened until it filled her entire face.

"Lower Pylon Five, Ensign," Mario said as he stood. He tossed back the rest of his drink. He gave the girls a wink and another one of his winning smiles before turning on his heel and leaving the bar.

The girls all watched Mario go with the general awe that he tended to generate in women. Sarah turned to the other three girls with a triumphant look on her face.

"So," she grinned broadly at them. "Do you know who that was?"

"Wow!" was all they could say at first. They all looked at her with an open-mouthed expression of awe.

"I guess you weren't pulling our legs after all, Sarah!" Kim said, shaking her head in complete disbelief. "Sorry we doubted you. Congratulations! Have fun!"

"Oh, I'm pretty sure I will," Sarah beamed as she finished her root beer. She stood and stretched. "I should go get ready to ship out."

The three girls watched Sarah go, looks of shock registering on their faces.

1.30.2136
0921
SLS White Knight
Captain Thala Ker'sal's office.

K'Alan Bryce stood quietly before Thala's desk. He'd been standing there for a couple minutes, waiting for her to acknowledge him. Even though he was standing at attention, he was fidgeting nervously. The captain did make him that uncomfortable.

"You wanted to see me, Captain?" he said quietly.

The captain looked up and leaned back in her chair. She looked K'Alan over and motioned to the chair across the desk from where she was sitting.

"Have a seat, Commander," she said, equally as softly as he'd spoken.

"Captain," K'Alan started without moving. "If you have a problem with me..."

"If I had a problem with you, Commander," Thala interrupted K'Alan. She placed the pen she was holding on the desk and steepled her fingers. She stared at the commander over her long steepled finger. "I would not have requested you as my executive officer."

"But the way that you..."

[31]

"My personal feelings for you have absolutely no relevance," Thala interrupted again. She leaned back in her chair and tugged on the bottom of her uniform tunic. "All I can and will tell you is that I would much rather have you as my exec than any of the other equally and suitably qualified candidates for the position. Is that clear, Commander?"

"As crystal, ma'am," K'Alan said sharply, an almost imperceptible nod the only motion he made in acknowledgement of her words.

"Good. Now take a seat before you break," she smiled.

It was the first smile he could remember ever seeing from her. It was enough for him to lower his guard slightly. But only slightly. He took the offered seat, turned it around and straddled it, leaving the chair back between himself and the Captain. It allowed him a slight amount of comfort to have the safety net.

"So," K'Alan asked, his voice rock solid despite how nervous he was still feeling. "What did you want to speak to me about, Captain?"

"I have some things to go over with you," Thala said. She picked up a datapad and glanced at it. "First of all, our Mr. Bonetti. Do you trust him?"

"Mario?" K'Alan laughed. it was a strained laugh but a laugh nonetheless. Thala nodded. K'Alan sighed and rubbed his chin before continuing. "Well, I've known Mario about fifteen years. We've served together a couple times. To be honest, I'd rather have him on some of the hell hole missions we're likely going to get than almost any of the highly trained ground troops we've been assigned. And yes, I've gone over the records of our ground troops. He's a hell of a pilot too. Almost as good as me." The last was said with a touch of pride in both his and Mario's piloting abilities.

"Good," Thala nodded. She laid the datapad back down on the desk. "He's your responsibility. I'm afraid he was pushed on me by his father. I don't much like having my teams picked for me."

[32]

"Captain, if I may," K'Alan began. He was a bit amused by the fact that Mario had to be pushed on Thala. But he refused to let his amusement show. "I know Admiral Bonetti. He and Mario don't see eye to eye on a lot of things. The admiral was none too pleased when Mario decided to go career enlisted. He was the first of his family to refuse to take the officer's exam. He still gets offered it every year, and he turns it down every time. If Admiral Bonetti did request Mario be assigned to this unit, then he must have had a very good reason."

"Be that as it may," Thala shrugged. "I still don't like it any."

"Trust me," K'Alan smiled. "Mario will grow on you in time."

"We'll see." Thala flicked her glance back to the datapad then to the computer screen on her desk. "Commander, are you rated to fly combat missions?"

"My personnel jacket should have told you that I was a squadron leader on my last two assignments," K'Alan noted.

"Good," "Thala smiled. She made an entry on her computer. "I'm assigning you as my strike leader."

"I want Mario as my wingman," K'Alan said simply.

That brought Thala's raptor gaze back up to meet K'Alan's gaze, telling him that his comment had had the desired effect. "Is he combat rated? I know you mentioned he was a good pilot, but I don't remember ever hearing he was combat rated."

"He was first in his class at the Academy," K'Alan shrugged. He stroked the cleft on his nose thoughtfully before continuing. "I once saw him fly between two Brentax Kovat class light cruisers without a scratch. The two cruisers... Well, they weren't so lucky."

"Whatever. It's your neck," Thala shrugged. She slid a datapad across the desk to K'Alan. You've been given the best pilots. I want you to be tough and consistent in your leadership. It's your responsibility to make sure we have the best fighting team we can possibly expect to have."

[33]

"What do we have for fighters and pilots?" K'Alan asked as he picked up the datapad and looked over the data.

"7 Starhawks and 56 Starfires," Thala responded as she checked the stats on her terminal. "And a full complement of 70 combat rated pilots, including yourself and Mr. Bonetti."

"All right," K'Alan nodded as he looked over the list of pilots. "I think the best way to do this would be to have 7 squads of 10 pilots each. One Starhawk and 8 Starfires per squadron. Squad leaders and their wings assigned to the Starhawks. I'll draw up the squadron rosters and have them to you within the hour."

"Good," Thala nodded. She glanced at the datapad again before continuing. "I'm sure you're wondering what our first mission is."

"Of course I have," K'Alan nodded. He slipped the datapad with the pilot information into a pocket of his uniform.

"So have I."

"You mean you haven't been given our orders yet?" K'Alan furrowed his brow.

"SLDF Command in their infinite wisdom has decided to give us a couple days shakedown time before giving us our first assignment." There was a touch of disdain in her voice, implying that she didn't agree that they needed the extra shakedown time.

"Great," K'Alan said with a rueful smile. "Just what I've always wanted. More time to sit around and worry."

"I wouldn't worry too much," Thala chuckled. "This will just give us a chance to make sure everything is fully functional on board. Not like we haven't already tested everything three times already."

"Always a good thing," K'Alan nodded, chuckling softly. "Is there anything else, Captain?"

"There's one other thing that's bothering me." Thala pulled up a schematic of the White Knight and turned the computer screen around so that K'Alan could see what she was talking about. "That blank area near the back of the ship. I have no idea what it is."

"Interesting," K'Alan muttered. He quickly scrolled through the schematics. As he looked the schematics over, he noted exactly how much of the ship was taken up by this strange blank area. "Why not just go check it out? That's a large part of the ship, almost half the total area!"

"I can't go check it out," Thala shrugged as she turned the computer screen back to face her. "Only two people are currently allowed access to that area: Admiral Bonetti and Ensign Hodge."

"Very strange indeed," K'Alan said, frowning. "What do you suppose is in there?"

Thala closed the computer screen and shrugged again. "I have no idea. I don't much like secrets on my ship."

"Well, I'm sure we'll find out what that section is for sooner or later," K'Alan shrugged, an almost perfect imitation of Thala's.

Thala came around the desk and sat down on the edge of the desk closest to K'Alan. She looked deep into his eyes. "I want you to know that this will work out fine, K'Alan." Her voice was soft and almost comforting.

K'Alan returned her gaze and held her gaze for several long seconds. "You still don't like me very much from our time at the Academy, do you?"

"If you only knew, Commander," Thala snapped as she jumped back to her feet. K'Alan could swear the temperature in the office dropped by thirty degrees. "Dismissed."

"Yes, ma'am," K'Alan barked. He wasted no time in leaving Thala's office.

* * *

K'Alan couldn't help himself. He just had to laugh when he entered Mario's quarters. All of his belongings, except his weapons collection of course, were already in all their proper places. But it looked like someone had inadvertantly put the armory in the morale officer's quarters by mistake. There were weapons everywhere, covering everything. That is, where there was room for them to cover everything. Mario's quarters were the standard size for someone on the command staff, but it looked like he was trying to maximize every inch of space in the quarters. A series of shelves in the main living area housed his collection of twentieth century memorabilia, including his most prized twentieth century possessions, a portable CD player complete with headphones and a stack of Billy Joel CDs. There were weapons hangers all over the walls, but most of them were empty as Mario tried to decide which weapons went where.

As K'Alan was looking around the main living area, Mario came out from the bedroom carrying a wicked looking spear in one hand. Mario's usually carefully combed hair was slightly disheveled, bordering on completely messy. His hazel eyes darted around the room, trying to decide what weapons should go where. The front of Mario's uniform tunic was open, showing the white undershirt the Colonel was wearing underneath. He smiled at K'Alan when he saw his friend.

"You know, Kal," Mario motioned for the Duterian to come further into the room. "There's definitely one major problem with transfers."

"What's that, Mario?" K'Alan asked, an amused expression on his face.

Mario spread his arms indicating the mass of weapons everywhere. "My weapons collection is getting too damn big! I ask you. Where am I going to store all these weapons? There is a definite lack of wall space here!"

"I'm sure you'll manage," K'Alan laughed. He picked his way carefully across the room. "I don't suppose you have that drink?"

"Nope. I haven't gotten any drinks in here yet," Mario shrugged. He put the spear into one of the weapons holders. "Is that straight?"

"Yeah," K'Alan lied.

"So," Mario asked as he turned back to K'Alan. He cleared off a chair and offered it to his friend. "What did the old battle ax want?"

"How would you like to be my wingman?" K'Alan said as he took the offered chair. He was barely able to keep a straight face.

"She's putting you in a fighter?" Mario asked with a raised eyebrow. He picked up a pair of blasters and looked for a suitable place to put them.

"A Starhawk even," K'Alan said. This time, he wasn't able to keep the smile off his face.

"Sweet deal." The blasters found themselves in weapons hangers on the wall across from the spear. "How did you manage that?"

"She made me strike leader," K'Alan mumbled.

Mario stopped and looked at his friend. "I'm sorry, bud. I didn't quite hear that. What did you say?"

"I said," K'Alan said, much louder this time. "She made me strike leader."

"Oh, that's a good one," Mario roared with laughter. When he'd composed himself, he started to pick up another weapon, then he turned back to the wall to find a place for it to go.

"Well," K'Alan shrugged. He picked up a wicked looking dagger and turned it over in his hands. "At least she doesn't hate me."

"She say as much?" Mario asked. He put he weapon he was holding in another weapons holder and turned back to K'Alan.

[37]

"Yeah, but I just don't know." K'Alan tossed the dagger lightly to Mario.

Mario caught the dagger by the hilt and put it in a holder near the spear. He started searching through the piles of weapons for something specific. "Listen, Kal. I missed your last birthday, so I want to give you your birthday present now if that's all right with you?"

"Sure," K'Alan laughed as he watched his friend. "You know me. I never turn down a present."

"Well, if I can find it, it's yours," Mario said. He continued digging through the piles of weapons. After a few moments of Mario's frantic searching, a pile of weapons toppled over, revealing the specific item Mario was looking for. He picked it up and offered it to K'Alan hilt first. "Ah, here it is! Forged from the same meteor as Wildfire."

K'Alan took the offered blade and examined it closely. It was a fine blade, crafted by one of the finest Spanish blacksmiths to what would have been K'Alan's exact specifications if he'd had the blade made himself. It was a thirty inch long blade that was sharp enough to split a hair. The hilt was made of steel inlaid with gold. It was crafted to depict two dragons interlocked in battle; the wings of the dragons formed the hand guard. It was perfectly balanced and surprisingly light. And the hilt felt extremely comfortable in his hand.

"Nice," K'Alan whistled as he looked the blade over. "Think the Ice Bitch will let me wear it?"

"The beauty of it is that she has no choice," Mario grinned. "It's in the regs."

"Thanks, buddy," K'Alan said as he stood up. He saluted Mario with the sword then attached the scabbard to his belt. "I have to go call Kit. I'll see you at the briefing later on."

"Sure thing," Mario grinned as he grabbed another weapon to try to find a home for it. "Later, Kal."

* * *

[38]

1.30.2136
1029
SLS White Knight
Captain Thala Ker'sal's office.

Jewel Kazin, Thala's long time friend and confidante, sat in the chair across the desk from Thala where K'Alan had sat facing down the captain not long before. Her dark green hair, dark almost to the point of being black, was pulled back into a ponytail. She sat with one leg dangling over the arm of the chair, rhythmically moving her foot to a beat only she could hear. Her deep blue eyes, an exceedingly rare eye color for a Jaradan, were locked with Thala's emerald eyes, and she decided that she didn't much like what she saw there.

"You're worried, aren't you, Thala." It was not a question so much as a statement of fact. She watched for a reaction in the other woman's face, and was not surprised to see none at all.

"You've known me a long time, Jewel," Thala sighed deeply. She closed her eyes and turned away from the other woman. "You know how I feel about a certain person under my command."

"I also know you cannot have him," Jewel reminded the captain. The rhythmic moving of her foot stopped to emphasize her point.

"If he weren't married..."

"If he weren't married, you still wouldn't be able to have him," Jewel interrupted testily. She turned her body and placed both feet on the floor. "You know that as well as I."

"Yes, I know. I suppose I'm just destined to love him without being loved back. How lonely," Thala grunted. She opened her eyes and looked at Jewel with a sad expression.

"That's not the only problem, is it, Thala?" Jewel asked after studying her friend for a few moments. Sometimes it amazed Thala how well Jewel knew her.

[39]

"I've been having the nightmares again," Thala frowned. She sighed again and shook her head. "Every night for the past two weeks."

"I thought they had stopped," Jewel frowned.

"No," Thala groaned. "They never really stopped. And I feel like I'm going to be seeing him again very soon."

"Who?" Jewel asked. She recrossed her legs and pulled her tunic down a little.

"The creature in my dreams," Thala sighed. She closed her eyes again and gently rubbed her temples.

"Are you sure?" Jewel cocked her head to the side and looked at her friend with a concerned look.

Thala's eyes snapped open. She slammed her hands against the desk and stood up. She began to slowly pace, each step punctuating her words. "That's just it, Jewel. I'm not so sure of anything anymore. Hell, I'm not even sure I'm the right person to be commanding this ship." She whirled around and locked her eyes with Jewel's. "And that doesn't leave this office, Lieutenant."

"I understand. Captain, I hate to do this to you. Especially so close to launch time," Jewel said. She stood up and returned Thala's steady gaze. "I want you to come by sickbay for a full physical and psychological workup. And you can't tell me no. This is official doctor's orders."

"It'll have to be right now then," Thala grumbled unhappily "We're due to launch soon and I still have quite a bit of work to do before we do."

Then I'd suggest you accompany me to the sickbay now, Captain," Jewel said. She motioned for Thala to head out of the office first.

1.30.2136
1147
SLS White Knight
The Bridge

K'Alan walked onto the bridge for the first time and stopped. He looked around at all the activity and whistled softly to himself. The bridge was fairly large, and it spanned two levels. He noticed he was on the upper level. The upper level was a ring of stations surrounding a vast opening. Around the wall of the upper level were engineering and tactical stations as well as the main communications station. The captain and executive officer stations were on opposite sides of the ring, jutting out into the open area just slightly and facing each other. There was a steel railing around the opening to prevent people from falling over into the lower level. Looking down to the lower level, K'Alan could see the helm and navigations station, as well as more engineering, tactical and operations stations. Everywhere he looked was a bustle of activity.

"Can I help you, Commander?" a slender woman asked from the nearby communications station. Her curly auburn hair bounced around as she moved.

"Lieutenant Commander Yeuid, is it?" he asked, still in awe of the bridge. He tore himself away from the bustle of activity to focus on the young woman. He extended his hand in a friendly greeting.

"Yes, sir," she grinned taking his hand in a surprisingly firm grip. "Katherine Yeuid. But you can call me Kath."

"K'Alan Bryce," K'Alan returned the grin. He took back his hand. "You can call me whatever you like, so long as you don't call me too late for dinner." He chuckled softly at his own little joke.

"That a line, sir?" Kath asked, raising a carefully manicured eyebrow in a slightly confused expression.

"I'm married, Kath," K'Alan laughed. He waggled the finger with his wedding ring for emphasis. "Seriously though, call me Kal. Everyone else does. Well, everyone except the captain that is."

"All right then. Kal, it is," Kath smiled broadly. "Now. What can I do for you?"

K'Alan headed over to his station and looked over the board, noting new controls he hadn't seen on a command board before. After a few moments, he turned back to Kath. "I need a comm channel open to Duterius Prime."

"I'm going to need a little something more specific than that, Kal," Kath laughed as she headed back to her station. "Duterius Prime's a big planet you know."

"I know," K'Alan laughed also. It was a good feeling to be able to just laugh with other members of the bridge crew. Especially since he knew there'd be no laughing with the Captain. "I grew up there. I need a channel opened up to the High Gentlewoman."

"Consider it done," Kath smiled as she set to work patching the call through.

"Patch it through to the conference room, please," K'Alan nodded. He took one last look around the bridge. He shook his head in disbelief and awe. Then he turned around and headed off the bridge.

1.30.2136
1152
SLS White Knight
Medbay

Jewel frowned deeply and shook her head as she draped her stethoscope around her neck. She made a quick entry into the computer, saved Thala's file and then walked over to the bed where Thala was sitting. She chuckled slightly to herself when she saw Thala fidgeting with the hem of her hospital gown.

"Well, Captain," Jewel began. She dropped Thala's chart onto the bed and crossed her arms. "Here's the scoop. I can't find anything wrong with you physically or psychologically."

"So I'm healthy and sane," Thala mumbled. She crossed her arms, unconsciously mimicking Jewel's posture, and grumped. "Good to know."

"I do want to run periodic workups on you to make sure," Jewel picked the chart back up and made a couple notes on it.

"Yes, Jewel," Thala rolled her eyes.

"And I'd strongly suggest that you talk to a counselor about those nightmares," Jewel ordered. Then she smiled, knowing what she was about to say would make Thala fairly happy. "Now go on and get out of here."

"Right. Thanks, Jewel," Thala grunted. She hopped off the bed and put her uniform back on. She nodded to Jewel then headed back up to her office.

1.30.2136
1132
SLS White Knight
Gymnasium 12

The two fencing foils clashed together again and again. Each time they touched, the metallic clang reverberated throughout the gym. After a few quick parries, the smaller of the two fencers parried the other foil aside and thrust his foil into the other fencer's now unprotected middle, scoring a touch.

"Nice steady start, Masha," Mario said as he removed his mask. "But as usual, you got off balance too easily, allowing me to score the easy touch. Try spreading your legs a little further apart. It'll give you a better base and a lower center of gravity."

They'd been fencing for over an hour. Masha Omega had always been one of Mario's favorite pupils over the years, but she'd never really been able to get the hang of fencing. She kept trying very hard, but it wasn't easy for her.

"That's easy for you to say, pretty boy," Masha smirked as she removed her own mask. The large Sandarian tossed the mask at Mario. "You've got those nice spindly legs. I got tree trunks remember? Besides. I got no use for little pointy swords. They just bounce off my body anyway. Now bombs. Those are fun!"

"Bombs are not a finesse weapon," Mario smiled as he picked up Masha's mask and tossed it back to her.

"Swords are. Now just try a little harder and I'm sure you'll get it."

"Mario," Masha chuckled as she caught the mask. "With all due respect, you've been trying to teach me to fight with swords off and on for ten years. I ain't learned yet. What makes you think I can learn now?"

"Because I have the patience of a saint," Mario grinned as he tossed off a salute to Masha with his sword. "Or because this is likely to be a fairly long assignment. Take your pick. Whichever reason you choose, I believe you can do it. Now try again."

"Forget it, but." Masha tossed the mask onto a nearby bench and put her foil on the rack. "I have to go back to my weapons inventory. I'll be really upset if we leave without a full compliment of weapons. And you know how I am when I'm upset."

"Yes, I do," Mario laughed. He put his own foil back on the rack and turned back to his pupil. He gave her a nice long glare. "Which reminds me. Why did you give me such a hard time with my weapons collection? It's saved your butt more times than I can count."

"Call it the fact that I like giving you hell, bud."

She patted him on the back, causing him to stumble. She smiled sweetly then strode off in the direction of the ship's armory.

K'Alan groaned loudly. Every time he called Kit he was invariably put on hold indefinitely. He knew it was first come first served, but sometimes he just hated the holding and waiting. One of these days he was going to have to find a way to let her know it was him calling.

"Your call is being processed to the High Gentlewoman in the order that it was received," the male voice on the recording droned on for the twelfth time. Your call is very important to her and it will be answered as soon as possible. However, it may be some time before..."

"This is the High Gentlewoman of Duterius Prime," Kit's voice floated into the conference lounge. She hadn't bothered to activate the video display, so K'Alan was still watching the Great Seal of Duterius Prime rotating slowly on the screen. She sounded completely bored. *Well*, he thought. *She's about to get some excitement! That's for sure.* "Please state your name and how I may be of service."

K'Alan chuckled softly to himself, knowing it was going to be fun springing this surprise on his beloved. "You know, Kit. If you turned on your video display every once in a while, you might not have to ask that question all the time."

"Kal?" K'Itea Bryce asked. The video flared to life showing Kit in all her regal beauty. Long curly golden hair flowed in waves around her. Bright blue eyes blazed from under thin eyebrows. But her most beautiful feature as far as K'Alan was concerned was the broad smile that broke over her features as soon as she saw who was on the viewscreen. "That really you?"

"Yes, my beloved," K'Alan's grin broadened even further. He reached over and touched her face on the viewscreen. "It is I."

"You have no idea how happy I am to hear from you." K'Itea reached up and placed her hand against K'Alan's on the viewscreen. "I was afraid you'd been killed." Her voice turned to a sad note when she mentioned that she thought he'd been killed.

K'Alan nodded reassuringly. "You'd have known if I'd been killed, Kit." He grinned conspiratorily and gave her a knowing wink. "Besides., you know as well as I do that the Brentax don't have anything that can touch me."

"Don't get cocky," K'Itea smirked. "Anyway, it's been far too long since we've talked."

"Forget talked!" K'Alan chuckled. He took his hand back down off the viewer. "It's been way too long since I've been there to visit you."

"Yes," K'Itea nodded sadly. "Eleven years is way too long a time. I miss you greatly."

"And I miss you," K'Alan sighed. Then he brightened as an idea hit him. "But I'm going to come see you soon. I've got a lot of personal time saved up. I'm sure my new CO will let me take some time off."

"New CO?" An eyebrow raised in surprise. "Did you get transferred again?"

"And promoted," K'Alan grinned, tapping his new rank insignia. "They made me a full commander and made me the executive officer on this tug."

"Congratulations, Kal!" K'Itea smiled broadly at K'Alan. The smile was touched with a hint of sadness, though, although K'Alan didn't recognize it as such. "I am so happy for you."

"There's only one thing that would make this better," K'Alan said, suddenly sounding very sad. "I wish you could be here with me."

"Someday we'll have a chance to travel the stars together, my love," K'Itea said. She smiled again, but this time, there was no trace of the sadness from before. "When do you think you'll be able to take time off?"

K'Alan shrugged and tapped a finger lightly on the table as he thought about his answer. "Not until after our first mission, but I don't really know how long that will be."

"Well, I look forward to seeing you, my beloved," K'Itea said. She looked down for a few moments, as if wrestling with whether or not to say something else. "There is something we need to discuss," she said finally, apparently having decided to just go ahead and say whatever it was that was on her mind. She tapped a few commands on her terminal and sighed again. "But it's something far better discussed in person. I've just sent you an encrypted message. Promise me you won't view it until you're on your way here."

"I promise." He checked his chrono quickly. "Listen, we're due to launch soon, and I still have things I need to do here before I go up to the bridge."

"I understand," K'Itea pouted, obviously wanting to prolong the conversation. "We both have things we need to do. I'll see you soon?"

"Count on it," K'Alan grinned.

"I love you K'Alan Ilan Bryce."

"And I love you now and always, K'Itea Alana Bryce." He kissed the tips of his first two fingers and touched them to her lips. "Commander Bryce out.

1.30.2136
1221
SLS White Knight
Main Engineering

Sarah stood just inside the doorway to her office looking out at Main Engineering. She had an ice cold root beer in her hand. She took a sip as she watched her crew performing final checks in final preparation for departure.

"Any problems, Major?" she asked one of the techs as he walked by.

"No, ma'am," the major grinned. He waved at a display panel nearby for emphasis. "Everything is working just the way you designed it." There was a touch of pride in his voice. He felt the pride Sarah felt in the engines. It was the brotherly pride all engineers feel in their engines.

"Glad to hear it," Sara smiled at the major and took a sip of he root beer. She looked over the display the major had indicate a second time and nodded thoughtfully. She made a small adjustment to the fusion drive and raised an eyebrow at the results.

"What did you just do, Ensign?" a nearby ensign asked as he looked at the display he was working at. "Fusion drive efficiency just jumped two percent."

"I know. I see that. I just made a slight adjustment to the Harstrom couplers," Sarah shrugged as she checked

[47]

over other settings on the display. "It shouldn't have made that big a difference unless something else is out of whack." She turned to the ensign that had asked her about the efficiency jump. "Ensign Scherma, run a level three diagnostic, please."

"Consider it done, Chief," Ensign Scherma nodded. He turned back and got right to work on the diagnostic.

"Bridge to Engineering," Captain Ker'sal's voice came floating in from the intercom.

Sarah took a sip of her root beer then punched the intercom button. "Engineering here."

"Status check," Thala ordered.

"We should be good to go on time, Captain," Sarah said. She looked over Ensign Scherma and nodded. "We're currently running a Level Three diagnostic on the Harstrom couplers. I made an adjustment and it made far too much of a difference in my opinion. I wanted to make sure nothing else was wrong before we got ready to ship out."

"Let me know," Thala responded. "Let's just hope it's nothing serious this close to launch."

"Whatever it is, we'll be able to deal with it down here, Captain," Sarah grinned. She had a great deal of confidence and pride in her team. She looked at the display and waved at Ensign Scherma to get his attention. "We've got a great team down here. Engineering out."

"What do you have, Chief?" Ensign Scherma asked as he came to stand by Sarah's side.

"Look here," Sarah pointed to a readout on one part of the display board. "The neutrino flow is misaligned. No wonder the Harstrom couplers were out of whack."

"I'm on it," Ensign Scherma said as he ran over to another console. "I never would have caught that in my diagnostic, Chief."

"I know," Sarah nodded. "Not your fault that it wouldn't have shown up. I'm just glad we found it."

"And it should be fixed now," Ensign Scherma smiled as he finished making a couple of adjustments. "We should be functioning at pretty close to one hundred percent. now."

[48]

"Good work," Sarah grinned. It was exciting to see her engines working. She'd put a lot of time and energy in their design and now to see them coming alive was like a dream come true. She took a sip of her root beer and punched the intercom button. "Engineering to Bridge."

"This is the bridge," Thala's voice came back. "Report, Ensign."

"We've found and corrected the problem, Captain. There was a slight irregularity in the neutrino flow. It might have caused us some problems, but it's fixed now," Sarah replied. She took another sip of the root beer and looked at the now empty bottle, frowning.

"Good work, Ensign," Thala said approvingly. "To you and your team."

"Thanks, Captain!"

1.30.2136
1457
SLS White Knight
The Bridge

Captain Thala Ker'sal made herself comfortable in her command chair. She looked out over the bridge and watched the bridge crew working at their consoles. It was a good crew, she decided. They would work well together. She allowed herself a satisfied smile at having put together such a good team.

"Take us out, Ms. Barros," Thala said to her Chief Helmsman. She settled further back in her chair and glanced across the upper level of the bridge to K'Alan's station. She frowned at his not being at his station when they were leaving space dock like he should have been. "Nice and slowly, please."

"Aye, Captain," Tyla Barros nodded. "Securing docking clamps. Taking her out." She manipulated controls on her station. The deck shuddered slightly as the ship accelerated away from the Gamma Epsilon station. "We have cleared the Gamma Epsilon station."

"Sorry, I'm late, Captain," K'Alan called as he ran onto the bridge. The sword Mario had given him hung off his left hip within easy reach. "I had a few last minute personal matters to attend to."

"What is that you're wearing, Commander?" Thala asked, pointing at the sword.

"What?" K'Alan frowned, then looked where Thala was pointing. "Oh. Late birthday present."

"What is it doing on your uniform, Commander?" Thala frowned. She hated flippancy. Especially on her bridge.

K'Alan tapped his finger on the hilt of the sword. "Star League Regulation 342.571 paragraph C clearly states that a duly appointed member of the Star League Defense Force may wear on their duty uniform a melee weapon for the purpose of ceremonial or functional use. I assure you that this is a fully functional melee weapon, and I am quite proficient in its use."

"Very well, Commander," Thala groaned, rolling her eyes. "Take your station.

"Aye, Captain," he saluted. K'Alan strode over to his instrument panel and checked it over. He noted with satisfaction that everything on the board was clear and in the green. He nodded to Kath, who was manning her communications station right near his own station.

"How was your call, Kal?" Kath whispered, leaning over so that only K'Alan could hear her.

"Pretty interesting, Kath. Thank you," K'Alan smiled.

"All right, people. This is what we've been waiting for," Thala rubbed her hands together in anticipation. "Let's see what this baby can do. Ms. Barros, take us to the edge of the solar system."

"Aye, Captain," Tyla nodded. She manipulated some controls on her board. Now reading a course of 321 mark 3. Speed: one quarter fusion drive."

Time passed quickly as the ship made its way out of the solar system. The subtle sounds of vibrations and the normal beeps and clicks of the consoles were the only sounds. An hour later, the crew found themselves at the edge of the solar system.

"We're now leaving the Gamma Epsilon System, Captain," Tyla reported without looking up from her helm.

"Status, Commander?" Thala inquired as she looked over at K'Alan.

"All systems reading normal, Captain," K'Alan called out after running another check of his board.

"Good," Thala nodded. She turned to face the navigations officer. "Ms. Silvermaine, set course for—"

"Captain," Kath interrupted from her station. She turned to face the Captain. "Distress call coming in from Duterius Prime."

K'Alan whirled to face Kath, a look of panic on his face. He turned back to his own station and pulled up a copy of the transmission.

"Holo!" Thala barked.

In the open area in the center of the bridge, a holographic image of K'Itea Bryce appeared and began to slowly rotate so that everyone could see her. Even though he'd already seen the transmission, K'Alan had to restrain himself from reacting as she looked as if she were positively panicking.

"This is High Gentlewoman K'Itea Bryce of Duterius Prime requesting assistance from any nearby Star League Defense Force vessel. We are under attack by unknown attackers. I do not know how much longer planetary defenses can hold out."

"Masha, are there any closer ships that can respond?" Thala asked, pointedly ignoring K'Alan's pained expression.

"We're the closest ship, Captain," Masha reported after checking long range scanners.

"Lieutenant Commander Yeuid, open a channel to Duterius Prime," Thala ordered. She stood up to face the holo.

"Channel open, Captain," Kath reported.

[51]

"High Gentlewoman, this is Captain Thala Ker'sal of the SLS White Knight. We have received your distress call and are en route."

"Thank you, Captain," K'Itea said, relief flooding through her voice.

"Captain, may I?" K'Alan asked after going over what little information was provided.

Thala nodded to K'Alan, indicating that he should say what he needed to say. She only hoped that he'd stay professional and not go all mushy on her.

"Kit, can you send us whatever the planetary scanners have been able to record of the attackers?" K'Alan asked. His tone was all business, even though his eyes clearly betrayed how worried he was.

"Kal?" K'Itea's voice registered a pleasant surprise at hearing her husband's voice. It was a comforting sound to her. "Consider it done. Just hurry please!"

The holo fizzled out and K'Alan started going over the data K'Itea had sent.

"Holo disconnected on their end, Captain," Kath reported.

"Ms. Silvermaine," Thala turned back to her navigations officer. She gripped the railing as she looked down to the lower level. "How far away is the nearest jump gate that will take us to Duterius Prime?"

"About ten minutes at maximum fusion drive, Captain," Mara Silvermaine reported after checking what jump gates were in the area.

"Set course and feed it to the helm. Ms. Barros, I want maximum fusion drive immediately," the captain barked out orders fast and furious. "And prepare the jump engines."

"Aye, Captain," Tyla reported. "Maximum fusion drive is ready on your mark."

"Go," Thala nodded. She began drumming her fingers on her chair's armrest impatiently.

"Kit?" Kath whispered as K'Alan stepped over to her station. "You speak so informally to the leader of your people?"

"Only because I'm married to her," K'Alan smiled broadly. He activated the shipcall. "Lancer, Falcon, and Hawk squadrons, scramble and meet in the flight deck in twenty minutes in full flight gear. This is not a drill. I repeat. This is not a drill."

"Jump engines are ready, Captain," Sarah reported from an engineering station.

"Good," Thala nodded tersely.

Minutes ticked by slowly. The bridge crew focused on the task at hand and K'Alan fidgeted nervously. The wait seemed almost forever. Soon the jumpgate loomed ahead of the White Knight, its iridescent gray energy swirling angrily. Thala closed her eyes and took a deep breath, steadying her nerves for the first jump in a new ship.

"Jump!" she ordered.

K'Alan ran off the bridge towards the flight deck as the ship lurched towards the yawning jumpgate.

"ETA to Duterius Prime, Ms. Barros?" Thala asked.

"Thirteen minutes, Captain," Tyla reported.

"Brentax," Thala growled. She punched the armrest for emphasis. "I can feel it."

The Dawning of a New Age

CHAPTER / 2

THE High Gentlewoman of the Duterian people fumed as she watched the monitors show wave after wave of enemy fighters firing on her people.

"What's happening to my planet?" she demanded. She said it softly. So softly, in fact, she doubted anyone heard her.

"K'Itea," S'Era Bryce, K'itea's most trusted advisor came up to her. S'Era was not only her advisor, but she was also the sister of her husband. "The White Knight will be here in 15 minutes."

"I hope that's soon enough, S'Era."

"Excuse me, High Gentlewoman," another aide puffed as he came up to her. This aide was far older than S'Era.

"What is it, J'Anai?"

"Planetary defenses are almost down."

[55]

"Damn," K'Itea swore as the Capitol building rocked with the impact of a proton shell. Dust fell from the ceiling as the room shook.

"We must evacuate to the shelter, K'Itea," S'Era took K'Itea's arm. "It's imperative that you are safe. You are the leader of our people. We need you."

"Yes, of course you're right, S'Era," K'Itea nodded. She looked her sister in law in the eye to make sure she understood how important the next order was. "Make sure Elam gets to the shelter. He's too important to me to lose him. Your brother still doesn't know about him. J'Anai, signal the evacuation then head to the shelter yourself."

"No, my child. I will remain up here and try to maintain the planetary defenses as long as I can," the elderly aide said. Only J'Anai could get away with calling her child. He had trained both her and K'Alan when they were children. In many ways, he was a second father to her.

"May the gods look over you and protect you, old friend," K'Itea said softly as she took his hand.

"And may they protect you as well, High Gentlewoman," J'Anai smiled at her. "I think you shall see your husband very soon."

K'Itea did not have a response to that. She sniffled once and fought back tears. She did not think it would be seemly for her attendants to see her cry. She was the leader of the Duterian people after all.

"Come, K'Itea," S'Era took her friend's arm. "Let's get you to the shelter."

K'Itea took one last look around her command center and sighed. She nodded and led the way to the shelter.

* * *

1/30/2136
1610
SLS White Knight
Launch Bay Alpha

Mario was still zipping up his flight jacket when he ran into the launch bay. He skidded to a halt next to K'Alan and looked at his friend. He could tell from the look on K'Alan's face that whatever was going on was serious.

"What's the drill?" the colonel said. "We never get a drop this quickly.

K;Alan clapped Mario on the shoulder and shook his head. He stepped into the center of the circle of pilots and cleared his throat. This was one of the hardest mission briefings he had ever given.

"As you know, we are on fast approach to Duterius Prime. Some of you, like myself, call it home. The planet is under attack by forces unknown, but we presume Brentax involvement. Planetary defenses are almost down.

"Our primary goal is to repel the attackers. Attack targets of opportunity only after you have driven off the attack force. Falcon and Hawk Squadrons, you are to patrol the entire planet attacking any hostiles. Silver Eagle squadron, we will concentrate on protecting the Capitol City. We hit space in five minutes. Mount up!"

The pilots rushed to their fighters, donning helmets and saying prayers as they did so.

"You're worried about Kit, aren't you?" Mario said, as the two friends climbed into their Starhawk.

"How could I not be? This is an attack against my home, Mario." K'Alan growled as he placed his energy bow in its charger. He looked over at his friend. "Right now, all I can be concerned with is saving my home. I can't let myself worry about Kit."

"It's not gonna be easy, Kal. Look at the situation monitor in the launch bay," Mario pointed at the display. "There sure are a lot of them."

[57]

"I know," K'Alan said. He punched up the weapons display and primed all weapons. "All weapons primed and ready. Comms and scanners are online."

"Engines are online," Mario reported, then added soothingly, "She'll be OK. Kit's a fighter. She'll pull through."

"She better." K'Alan flicked on the comms system. "Strike Leader to bridge. Lancer, Falcon, and Hawk strike wings requesting permission to launch."

"Transferring launch control to fighter wings," Kath called from the bridge. "You may launch when ready."

"Well, she sounds cute," Mario grinned.

"You think she sounds cute, just wait 'til you meet her, buddy," K'Alan laughed.

"Just keep your mind on Kit, old buddy, let me worry about the young cute ones."

K'Alan laughed as he checked his straps and gripped the control yokes. "All fighters launch on my mark." He took a deep breath to steel himself before the g-forces of launch. "MARK!"

He felt the g-forces push him back in his chair as Mario hit the thrusters and they hurtled down the launch tube. Fighters soared out from all of the launch bays and formed up into squadrons. Each squadron formed a pyramid with the squad leader's Starhawk as the capstone. Each squadron located a phalanx of enemy fighters and got to work.

K'Alan took a deep breath and started firing.

1.30.2136
1621
SLS White Knight
The Bridge

Thala scowled in her chair.

"Status report!" she barked.

"Duterius Prime is in flames, Captain," Masha reported coolly from tactical. "Planetary defenses are totally down.

[58]

Our fighters are cutting through the enemy, but there are an awful lot of them out there. I estimate that we'll suffer very heavy casualties."

"How many of them are there, Lieutenant?"

"For every one of our fighters out there, they have five," Masha reported.

"Damn! Kath, open a channel to K'Alan's Starhawk."

"He's on the line, Captain," Kath replied.

"K'Alan, I'm mobilizing three more squadrons to try and help you out a little."

"Much obliged, Captain. Scramble Lancer, Crusader, and Warhammer squadrons."

"Consider it done. They'll be out there helping you within five minutes."

"Thank you, Captain. Bryce out."

"Kath, sound the alert. Masha, try to locate that base ship. I want to know what we're dealing with."

"Aye, Captain."

"Captain, incoming transmission from Duterius Prime," Kath reported.

"Holo."

"No holo available. It's audio only."

"Put it on the line, then."

"Captain Ker'sal, this is J'Anai Sirrus of the Duterian cabinet. I'm not sure how much longer we can—" The commline fizzled to static.

"Kath? What happened?"

"Transmission was cut off at their end, Captain," Kath reported, her tone terse and clipped. "I'm trying to reconnect."

"Captain, the Capitol building just took a direct hit," Masha reported.

"Life signs?" Thala asked, suddenly very concerned.

"Inconclusive. There's too much dust, debris and low-level radiation for the sensor to be accurate on life signs."

"Great," Thala grumbled. "Relay that info to K'Alan. Tell him to make searching the Capitol building for

[59]

survivors a priority when the attackers have been driven off."

1.30.2136
1652
K"Alan's Starhawk

"K'Alan!"

"I see him, Mario. Angle down so I can get a clear shot."

"Hang on to your stomach," Mario called. "This is likely to be a bumpy ride."

K'Alan gritted his teeth and tracked the raider on its strafing run. His thumbs were lightly caressing the firing stubs, just waiting for the shot to line up.

"He's headed for the Capitol Building, Mario. Will you hurry it up, please?"

"Hey, I'm flying this thing as fast as I can.. If you're not happy about how fast I'm flying, you can always get out and push," Mario growled.

"Switching to quad lasers," K'Alan said, ignoring the barb. He flicked a switch on his weapons display.

"You should have a clear shot now, Kal." Mario said softly.

K'Alan grunted as he fired. He kept his finger on the firing button until the raider was reduced to ash.

"Hey, buddy!" Mario called. "You can let up. You got him."

"Yeah, I did," K'Alan said, a tear in his voice. "But we're too late. Look."

"Oh, Lord!"

* * *

Rick Bentsen

1.30.2136
1643
Brentax Duhari class cruiser Torellia Corvax
Bridge

M'Bek Tarmos, Supreme Commander of the Brentax Empire, smiled with sadistic glee as he watched the carnage on the forward view screen.

"Supreme Commander," the weapons officer reported. "The planet is in flames."

"Excellent, T'Marik. And the Capitol City?"

"The Capitol City has been reduced to rubble, Commander," T'Marik said with pride.

M'Bek leaned in his chair and looked at his cold kamarat root tea, and he sent the cup skidding along the floor of the bridge. He looked at the young Brentax female standing by the door.

"Y'Ada, fetch me a new cup of tea, and clean up this mess," M'Bek barked.

"Yes, sir."

Much to his delight, she set right to work cleaning up the spilled tea from the deck.

She might just be my victory celebration, he thought with glee as he watched her.

"Supreme Commander," T'Marik caught his attention. "I have some schematics of the Star League ship for you."

M'Bek sighed, wishing he could watch the young woman finish her work. *Yes,* he thought. *She will definitely share my quarters with me this evening.*

"On screen," he barked.

Images of the White Knight scrolled across the screen along with size and weight statistics. Unfortunately for M'Bek, there wasn't any information about weapons or engine systems, but he would take whatever information he could get.

"So, it's big," he growled. "Why can't I get any more information than that?"

[61]

"The hull is made of an alloy that we've never seen before. Scanners are having trouble locking onto the ship let alone probing it," T'Marik shook his head. "And before you ask, I've tried everything I can, but nothing I try can get through that hull."

"Very well," M'Bek rumbled. When he looked over and noted that Y'Ada had finished scrubbing the floor and was fixing his tea, he growled. "Status of the planet?"

"Planetary surface destruction is ninety-one percent. Eleven percent over the success guidelines for this mission," T'Marik reported proudly.

"Very good. Have our raiders do one more strafing run then have them retreat back to the ship. Tonight, we celebrate the destruction of one of the Star League's homeworlds."

And tonight, Y'Ada, you will be mine, M'Bek thought with glee.

1.30.2136
1650
SLS White Knight
The Bridge

"Where's that base ship, Masha?"

"I haven't been able to locate it yet, Captain. I think it's probable that they're hiding in the asteroid belt near Duterius Six."

"I want them found. Is that clear, Lieutenant?"

"Yes, Captain," Masha said. She checked her scanners again. "Captain, they're retreating."

"Track them. Kath, recall the squadrons. Have them refuel and relaunch to join the search for survivors. Scramble teams to search. Jewel, prepare for heavy casualties."

"Aye, Captain," came the call from medbay. "How heavy are we talking?"

"Call in all off-duty medical personnel. It's likely you'll need all of them."

[62]

"Understood."

"Captain, K'Alan is requesting permission to search the Capitol Building for survivors."

"Acknowledge the request and wish him good luck," Thala sighed.

"Aye, Captain."

"Captain," Masha growled. "The enemy raiders are escaping into the asteroid belt. We are losing sensor contact."

"Let them go, Lieutenant," the captain said after a moment. "As much as I want that ship, our priority is finding and rescuing any survivors."

"Captain," Kath called. "I've got ten search crews ready to launch and begin the search."

"Clear them for launch, Lieutenant Commander."

And good luck, she thought.

1.30.2136
1711
Duterius Prime
Outside the Capitol Building

K'Alan fought back the tears as the fighter landed near the rubble that used to be the Capitol Building. There was no time to let the worry about K'Itea get to him. He had a job to do. Readying himself for the task at hand, he pulled his energy bow off its charger and attached it to his belt. He clipped a couple extra power cells and growled impatiently as he waited for the engines to cycle down and the hatch to open.

"Maybe she wasn't here, Kal," Mario looked over at him.

"She was here. This would be the only place she'd be during a planet-wide emergency."

"Can you still sense her?"

K'Alan closed his eyes and focused on the bond he shared with K'Itea. "Barely," he said after a moment. He hopped out of the fighter. "We've got to hurry. I don't know how long she can hold out."

[63]

"We'll make it, Kal," Mario said softly. "We'll make it."

1.30.2136
1723
SLS White Knight
Medbay

Captain Ker'sal smiled as she walked into the medbay. When she had visited medbay earlier, it had been just her and Jewel, but now there was a bustle of activity, as a full complement of doctors and nurses prepared for the influx of casualties.

"What can I do for you, Captain?" a nurse asked as she hurried by.

"I was just checking on the ready status of medbay."

"We're just about ready," Jewel appeared out of nowhere. "This is probably the best crew I could have hoped for. The only reason it took so long to get ready was that some of the equipment hadn't been unpacked yet."

"Kath reports that the first shuttle of casualties just launched from the planet. That gives you about fifteen minutes before they get on board."

"Understood. We'll be ready."

1.30.2136
1730
Duterius Prime
The Capitol Building

K'Alan and Mario moved along a ruined corridor towards the command center of the Capitol Building.

"Do you know where you're going, Kal?" Mario asked, grunting as he nearly tripped over a pile of rubble.

"Nope. But I figure that this is the best place for us to look."

"I hope that this room is better than the others we've already been through."

"I know what you mean, Mario," K'Alan looked back at his friend.

So far they'd been through about fifteen rooms, but they hadn't found any survivors. Still, K'Alan clung to the belief that Kit was still alive. He could still feel the bond he had with her. As long as he continued to feel that bond, he knew he would move mountains to find her.

They carefully entered the command center. K'Alan almost tripped over a body right as they entered the room. The body, that of an elder Duterian male, groaned, and K'Alan knelt down next to him. Although it had been many years since he had seen the old man, he recognized him immediately, even though the old man's face was a mask of blood.

"J'Anai? J'Anai Sirrus?"

"K'Alan, my boy?" J'Anai asked weakly. "Is that really you?"

"Yes, old friend, it's me. Mario, call for a shuttle. We've got a survivor here."

"Do not waste your energy on saving me, K'Alan," J'Anai rasped. "I don't think I'd survive the journey back to your ship. The council...." J'Anai broke off into a fit of coughing.

"Take it easy, J'Anai. Try to conserve your energy," K'Alan soothed. "Do you know where Kit and the Council of Elders are?"

"In the bunker located through the door behind the throne. Now go. Save them. Leave me to die." Still serving the Duterian people with his last breath, J'Anai Sirrus was no more.

"You're not giving up that easy, J'Anai. You always taught Kit and I never to give up. Don't give up on me now." K'Alan tried in vain to start the old man's heart. Mario put his hand on his friend's shoulder and shook his head.

"K'Alan, he's gone," Mario whispered. "There's nothing you can do for him. We have to go look for Kit."

"You're right, Mario," K'Alan said, slowly getting to his feet. "It's just that J'Anai was so good to Kit and me."

"I know. J'Anai was a good man. But Kit has to be your priority, Kal. She needs you."

The two men slowly made their way to the throne room. Mario looked around, making sure the area was secure while K'Alan looked for the door to the bunker that J'Anai had mentioned.

"K'Alan?" a woman's voice called from the shadows near the throne. A young woman came from the shadows and ran to hug K'Alan.

"S'Era? It's good to see you!"

"Not as good as it is to see you, brother."

"Where's Kit?" K'Alan asked, a sense of urgency in his voice.

"She's in the bunker. She's in bad shape though. You're going to have to hurry."

"As soon as we get a clear picture of the casualties, I'll get a shuttle down here," Mario said.

"S'Era, how many people are down there?"

"Counting me? Thirty-three," she said sadly.

"J'Anai is dead. We found him in the control room."

"He was trying to bring the planetary defenses back online. He wouldn't let anyone drag him to the bunker."

"Take me to Kit, S'Era," K'Alan said, doing his best to hide his fear and worry from his sister.

"Follow me, brother."

S'Era led them behind the throne to a steel door. Mario and K'Alan helped pull the door open. S'Era took the lead with Mario and K'Alan following behind.

"I forgot how pretty your sister is, Kal," Mario grinned.

"Stow it, flyboy. She's still my sister."

They followed S'Era down a long gently sloping passageway to a large concrete room. There was a group of people sitting off to one side and a couple injured people lying around. Kit was lying on her back with her eyes closed. K'Alan walked over and knelt beside his fallen wife.

[66]

He put his hand gently on her face, happy to still feel her warmth.

"Don't touch her!" an angry voice next to him growled. He looked up to see a boy no older than ten staring at him. "I said, don't touch her."

"Elam, that's no way to talk to your father," S'Era admonished.

K'Alan and Mario looked at each other briefly then K'Alan looked at his sister quizzically, a look of shock registering on his face.

"I'm a father?" he said.

The Dawning of a New Age

CHAPTER 3

"CAPTAIN, we're receiving a transmission from Mario Bonetti. They found a bunch of survivors and are requesting a shuttle," Kath called from her station.

"Launch a shuttle immediately. What are their conditions?" Thala asked coolly.

The communications officer listened as Mario relayed the casualty information. "They have one very severe casualty. They are requesting immediate triage for her."

"Who is it?"

"It's the High Gentlewoman, Captain. She is unconscious and looks to have lost a lot of blood. She is as stable as she can be to transport up to the ship, but she will need immediate medical attention."

"Understood. Tell them I'll have Jewel herself take care of her. If you need me, I'll be in the medbay. You have the conn, Kath."

[69]

"Aye, ma'am."

K'Alan looked up as Mario returned to the shelter and headed over to where he was kneeling by K'Itea. He closed the scanner he was looking at and put it back on his belt.

"What's the news, Mario?"

"Kal, they're sending a shuttle down now. Captain said that Jewel will treat Kit immediately," Mario said.

"I've got her stabilized enough to move her out of the shelter," K'Alan grunted, tired from the effort he'd put in to save his wife. "But she's in bad shape. We have to get her up to the White Knight quickly."

"Understood. We'll get her there, buddy." Mario clapped him on the shoulder. He helped K'Alan to his feet, giving his friend a shoulder to lean on.

"All right everyone, listen up," K'Alan shouted. "A shuttle is on its way to bring us all back up to the White Knight. I want a nice orderly exodus from this bunker. The stronger people should help the injured along. We'll all make it through this."

"What about the High Gentlewoman?" a voice called from the back. "She's our only hope."

"Mario and I will personally get her to the shuttle. Once she reaches the White Knight, she will receive care from the Chief Medtech herself."

"Why should we trust you to help her?" the same voice called. "You're not known to any of us. We cannot risk the High Gentlewoman to just anyone."

"He is known to me. You can trust him," S'Era stood next to K'Alan and stared down the voice in the back. "He is my brother. And he is the husband of the High Gentlewoman. And anyone with him can be trusted too."

"Thanks, S'Era," K'Alan said quietly. "Right now, all I want to do is just save as many of our people as we can."

"Let's move on out!" Mario called.

1.30.2136
2215
SLS White Knight
Medbay

K'Alan hobbled into medbay on makeshift crutches ahead of the group of antigrav stretchers and other Duterians. He hobbled over to an empty chair out of the way and sat down. He winced as he landed in the chair.

"What happened to you?" Jewel asked, coming over to him.

"Rockslide. Snapped my shin in half," K'Alan winced as she touched his leg. It's set for now. No need to bother with me for the moment. Take care of the survivors first. I'll still be here when they're all treated."

"All right." She turned away and headed towards the group of stretchers. "Which one is K'Itea Bryce?"

S'Era walked over to the antigrav stretcher that K'Itea was lying on. She put her hand on the woman's shoulder and closed her eyes.

"This is she," S'Era said quietly. She draped her arm around Elam. "The child and I will go to our quarters now. Please notify us when she wakes up."

"And you are?" the doctor asked.

"My sister," K'Alan croaked from where he was sitting. "And do as she asks, please. I have no desire to see S'Era angry."

"Very well, as soon as she wakes, I'll inform you and the Commander."

"Thank you, Doctor," S'Era smiled. She led Elam out of the medbay.

"Doctor, would it be alright if I sat with her when you finished treating her?" K'Alan asked.

[71]

"Of course. I'll let you know. Having her loved ones by her side can only help her recover."

"Thank you. I'll be in my quarters."

1.30.2136
2245
SLS White Knight
K'Alan Bryce's Quarters

K'Alan winced as he turned on the lights in is quarters. He sat down at his vidterminal and flicked it on. He brought up his messages and selected the unread one that K'Itea had sent him earlier that day.

"Decode and display message. Authorization: Bryce-one-one-oh-seven-gamma. Password: Braga."

"Decoding in process," the computer droned. "Estimate display in two minutes."

K'Alan sighed as he waited. He fidgeted nervously as the computer noiselessly set to its task. He drummed his fingers on the edge of his desk. It seemed like it was taking far longer than two minutes to decode the message. Even though he knew what the message was about, he was impatient to get answers to some of his questions.

"Message decoded," the computer announced finally.

"Play."

The screen shimmered and changed to show K'Itea's face. He traced her cheek with his finger and had to fight tears, knowing she was lying in the medbay gravely injured.

"K'Alan, if you're watching this message, then you're obviously on your way to Duterius Prime. Good. I can't wait to see you.

"But there's something that you should know before you get here. Something that neither S'Era nor I have told you until now.

"You have a son.

"His name is Elam Jarron Bryce. He was born ten months after you were here last, eleven years ago.

"I should have told you years ago. But I always felt that this was something best told to you in person. And I didn't want you to leave the Defense Force because of me.

"I hope you're not too mad at me, although I'm afraid Elam might be more mad at you than you are at me. And that's the worst part.

"K'Alan, I love you. I never meant for this to be hidden from you for so long. I hope that you will forgive me.

"I'm sorry, my love. I will talk to you when you land. All my love."

K'Alan shut off the vidterminal and slumped back in his chair, his breath escaping in a huff. The message hadn't answered any questions. Now, he could only wait and get the answers he wanted from K'Itea.

He could only pray that she would awaken.

She was floating in a timeless, spaceless void. Up was down and down was up. She had no idea where she was, nor did she really care. All she knew was that she was cold. Why had K'Alan not come and saved her? Was he even still alive? For that matter, was she even still alive?

All questions pushed themselves out of her head, and she forced herself to stay awake. She tried hard to keep herself calm, but it was not easy, because, as realization of what had happened set in, she became more and more afraid. She remembered ordering everyone to the shelter. She remembered the blast that set the ceiling crumbling, but after that, it was all black.

"K'Alan!" her mind screamed frantically.

It was a sunny day in the middle of the harvest season on Duterius Prime. Two fifteen year old children ran hand in hand across a dijarin field in the Braga Valley province. The boy had a picnic basket, and the girl carried a small blanket. They laughed and ran without any care in the world.

"Kal, I'm so glad we were able to get away today," the girl said to her companion. "I'm not sure I could take another

[73]

day of learning how to become a Gentlewoman. It's so boring."

"I know. J'Anai has been going nuts with both of our lessons lately. I don't think I could take another combat class either. Tell you what. For today, let's forget about all of them. Let's just focus on us."

"Sounds good to me!" Kit said. "I'm hungry!"

The boy laughed as he spread out the blanket and gently laid out the food. They ate and laughed for hours. Eventually, the suns set, and the two children found themselves lying on their backs in each other's arms.

"Someday, I wish I could travel among the stars," Kit said, as the two watched the stars twinkle in the night sky.

"Someday, Kit, we'll travel the stars together," Kal smiled.

"I doubt it," Kit sighed. "Once I become a Gentlewoman, all my hopes of getting off of Duterius Prime for any length of time are gone."

"Have faith, Kit. I believe."

"I hope you're right, Kal."

The two stayed like that for the entire night.

The Great Hall of Braga Valley was full of light from the large windows over looking the gardens. The newly ascended Gentlewoman, K'Itea Alana Bilso, sat on the throne with a bored expression on her face.

"Your Excellency, there are two representatives from the Star League Defense Force here to see you," J'Anai Sirrus said as he entered the main chamber.

"Show them in, J'Anai," she whispered.

"At once, Excellency," he bowed and left.

Moments later, he returned leading two men in uniform. One was wearing a flight helmet, the other, a man wearing the rank insignia of Captain, was not.

"Ensign, I must ask you to remove your flight helmet," K'Itea said. "It is a measure of disrespect for the court to hide one's face in my presence."

"I'm sorry, Kit," K'Alan said as he removed his helmet. "I did not mean to offend. I did mean to surprise you though."

"Kal!" she shrieked as she bolted across the room into his arms. "It's so good to see you!"

"K'Itea Bilso, may I introduce Captain Thane Starlos, my commanding officer. He refused to let me take leave unless he came with me."

"I've always wanted to see Duterius Prime," the captain bowed. "I've head time and again of its endless beauty, and I've wanted to see for myself if what I have heard is true."

"And what do you think, Captain?" K'Itea asked, a light smile playing across her face.

"I think that what certain people have told me about how beautiful this planet is can't come close to the reality of its beauty," Starlos smiled. "It rivals my home planet of Earth as the most beautiful planet I've seen."

"Well, I'm glad you approve," K'Itea smiled. "There is a dinner tonight. I would like you to join us. As a guest of K'Alan, you will be accorded the utmost respect."

"I understand that you two are to be married," Starlos said. "I wish you both the best."

"You are, of course, welcome to attend the wedding," K'Itea smiled. "A friend of K'Alan's is a friend of mine."

"Thank you, good lady. I am honored."

"I think I will take the rest of the day off. J'Anai, see that Captain Starlos is given the best accommodations available. When they have settled in, I think we four shall go on a picnic."

"Would the Gentlewoman allow me the honor of a kiss?" K'Alan said formally, trying hard not to grin.

"Would the Ensign like a boot in the butt for being so formal with me?" K'Itea grinned.

K'Alan smiled and took Kit in his arms. He held her tight and kissed her gently.

"I've missed you so much, Kit," he whispered.

"And I've missed you. Now go get settled. I want to go on a picnic!"

The Great Hall was decorated with all manners of colors and banners. Crowds of well wishers lined both sides of the main aisle and smiled as the two officers walked down the aisle in full dress uniform.

"I've never been to a Duterian wedding before," Captain Starlos noted.

"They're not too much different from an Earth wedding. Well, there are some minor differences, of course. But it's not too different."

"Fair enough."

The two officers stood before the priest. The priest wore long, elegant white robes. He was very plain, his pale skin almost as white as his robes.

"Which one of you is the intended?" he intoned.

"I have that honor," K'Alan said boldly.

"Have you proven yourself?" the priest asked.

"I have walked through fire and flood. I have breathed where no air exists. Through it all, my love remains. I have conquered great giants. I have helped the simple lion. Through it all, my love remains," K'Alan recited. The words came easy to him.

"Then walk where there is light, my child. Take comfort in the one you shall share your life with. Become one with her."

"This I would gladly do," K'Alan bowed.

"I see. Where is this man's betrothed?"

"I am here," K'Itea called from the end of the aisle.

"And has he proven himself to you?"

"He has won my heart with kind words and with fierce battles. He has roped the moon for my chariot and the stars for my steeds. He has built my castle and torn down the mountains that upset my view."

"Then join him here and take comfort in he whom you shall share your life with."

K'Itea walked down the aisle and stood next to K'Alan. She did not look at him. She looked straight at the priest and stood straight, her hands clasped in front of her.

[76]

"These two come before the gods of Duterius to be bonded for life and beyond. They have proven their worth to each other and to the gods. They are about to embark on a journey that only they can go on. Should anyone disapprove of this bonding, speak now or forever hold your peace." The priest waited a few minutes before continuing. *"K'Alan Ilan Bryce, will you honor and protect this woman? Will you walk through fire for her? Will you walk through darkness for her? Will you stay with her through all time?"*

"I will," K'Alan said, looking at the woman he loved.

"K'Itea Alana Bilso, will you honor and obey this man? Will you follow him though fire? Will you follow him through darkness? Will you stay with him through all time?"

"I will," K'Itea smiled.

"Take each other's hand." He waited until they had complied. He took a blue and red scarf from the altar and began to slowly bind their hands together *"Through all time, these two shall be bonded. They shall be able to feel each other across the vastnesses of space and time. They shall be together for all time. This is witnessed by the gods. Let their love be a beacon for all Duterians for years to come. This ceremony is concluded. Go in peace."*

The priest turned around and walked out. K'Alan and K'Itea started towards their quarters when the scene misted out into blackness.

1.31.2136
0012
SLS White Knight
The Medbay

K'Alan hobbled in on his crutches and sat down in a spare chair. Medbay had calmed down quite a bit from when he had been there earlier. The medtechs had cleared out all the casualties. Their work had been good; they'd only lost one patient. So far.

[77]

"Good. You're here, Hopalong," Jewel said as she walked up to where he was sitting. "I was just about to send Security to go get you."

"How is she?" K'Alan asked as he looked over at the closed door to K'Itea's isoroom.

"She's in a coma, K'Alan," Jewel said as she ran the bone fuser over his leg. When she was done fusing his leg, she put the fuser down and sat next to him. "At this point, all we can do is wait. If she wakes up, she'll be ok. But the body is a funny thing. She may just give up."

"I hope she doesn't. I don't know what I would do without her."

"Me too. I promise that I'll do everything I can for her. In reality, though, there isn't much other than keeping her comfortable. She is at a point where she is the only one who can help her."

"You're doing all any of us can ask of you, Doctor," K'Alan flashed a weak smile. "But you need to get some sleep too."

"I know, and I will," Jewel nodded. She patted his leg. "Your leg should be just fine. You'll still have a little pain for a couple days, but you should be just fine."

"I won't be just fine until she's back, Jewel." K'Alan stood and stretched his leg. "Now, I need to go check on my sister and my son."

"Your son?" Jewel asked.

"It's a long story. But that boy that was with my sister was my son."

"I didn't know."

"Neither did I," K'Alan said as he walked out of the medbay.

She was back in the timeless spaceless void.
"Where am I?" K'Itea called to no one.
"You are here," a male voice called.
"I don't think I understand," K'Itea looked around. There was no one that she could see, just darkness.

[78]

"We are here too," the same voice called as two grey robed figures appeared out of nowhere.

"We have been watching," the other figure said. "We know all that has happened."

"What is this place? And why am I here?" K'Itea asked.

"This is here. You are here by accident," the first voice said.

"Well that makes sense," K'Itea snorted.

"You are not alive, yet you are not dead," the second voice said. "You are stuck in the middle."

"How do I get unstuck?" she grumbled.

"You must choose," the first man said.

"So, I choose to live. What's so hard about this?" she asked.

"Why do you choose to live?" the second man asked.

"My son needs me."

"It's funny that you focus on your son, yet your thoughts are only for your husband."

"How..."

"Like we said, we've been watching for a long time," the first man said. "We know quite a bit."

"I'm a little confused," K'Itea said.

"I imagine you are," one of the men said as he lowered his hood. "My name is Alan. We are here to watch. And to help."

"Help with what?" K'Itea furrowed her brow.

"There is a great darkness ahead. This war with the Brentax is only a distraction from the upcoming issues."

"What are you talking about?"

"You will all know soon enough." Alan waved his head in front of her eyes. "You won't remember any of this when you awaken."

"But....." She fell asleep.

* * *

A nurse was checking over the equipment in K'Itea's isoroom. She noted all of K'Itea's current vitals in the chart. The nurse looked sadly at the woman in the bed. Everything that could be done was being done, and the nurse knew it. Still, nurses tended to hurt a little when they saw someone else hurting. But there was nothing else she could do for K'Itea other than just make a note of her condition.

This was one fight that could only be fought by the patient.

The nurse started to turn and leave the room, but she was startled by a noise. She wasn't sure what had brought her up short. She turned back to the bead and frowned. Had her patient moved slightly in bed?

K'Itea moaned. There was no mistaking it for what it was. The nurse watched as K'Itea's eyes fluttered open. K'Itea closed her eyes again just as quickly, moaning against the pain of the bright light in her eyes.

"Doctor!" the nurse called. "She's awake."

Jewel came running into the room. She looked over her vitals then looked over at the bed.

"K'Itea, are you awake?" Jewel said.

"Unh," K'Itea said. "I'm... awake."

"How are you feeling?"

"I feel like an entire building fell on top of me," K'Itea whispered, her voice hoarse. "But that beats being dead."

"Good. I'll get your husband down here right away," Jewel smiled.

"He's here?" The thought of seeing her husband again looked to have a better affect on the young woman than any medicine could have.

"Yes, and he's anxious to see you."

[80]

⟨CHAPTER /4⟩

THE only light in the room came from the faint starlight coming through the windows of his quarters. K'Alan sat in solitary contemplation, his eyes closed and his breathing shallow. While he had not been doing so often of late, K'Alan liked to meditate to try to work through issues. Meditation had helped him through many difficult periods over the years. He could only hope that it would help him through this one.

There had not been a more difficult period than this one. It had been a long two days since the White Knight had rescued the survivors on Duterius Prime. All in all only 14,150 people that had been on the planet had survived the catastrophe. And his wife, the woman he loved more than anyone, was lying in medbay in a coma. He had no idea if he would ever get to see her smile again.

And then there was Elam. He could surely understand why the child resented him, but he had not known about the boy. Kit hadn't told him. Neither had his sister. In Kit's last message, she had told him that there was something that she had been keeping from him. That it was something better said in person. Now that he knew what it was, he wished she'd told him years before. He doubted things would have changed, though. He would not have been able to leave the Defense Force. Not with the way the war had gone.

There was a knock on his door that knocked him out of his silent retrospections back into the present.

"Come in," he called.

Admiral John Bonetti, the commander of the Gamma Epsilon sector of the Star League, walked into the room. He stopped just inside the door as if unsure of whether or not he should be there.

He looked over at the younger man and tried to gauge what the commander was thinking. It was hard to see K'Alan clearly in the darkness, but John could make out the medium length brown hair and the pale pale skin so common amongst the Duterians. He marveled to himself again how similar in appearance the Duterians were to humans. If it weren't for the small cleft right on the bridge of K'Alan's nose, John might have mistaken him for human.

"Have a seat, John," K'Alan said quietly. He did not look in the admiral's direction. He had been expecting the visit, so he was not surprised that the admiral had made the visit unannounced.

"When you weren't in the party that greeted me, I knew that the situation was bad. How's Kit doing?" John asked as he took a seat opposite where K'Alan was sitting.

"Jewel says that if she wakes up, she'll be OK." K'Alan took a sip of tea. The tea had long since gone cold and K'Alan winced at the taste. "Did you know I had a ten year old son?"

"No, I didn't," John frowned.

"Neither did I until two days ago," K'Alan shrugged. "Neither my sister nor my wife wanted to tell me unless I was there to hear it in person."

"So they've been keeping this to themselves for ten years?"

"Yeah," K'Alan nodded. "I don't even know whether or not to be angry about it. I cannot change the past ten years. I don't know if I would even if I were able to."

"Unreal. Listen, I need you to be at the mission briefing today."

"Of course I'll be there, but why are you saying I need to be?"

"We need to address the issue of what to do with the survivors of the Duterius Prime tragedy. Now I have a proposal, but I doubt that Captain Ker'sal will agree, at least not without a fight. Since it's your people that are affected, I think you need to speak for them." John pulled out a datadisc and tossed it to K'Alan. "This datadisc has all the details of my proposal. I think..." John was interrupted by K'Alan's wristlink.

"K'Alan here," he said as he switched on his com.

"K'Alan, this is Jewel," the medtech's voice floated in through his link. "You need to get down to medbay ASAP. K'Itea is awake and she's asking for you."

"I'll be right there." He switched off his com and looked at John. "I'll be at the briefing, but this is my wife. She must take precedence."

"I wouldn't have expected any less."

2.1.2136
1011
SLS White Knight
Medbay

K'Alan Bryce raced into the medbay, almost knocking over a nurse in his haste. He nodded in apology to the nurse and hurried to the isolation room where his wife was being treated.

Jewel was the only other person in the room. She was checking over some readings when he raced in. Smiling to K'Alan, she motioned him over to the bed.

"I'll give you two some time alone," she smiled. She laid a hand on his arm. "But you have to remember, Commander, she's been through a lot in the last couple days. Take it easy." She smiled again before leaving, closing the isoroom's door behind her.

K'Alan sat on the edge of the bed and looked down at the woman he loved. She still had a sizeable greenish-blue bruise on her forehead, but other than that, she was as beautiful as she had ever been. Her long curly golden hair spread out across the pillow, and her fiery green eyes twinkled with an odd combination of humor and wisdom.

"Hi," he said.

"Hi!" she exclaimed.

"So, I guess you know how bad it is," he began.

"Were you able to drive the attackers off?"

"Yes," he nodded. He hesitated a moment, not wanting to be the one to tell her just what had happened. "But, Kit, we were just too late. I'm sorry."

"How bad?"

"Duterius Prime is uninhabitable," he turned away, a tear rolling down his cheek. "And counting the members of our race who are currently serving in the Star League Defense Force, there are just over 15,000 of us left."

"Oh, gods!"

"Admiral Bonetti has a proposal about how to help our people." He held up the datadisc. "I haven't taken a look at this yet. When I'd heard you'd woken up, I raced right here. I thought we should look at it together."

K'Itea nodded, and K'Alan placed the datadisc in the room's reader. They watched the proposal in silence, each one lost in their own thoughts. When the datadisc finished playing, they just looked at each other for a few minutes.

"They have to agree to this, Kal. It's probably our only hope," she said softly.

"I'll do my best to convince them." He paused and looked at her with sad eyes. "Kit, I know about Elam."

"I should have told you years ago. He needed you to be in his life."

"Well, at least now he'll have that chance. He's staying with my sister for the time being. I haven't exactly been the most pleasant of people to be around the past couple days." He smiled a sad smile. "And he's quite an angry young man."

"Just be there for him," she said quietly, as she put her hand on his.

"We both will. Doc says you're gonna be OK."

"Yeah, I am. Thank you for being there when I needed you the most."

"I did promise that I always would be," he leaned down and kissed her forehead gently. "And now I need to go be there for us again and knock some sense into the command crew."

2.1.2136
1030
SLS White Knight
The Conference Room

Thala looked at the empty chair to her left where K'Alan should have been sitting and frowned. It was the third time she had looked at the chair. And the third time it had been empty. It was time for the briefing, and her XO was late. In all the time she had known him, Thala could not remember K'Alan Bryce being late for anything.

"He'll be here," Admiral Bonetti said softly, noticing her look. "I know where he is and I have excused him from being on time to the briefing. Meanwhile, I suggest we get started."

"Agreed, sir," Thala nodded. She turned to her command staff and looked them over. "Ladies and gentleman, thank you for coming. Admiral Bonetti, would you care to begin the briefing?"

"Before I go over Gamma Strike's first mission, there is a proposal that I would like to make," the admiral said. He stood up and strode over to the room's viewer. He slipped a datadisc in the reader and graphics, statistics, figures and graphs scrolled across the screen to support his proposal as he spoke.

"With the destruction of Duterius Prime, a critical situation has arisen," the admiral began. "There are currently exactly 15,132 Duterians left alive."

"Fifteen thousand?" Kath gasped, looking pained. "Duterius Prime was home to over four billion people."

"I know," Admiral Bonetti began. "And we know who is responsible. But that information is irrelevant to this part of the meeting.

"Due to a cultural taboo and a lack of necessity, the Duterian people never developed the abilities and technology necessary to colonize a planet. Without colonization abilities, the Duterian people will not survive any new planet that they attempt to colonize."

"What does this have to do with Gamma Strike?" Thala rolled her hand as if telling the admiral to get to the point.

"When the White Knight was designed," Sarah Hodge said. "She was designed to carry diplomats from all of the major governments of the Star League as well as diplomats from non-aligned worlds, such as the Brentax when the war ends. The goal was to have a place where issues can be discussed and resolved before they lead to war."

"It's a self-contained city inside the ship," Admiral Bonetti continued. "It can hold a quarter of a million people comfortably.

"The area was labeled Top Secret. That's why only Sarah and I were allowed in the area. But with the recent catastrophe on Duterius Prime, I propose that we use this space to house the survivors while scientists from all of the other major governments teach those survivors how to survive when colonizing a planet."

"This is your proposal?" Thala said incredulously.

"The Duterian government respectfully requests that the Star League implement Admiral Bonetti's proposal immediately," K'Alan said as he slipped into his chair.

"Nice of you to join us, Commander," Thala said dourly.

"I apologize for being late, Captain. The High Gentlewoman of the Duterian people has regained consciousness and I had to confer with her about the Admiral's proposal before I came to the briefing."

"Very well. Continue, Admiral," Thala sighed.

"We can't force Gamma Strike to implement this proposal," Admiral Bonetti said. "A vote is required by the command staff, and one vote will be allocated to the Duterian government."

"Very well," Thala said. "I cannot vote in favor of this proposal."

"Well, the Duterian government votes for the proposal," K'Alan said. "And so do I."

"I have to side with the Commander," Colonel Bonetti said.

"For," Kath said simply.

"We have to," Tyla Barros said.

As the votes were cast one by one, Thala realized she was going to be the only dissenting voice. With each vote, she slumped a little further against her chair.

"The proposal passes," Admiral Bonetti said. "The housing of the Duterian survivors will begin immediately. Now, we need to discuss Gamma Strike's first mission."

"Admiral Bonetti, with all due respect," K'Alan interrupted. "I want to go after whoever did this to my people."

"Funny, that's what I had in mind, Commander," the admiral smiled. "We know that the Brentax are responsible. We were able to determine that the base ship involved in the attack was the Torellia Corvax under the command of M'Bek Tarmos himself. I want this man brought to justice."

"It will be my pleasure," K'Alan grinned.

[87]

"Don't get too cocky, Commander. This will not be an easy mission," Admiral Bonetti warned the commander. "But it may mean the end of this war. It may mean peace in this quadrant."

"Well, that's reason enough to want this mission to succeed," K'Alan nodded. "I assume you want him alive."

"Yes, Commander. Alive."

"Darn. Alive wouldn't have been my first choice, but I guess I can do alive."

"Good. Well, that concludes this briefing. Dismissed," Admiral Bonetti said.

Thala stormed out of the conference room even before the admiral had finished speaking. K'Alan and Mario just looked at each other.

"Listen, Kal," Mario said. "I know you've been busy worrying about Kit for the last two days, but I was hoping we could talk. Wanna meet at the lounge in a few minutes?"

"Sure," K'Alan smiled. "I could use a little drink."

"No alcohol, remember," Mario shook his head.

"Yes, Dad," K'Alan snickered.

"K'Alan, I want to talk to you later," Admiral Bonetti said. "There are some things about this mission we need to discuss."

"Why aren't you taking them up with the Captain?" K'Alan asked.

"Because I think she has some other issues she's going to be dealing with. And besides, you're probably the one who's going to be bringing him in."

"All right, John," K'Alan sighed. "Let me know when."

"Good. Now if you'll excuse me, I need to go talk with the captain," Admiral Bonetti said as he turned to leave.

"Shall we head to the lounge, Colonel?" K'Alan grinned.

"Yes, we shall, Commander."

* * *

2.1.2136
1200
SLS White Knight
Forward Observation Lounge

Thala Ker'sal stared out the window at the Gamma Epsilon station. It had been a difficult day. With the Duterian situation and the mission briefing, it had been a really rough morning for her. She wasn't sure what she was going to do about the situation. All she wanted was some time alone to think and figure it out.

"Captain, I was hoping I might have a word with you," Admiral Bonetti trod on her interspection.

"I'm not in the mood right now, Admiral," Thala snapped. She kept staring out the window. She saw his reflection start to cross the observation lounge towards her

"That's too bad. You stormed out of the briefing in a bit of a huff. Why?"

"I said I don't want to talk about it," Thala growled.

"You're about one step away from insubordination, Captain," Admiral Bonetti snarled.

"Well, then, maybe you should bring me up on charges," Thala whipped around to face the admiral. "It sure wouldn't be the worst thing to happen to me today. And, by the way, you'll have my request for a transfer within the hour."

"Transfer?"

"I won't stay on this ship. And you can't force me to stay. If you deny my transfer, I will resign my commission."

"I'm not sure I understand, Captain."

"Let me put it bluntly, Admiral. You have placed me in a very awkward position and I don't want to deal with it. So, I'm doing what I must in order to get myself out of that situation."

"Not until I get a straight answer from you, Captain. I thought you would be happy about the mission."

"I am. It's ferrying the Duterians around that I'm having a problem with."

[89]

"Are you sure it's the Duterians you have a problem with?"

"No," Thala exploded. She flung the datapad she was holding across the room. It shattered against the wall by the door. "It's not the Duterians. It's HER! It's his wife. I wish she had never pulled through."

"What?" Admiral Bonetti asked incredulously.

"Ever since the Academy," Thala slumped in a chair and closed her eyes. "I've been hopelessly in love with K'Alan Bryce. And when I'd heard that she was injured, I was filled with hope. Hope that maybe there was a chance that he and I might be able to eventually get together."

"I'm not sure I believe what I'm hearing," Admiral Bonetti said. He walked over to the viewport. "All right. I'll approve your transfer. But I suggest you talk to someone about these feelings, Captain. I'm putting you on detached duty until you work this out. When you do, I'll assign you a new command."

"Thank you, Admiral."

"I would like you to consider staying on for this one mission though," the admiral turned back to her.

"Admiral, as tempting as it is to go after M'Bek Tarmos, I just don't think my staying on this ship is a good idea. Commander Bryce can handle this ship and her crew."

"Very well," Admiral Bonetti sighed. "You stand relieved. I'll brief the Commander later. And, Captain, I'd suggest you be off the White Knight within six hours. They're going to be shipping out that soon."

2.1.2136
1210
SLS White Knight
The Lounge

"I still can't believe that Soran is on the ship," K'Alan laughed. It was good to laugh after the events of the past couple days.

"Well, the Captain told me she wanted the best people on here, and Soran is the best barman we've ever seen," Mario grinned.

"Well, I just want you to know that even with Kit and Elam living on board, nothing's going to be different between us," K'Alan sighed, sipping his Duterian Sunmist.

"How are you holding up with everything that's been going on, Kal?"

"Not very well, to be honest, Mario. Can you imagine what it's like to suddenly find out that you've had a son for ten years?"

"Nope. No one could ever prove that in my case. And I will call anyone that tries a big, fat liar."

"You're incorrigible, my friend."

"In all seriousness, I'm sure it's not easy on Elam either."

"Oh, he just hates and resents me. Can't say I blame him," K'Alan sipped his drink. "If I were him, I'm not sure I'd like me too much either."

"But you didn't know, Kal."

"But he's a kid. To a kid, that doesn't matter, Mario. I wasn't there. That's all he knows."

"But you're here. He's here. Kit's going to be OK. You can be a family again."

"I hope so."

"Commander Bryce?" a young ensign said as she approached the table the two friends were sitting at.

"Yes, Ensign?" K'Alan raised an eyebrow at the unexpected interruption.

"Admiral Bonetti sent me to find you. He needs to speak to you immediately." The ensign shifted uncomfortably. "It's quite important."

"Tell him I'll be there presently."

"With all due respect, sir," the ensign blushed. "I'm not supposed to return without you."

"Well, then I guess I better follow you then, Ensign. Mario, I'll talk to you later. Will you be here for a while?"

[91]

"Oh, I'll be here for a couple hours at least, K'Alan," Mario smiled. "The day is young, and there are so many credits to win."

"I'll be back before you know it," K'Alan laughed.

The commander tossed back the last of his drink and stood up. He motioned for the young ensign to lead on.

2.1.2136
1244
SLS White Knight
The Conference Room

K'Alan fidgeted nervously as he stood just inside the door of the conference room. Admiral Bonetti was doing paperwork. K'Alan couldn't make out what file the admiral was working on, but it appeared to be a personnel file.

"You asked to see me, sir?" K'Alan finally gathered up the courage to interrupt.

"Yes, Commander. Have a seat." The admiral finished making a note in the file he was reading and looked at K'Alan. "I have a problem."

"Is there anything I can do to help you, John? I mean, I know things have been kind of hectic lately, but you know that if there's anything I can do to help out, I will."

"Well, I find myself having to make a very difficult decision," Admiral Bonetti sighed. "Captain Ker'sal will not be staying on as commanding officer of Gamma Strike."

"What? Why?" It was the last thing K'Alan had expected to hear. Despite the issues he and Thala had had, he knew she was an excellent commanding officer. He couldn't believe she would just walk away without a really good reason.

"I'm not at liberty to say why, but she's been put on detached duty. Unfortunately, this leaves Gamma Strike with no CO."

"I'm sure that there are plenty of Captains that would jump at the chance at commanding this squad," K'Alan noted. "Captain Perrin Hawks would be a good choice.

[92]

She's been looking for a new command since the Grange was lost last year."

"Captain Hawks is not available. She just got a new command this morning. No, I'm afraid there's only one thing I can do. Commander, Gamma Strike is yours."

"Uh, sir, with all due respect, I'm afraid I may not be the best person to command this unit."

"Why do you say that?"

"Well, first of all, regulations call for a Captain or higher to lead a unit. I doubt that I can be promoted so soon after my last promotion. And second, with all of the recent issues with my people and especially with what has happened concerning my family, my mental state may not be the best at the moment."

"Well, as for your second concern, your mental state is not an issue. I believe that you can handle this new assignment, or else I wouldn't have given it to you. As for your rank.... Congratulations, Captain Bryce."

"Um, thank you, Admiral. About my new XO. Is Commander Erin Sykes available?" K'Alan asked. "She's one of the best officers I've ever worked with."

"As a matter of fact, she's available. I can have her on board in six hours," the admiral smiled. With how quickly he agreed to the suggestion, K'Alan wondered if Admiral Bonetti hadn't already anticipated who he would choose as his XO. K'Alan, honestly, would not have put it past the admiral to know. "Congratulations, Captain. I believe Gamma Strike is in good hands. Oh, I believe you'll need these." He handed K'Alan his new rank insignia.

"Thanks, Admiral. I hope I don't disappoint you," K'Alan said slowly as he changed his rank insignia on his uniform.

"You won't. Dismissed."

"Yes, sir."

* * *

Mario was sitting at the same table carefully counting several stacks of credit chips when K'Alan came walking back into the lounge. K'Alan was always amazed at how fast his friend could bilk his fellow crewmembers out of their credit chits.

"Barman, my usual," K'Alan grunted as he walked over to their table.

"Hey, Kal," Mario grinned, tossing a credit chip to K'Alan. "Don't worry about it. This one's on Lieutenant Ramierez."

"Only you, Mario," K'Alan laughed. "How many credits did you win this time?"

"Full week's pay from two lieutenants and three ensigns," Mario grinned.

"I'm going to pretend I didn't hear that."

He flopped down opposite Mario. Exhaustion from dealing with everything so far today set in fast as he sat down, and he put his arms on the table and laid his head down.

"So what did my father want, Kal?"

"Ice is gone."

"What?" Mario yelped. "What happened?"

"Not sure," K'Alan said as he sat back up. He fingered his new insignia. "But she's no longer in command of Gamma Strike."

"So who is?"

"I am."

CHAPTER / 5

ORIN Minaya hurried down the hall towards the Emperor's personal library. The young ambassador had been summoned to the library. And he knew that ignoring such a summons would not be received well.

He had no idea what the Emperor wanted to see him about, however. He knew that whatever it was had to be important. It was the Emperor after all.

The thing that surprised him, though, was that the Emperor clearly knew who he was. Orin was a relative newcomer to the ambassadorial corps. He doubted that the Emperor got a report on each and every member of the ambassadorial corps. That made the summons even more curious and potentially worrying.

As he hurried down the hallway, he worried about what the summons could be about. Was he in trouble? If he was, what had he done. Orin was a quiet, nervous sort that, unless out and about doing his job, kept to himself.

When he got to the Emperor's private library, he was stopped by two of the Emperor's private guards.

"Name?" one of the guards demanded.

"Ambassador Orin Minaya," the young man's voice quavered slightly. "I was summoned."

"You are expected," the other guard rumbled. "Leave your weapons here. You may pick them up on the way out."

"One does not customarily come before his Emperor armed," the young man said quietly. He unhooked his dagger from his belt and handed it over to the first guard. "Save for this knife, I am unarmed."

The first guard pulled a small hand scanner from behind his back and ran it over the young man. When the scanner finished, the guard looked at the readings and grunted.

"Can never be too careful," the guard muttered as he put the scanner away. He looked at the other guard. "He is clean."

Nodding, the second guard opened the door to the library, motioning for the young man to enter.

"Have a seat and wait," the guard said. "The Emperor will be with you presently."

After Orin walked through the open door to the library, he heard the guards close and bar the door. He tried the door handle, but there was no way out. He was there until the Emperor was through with him.

Not knowing what to do with himself until the Emperor arrived, Orin walked over to one of the shelves and started looking over the titles of the books on the spines. He quickly realized what books were stored in the personal library of the Emperor.

The diaries of previous Emperors.

When he realized what the books were, he felt an immediate and immense sense of guilt for having looked.

He felt it an invasion of the Emperor's privacy, a crime that some felt should be punishable by death.

Curiosity was Orin's one big flaw, though. Some would say that his curiosity had served him well in the ambassadorial corps, as it had focused him when he did research on another race. His supervisors in the ambassadorial corps had always found his research helpful.

He turned away from the bookshelf and walked over to the small window that overlooked the capitol city. The young ambassador watched people in the street far below going about their business. If he had not been summoned to see the Emperor, he would have been one of the people down in the hustle and bustle.

"Ah, good," a soft voice from behind Orin said. "You are here finally."

Orin slowly turned around to see the Emperor watching him. He bowed low in a formal bow.

"I have come as you have bid, my Emperor," Orin spoke the traditional words of greeting to the Emperor of the Furitan people.

"Oh, posh," the Emperor laughed softly. "We are in private, Orin Minaya. There is no need for the formal bowing and scraping. To be honest, I hate the pomp and circumstance of my office."

Orin straightened and looked at the Emperor, clearly confused. "You do?"

"Of course I do. How would you feel if people came up to you and said 'I have come as you have bid.' hundreds of times each day?"

"I imagine I would get tired of it rather quickly, to be honest," Orin shrugged.

"And so have I."

The Emperor smiled at Orin and indicated a chair across a small table from where the Emperor was now sitting.

Orin slowly moved over and took the offered chair. He was still nervous about being in the presence of the Emperor by himself. If he had known what the Emperor wanted, he did not think he would have been quite so nervous.

"You asked to see me, Your Eminence?" Orin said quietly after settling in the chair.

"Please, Orin," the Emperor shook his head. "We are alone. You may call me Tarmin."

"I don't think I can do that, Your Eminence. You are the Emperor, after all," Orin sighed. "I'm just a lowly peon in the ambassadorial corps."

"Hardly lowly, and hardly a peon." The Emperor pressed a button on the table and a *tangu* table appeared. "Tell me, Orin. Do you play *tangu*?"

"I have not played in some time, but yes," Orin nodded. "I doubt I shall be any competition for you."

"You may have first move," Emperor Tarmin waved at the board. "You are here because I have need of your opinions."

"My opinion on what, sir?" Orin moved one of his forward soldiers two spaces. "As I said, I'm just a lowly member of the ambassadorial corps. I don't even have access to anything important right now."

"Ah, but that is not exactly true, my young friend," Tarmin smiled. "You have access to exactly the most important thing. To me at any rate."

"I don't think I understand."

"You did research on both the Star League and the Brentax Empire," Tarmin shrugged. He moved a forward soldier to match Orin's opening move.

"I did, yes," Orin nodded. "I was asked to do a threat assessment on both governments."

"I have read them," Tarmin smiled. "Excellent and thorough work."

"Thank you, sir," Orin bowed his head slightly. "I was unaware that you would get a copy of the reports."

"Who do you think asked for the threat assessments in the first place?"

Orin looked stunned, but said nothing. He looked over the game board, finally moving one of his guards, capturing one of the Emperor's forts.   The Emperor nodded in approval at the move.

"If you have read my report, what more do you need from me?" Orin asked.

"Which side will win the war?" the Emperor asked simply.

Orin leaned back in his chair and stroked his chin in thought. He wasn't sure how to answer, as he did not know who would win the war between the Star League and the Brentax Empire. He had given it a great deal of thought since the original threat assessments, but he had no more idea now which side would prevail than he had before. He had to say something though. The Emperor was expecting an answer.

"I believe that the Brentax Empire currently has the superior military," Orin said, choosing his words very carefully.

"So you think the Brentax will win, then?" Tarmin pressed.

"We received a report earlier today that the Brentax Empire had brutally attacked one of the Star League homeworlds," Orin said. "I don't know how the Star League can stand up to the Brentax. And yet..."

"And yet, what?" Tarmin prodded.

"And yet, I cannot help but think that the Star League will be the last ones standing at the end."

"I see." The Emperor got up and walked over to the shelf of books that Orin had looked at earlier. He scanned down the row of books and pulled one from the shelf. "What do you know of Emperor Kyn Cartha?"

"They say the prophecies his star guide gave him made him go mad. Beyond that, I don't know much, I am afraid."

"The books on this shelf are the collected journals of past emperors," Tarmin said softly.   "I have read all of them." He held up the book he pulled off the shelf. "This one was written by Kyn Cartha."

"Why are you telling me about these diaries?" Orin furrowed his brow. "I would assume that these are not for people like me to know about."

"Normally, that would be true," Tarmin nodded. He sat back down at the table. "And if you were to tell anyone about the diaries, I would have no choice but to have you executed. Still, I think I can trust you not to spread this around."

"I shall take this secret to my grave," the young ambassador nodded.

"Good." Tarmin flipped through the book to get to the passage he wanted. "Emperor Cartha did, indeed, get a vision from his star guide. And it disturbed him greatly. I don't know that it exactly drove him mad, but it did cause him to lose sleep."

Orin looked uncomfortable at the table. He tried to cover his discomfort by studying the game board. He saw an opening that he wasn't sure that the Emperor knew was there, and so he took it, moving one of his clerics into a position causing the Emperor's lord to be in danger.

"What does a vision from a star guide from hundreds of years ago have to do with the war between the Star League and the Brentax Empire?" Orin asked after making the move.

"Because, this war is referenced in the vision," Tarmin shrugged. "As is one other war to come." He moved his lady to capture Orin's clergy. "The vision, which I will not relate as the details are not important, stated that the Furitan Empire must ally itself with whichever side wins this current war or we will be lost."

"I can see why you wanted to know about the two sides, then," Orin nodded.

"There is one other reason I summoned you," the Emperor said after a few moments.

"What else can I do for you, Emperor?"

"When this war is over and the winner is known, you will be my ambassador." Tarmin moved his lady to a position on the board where it put Orin's lord in danger, one that Orin could not escape from. "I am raising you to full ambassadorial status as of now. The only question is whom you will be the ambassador to."

Orin slumped back in his chair as he realized he lost to the Emperor. Then he smiled broadly.

"I shall endeavor not to let you down, Emperor," Orin chuckled, knowing he had been outmaneuvered in life as in the game. "I shall keep you informed as to the developments of the war."

"Excellent," Tarmin nodded as he reset the game board. "You may go, Ambassador."

"Thank you, Emperor," Orin stood and bowed. He made his way out of the library quickly, before the Emperor could call him back.

The newly minted ambassador smiled as he left the library, knowing his star was, once again, on the rise.

The Dawning of a New Age

⟨CHAPTER 6⟩

"HEY, Kit. How are you feeling?" K'Alan asked as he sat down next to her bed. He reached over and took her hand, which elicited a growl from the other side of the bed. K'Alan looked up and saw his sister and Elam sitting on the opposite side of K'Itea.

"I've been better," K'Itea smiled. She squeezed his hand gently. "But I am going to be fine. I hear that the admiral's proposal passed."

"That's right," K'Alan nodded. Then he smiled at his wife. "The Duterian survivors are all going to be living on the White Knight for a while. Under my protection."

"Your protection," S'Era furrowed her brow. "I thought you were the exec."

K'Alan leaned back in his chair and sighed softly. "I was," he shrugged. "But the captain decided that she did not want to stay on and left. Admiral Bonetti decided that I was the best person for the job, so he just promoted me and made me the commanding officer."

[103]

"Good," K'Itea smiled at him. "You deserve it. And I am sure all of our people will feel safer having you in charge."

K'Alan gazed at his family, lost in though. He had had a lot dumped on him in a short amount of time and he was doing his best to deal with it all at once. Having the people he loved most in the galaxy on the ship with him made it easier.

"I'm going to move my quarters into the City with the rest of you," he said after a while. "I think it's only proper."

"I think it's a good idea," his sister said. A smile spread across her face as a thought entered her mind. "It would be good for you, Kit and Elam to finally spend time together as a family."

"I don't like him," Elam whispered in S'Era's ear.

"Elam Jarron Bryce," S'Era admonished him in a stern voice. "In time you will grow to like your father. He is a very good man."

"If he's such a good man, then why has he never once visited me?" Elam shot back.

The words hit K'Alan like daggers. He knew why Elam was so angry, but it did not make it any easier for him to hear it. He hoped that there would be, someday, a way for him to make those ten years up to his son.

"Because I never told him that you were alive, my son," K'Itea's words were soft, but did not cut K'Alan any less than Elam's. "He did not know to visit you."

K'Alan's gaze caught his son's, pain mirrored in eyes so much like his own. "Elam, had I known I would have been home long before now." K'Alan's voice was soft and, he hoped, comforting. "I would have never wanted to hurt you. I'm sorry I never met you before now. I am so, so sorry."

"Yeah. Sure you are," Elam snarled at his father. The boy stormed out of the room.

"Elam," K'Alan called after him. He turned back to K'Itea when she squeezed his arm. A single tear rolled down his cheek.

"Let him go, Kal," she said, her voice sad. "He will come around in time."

[104]

"I hope so."

"Commander Bryce to the bridge, please," the voice of Katherine Yeuid floated into the isoroom over the shipcall.

K'Alan looked up at the speaker and sighed. He thumbed his wristlink. "On my way, Kath," he said. "Actually, it's Captain Bryce now."

"Sorry, Captain," came back the quick reply. "Didn't know."

"Don't worry about it. The official announcement isn't until 2000 hours." He thumbed his wristlink off and looked at his family. "I don't want to, but I have to go. Duty calls."

"I understand, my love," his wife smiled at him. "I will be here when you are done. I doubt I am going anywhere anytime soon."

2.1.2136
1700
SLS White Knight
The Bridge

Thala sat at her station on the bridge. It would be the last time she would sit in the command chair of the White Knight. Even though it was her decision, she hated the thought of leaving. She felt like she had lost something. It was not the first time she had felt that way when it came to K'Alan Bryce.

She was checking over some of the controls on her station when he walked onto the bridge. She watched him walk to his station, check some controls and then head for her.

"I hear you're leaving," he said when he got to her station. He kept his voice soft out of respect for her. It would be touching if he hadn't driven the knife into her back one more time.

"I hear you're taking over for me," she replied in a terse voice. "Congratulations."

"This is not exactly what I had in mind to get a command of my own," he shook his head. Damn him for looking sad! "In fact, I want you to know, I protested strenuously at first."

"I'm sure you did." Her voice was distant. She was already trying to figure out what she was going to do next. "I suppose it is time for me to go."

"Captain, I relieve you," he said in a quiet voice. He'd snapped to attention as the custom dictated.

"I stand relieved," she sighed after a pause. After a moment, she clapped her hand on his shoulder. "Good luck, Captain Bryce. I know you will succeed in your mission to bring M'Bek Tarmos to justice."

"Good luck to you as well, Captain Ker'sal. I hope you find what it is you're looking for."

Thala strode off the bridge. She was fighting tears as she walked. She would not cry in front of him. She had never cried in front of him, and she would be damned if she did now. She could feel his eyes bore into her back like daggers all the way off the bridge.

2.1.2136
1837
SLS White Knight
Soran's Bar

Captain K'Alan Bryce was halfway to the bar to get a drink when he heard his name being called from a different part of the bar. He recognized the voice right away, and changed his course from the bar to where Mario was sitting with his father.

"The captain's bars look good on you, Kal," Mario smiled at his friend.

"Not the way I wanted to earn them, Mario," K'Alan grunted.

"Well, congratulations anyway," Mario laughed.

"It's well deserved, K'Alan," the admiral added. "I did not give you the promotion lightly."

"I appreciate the vote of confidence from both of you," K'Alan shared a weak smile with the two men. "Listen,

[106]

Mario. I'm going to be leaning on you quite heavily over the next couple of weeks."

"Of course, Kal," Mario nodded. "Anything you need."

"I was hoping you would say that," K'Alan's smile grew. "Now, here's my plan..."

2.1.2136
1925
SLS White Knight
Flight Bay Alpha

Commander Erin Lyn Sykes stepped off a shuttle from the Gamma Epsilon Station and grunted. She looked around the flight bay, impressed with the size. Her kit bag was still slung over her shoulder. When she heard running boot falls, she looked over to the entrance to the flight bay and chuckled softly to herself as she watched K'Alan come running on the flight deck at full speed.

The two had been friends for years and had served together several times. Still, there was a distance that Erin had never understood between them. It was a shame, because she had always counted him amongst her friends. And she did not have many. She could ill afford to have one of her friends walk out of her life.

"Commander Erin Lyn Sykes reporting for duty as ordered, sir!" she barked a she snapped a crisp salute to her new commanding officer.

"Welcome aboard, Commander," K'Alan returned the salute. Then his stance softened and he smiled at her. "I'm glad you're here, Erin."

"Thank you, K'Alan," she returned the smile. "I must say, I was quite surprised when I got the call from Admiral Bonetti ordering me to report to you as your new XO. I rather got the impression that you didn't want me around."

"If you're referring to the way that I keep pushing you away whenever you get too close, you need to know that I am married and am very faithful to my wife."

"Ooooooh."

[107]

Well, that wasn't what she had expected. Ten years of friendship had just come into focus for her with that statement. She now understood all the distance he had put between them. More, she could not say that were their situations reversed that she would not have done the same.

"Besides. It was always Tom Keevan that was interested in you." K'Alan broke into a merry laugh. "You know that as well as I."

"How is Swamp Rat?" Erin asked. "I have not heard from him in a while."

"Last I heard, he was good. Just took command of the Creighton three months ago." He motioned towards the entrance to the flight bay. "On to business. Allow me to give you a quick tour of the ship while I give you the rundown on the situation."

"That would be great," Erin nodded. "I take it, the situation is bad."

"Yep," K'Alan nodded.

He led her out of the flight bay and down a corridor. The corridors were shiny and new with muted grey carpeting. They were wide enough for three people to walk side by side comfortably. The walls slanted down slightly from the ceiling so that the floors ended up about a foot wider than the ceilings. It was an odd shape for the corridors, but she had seen it on other Star League ships.

"I'm going to be depending on you on the bridge a lot, Erin. I'm going to be retaining my position as strike leader."

"Is that wise, Captain?" she looked at him with a concerned look on her face. "Part of my duties are keeping you safe, after all."

"No need to Captain me in private, Erin. We are old friends after all," he chuckled at her. "And it's not a matter of whether or not it's wise. I'm the best damn pilot we have and I will be damned if I am going to stop flying just because Admiral Bonetti decided I'd look better with captain's bars on my chest."

"I can see our command styles are going to clash a bit, K'Alan," Erin suppressed a chuckle.

"That's all right. I'm used to that. My command style clashed with the last CO too." He pointed down a side corridor to a large hatch. "Down that corridor is a city."

"A city? On a spaceship?"

"When Duterius Prime was destroyed, we brought the survivors on board this ship," K'Alan explained. "This area is where they live. It's a small self contained city."

"How many survivors are we housing?" She did not want to know the answer, but she had to ask the question.

"Just over fifteen thousand," K'Alan said, his voice racked with pain for his people.

"My God!" she exclaimed. "I assume the Star League Defense Force is sending someone after whoever was responsible?"

"They are," K'Alan nodded. He guided them back down the hallway to the lift. "Us. That's our first mission."

"Great," Erin nodded. She was enthusiastic for the mission. A woman of action, she would have hated to have been on the sidelines for a mission like this. "Who is it?"

"M'Bek Tarmos."

"Wait," she put her hand on his arm and turned him to face her. "We're going after the Supreme Commander of the Brentax Military?"

"Yes. We are."

"Oh, hell," she said, starting to walk down the corridor again. "I didn't want to live forever anyway."

"This will be a simple insertion and retrieval mission," he shrugged. "Nothing to worry about."

"I don't like the way you said simple, K'Alan," she looked at him sideways. "Nothing like this is ever simple."

"True enough. But this mission is actually very simple. I can promise you it has been well thought out and no one should be hurt or killed during the insertion or retrieval process."

"Don't make promises you can't keep, K'Alan," she admonished. "No one can guarantee that no one will be hurt during a mission."

"True," he said again. He pointed at a door they were passing. "Medbay. Important to know where that is."

"I must say, you have inherited quite the impressive ship, K'Alan," she smiled at him.

"It is indeed," he smiled proudly. "Just wait until you see the bridge though."

2.1.2136
2000
SLS White Knight
The Bridge

When K'Alan walked onto the bridge, most of his alpha shift crew were at their stations even though they would normally be off duty at that time. He looked around at the assembled crew. His crew now. He knew that he had inherited the best crew. He'd spent some time looking over all their files after he'd first come aboard, but it would take some time to truly learn all of their capabilities.

His eyes locked on Admiral Bonetti's at the command chair when he was finished scanning the bridge and nodded once. He made his way over to what was now his station on the bridge.

"Captain Bryce," John acknowledged when he got there.

"Admiral Bonetti," K'Alan bowed his head just slightly in respect.

"Captain K'Alan Ilan Bryce, do you now accept the responsibility of this unit?" the admiral asked, his voice loud and clear so that it carried through the now silent bridge.

"Yes, Admiral. They are now my responsibility," K'Alan nodded once.

"Good." John pressed a button on the command console. A soft whistle followed. "Let it be known that on this date and time, I, Admiral John Bonetti, do bestow upon

Captain K'Alan Bryce the command of the Star League Defense Force unit known as Gamma Strike."

"I accept command," K'Alan said, his voice firm but grim.

The bridge broke into cheering. K'Alan had to wonder if they would have cheered like this for Thala. He did not think, as good an officer as she was, that she could command this kind of respect from the crew.

John shook his hand warmly and smiled at him.

"Good luck, Captain."

"Thank you, Admiral."

John lowered his voice and leaned in so that the conversation would be between only himself and K'Alan.

"As soon as the Creighton gets here, I will be off your ship," he said.

"How soon?"

"They'll be here in about two hours," John said after checking the chrono. "Then you will be free to embark on your mission."

"Do me a favor, John?" There was a twinkle in K'Alan's eye. "Tell Swamp Rat that I swiped his girl. He'll know what I mean."

"I will," John laughed. Then he turned serious. "I can't tell you how important it is that you bring M'Bek Tarmos in alive. The plan you have is good. You just need to be careful."

"We'll get him, Admiral. I swear it."

2.1.2136
2111
SLS White Knight
Hydroponics Bay 1

Elam sat quietly on a wooden bench in the hydroponics bay. His eyes were closed and thoughts swirled in the boy's head.

He had finally met his father after ten years. He wanted to like K'Alan, but he could not get past the fact that there had not been one visit in his entire life. Why had

[111]

it taken such a monumental disaster to get his father to visit him?

He did not see Mario Bonetti walk into the hydroponics bay. Nor did he see Mario walk over to him. So it took him completely by surprise when the ship's morale officer spoke to him.

"Elam?"

Elam's eyes snapped open and his head whipped around to see who had called him. When he saw who it was, he snarled.

"Get away from me."

"Elam, I want to talk to you," Mario said, his voice calm.

"I don't know you," Elam growled. "I have nothing to say to you."

"I want to talk to you about your father," Mario continued in his calm voice.

"Did he send you?"

"No," Mario shook his head. "K'Alan doesn't even know I am here."

"Good," Elam crossed his arms and turned away from Mario. "Then if I send you away, he won't care."

"But he does care, Elam," Mario walked around to be in the boy's line of sight again. "Give him a chance. Let him be the father he wants to be."

"He had ten years to be a father!" Elam shouted. He let all his anger out on this friend of his father. "Ten years. But he'd rather roam the stars than care for a kid. Where was he all those years? Why couldn't he come visit before now? What was so important that he did not care about me?"

"Elam, he did not know about you," Mario shook his head. "I've known your father a long time. Longer than he's been married to your mother. I know that he's always wanted a son. And I know that, if he had known you were his son, he would have made the time to be with you. He may even have resigned from the service."

"You don't really believe that," Elam scowled in accusation.

"Actually, I do. He told me some time ago that he would love to settle down with a family. I mean, he's always had your mother, but he has always wanted to settle down with kids."

"He really told you that?" The boy furrowed his brow. This man could claim to know his father's wishes all he wanted, but Elam still wasn't convinced. He wouldn't be convinced until he heard it straight from his father's mouth.

"Yes, I did," K'Alan said. He came out from the tree he'd been behind while watching the conversation. Elam had never noticed him standing there. The boy watched as his father walked across the hydroponics bay and knelt down in front of him. "Your aunt and mother thought they were doing the right thing by not telling me about you, because they knew that I would have resigned from the Defense Force and come home to settle down with you. They didn't want to let me put my family over my career even though I would have in a heartbeat. But I guess now it doesn't' really matter."

"What do you mean by that, K'Alan?" Mario asked. The morale officer creased his brow. "You're not thinking about resigning too, are you? I'd hate to have to break in yet another commanding officer."

"No, I'm not," K'Alan smiled. It was a very sad smile, but it was a smile just the same. "But now I can have my career and have my family close to me. I can't think of too many silver linings in this tragedy, but I think that's one."

Elam almost believed him. But he was afraid. He knew that it was too good to be true that he finally had his father around. He was afraid that something would happen and K'Alan would be snatched from his life again.

"Promise me that you'll never leave me again," the boy whispered to his father.

"I wish I could promise that, Elam, but I can't," K'Alan sighed softly. It wasn't what Elam wanted to hear. "With my job, there is never a guarantee that I'll be able to stay here all the time. But I can promise you that I will do the best I can to make up for all the time that I was not in your life."

Elam knew that it was the best promise he could get from K'Alan. And it was enough. He slowly stood up and walked over to his father. He buried his face in K'Alan's shoulder and started to cry, letting all the pain and anger that had been building out.

⟨CHAPTER 7⟩

2.1.2136
2237
SLS White Knight
The Bridge

K'ALAN Bryce closed his eyes and tried to block out the bustle of activity going on around him. It had been a very long day for the young Duterian

After finally getting through to Elam, he'd held his son and let him cry on his shoulder until he'd fallen asleep like that. He'd carried the boy to his sister's quarters and tucked him into bed. S'Era hadn't said anything to him, but the smile on her face at seeing her brother with Elam told him volumes.

There was only one thing left for him to do before he could go find his own bed. He smiled to himself in anticipation of finally getting some sleep. His wife was on the mend and his son had finally accepted him. He knew he would sleep well this evening.

"Captain," Kath called from the communications station. "Admiral Bonetti is on the line for you."

"Put him through to my station, Lieutenant Commander," K'Alan nodded.

The small monitor on his station flickered to life in short order. Admiral Bonetti's face appeared on the monitor replacing the Star League logo.

"The Creighton has arrived, Captain," the admiral said. "Permission to disembark."

"Permission granted, Admiral," K'Alan smiled at his friend. "Good journey to you, sir."

"Good hunting to you, Captain Bryce," the admiral returned the smile.

"Thank you, Admiral. Captain Bryce out."

K'Alan reached over and flicked a switch, disengaging the monitor. The screen went back to the standard Star League logo. The captain stood and looked out over the bridge. His alpha shift crew was still on duty from earlier. They were the best crew he had, and it was only fitting that they were the ones that were on the bridge when they left Duterian space to head out on their mission.

"Orders, Captain?" Erin called from her station directly across the bridge from him. It felt weird to see someone else at what just yesterday was his station.

"Navigator, set course for the nearest jumpgate to Brentax space," he ordered. He looked from the navigator to the pilot sitting next to her. "Prepare to engage maximum fusion drive."

"Aye, Captain," the navigator, Mara Silvermaine, reported as she made some calculations. "Course plotted and laid in."

"Ready to engage maximum fusion drive on your mark, Captain," the pilot, Tyla Barros, added.

"Good. Engage," K'Alan ordered. He was pleased with how quickly the course had been laid in. His navigator and pilot worked well together. He would remember to keep this team together. "Navigator, ETA to jumpgate?"

"Just over 36 hours, Captain," Mara said after checking her calulations. "The nearest jumpgate to the Brentax Empire is in the Proxima sector."

"Understood," K'Alan nodded. He flicked the shipcall button on his station. "Delta watch to the bridge." He looked out over the bridge. "Get some rest when Delta watch arrives, people. Mission briefing is at 0900 hours tomorrow morning."

K'Alan was dreaming. At least he thought he was dreaming. He was floating in a void of blackness. There was a definite feeling of timelessness in the void. He was fascinated by the blackness around him. It felt like it was almost alive.

"Where am I?" he asked, although there was no one there to answer. Or at least no one he could see.

"You are in the midst of the fabric of time, my child," a soft female voice called from the darkness.

"Who are you?"

"I am one who watches," the woman's voice said. She stepped out of the darkness in front of him. K'Alan looked her over, although he could not tell much. She was wearing long grey robes with a hood drawn up over her head. "There are some few of us. We watch, and we wait."

"I don't think I understand," K'Alan frowned.

"No, I should imagine that you do not," the woman chuckled. She pulled her hood back, revealing shoulder length jet black hair and eyes so dark they were almost black. "My name is Kiara. I have come to warn you."

"Warn me?" K'Alan's frown deepened. "I don't understand. Warn me about what?"

"It is natural that you do not understand. You do not see the flow of time as we do. I have come to warn you not to follow your intended mission. It can only end in bloodshed."

"I can't abandon my mission," he protested. "If I don't continue the mission, this war will continue."

"That is true," Kiara nodded. "And this war cannot continue. I did not mean that you should abandon your mission. I meant that you should not go to Brentax III yourself."

"Why?"

"I cannot answer that. But heed my warning, child."

Kiara slowly started to fade back into the darkness of the void. K'Alan was left with more questions than he started with.

2.2.2136
03013
SLS White Knight
K'Alan Bryce's quarters

K'Alan awoke with a start with Kiara's words still ringing in his ears. Had he only imagined her? Or had he really somehow transported to that timeless, spaceless void? There was no way of knowing for sure.

He shook his head and flicked the switch for the lights. There was no one in his quarters. He hadn't expected anyone to be there, though.

"Probably just nerves," he muttered to himself. "Too much happened today. Probably, it's nothing to worry about."

He walked over to his personal bar and made some tea to calm himself. When he finished the tea, he put himself back to bed. He did not go back to the void and slept the rest of the night in a fitful peace.

2.2.2136
0847
SLS White Knight
Main Conference Room

K'Alan sat in the conference room by himself with his eyes closed. He was waiting for his command staff, but he had gotten there early so he could have some time to himself.

He could not get the memory of the dream of the void out of his head. There was something that kept nagging at him, but he could not figure out what it was that was bothering him.

"Sleep OK, Kal?" Mario asked him as he walked into the conference room. There was something annoying about how cheerful Mario was first thing in the morning.

"No," the captain said, opening his eyes. "But I will be all right." He took a sip of the coffee in front of him and forced a smile. "How did you sleep?"

"Like a rock, as usual," Mario flashed his insufferable grin.

"Don't make me throw this coffee at you," K'Alan growled.

Mario laughed as he took his seat at the table. They waited as, one by one, the other members of the command staff slowly began filing into the conference room. Erin Sykes was the last one to arrive, and she sat next to K'Alan as was her right as executive officer.

"Before we begin, I would like to introduce our new executive officer, Commander Erin Sykes," K'Alan began. He waved his hand at Erin as he introduced her. "I have known Commander Sykes a long time. She is a fine officer and will fit in well with this crew. She will be covering for me quite a bit on the bridge."

"I'm glad to be a part of Gamma Strike," Erin said, keeping her remarks as short and sweet as she tended to.

"Now, let's get right down to the mission at hand," K'Alan said as he stood and slid a disc into the wall display slot. "I'm not going to lie to you. Our first mission will not be an easy one. We are being sent into Brentax space to retrieve the Supreme Commander of the Brentax Empire, M'Bek Tarmos. For those that are unaware, this man was responsible for the destruction of the Duterian homeworld."

"This sounds like a suicide mission, Captain," Sarah Hodge piped in from her end of the table.

"We're taking a small two man team to infiltrate the Brentax Empire, retrieve the Supreme Commander, and get out," K'Alan continued as the viewscreen showed the essense of the plan.

"A two man team?" Erin looked hard at K'Alan. "That really *is* a suicide mission. Which two crazy people are being sent on this suicide mission?"

"We can't afford to send anyone else. Mario and I will go in by ourselves," the captain said.

"I have to protest as your executive officer," Erin glared at him. "Your place is on the bridge."

"I understand your concern, but this mission has been approved already," K'Alan fired back. "I'm going. That's final."

"What makes you think you two will be successful?" Erin asked. "It's a huge risk."

"We did a lot of statistical analysis on the best way to accomplish the mission," Mario said from his end of the table. "We ran permutation after permutation. By the end of all the simulations, we discovered that having K'Alan and I on this mission increased the chance of this mission being successful by fifty percent."

"I still think it's a bad idea," Erin shrugged, but ended her protests.

"Commander Sykes will retain command of the White Knight while I am off ship," K'Alan added. "I don't anticipate any problems, although we all know problems can crop up."

"Captain, we received the specs you forwarded to engineering on the way you want the shuttle prepared," Sarah spoke up. "We'll have to push engineering teams around the clock, but we can definitely have the shuttle ready by the time we reach Brentax space."

"Good," K'Alan nodded. "This concludes the mission briefing. Dismissed."

K'Alan turned to remove the disc from the wall reader while his command staff filed out of the conference room. When he turned back around, only Mario was still there. The morale officer had not gotten up from the table. The normally affable young man looked serious. It struck K'Alan as and odd look for his friend. He could count on one hand the number of times he had seen such a look on

Mario's face. He thought there might be some fingers left over too.

"You know, K'Alan," Mario began in a somber voice. "She might be right. This could well be a suicide mission."

"You're the one that ran the simulations, Mario," K'Alan shrugged. "You know as well as I do that we are the best people for the job."

"Just because I ran the numbers doesn't mean I have to like it any," Mario shook his head. Then, like someone had flicked a switch, the serious moment was over and the cocky, self-assured grin that K'Alan was used to was back. "By the way, Kal. Nice choice on the exec. She's a real cutie."

"I thought you were interested in my sister," K'Alan glared daggers at his friend.

"Just because I have one target in mind doesn't mean I can't look at others!" Mario gasped in protest.

"Only you, Mario," K'Alan rolled his eyes. "Only you."

2.2.2136
1124
SLS White Knight
The Medbay

K'Alan Bryce slipped into K'Itea's isoroom. She was sleeping soundly when he walked in. As it always did, the sight of his wife made his heart beat a little faster in his chest. One more time, the young man wondered how he could have gotten so lucky to land this beautiful woman to be his bondmate.

The customs of the Duterian people were important to them. And, in many ways, the most important was the bonding. It was the way that the Duterian people continued their species. It had come all the way through ancient times. No one fully understood exactly what happened during the bonding, but there was a connection between a bonded pair of Duterians through which they could feel where each other was when they were close. At longer distances, they could at least tell if their bondmate was still alive.

In the higher caste, such as the *Karta* and *Serata* castes, bonds were traditionally arranged by the parents. K'Alan and K'Itea's bonding had been such an arrangement.

He could not imagine having been bonded to a better person.

K'Alan felt sorry for his sister, though. The man that their parents had chosen for her had been killed during the war. It was rare that a pair that had had their bonding arranged did not make it to the ceremony. When that happened, the survivor was free to bond with anyone of his or her choosing.

The problem was, there were few eligible Duterians of an appropriate caste for her to bond with. It was why Mario's interest in S'Era had been so well received by her. There was a chance for happiness.

K'Alan was afraid she was going to get her heart broken by the handsome young human, though.

Smiling to himself, he shook off his musings about his sister, and made his way over to the bed. Leaning over, he barely pressed his lips to her forehead.

"Hey," she opened her beautiful eyes. "When'd you come in?"

"A few minutes ago," he admitted with a smile. "I couldn't help but watch you sleeping. On my way in, Jewel said you can probably leave the medbay today, but that you'd have to take it easy for a few weeks."

"Have you talked to Elam?" she asked. There was a trace of urgency in her voice.

"Yes, my love," K'Alan nodded. "We've talked. He and I have come to something of an understanding."

"Good. I hate to think that my son hates his father."

"He's still angry, but he'll be all right," K'Alan smiled. "We'll all be all right."

K'Itea nodded and smiled.

* * *

Mario had the gym to himself when he stepped out on the mat. He slowly began going through his kata, allowing it to soothe him like it always did. He closed his hazel eyes as he slowly went through the motions, one move flowing into the next. The young colonel's tall thin frame swept gracefully through the complicated moves that he had practiced so many times before, his long fingers cutting through the air as cleanly as if blades. His short black hair was plastered to his head with a light coating of sweat.

"Nice moves," a female voice called out to him, almost causing him to miss a step. But only almost, as he had been expecting the visit.

Mario opened his eyes, and, as expected, he saw Erin Sykes standing there.

"Commander," he nodded.

"Oh, don't be so formal, Mario. We're both off duty," Erin laughed a little laugh. He decided that she looked even better when she was smiling. "Call me Erin."

"Sure," Mario grinned. "There something I can help you with, Erin?"

"I just thought we might talk for a little while, Mario." She looked around for a place to sit, but with the gym set in dojo mode, there were nothing but mats on the floor.

"Sure," Mario nodded as he picked up a towel and dried his face. "You have something specific on your mind, I would assume."

"I want you to do me a favor," she said to him, still trying to figure out where to sit.

"What's that?"

"Make sure nothing happens to the Captain on this mission."

[123]

"That would be my intention," Mario wiped his face again. He tossed the towel down on top of his gym bag and sat on the mat. "Why?"

Erin followed his lead and sat down on the mat, crossing her legs under her. "I have no desire to have a command of my own. Least of all at the expense of someone like K'Alan. He's been a good friend for a few years, and I have the utmost respect for him. But I don't ever want to replace him."

"Erin, I can't promise nothing will happen to him, but I'll do my best."

"That's all I ask." She looked Mario over. "So, you any good at martial arts?"

2.2.2136
1300
SLS White Knight
The Lounge

Sarah Hodge sat in a corner of the lounge, nursing a root beer. She'd been working on the shuttle modifications that the captain had requested, and her teams had just finished as much work as they could handle for the time being. The work would have to continue after they'd all had a chance to get something in their bellies. She expected that it would be another very long day of modifications. All she wanted at that point was some rest and relaxation.

"Mind if I join you, Sarah?" Katherine Yeuid asked as she approached the table.

"Am I falling apart?" Sarah smiled at her own weak attempt at humor.

"Cute," Kath chuckled as she sat down. She motioned for the bartender to bring her a drink. "Real cute."

"What can I do for you, Kath?"

"I just thought you could use some company," Kath smiled. "You look like hell."

"I spent the morning working on the shuttle modifications for the Captain," Sarah groaned. "I'm exhausted. And we have so much work still to go if the captain's plan is going to be successful."

"Do you want me to leave?" the older woman asked.

Sarah looked over at the woman who had so quickly become her friend over the past couple weeks and smiled broadly. "No, you're right. I could use the company."

"So, tell me about these modifactions..."

2.2.2136
1344
SLS White Knight
The City

K'Alan walked through the city inside his ship. The sights of the city tormented him. Duterians, some still injured, moved through the city still looking dejected and lost. No one noticed that the ship's captain was in there walking among them. He walked straight to the temple in the center of what would be forever known on the ship as the Duterian sector.

"I come seeking the blessings of the gods," K'Alan said, his voice suitably reverent.

"Then come inside," an acolyte said from the door of the temple.

"Thank you." K'Alan bowed as he walked inside the temple. He looked, amazed. In a little over one day, they had managed to completely and accurately recreate the temple from the village that he and K'Itea had grown up in.

"We've been expecting you, Captain," a priest said. "You carry a great burden."

"Yeah, you can say that again," K'Alan grunted. "It's been a rough week."

"And yet you remain here. To protect your people."

"Yeah. Seems pretty strange to me how things work sometimes."

"Not really, Captain Bryce," the priest gave him a kind smile. "Your soul tells me many things."

"My soul and I aren't on speaking terms."

[125]

"Yes, I see that too," the priest sighed. "It is a shame. Your soul can tell you a great many things, Captain. Your soul will save your life one day."

"I'm sorry, I just can't believe that," K'Alan shook his head. "My wife believes. Her faith has always been stronger than mine. But of late... I just don't know."

"You will," the priest turned away. "And very soon."

2.2.2136
1500
SLS White Knight
The Lounge

"So, have you seen the Captain today, Lieutenant Commander?" Soran's pleasant baritone greeted Kath when she came up to where he was tending bar.

"Not since the mission briefing," the young woman replied. "Why?"

"I'm looking for him," the bald barman shrugged. "He hasn't been in, so I'm a little worried."

"You're worried because he hasn't come in for a drink?" Kath raised an eyebrow. "That's odd. What makes you worried?"

"Well, among other things, the captain is a creature of habit. He usually comes in and has lunch here around 1200 hours. He hasn't been in yet today." The large barman crossed his beefy arms across his chest. "I worry when people I know do things contrary to normal."

Kath chuckled and looked around. She inclined her head towards the door.

"His wife just walked in. You might ask her," Kath smiled. "But I'm sorry, I can't help you."

Kath took her drink and walked off towards a table, where a couple other bridge officers were sitting. Soran shrugged his shoulders again and started to wipe down the bar. K'Itea Bryce slipped onto a stool at the bar, still a little unsteady on her feet.

"What can I get for you?" the barman asked.

"Duterian Sunmist," she said, her voice tired.

"One Duterian Sunmist coming up," he smiled. "If you don't mind my asking, are you K'Itea Bryce by any chance?"

"Yes," she said, startled. "How did you know who I am?"

"I cheated. Your husband showed me a picture of you once," he admitted. "He's a good man."

"Yes, he is," K'Itea smiled. "I love him very much."

"And he does you, I'm sure," the barman smiled again. He started wiping the bar some more, although the bar was as clean as it always was. "I have to admit I'm a little worried about him."

"Why?"

"He's been very distant the last couple days. I'm sure he's just worried about the situation, but as I said, I think he's a good man, and I worry."

"I've never heard of a bartender worrying about one of his clients before," K'Itea laughed. "Why are you worrying about Kal?"

"He saved my life once. I never forget something like that."

"Well, thank you for your concern..."

"Soran," the barman said, pausing from wiping the bar.

"Thank you for your concern, Soran. I'm sure he'll be all right."

2.3.2136
1049
SLS White Knight
The Bridge

K'Alan settled into the command chair. He wanted to get this mission over with, and he fidgeted with a loose thread on his uniform jacket.

"Approaching jump gate," Tyla Barros announced.

"Jump engines reading normal, Captain," Sarah called.

"Jump!"

The Dawning of a New Age

⟨CHAPTER 8⟩

HYPERSPACE is a layer of space under our own that we can tap into. Distances in our galaxy between two points are greatly reduced by going through hyperspace. In order for a ship to go into hyperspace, it must engage jump engines while going through a jump gate.

Hyperspace itself is nothing special to look at. Black against black, there are no stars, no planets. Nothing but an endless void. Navigating in hyperspace is usually done by computer because it's so tricky. Jump gates have a hyperspace homing beacon attached to them that ship computers can lock onto to navigate in hyperspace.

Hyperspace can be a very lonely place.

"ETA at the Brentax jump gate?" K'Alan asked.

"About 24 hours, Captain," Tyla Barros reported after doing the calculations. "It's just amazing. Just fifty years ago, this trip would have taken twelve years."

"Yeah. And we weren't at war with the Brentax either," K'Alan reminded the young woman. "You have the bridge, Ms. Barros. Call me when we reach the Brentax jump gate."

"Yes, sir."

K'Alan walked off the bridge and headed for the nearest lift.

2.3.2136
1222
SLS White Knight
The Gym

"Hey, pretty boy," Masha called. "Wait up."

Mario turned and looked at his friend. While he had been expecting her to find him, he was not sure he really wanted to talk to the large security chief. But the two had been friends for a while, so he would at least be polite to her.

"What do you need, Masha," he asked. "I'm getting ready for the mission."

"Captain says you got almost 24 hours to get ready," Masha said. "How about a little sparring session?"

"Not right now, Masha."

"All right, bud. What's wrong?" she growled. "You never pass up an opportunity to spar."

"I'd rather not talk about it." He started to turn away, but stopped when she put her hand on his arm.

"Mario, this is me you're talking to," she reminded him. " You know I won't just let this go."

"It's just..." he started to say. He almost told her that he had a bad feeling about the mission. But he knew that she would try to stop them from going, and he knew that this was the best chance of the mission succeeding, so he changed his mind. "Nothing. Never mind."

Rick Bentsen

"All right, bud. I'll let it go for now. But we will talk about this some other time."

"I gotta go get ready."

2.3.2136
1442
SLS White Knight
The City

K'Alan grunted. He really didn't want to do this, but he knew that it was better to get it over with now then to try to have this conversation when he was getting ready to leave for Brentax III.

He walked along the various corridors of the city until he came to the area that served as the palace. It really didn't look like the palace from Duterius Prime. But it served its purpose.

The royal guard, one of a very few that had survived the destruction of Duterius Prime, at the palace entrance nodded at K'Alan and let him pass. He smiled at the guard as he entered. He remembered that the man had been one of the guards watching over the survivors when he and Mario had found and rescued K'Itea.

K'Alan walked down a hall looking for where his sister or wife were. He saw K'Itea sitting in a room, watching out a viewport. He walked up behind her and gently folded his arms around her from behind. She looked up at him and smiled taking great comfort from being in his arms.

"Why are there no stars, Kal?" she asked.

"There are no stars in hyperspace."

"It looks so empty," she observed. "So lonely."

"It can be," he said as he kissed her forehead.

"You're leaving, aren't you?" she said, sadness creeping into her voice.

"Mario and I are going on a mission, yes," he admitted.

"Elam will be mad."

"He'll understand in time," K'Alan said, his voice betraying his lack of certainty in his words.

[131]

"He may." K'Itea looked at him. "Where are you going?"

"Brentax III."

"Are you crazy?" she thundered. She pulled away from his embrace. "K;Alan Bryce, that's the homeworld of the Brentax Empire!"

"I know," he said.

"Why are you going?" she demanded.

"Because I'm tired of war," he exploded. He regretted his tone at once. Sitting down next to K'Itea on the bench, he took her back in his arms and held her tight. "All I want is for this war to end so I can spend more time with my family. And this is a way to end it once and for all."

"Oh? Is that the only reason you are going?"

"Plus I'm going to kidnap the person who destroyed our planet," he admitted after a moment.

"So it's revenge."

"Basically, yes."

"I don't want you to go, Kal." She buried her face in his shoulder, and he could feel the tears starting to soak through his uniform jacket.

"Kit, I have to go." He kissed her hair and squeezed just a little tighter. What he really wanted to do was just hold her for the rest of his life, but he knew that he would have to go on this mission before that could really happen. "If Mario and I are successful, we could end this war and start an era of peace here in the quadrant."

"I just don't want to lose you, Kal." She looked up at him with her big tear filled eyes. "And I'm afraid if you go, you won't come back."

"I'll be back, Kit. Count on it."

* * *

2.3.2136
2000
SLS White Knight
Forward Observation Lounge

Mario stood looking out a viewport. He'd been there for half an hour, just staring. He watched the blackness as it rolled past the viewport. His thoughts were turbulent and troubled.

"Mario? Are you OK?" Kath asked as she walked into the lounge her bootfalls muted by the plush carpeting.

"Hmm?" Mario was startled from his musings. "Oh, yeah, Katherine. I'm fine."

"You sure? You're staring out the viewport like you've never seen hyperspace before," Kath chuckled.

"Looking out into hyperspace is like looking into one's soul, Katherine," Mario reflected.

"Getting philosophical in your old age, Mario?" Kath laughed.

"No, Katherine," Mario chuckled. "I just get this way before a mission."

"You know, you're the only one who calls me Katherine. Why?"

"A beautiful name for a beautiful lady," Mario smiled.

"You think I'm beautiful?" Kath blushed. "No one's ever said that to me before."

"They must all be blind then," Mario said, flashing his famous winning smile.

Kath blushed further and turned away. "You probably say that to all the girls."

"No, Katherine. I haven't said that to anyone in years," Mario shook his head. "Aw, hell. Can't a guy give a girl a compliment anymore?"

* * *

K'Alan sat reading over status reports. He'd been having trouble getting to sleep so he thought he'd do a little work. He knew that the nerves he was feeling about the mission were behind the lack of sleep.

There was a soft knock on his door. Frowning, he looked at the door and then at the chrono on his desk, wondering who could be visiting him at this hour.

"Come on in," he called.

The door opened and K'Itea and Elam walked in. A broad smile lit his face when he saw who it was.

"We couldn't sleep either," K'Itea said in answer to his unspoken question as to why they were there.

"Well, if I were going to have two midnight visitors, I couldn't have picked a better two," K'Alan said. He moved over to the couch and motioned for his family to join him.

"You don't mind us being here?" Elam asked.

"Nope," K'Alan said. "Not at all. In fact, I have something for you, Elam."

"You do?" Elam furrowed his brow.

"Yes, I do." K'Alan took a baseball glove and baseball off of a small table by the couch. "I wanted to give these to you. I've had these a long time. I used to use these at the Academy."

"What is it, K'Alan?" K'Itea asked. "I've never seen anything like it."

"It's part of a game from Terra called baseball. I thought maybe I could teach the game to you, Elam. Or at least the basics."

"Is it fun?" Elam asked, his eyes lighting up.

"I've been told that it's actually more fun to watch it than to play it, but yes, I've had a lot of fun playing baseball."

"Maybe you should explain the game to us, K'Alan," K'Itea said with a twinkle in her eyes, knowing that K'Alan had finally found the thing to connect him to his son once and for all.

"All right," K'Alan smiled. He wrapped one arm around his son and his other arm around his wife. "There are two teams..."

2.4.2136
1103
SLS White Knight
The Bridge

"Captain, computers are reading that we have reached the Brentax jump gate," Tyla Barros reported.

"Prepare to jump to normal space," K'Alan ordered.

"Ready to jump on your mark, Captain," Tyla said.

"Jump!" K'Alan said after a moment.

The ship shuddered once as it entered the jump gate. Almost as soon as they cleared the gate, K'Alan could see stars through the stardome.

"Navigator, please confirm that we are near Brentax space," K'Alan said.

"Yes, sir," Mara Silvermaine said. She made a quick check of her scanners. "We are just outside Brentax space. Brentax III is two days travel time at the shuttle's max speed."

"Prepare the shuttle for launch. We leave in an hour. Commander Sykes, you have the bridge," K'Alan said as he headed to the lift.

The Dawning of a New Age

CHAPTER / 9

Brentax Duhari class cruiser Torellia Corvax
Bridge

M'BEK Tarmos was insufferably pleased with himself. In the span of one week, he'd managed to destroy one of the Star League home worlds, and gotten himself a slew of medals and acknowledgements. Now the Torellia Corvax was patrolling the Empire's southern border. He almost wished that the Star League would launch an attack to retaliate. It would mean many more medals and acknowledgements.

"Supreme Commander, we have jump gate activity," T'Marik announced.

"Really?" M'Bek mused. "Which jump gate?"

"Number 37, sir," T'Marik noted. "That is the one that the Star League would most likely use to launch an attack on us."

"Can your scanners detect any ships that may have just come through the gate, T'Marik?" the commander asked.

"No, sir," T'Marik said after checking over all his systems. "But at this range, our scanners are very limited."

"Flight deck," M'Bek growled as he punched a button on his console. "I want a single fighter prepped and launched. Send him to investigate jump gate 37."

"Yes, sir," came the response from the flight deck.

2.4.2136
1202
SLS White Knight
The Bridge

Commander Erin Sykes did not think she would ever get comfortable sitting in the command chair. She shifted around for a couple minutes trying to get comfortable and sighed when she finally gave up.

"I don't like this chair," she said to no one in particular. "I hope they hurry back."

"Commander, I have Captain Bryce on the line for you," Kath said.

"Holo," the commander ordered.

"Shuttle Kiarin requesting permission to launch," K'Alan said.

"Shuttle Kiarin..."

"Commander, contact on long range radar. Single Brentax fighter. We have not yet been scanned," Masha interrupted.

"Defensive screens full. Full scanner and visual cloaking. Make us invisible, Masha," Erin ordered.

"Done, Commander," the lieutenant smiled. She had anticipated the order and had set it so that she only had to execute the order.

The lights on the bridge dimmed as the cloaking went into place. As part of the procedure, the ships power signature was lessened. But that meant that the power savings had to come from somewhere.

"Captain, hold off on launching," Erin ordered. "We have a long range Brentax contact."

"Understood. Let me know when the pattern's clear, Commander," K'Alan said.

"Acknowledged." She turned to face Masha. "Any chance that pilot can see us?"

"Not likely. To him, we look like space. Both visually and electronically," Masha confirmed. "There's no chance that we can be seen. Unless the fighter bumps into us, that is."

"Good work. Let me know the moment he's gone," Erin said, settling back in the command chair.

The minutes ticked by slowly as the Brentax fighter continued to survey the area looking for whatever. The fighter was doing a very thorough scan, and they were getting fairly close to the White Knight's location. After about twenty minutes, the fighter turned around and headed back the way it came.

"Commander, the fighter's retreating," Masha reported. "Passing off long range sensors now."

"All right, Captain," Erin said as she turned back to K'Alan. "You're cleared to launch. We'll maintain the cloak and silent running until we get the signal from the shuttle. Good hunting."

"We'll be back in five days," K'Alan smiled. "Shuttle Kiarin out."

"And don't die on me," Erin added after K'Alan had severed the transmission. "I don't want your chair."

2.4.2136
1344
Brentax Duhari class cruiser Torellia Corvax
Bridge

"Any word from our fighter?" M'Bek Tarmos asked. He drummed his fingers on the arm of his chair in impatience

"She's requesting landing clearance now, Supreme Commander," T'Marik said.

"Grant clearance and have the pilot report to me on the double," M'Bek growled.

"Aye, sir," T'Marik turned back to his board. "Fighter recon cleared for landing. The Commander wishes to speak to you immediately."

M'Bek stood up and started to slowly pace around the cramped bridge

"Someone get me a cup of kamarat root tea," he growled as he plopped back down in his command chair.

A steaming cup of kamarat root tea appeared next to M'Bek Tarmos as a female in a flight suit rushed onto the bridge.

"Pilot Y'Edera reporting as ordered, sir," the female said.

M'Bek looked over the lithe, as much as lithe could apply to any member of the Brentax race, female with a lecherous glint in his eye. He nodded approvingly and smiled.

"Y'Edera, report on your mission," M'Bek hissed.

"As I approached the jump gate, I had a momentary contact on my scanner. But it was not there long enough for me to be able to tell what it was," Y'Edera shrugged. "I ran a diagnostic on my scanner just to be sure. There does appear that there is some sort of power glitch. I have requested the engineers to look at it."

"Good."

Y'Edera turned and walked off the bridge, M'Bek Tarmos' eyes on her the entire time.

2.4.2136
1604
Shuttle Kiarin

K'Alan grunted as he worked the navigations console. One of the things he had been doing had been to monitor Brentax activity. They were in enemy territory, and it would have been foolish to not pay attention. He'd been hoping to catch a break and end up having little Brentax activity in the area.

Unfortunately, the Brentax seemed to be anticipating a retaliatory strike from the Star League for the destruction of Duterius Prime. It seemed to K'Alan that every ship in the Brentax Armada was going to be in range of them on their way to Brentax III. He only hoped the work that Sarah did on the shuttle would hold up.

"This doesn't look good," he said finally.

"What's wrong, Kal?" Mario asked from his seat on the opposite side of the small cabin.

"It looks like a Duhari class cruiser has been dogging our six," K'Alan sighed.

"You sure?" Mario turned around to look over the readings.

"Well, it looks like they're heading to Brentax III. Not in any hurry either. They could have long outrun us. I think they're following us in on purpose."

"It's a long ride in, Kal. Maybe they'll peel off and head wherever they're heading before we get to Brentax III."

"We can hope," K'Alan said.

2.4.2136
1822
SLS White Knight
Soran's Bar.

Soran was polishing the bar, gently rubbing it, smiling to himself as he admired the polish.

"Hi, Soran," K'Itea smiled a sad little smile as she sat down at the bar.

"Kit, it's good to see you," Soran smiled. "How's Elam?"

"All right. He's with K'Alan's sister."

"How are you holding up?" he asked as he reached under the bar and grabbed a clean glass. With a flourish, he poured her a Duterian Sunmist.

"Not well," she admitted. "I'm worried about him, Soran."

"I'm sure he's fine, Kit," Soran said, his smile broadening. "K'Alan has a way of always coming back."

[141]

"I know. But I still worry."

"Well, he and Mario can take care of themselves," the barman shrugged. He went back to polishing his bar. "They're quite a team. Mario'll watch his back."

"Do you think they'll be successful, Soran?" K'Itea leaned forward and asked. "I understand that if they can do what they're trying to do, it could end the war."

"I hope they do," Soran said, pausing from his polishing to look at her. "I for one am tired of war."

"Me too," K'Itea sighed. "Me too."

"Yes," he nodded and went back to rubbing the soft towel on the hardwood top of the bar. "I would imagine you are."

2.4.2136
1900
SLS White Knight
The Bridge.

"Commander, you should go get some rest. It'll be quite a while before we hear from them," Kath said.

"Yeah, you're right," Erin said, not moving from the command chair. There were several Styrofoam coffee cups scattered around the command chair. All of them were empty. There was a full cup on the arm of the command chair.

"So, why aren't you going off the bridge?" Kath said.

"I'm a little nervous with the Captain going off on a mission like that," the commander shrugged. She took a sip of the coffee and put the cup back on the arm.

"We all are, Commander," Kath shook her head. "But the captain's a survivor. He'll be back."

"The captain is a very special man, Kath," Erin smiled. "Hell, if it weren't for him, I doubt I'd be a Commander right now."

"Really? What do you mean?"

"We were assigned to the Prometheus. It was a tough assignment. The captain was a real hard case. Had his

[142]

'special cases' that were the only ones he gave the cushy jobs to. And the only ones he ever promoted. I was fed up, and ready to quit the SLDF altogether.

"K'Alan, even then, was the same kind of guy he is now. He was easy going and very easy to turn to with a problem. I told him I was quitting and why. He talked me out of it. He said that I'd long since earned his respect and that he believed in me. He helped me fight within the rules and start getting the recognition I deserved.

"We were both transferred off the Prometheus at the same time. My new CO saw how hard I worked and immediately gave me the promotion to Lieutenant that I should have received months before. K'Alan was one of the first to congratulate me. I would have given up if it weren't for him."

"He really cares about his people, Erin," Kath said. "That's probably one of the reasons Admiral Bonetti gave him this command when Captain Ker'sal left."

"Yeah, probably," Erin nodded. "But I don't intend to let Gamma Strike lose two Captains in a month."

"We won't, Erin. If my read on Mario is correct, he will do whatever it takes to keep the captain safe."

"Let's hope so."

2.4.2136
2355
Shuttle Kiarin

"Mario, the cruiser's accelerating. It looks like she is going to go right past us." K'Alan's eyes were glued to the scanner watching every move the Brentax cruiser

"I told you. And you were worrying about nothing."

"Unidentified freighter," the comms systems crackled. "This is the Brentax warship Dorania Toran. You are in Brentax space. You are ordered to submit a complete cargo manifest and flight plan immediately. Failure to comply or an attempt to run will result in your immediate and painful termination. You have ten standard minutes to comply."\

The Dawning of a New Age

"Or you may have good reason to worry," Mario sighed. "Dammit, why can't I keep my big mouth shut?"

CHAPTER 10

2.5.2136
0001
Brentax Duhari class cruiser Torellia Corvax
The Bridge.

M'BEK Tarmos growled as he stumbled onto the bridge. The summons from the bridge had awakened him from a sound sleep. M'Bek Tarmos was not a man that liked being woken up.

"You had best have a good reason for interrupting my sleep period, T'Marik," the Brentax commander roared.

"We are approaching Brentax III, Commander," T'Marik replied. He had seen his commander angry before, so the outburst was nothing new to him. And he knew how to handle it. "You asked to be alerted the moment we were this close to home."

"Ah, good man, T'Marik," M'Bek smiled. "Because you were following my orders, I will not have you beheaded for waking me this time." He strode over to his command chair. "It is good to be home, wouldn't you say, T'Marik?"

"Yes, sir. My wife will be pleased to see me," T'Marik said. "And I'm sure my pouchling has grown quite a bit."

"Yes, I had forgotten that you had family," M'Bek nodded. "Well, we'll be on Brentax III for about a month. You should be able to spend plenty of time with them."

"Thank you, sir," T'Marik nodded and turned back to his console.

M'Bek smiled as he watched the main viewscreen as his home planet loomed larger and larger.

2.5.2136
0003
Shuttle Kiarin

"Your time is almost up, unidentified freighter. Do you truly wish to die this much? It can be arranged."

"Answer the man, Kal," Mario urged.

"Brentax warship, this is the freighter Torian. I apologize for the delay in replying to you. I've been having intermittent computer problems. We are carrying a small shipment of katarrh root for Supreme Commander M'Bek Tarmos on Brentax III," K'Alan closed his eyes as he talked to the unseen cruiser. He said a small prayer to the Duterian gods that this would work.

They had the paperwork to prove that it was a legitimate order. In fact, it had cost the Star League a pretty penny to take this run over from the purveyor that was originally supposed to bring the catarrh root to Brentax III.

"Freighter Torian, prepare to be boarded for shipment inspection." The Brentax sounded like he was grinning in anticipation.

"Sir, I must protest," K'Alan said. "If we don't get this katarrh root to Brentax III soon, the Supreme Commander will be most displeased. We are already running behind due to the computer issues. I would be happy to transmit the shipping order signed by the Supreme Commander himself."

"Transmit your paperwork, freighter," the Brentax officer ordered.

K'Alan fiddled with the controls in front of him, preparing the documents for transmission. As soon as he hit the send button, he turned back to the transmitting mike. "Sent. You should be able to confirm that it is, in fact, the Supreme Commander's signature on that paperwork."

"It is indeed," the Brentax growled. K'Alan wasn't sure, but he thought he detected a note of disappointment in the voice. "Very well, you may proceed to Brentax III. But remember this, Freighter Torian. We will be monitoring you. If you deviate from your planned flight path to Brentax III, we will be forced to open fire on your freighter."

"Understood. Thank you, sir," K'Alan acknowledged as he flicked the comms system off. He breathed a sigh of relief and looked at Mario.

"That was close," Mario said, his eyes wide.

"Too close," K'Alan nodded. "Let's just hope that the rest of this trip is uneventful."

2.5.2136
0944
SLS White Knight
The Gym.

Masha was angry.

She'd protested K'Alan and Mario going on the mission by themselves, but they left her behind. She pointed out that it was her job to protect the Captain at all costs. They had ignored her recommendation. She knew that they were going to get in trouble, and that she wouldn't be able to help them.

So, she was angry. And she was taking out her anger on the punching bag, taking out all her aggressions on an inanimate object rather than her usual sparring partners. She was too afraid that anyone she sparred with would end up in the medbay.

[147]

"Lieutenant?" Tyla Barros said as she walked into the gym. "I don't normally see you in here."

"I usually only come down here when I'm upset, Tyla," the big woman growled. "And call me Masha."

"Masha it is then," Tyla grinned. "Let me guess. You're upset about the Captain and Mario going on this mission."

"You got it, sugar," Masha said as she gave the bag a particularly hard punch. "They should have taken a security officer or two along. They certainly should *not* have gone on the mission by themselves."

"I think we all agree, Masha," Tyla nodded. She began to stretch to prepare for her own exercise. "But beating up a punching bag won't help them."

"Neither will worrying about them, sugar, but I'm doing that too," Masha said, grinning and baring her sharp teeth. "Say, sugar. Do you know how to fence?"

> **2.5.2136**
> **1408**
> **Gamma Epsilon station**
> **Admiral Bonetti's office.**

Admiral John Bonetti was bored. Very bored. He was looking over acquisition and budget reports. He hated this part of the job, looking over and approving budgets for the units under his command. It was a necessity, but none of the Admiralty particularly enjoyed it. Except for Admiral Bryce Hawkes. He kept thinking about seeing if Hawkes would do his for him.

There was a knock on his door, and he sighed.

"Enter," he called.

"I hope I'm not interrupting anything, Admiral," the newcomer said.

"No, not at all," John said looking up. *Dear lord, did the man have a psychic connection or something? How did he know that I was literally just thinking about passing off paperwork to him?* "In fact, I'm glad for the interruption, Admiral Hawkes. What can I do for you?"

[148]

"I wanted to talk to you about the Gamma Strike mission, John," Bryce Hawkes took a seat without it being offered. It was one of the privileges of being the same rank. "I wanted to talk to you outside of the council chambers."

"What do you want to talk about?" John leaned back in his chair, taking a clearly defensive posture.

"Is it wise to send men off to abduct M'Bek Tarmos like that?" Admiral Hawkes spoke in a soft voice, measuring his words carefully.

"Bryce, you and I disagree on a lot of things, but one thing we don't disagree on is that this war has gone on way too long," John suppressed the urge to sigh. "It's my intention to stop this war once and for all."

"By sending some of our best men on what could very easily be a suicide mission, John?"

John stood up and walked around his desk. He sat on the edge of the desk and looked down at Bryce Hawkes.

"It won't be a suicide mission because of who I sent on it. You're right. They are the best we have for this mission, Bryce."

"John," Bryce closed his eyes. "It's suicide. They're not going to just be able to saunter onto Brentax III, grab M'Bek Tarmos, and saunter back out. They'll get caught. And when they get caught, they'll get executed."

"I have a feeling that they'll make it, Bryce. I wouldn't have sent them otherwise. Besides. Do you think I'd consent to my son going on a suicide mission?"

"Mario's on the mission?" Bryce's jaw dropped. "That's just pure insanity! He's a morale officer, for Christ's sake!"

"There's more to Mario than you know, Bryce," John smiled. There was a twinkle in his eye. He was proud of his son, even if Mario's insistence on staying an enlisted man infuriated him. "Mario is a martial arts master and a tactical genius. If he'd only take the officer's exam, he'd have a command of his own by now."

"Well, I'm still not sure if it's the brightest move we've made," Bryce shook his head.

[149]

"Bryce, if this works, we'll end this war once and for all. A new era of peace can begin," John said.

"And if it doesn't work, we've lost some of our best men," Bryce countered.

"It'll work, my friend. It has to work."

2.5.2136
1818
Shuttle Kiarin

K'Alan was dozing at the navigations station. He'd been dozing a couple minutes here and there whenever he could. Unfortunately, the shuttle seemed to have a mind of its own and needed almost constant course correction. He grumbled as the computer beeped to get his attention.

"You know, I can pilot the shuttle for a while, K'Alan," Mario said.

"You just keep your eyes on the scanners. If we run into another Brentax cruiser that wants to inspect our cargo, I doubt I can pull off the same trick twice," K'Alan grunted. "We may have legitimate paperwork, but if one of them gets it into their head that they need to search us even with M'Bek Tarmos's signature on the order request, we're done for."

"Good point."

The two men were quiet for a while, each one concentrating on his individual duties. Finally, K'Alan broke the silence.

"You know, Mario," he said, with a wry smile on his face. "I think Kath likes you."

"Huh?" Mario said, caught off guard. "What are you talking about, Kal?"

"Kath from the bridge," K'Alan specified as his fingers flew over his console, as he adjusted their course yet again. "You know. Tall. Lithe. Kind of a light brown hair. Pixie face."

"What about her?" Mario turned in his seat to look at his friend.

"I think she likes you." K'Alan looked at Mario and winked.

"Oh." Mario turned back to his console and continued to scan. Suddenly he turned back to K'Alan. "She's the cute one, right?"

"Yup."

"Oh."

K'Alan chuckled as he finished making the course corrections and closed his eyes to try to get a couple minutes sleep.

2.5.2136
1911
SLS White Knight
The Bridge

Kath was alone on the bridge. She'd opted to take a shift monitoring the bridge. Because of the current circumstances, a full bridge crew wasn't necessary. Kath didn't mind the time by herself. It gave her time to sort out her thoughts.

She was worried about the two men, of course. She knew that the outcome of this war may well hinge on those two men. But even more, she found, much to her dismay, that she was more worried about not seeing them again. Particularly Mario. It was a disturbing thought for her. She'd never felt anything for a man before. She wasn't sure how to deal with it.

Shrugging to herself, she checked over her readings again. Nodding to herself as she noted that everything was reading normal, she tried to get her mind off the engaging young Colonel.

"Katherine?" a tentative voice from behind the young woman said, startling her. Kath turned around...

...and looked into a mirror image of herself.

The Dawning of a New Age

CHAPTER 11

2.5.2136
1912
Shuttle Kiarin

M ARIO gently nudged K'Alan awake.

"Dinner time, Kal," Mario said as he handed K'Alan a small tray.

"Great," K'Alan yawned. "I'm hungry."

"Too bad. It's not great," Mario grunted. "I'm afraid K rations are about all I could make. Even I, with all my skills, can't make K rations taste good."

"They'll do," K'Alan said as he tore into the food.

They ate in silence, the quiet hum of the engines the only sound in the cabin.

"What are you going to do when the war's over, Kal?" Mario said after a while.

"I don't know," K'Alan shrugged "Your father has a great idea as far as the White Knight becoming a place of diplomacy. I think we'll work on that when it's over. I guess I'll travel for a little while afterwards. I have some

[153]

personal time saved up. Maybe Kit, Elam and I will take a trip."

"Sounds like a good idea," Mario nodded. "Me, I don't think I'll take any time off."

"You should, Mario," K'Alan smiled. "Once the delegates start arriving, I don't know when any of us will get a chance to take a vacation again."

"You're kidding, right?" Mario said with a dead pan expression on his face.

"No, I'm not, Mario," K'Alan chuckled. "Once we start putting the delegates together, we're going to be very busy. And of course, there's the matter of relocating the survivors once a colony can be started for them."

"Aw, hell. We're going to be too busy to enjoy life," Mario rolled his eyes.

"Probably not THAT busy, Mario," K'Alan chuckled. He reached for his drink.

"By the way, K'Alan. S'Era asked me out today," Mario grinned as K'Alan took a swig of his drink.

K'Alan choked, sending his drink all over the cabin.

"That's not even funny, Mario," K'Alan said.

"Actually, she did. I wanted to talk to you before I gave her my answer. If it bothers you that much." He shrugged.

"It just caught me by surprise is all," K'Alan laughed. "If you want to go out with her, I won't stop you. Mostly because if she has her sights set on you, there's no way I could stop it anyway. Just tread really careful. I'd hate to pick up the pieces if she gets honked off at you."

"I promise I'll be careful, Kal. Hey, this is me we're talking about here," Mario flashed his winning smile.

"And that's what I'm worried about," K'Alan grinned.

* * *

"You can pick up your jaw, Katherine," the newcomer said. "I'm quite real."

"But you..."

"Look just like you?" the other woman said. It felt weird to Kath to hear her own voice come out of someone else's mouth. "Of course I do. I'm your twin sister. My name is Suela Yeuid."

"I didn't even know I had a twin sister," Kath shook her head in disbelief. "How long have you been on board?"

"I came on the same time as Commander Sykes," Suela made herself comfortable at a station near where Kath was sitting. "This is the first chance I've had to come try to talk to you."

"This is unbelievable. I never even dreamed I had a twin," Kath sank back into her chair, clearly still stunned.

"You were sent away when you were born. I've spent my entire adult life looking for you. And now that I've found you, I'm glad." Suela smiled a broad smile. It was eerie seeing her own smile on someone else's face. It was clear that having a twin would take some getting used to.

"I wish I had known, Suela. I would have been looking for you too."

"I know, Katherine. But you had no way of knowing. When our mother sent you away, she did so because she couldn't care for both of us. Unfortunately, that meant that you not only did not know about me, but also did not receive the proper training in your youth."

"Training?" Kath furrowed her brow in confusion. "I don't think I understand. What kind of training?"

"You're an empath, Katherine."

"What's an empath?"

"An empath is someone who can sense and affect other people's emotions," Suela explained. "It's a rare gift, but

[155]

one which requires great training to use properly. Angelian twins, such as we are, generally have the gift. I do. And so must you."

"OK, I'm dreaming right? This is all just the result of a very whacked out dream, right?" Kath asked, still disbelieving. "I fell asleep on watch. That must be it."

"It's real, Katherine. All too real."

She was floating.

Inwardly, she groaned, as she recognized the void. She didn't know why, but she recognized the void from somewhere in her subconscious. She must have been here before, The fact that she had been here confused her. And K'Itea was afraid.

"Is anyone there?" she asked aloud.

"We are here, K'Itea Bryce," a woman's voice.

"Show yourself," K'Itea said, looking around.

A lone figure stepped out of the shadows. She was wearing a long grey robe with the hood pulled back. She appeared to be young with shoulder length black hair and eyes so dark they appeared to be black. She had plain features and looked as if she had never smiled a day in her life.

"I am Kiara. I am one who watches," the woman said by way of introduction.

"What do you want with me?"

"Your husband is headed into trouble. He was warned not to go to Brentax III himself. He will likely be captured."

"Will he be killed?"

"I do not know. His path is difficult. I do not know yet if he will survive."

"Why are you telling me this?" K'Itea asked. "It will only make me worry more."

"Warn the others to prepare to take action, K'Itea. They will listen to you."

"But..." she trailed off. "I don't know if I can bear to live without him."

"You are important to the future, as is your husband. We will be watching."

Kiara faded back into the darkness.

2.6.2136
0313
SLS White Knight
Forward Observation Lounge

K'Itea sat in silence, meditating on what she had heard in her dream. She shook her head. K'Alan would be all right. He had to be. Mario would keep him safe. She believed Soran when he had said that. Or at least she'd wanted to.

"Couldn't sleep either, eh?" S'Era said behind K'Itea.

"No," she sighed. "S'Era, I'm worried about him. I'm afraid he won't come back."

"Kit, I'm worried about him too," S'Era said as she walked over and gently put her hands on Kit's shoulders. "But my brother is a survivor. You know that. He's going to be all right."

"I'm not so sure," K'Itea shook her head. She went on to tell the younger woman about the dream she'd had. S'Era listened intently, shaking her head as K'Itea finished speaking.

"Maybe he is in for some trouble on Brentax III, Kit," S'Era said. "But he'll make it through. I'm sure of it."

"I hope you're right, S'Era. For all our sakes."

"If it'll make you feel better, Kit, I'll go with you in the morning, and we can talk to Commander Sykes about it."

"Yeah, maybe that would be best," K'Itea nodded.

"Good. Now go get some rest. You won't do him any good by not sleeping."

* * *

The bridge was bustling with activity. Everyone was at their posts monitoring their stations with renewed interest. The shuttle was due to reach Brentax III shortly. And while everyone hoped that the mission went smoothly, they knew that, if it didn't, the White Knight needed to be working efficiently and had to be ready for anything.

Commander Erin Sykes oversaw the bustle of activity with pride. This was a good crew. They knew their jobs and knew them well. They would be ready for anything.

The only drawback was that Katherine Yeuid looked distracted. It appeared to be only a slight distraction, but any such distraction in this type of situation was enough to worry Erin. She hoped it wasn't enough of a problem to distract the young woman from her work. Maybe she'd talk to Katherine later about it. Or maybe she'd just file it away and report her concerns to K'Alan when he came back.

"Commander," Kath called from her console.

"Yes, Lieutenant Commander," Erin said as she looked at the young woman.

"Commander, K'Itea Bryce is requesting to meet with you. She says it's extremely urgent."

"Tell her I'll meet with her in the conference room. You have the bridge, Lieutenant Commander," she said, jumping off and heading off the bridge.

I just hope whatever's bothering you's not too important, Kath, Erin thought as she walked down the hall to the conference room.

* * *

[158]

K'Itea Bryce and S'Era Bryce sat patiently in the conference room waiting for the commander. The two women were in silent contemplation about what K'Itea had seen in her vision. It had been so real, and K'Itea worried about the implications. There was very little that she could do, other than warn Commander Sykes about what she had seen and hope that the commander took her warning seriously.

Not for the first time since she had woken up from the vision, she touched the bond she shared with K'Alan. She wanted nothing more than to feel it was there. Any more than that, and he would have felt it. The last thing she wanted was to distract him in the middle of his mission. She knew that such a distraction could be fatal. But she was comforted that the bond was there.

"I hope you're right about this, S'Era," K'Itea broke the silence after a while.

"You need to bring up your concerns to the commander, Kit," S'Era put her hand on her friend's arm in a gesture of comfort. "If you feel that this is something she needs to worry about, she needs to know."

"I know, S'Era." K'Itea twiddled her thumbs. "But what if it's just a dream?"

"Well, if it's just a dream, then they'll be prepared for nothing," S'Era gave K'Itea's arm a squeeze. "But what if it isn't just a dream, Kit?"

"That's what worries me even more."

Erin Sykes strode into the conference room. She looked over the two Duterian women and smiled a warm comforting smile. She sat down and looked at K'Itea.

"I understand you wanted to speak to me?" the commander asked.

"Yes, Commander. I wanted to talk to you about a vision I had last night..."

2.6.2136
1102
Shuttle Kiarin

"Mario, wake up," K'Alan said. "We're approaching Brentax III."

"And I was having such a good dream too," Mario groaned. "Can't I just go back to sleep, Kal?"

"Nope. We need to get down get this over with and get back," K'Alan shook his head. "Time to get up, lazybones."

"We do this and get back, right?" Mario opened one eye.

"Right. We get back as quickly as we can," the captain nodded. "In and out."

"Good. I have some new recruits that I need to bilk out of their pay!" Mario opened his other eye and sat up.

"I'm going to pretend I didn't hear that," K'Alan laughed.

"You better get our landing clearance, Kal. I don't want to have to deal with a bunch of angry guards just because we didn't land properly," Mario reminded his friend.

"Agreed," K'Alan nodded as he reached over to open a commlink. "Freighter Torian to Brentacchia Spaceport. Requesting landing clearance for supply offloading."

"Standby, Freighter Torian," the Brentax flight control officer said.

"We're screwed," Mario mouthed. K'Alan shook his head.

"Freighter Torian, you are cleared for landing pad 113. Enjoy your stay on Brentax III."

"Oh, I don't like the way he said that," Mario said after K'Alan closed the commlink.

"Well, you're the one who wanted me to get landing clearance," K'Alan shrugged. He set the course for the indicated landing pad and engaged the thrusters. "I could have just landed us somewhere and let the brush cover the shuttle."

"And it would have been found and destroyed," Mario sighed. "We'll just have to figure out how to go about getting M'Bek Tarmos into the shuttle without anyone noticing."

K'Alan looked over as the shuttle landed softly on the landing pad.

"We're down."

The Dawning of a New Age

⟨CHAPTER / 12⟩

2.6.2136
1117
SLS White Knight
The Bridge

ERIN stormed back onto the bridge. She wasn't sure what to make of K'Itea's vision, but she was now even more worried than she was.

"Yellow alert," she said. "Everyone set to full battle readiness. Maintain full defensive screens, and full visual and electronic cloaking."

"Yes, ma'am!" Masha barked as she set to making sure the cloaking field was in place and fully operational. "Cloak working at one hundred percent. Defensive screens are currently at ninety seven percent charge."

"Weapons status?" Erin barked.

"Lasers are fully functional. Proton torpedoes are armed and ready," Masha reported.

"Good," Erin nodded. She flicked a switch on her panel "Flight crews and pilots, stand ready. We may end up needing you."

[163]

"Commander, I hope you're wrong about needing all of these precautions," Kath said.

"Me too, Lieutenant Commander," Erin said. "Me too."

2.6.2136
1300
Shuttle Kiarin

K'Alan groaned as he looked over the cargo in the shuttle. Half of the katarrh root they had brought on board was destroyed.

"Well, at least our cover won't be totally blown," he sighed.

"What's the problem now, Kal?" Mario said as he came back into the cabin from outside where he'd been checking over the shuttle's status.

"Oh, nothing much," K'Alan said. "Half our katarrh root is bad."

"Could be worse," Mario smiled as he grabbed an antigrav sled and started to load the good cases of katarrh root onto it.

"How so?"

"All of it could be bad," Mario flashed his winning smile and stepped out of the shuttle, pulling the antigrav sled behind him.

"The moment this mission's over, the happier I'll be," K'Alan muttered as he stepped off the shuttle, closing the door behind him.

2.6.2136
1622
Gamma Epsilon Station
John Bonetti's office.

John sighed as he looked at the growing mountain of paperwork on his desk. All he really wanted to do was to run the entire pile through the shredder and be done with it. He grinned to himself as he thought about what the mound of shredded reports might look like. He shook his head and pulled the next report off the pile to read.

"Admiral, there's a hyperspace call for you," Sergeant Riggs, his yeoman called.

"Put it through, Riggs," John sighed, inwardly relieved at the interruption.

"Admiral Bonetti," Kerrin Jameson, President of the Star Leage, greeted the admiral.

"Madame President," he acknowledged.

"How goes the retrieval mission, John?" the president asked.

"It's still too early to know, Kerrin," John sighed. "The team should have gotten to Brentax III a few hours ago. I am expecting to hear a status update from Commander Sykes this evening. I will, of course, pass along what she says."

"This mission is very important, John," Kerrin reminded him. "I trust you put the best people you could on it."

"Of course, Kerrin. I know full well that the success of this mission could spell the end of the war," John smiled. "Frankly, I'd love this war to end. I'm getting tired of reading status reports with friends and loved ones in the latest list of casualties."

"I know, John. I feel the same," Kerrin said, a touch of sadness in her voice. "Thorrin Jade has agreed to mediate the treaty."

"How did you pull that one off, Kerrin? He's the best negotiator in this entire quadrant!"

"Very simply, he's tired of the casualty reports too, John. You get us M'Bek Tarmos and we'll get the treaty negotiated and signed."

"We'll get him, Madame President. Admiral Bonetti out."

The President smiled and blinked off the viewscreen.

"Sergeant Riggs, if the White Knight should report in, I want to speak to Commander Sykes as soon as possible,"

"Understood, Admiral."

John grumbled and picked the report back up.

A small park, vaguely reminiscent of K'Itea Bryce's favorite park on Duterius Prime, had been built near the center of the city. It wasn't very large, only about a thousand square feet. It was about all that they could allocate for such a park. But it was beautiful. Short green grass grew all over, and children could almost always be seen running around. There was talk that the Captain had something special in mind for the park, but no one knew what. There were some benches lining the sides of the park.

It was on one of these benches that S'Era Bryce was sitting dejectedly. She'd sunk into a depression over the past two days, ever since her brother and Mario had left for Brentax III. She didn't even really know why, which was what bothered her most.

She watched the children playing tag and sighed. She wanted children of her own. She knew that much. And yet she didn't have any idea about what she'd like in a mate. Nor had she ever really had any experience dating. Ever since her bondmate had passed away, she'd simply been turned aside, as any potential suitors always viewed her as simply a handmaiden. It did not matter that she came from a higher caste and chose the life she lead. Nor did it matter that she was the handmaiden to the High Gentlewoman herself. She never resented her role, never wished for another life for herself. She only wished that one day, a suitor might see her for who she was, rather than what her job was.

Maybe that was why she had fallen for Mario. He had no concerns over society. Indeed, he'd probably be more concerned with the social ramifications of having a beautiful woman by his side, rather than the ramifications of dating a handmaiden. No, he probably wouldn't care about her station.

She sighed. Despite all of the wonderful people in her life, she realized, for the first time, that she was truly alone. There were only four things in her life that kept her from being totally despondent, her brother, K'Itea, Elam...

...and Mario. She couldn't explain it to anyone even if she had wanted to, but she felt this kinship with Mario. Almost as if they were destined to be together. Of course, she hadn't told him that was how she felt. She was too afraid that he'd laugh it off as a childish fantasy. But her heart had soared when he hadn't said no to her request for a date. She hoped that he would say yes, but he'd said he'd needed to think about it. She suspected that he wanted to talk to K'Alan about it before giving her an answer.

And now he was off on Brentax III. And she was worried about him.

She closed her eyes and listened to the sounds of the children playing.

"Are you OK, S'Era?" a female voice near her said. She opened her eyes to see K'Itea standing nearby and watching her.

"No, K'Itea, I'm not," the younger woman shook her head.

"Well, if you need someone to talk to, I'm here," K'Itea said softly as she sat down.

"I'll be OK," S'Era smiled a sad smile. "So, I hear that K'Alan has plans for this park."

"Yeah, he does," K'Itea grinned. "He wants to turn it into a baseball field. It's not nearly a big enough park, though, so I am not sure what he will do instead."

"Only K'Alan would think of something like that," S'Era chuckled. "It makes sense though. Something like that is bound to be a real moral boost to everyone."

"I didn't even know what baseball was until two days ago," K'Itea sighed. "Kal had a ball and glove that he gave to Elam. He explained the rules to us. It sounds kind of fun."

[167]

"He played in the Academy, didn't he?" S'Era asked, vaguely remembering a letter from K'Alan describing the game.

"Yes. Apparently he was a pitcher. A fairly good one, especially since he had to learn the rules as he went," K'Itea smiled. "I would have liked to have seen him play."

"Me too, K'Itea." S'Era watched the children playing and smiled to herself. "I'd like to have children one day, K'Itea," she added softly after a while.

"I know, S'Era," K'Itea said, patting her friend's hand comfortingly. "I've seen how you are with Elam. I have no doubt you'd be a good mother."

"Thank you, K'Itea. That means a lot to me," S'Era smiled.

2.6.2136
1902
SLS White Knight
The Bridge

Erin settled into the command chair. She'd just come back from having an early dinner. She was supposed to report in to Admiral Bonetti sometime that evening, but she had nothing to report. It would have to be enough for the admiral.

"Lieutenant Commander Yeuid, prepare to initiate hyperspace communication with the Gamma Epsilon station," Erin said, her voice clearly bored.

"Yes, ma'am. Hyperspace communication initiated," Kath reported. "Holo activated now."

John Bonetti's head appeared in the gap made by the ring of the top level of the bridge.

"Admiral Bonetti, this is Commander Erin Sykes reporting in as ordered," Erin said, snapping off a quick salute.

"Commander, how goes the mission?" the admiral asked.

"Uneventful, sir," the young woman said. "No word from Captain Bryce or Colonel Bonetti, but that's to be expected. I doubt we'll hear from them for another twenty four hours or so."

"As soon as M'Bek Tarmos arrives on the ship you are to immediately bring him to my office on the Gamma Epsilon station." the admiral ordered.

"Understood," Erin nodded. "I'll report in as soon as I know more."

"Good," John nodded. "I'll expect to hear from you in about twenty four hours then, Commander."

"Yes, sir. Commander Sykes out."

The holo faded and Erin closed her eyes. She gently rubbed her temples. This was going to be a very long twenty four hours. She sighed and went back to monitoring the bridge.

2.6.2136
1722
Brentax III
Brentax Militia Headquarters.

M'Bek Tarmos strode purposefully through the building that served as the headquarters for the Brentax Militia. He headed to his office and closed the door behind him. He walked around and sat down behind his desk, looking with distaste at the pile of paperwork that awaited him.

"Supreme Commander, Chancellor G'Kiron is here to see you," one of his office staff called through his closed door.

"Send him in," M'Bek growled. He did not know what the elderly chancellor wanted, but it would be a good distraction from the paperwork.

Chancellor G'Kiron strode in, his large frame barely fitting through the door. G'Kiron had no last name. Some thought it was a symbol of dishonor for the elderly Brentax official, but G'Kiron had made a name for himself. Once he had been the Supreme Commander of the Brentax Militia, but he had retired, healthy and whole, to the world of politics. Although he knew that the strings were really pulled by the Militia and always would be, he did his best to influence things for the better. The Chancellor knew that this war was proving to be more costly than anyone had ever realized. And so, with heavy heart, he had decided to talk to M'Bek Tarmos, Supreme Commander of the Brenax Militia, about ending this war.

"Chancellor G'Kiron!" M'Bek oozed. "It's so good to see you. Care for a cup of kamarat root tea?"

"No thank you, Supreme Commander," G'Kiron shook his head. "I was hoping I could have a word with you about the state of this war."

"Glorious, isn't it?" M'Bek smiled.

"I'm not sure I'd use the term glorious to describe it," G'Kiron shook his head a second time. "The war has gone on for almost thirty years, M'Bek. Don't you think we've made our point?"

"And what point would that be, G'Kiron?" M'Bek leaned back in his chair to look at the Brentax official. His eyes slowly narrowed as he suspected the man of cowardice.

"That the Brentax are not to be crossed," G'Kiron said firmly. "I didn't say that I did not agree with the war, M'Bek."

"If you had, I would have had to have you executed for treason, G'Kiron. Watch yourself."

"The Star League knows that we are a dominant force in this quadrant and that we're not going to be going anywhere. They respect us, and even fear us. If we were to offer them a truce, they would not dare break it."

"Yes, but why should we trust the Star League, G'Kiron? They have not given us much reason to trust them. They sneak attack us. They send us peace envoys and use them as lures to destroy us."

"But we have destroyed one of their homeworlds. Surely they'll remember that and quiver in fear at the thought of our doing that again and again. We do have the firepower to destroy any of their worlds we so choose."

[170]

"So you would recommend that we throw down our arms and make peace with the sniveling worms? Is that what you are recommending, G'Kiron?" M'Bek scoffed.

"There is a great darkness on the horizon, M'Bek," G'Kiron sighed. He knew that his plea was falling on deaf ears but he continued anyway. It's one that can destroy even the great Brentax Empire. Surely you must remember the prophecies of the Great Thinkers."

"Great darkness indeed," M'Bek laughed. "Thank you for a good laugh, Chancellor. But this conversation is over. I thank you for your counsel, but the war continues."

"It will be on your head if we are swallowed up in the darkness, M'Bek Tarmos," G'Kiron warned gravely.

"An idle threat, I'm afraid, G'Kiron," M'Bek guffawed.

"We'll see, M'Bek."

G'Kiron turned on his heel and whirled out of the office. M'Bek continued to guffaw raucously as G'Kiron strode out.

2.6.2136
1735
Brentax III
An abandoned warehouse

"All right. So who are we supposed to be meeting here?" Mario asked with his arm crossed. He started tapping his foot without even realizing it.

"A Brentax by the name of Chancellor G'Kiron," K'Alan said as he checked his notes.

"You know anything about this G'Kiron?" Mario asked.

"Very little. Admiral Bonetti said that this Chancellor is interested in ending the war and may be able to help us get into the militia headquarters undetected."

"But you don't know more than that?" Mario grumbled.

"No," K'Alan said after a pause. "But I have a gut instinct that we can trust him."

"Let me just remind you, buddy," Mario clapped K'Alan on the back. "These are the same folks that destroyed your homeworld. How can you trust any of them?"

"I remember," K'Alan looked sternly at Mario. "But my gut instinct is to trust this Chancellor G'Kiron."

"It's your neck, buddy," Mario shrugged. He started tapping his foot again. "I hope you're right."

"We'll find out soon enough," K'Alan said. He leaned on a crate and crossed his arms across his chest. He had heard some scuffling, and he hoped it would turn out to be the Chancellor.

"Is anyone there?" a crackly voice croaked. "This is Chancellor G'Kiron."

Mario and K'Alan looked at each other. Mario shrugged and K'Alan slowly walked out into the open.

"Chancellor G'Kiron?" he asked in a tentative voice.

"Are you from the Star League?" the large Brentax male K'Alan saw asked.

"Yes, I am."

"We must hurry," Chancellor G'Kiron said. "This war must end soon."

CHAPTER / 13

CHANCELLOR G'Kiron sat on a crate looking at the two Star League soldiers. He leaned forward, his forearms resting on his thighs. A deep sigh rattled through the old man's chest.

"Long ago," the Chancellor began. "The Brentax Empire was not much different than the Star League. We were a peaceful empire dedicated to peaceful exploration. We were provoked into a conflict with the Tularian Empire."

"I've never heard of the Tularian Empire," Mario said.

"You would not have. We destroyed them a long time ago," G'Kiron continued. "Once we started into that conflict, we embarked on a path of military supremacy in this quadrant. A hundred years ago, I was named the Supreme Commander of the Brentax Armada."

"A hundred years?" K'Alan raised an eyebrow. "Just how old are you sir?"

[173]

"I have made over one hundred and fifty trips around my sun," the old man rasped. "If I am lucky, I will have another forty or fifty years left."

"Your people are long lived," Mario noted. "I never knew that about the Brentax."

The old Brentax man smiled at Mario.

"I suspect that we will find a great deal about each other's races that we do not know," G'Kiron noted.

"I suspect you are right," K'Alan nodded. "Please, continue."

"We first learned of the Star League when I was the Supreme Commander. We considered the Star League to be of little consequence. After I resigned as Supreme Commander and entered the political arena, I began to reread the old prophecies of our Great Thinkers."

"Great Thinkers?" K'Alan asked. "Who were they?"

"Back before we became a militaristic society, we were an idealistic and thoughtful society. We had seven Great Thinkers whose prophecies shape our society. One of our Great Thinkers, N'Ron Jukar, prophesied a great darkness that would engulf this quadrant. He said that the Brentax Empire would have to align itself with another power in the quadrant in order to save ourselves from this darkness."

"What does this have to do with the situation?" Mario asked. He turned from where he was watching out the window. "I mean, if we even believe this prophecy."

"I believe that the prophecy refers to the Star League," the old man finished. "We must end this war before there is no one left to stop the darkness."

"Chancellor," K'Alan said. "I have to tell you. Many of my people won't accept peace with the Brentax. After the destruction of Duterius Prime..." he trailed off.

"A tragic event. And one I do not condone. You have my sincere apologies for the destruction of your planet, Captain. I wish circumstances were different."

"So do I, Chancellor," K'Alan nodded. "I don't mind telling you, right after the assault on Duterius Prime, I wanted nothing more than to retaliate by destroying Brentax III."

"I understand," G'Kiron sighed, suddenly looking even older. "You must have lost many friends and loved ones in the destruction."

"Fortunately, the one person I love the most wasn't killed," K'Alan admitted. "Had she been, I doubt I'd be on a mission designed to end this war peacefully. I'd be leading the destruction of Brentax III myself."

"For your loved one being safe, I am grateful," G'Kiron said. "Love is a very powerful force, even for the Brentax. Our peoples have much in common. Hopefully in time, we will be able to work peacefully together as opposed to fighting amongst each other."

"Agreed," K'Alan nodded as he extended his hand. G'Kiron shook K'Alan's hand and smiled. It was a small step, but a step nonetheless.

2.6.2136
2010
Earth
President Kerrin Jameson's office.

The President of the Star League was an attractive woman. She had short-cropped brown hair and fiery green eyes. Those green eyes were deep and knowledgeable. She was usually jovial, her thin lips pressed together in an almost perpetual smile.

She was, however, not smiling at the moment.

In fact, she was scowling. She'd just finished reading yet another casualty report, the sixth such report since the destruction of Duterius Prime. It was as if the Brentax had stepped up their efforts in ending this war by force once and for all.

And Kerrin Jameson, President of the Star League, didn't like it one bit.

Once again, she wondered about the progress of the Gamma Strike mission to Brentax III, hoping beyond hope that it would be successful. She had no doubt in her mind that if it weren't successful, the Star League would be hard-pressed to stop this war before it destroyed them all.

She sighed as she looked over the casualty reports. Perrin Hawks, who had just been handed a new ship, was just barely clinging to life after a devastating attack by the Brentax killed over half her crew. Perrin had barely survived as the bridge was all but destroyed.

Kerrin was deeply troubled to see what had happened to Perrin. Perrin Hawks was a good friend. They'd grown up together in Chicago, had double dated a couple times in high school. Kerrin had laughed when Perrin had applied to the Academy, not knowing that Perrin would have a brilliant career in the Star League Defense Force. Indeed, Perrin had made Captain at just thirty years old. They refused to promote her again, saying that having someone as much of a tactical genius as Perrin Hawks anywhere but the commander of a unit was a big mistake.

In fact, there were a lot of people in the higher levels who were saying that, had anyone else been in command of the Charger, the entire crew would have been lost. As it was, the Charger would be in the space docks around Ventura Prime for several weeks, probably closer to a couple months.

The last thing Kerrin Jameson wanted to do was to have to phone Perrin's parents and tell them their daughter had been killed in the war.

"Madame President," a voice from her desk intercom called. "Thorrin Jade is here to see you."

"Send him in, Jane," Kerrin said, her exhaustion evident in her voice.

Thorrin Jade walked into the office. His diminutive stature belied the power his personality and voice exuded.

"Madame President," he nodded in greeting.

"Thorrin," Kerrin smiled warmly. "What can I do for you today?"

"I was hoping to get an update on the mission," he said, his dulcet tones almost swept away in Kerrin's large office.

"I'm afraid that there hasn't been any word yet," Kerrin said as she sat back in her chair. "I, for one, am hoping that this mission is quick and successful." She glanced at the latest casualty list and shook her head.

"I agree," he said as he looked towards the casualty list. "More casualties?"

"Yes, I was just looking at the list. It just came in. My dear friend, Perrin Hawks, was grievously hurt in one of the latest Brentax attacks. The doctors aren't hopeful that she'll recover."

"I'm sorry, Kerrin," Thorrin sighed. "We've all lost people close to us in this war. Captain Hawks is a very brave woman. I hope she pulls through."

"I hope so too. Now, let's get to the business at hand," she smiled.

2.6.2136
2236
Brentax III
Chancellor G'Kiron's home.

Chancellor G'Kiron smiled at the two Star League soldiers. They had gone to the Chancellor's home to discuss strategy. G'Kiron was a study in contrasts. On one side, he was a warrior. He'd admitted to K'Alan and Mario that he had believed at first that this war was correct. On the other side, he was a free thinker. He made it clear to the two soldiers that he felt that this war needed to end, and end quickly.

K'Alan and Mario decided that they should trust the Brentax Chancellor. After all, without his help, they would never get into the Militia Headquarters.

"Chancellor, what is the security like inside the Militia Headquarters?" Mario asked.

"Security is very tight. You will not be able to walk in uncontested," the chancellor said. "I would recommend that the two of you enter the building in two separate places and meet up at M'Bek Tarmos's office."

[177]

"I'm not sure I like the idea of splitting up," K'Alan said.

"You'll like the idea of a Brentax prison even less, Captain," G'Kiron said. "I assure you that such a stay would be unpleasant at best. The torture that would be inflicted on you would break even the heartiest of Star League soldiers."

"I think we'd like to avoid that," Mario grimaced. "K'Alan over there is too sweet and tender to hold up to torture." Mario ignored the glare his friend shot his way. "What are the security patrols like?"

"Two man patrols wander the halls randomly. There is no pattern. They are armed with heavy blaster rifles," G'Kiron said, his breath rattling in his chest as he spoke. "The guards usually have their blaster rifles armed at all times and they are usually set on heavy stun, but they sometimes are set on kill."

"Great," K'Alan said.

"It would be best if you went in right before dawn. The guards will not suspect someone trying to break into the building then. And be careful," the chancellor warned. "I know that peace in this quadrant hinges on this mission. It must succeed."

2.7.2136
0003
SLS White Knight
The City

K'Itea Bryce couldn't sleep. She hadn't been able to sleep since her vision the previous night. She sighed as she stared at the grey metal ceiling in her room. If only K'Alan were there to comfort her...

Elam was asleep in the other room. The boy had slept soundly the past two nights. K'Itea found that she envied her son. Even though he and K'Alan had seemingly made peace with each other, Elam seemed to have no sense that he might not see his father again.

It almost worried K'Itea.

It wasn't that he didn't care, for she knew he did. Elam had been very excited at the prospect of learning to play baseball. In fact, when K'Alan had demonstrated how to pitch, Elam had been totally fascinated and had wanted to try. His first few attempts had been very clumsy, and he'd bounced the ball in front of the plate. But K'Alan had been very patient with Elam showing him the proper grip for different pitches and working on Elam's mechanics. Finally, Elam had thrown a pitch over the plate. It didn't have great speed on it, but K'Alan assured the boy that speed and accuracy would come with practice. He had said that Elam was probably going to be a great pitcher in time.

Elam had soaked up the compliment with pride.

So why did he seem unconcerned about whether or not K'Alan was coming home?

K'Itea sighed softly to herself as she realized that she didn't have an answer. She stared up at the ceiling, wondering what she should do.

Finally, she got up and dressed. She moved quietly through the quarters she shared with her son, checked on Elam again and walked out into the City.

2.7.2136
0201
SLS White Knight
Medbay

K'Itea wandered into the medbay, her robes rustling around her body. A couple of the medtechs smiled at her and went about their business. She walked over to Jewel, who always seemed to be on duty and sat down.

"Let me guess," Jewel said, not looking up from the chart she was working on. "You're having trouble sleeping."

K'Itea nodded. "Any idea why?"

"Probably, I'm just worried about K'Alan," K'Itea said. "I had this dream last night, and I haven't slept since."

"Well, I'm sure K'Alan will be all right," Jewel smiled. "If you'd like, I can give you something to help you sleep."

[179]

"Maybe that would be good," K'Itea nodded.

2.7.2136
0415
Earth
President Kerrin Jameson's quarters.

Kerrin woke up with a start. She didn't know what caused it. All she knew was that suddenly, she was awake and panicking.

She looked around and sighed. Nothing different was evident in her quarters. She shook her head and told herself she was just imagining things.

But she couldn't just go back to sleep without checking, so she went through her quarters room by room. When she was satisfied that there was nothing out of place anywhere in her quarters, she went back to her bedroom.

She lay back down and fell asleep.

2.7.2136
0533
Brentax III
Outside the Brentax Militia Headquarters.

K'Alan crouched outside one of the entrances to the Brentax Militia Headquarters.

"I'm in position," he said into his wristlink.

"Waiting on your word, buddy," Mario replied.

"Go!" K'Alan said. He tightened his grip on his energy bow and slowly crept inside.

⟨CHAPTER 14⟩

2.4.2136
1214
Jarada V

THALA Ker'sal stepped off of a freighter that had brought her from the Gamma Epsilon Station to her homeworld. It felt good to once again be on the desert sands of her home planet. She slung her duffel bag over her left shoulder, and smiled a sad smile as she watched the dust swirl in the distance.

"Home," she said, closing her eyes and letting the sun caress her skin. "I've missed this planet."

She walked over to the transport station and walked inside. The Jaradan behind the counter smiled at her.

"Where do you want to go?" the man asked.

"Well," she gave it some thought. In the end there was only one choice for her. "I suppose I should go to Kentar."

"From there originally?" he asked as he wrote up the transport ducat.

"Yeah," she nodded. She wasn't able to muster up even a sad smile for this man. "I still have family there."

"Well, I hope you have a safe trip," the man smiled.

"Thanks," she said as she took the ducat. The man did not even notice her lack of enthusiasm for the trip. He simply turned to take care of the next person in line.

She walked towards her transport, looking around. The spaceport and transport hub had not changed any since she had been there last. She hadn't been there since she had passed her officer's exam and had been assigned to her first ship as an officer ten years before. She suspected that it was one of those places that would just never change.

As she walked across the tarmac to her transport, she thought about how she had gotten there. It had been a long three days since she had stepped down from commanding Gamma Strike. She still wondered if she had done the right thing. In her heart, she knew she had, though. She would never have been able to handle the constant reminder that K'Alan had chosen his wife over her.

She stepped onto the transport and found a seat near a window. She looked out the window and sighed to herself. She took comfort in the fact that Jarada hadn't changed since she'd left to join the Defense Force. Jarada was a mostly desert planet, its reddish orange sand kicking up into dangerous sandstorms regularly. The buildings always had been a rust colored brown. The Jaradan people had developed a thick outer skin to protect themselves from the sun and the sand.

She watched as the buildings slowly moved past her. Travelling to Kentar would take a few hours at best. It would be longer if they ran into a sandstorm and had to divert. Sandstorms were always a possibility this time of year. Unfortunately, that left her with too much time on her hands, something she was all too familiar with.

She closed her eyes, only to see his face in her mind. Lords, she resented him. She resented the fact that he was now the commanding officer of the squad she had been given command of. Resented him because he had found happiness with another woman. Resented him because he had no regrets. Resented him because she was the one who had left the ship not him. And she resented him for making her feel something she knew she shouldn't have.

And yet, she didn't know what to do.

She still wore her Star League uniform. She had no other clothes but her uniforms. That was something she would have to fix when she got back to Kentar. She thought of her home.

How would her family react to her being home? It had been a long time since she had seen them. Ten years since she'd visited. She wondered how her baby brother had turned out. He had been only seven when she'd last seen him ten years earlier. And her parents. How were they? Would they be happy to see her? She seemed to recall that they hadn't parted happily the last time she was home.

She shook her head, as if to clear her mind of all questions. It was pointless second-guessing herself. She was going home, whether she was ready or not.

The transport lurched, and she opened her eyes. A small sandstorm had kicked up on the horizon and the transport pilot had altered course to avoid it. She watched as the sandstorm swept over a nearby town, covering the town in reddish orange dust. She shook her head, trying to remember the name of the town.

She closed her eyes again, hoping to get a few minutes sleep before the transport landed, but knowing that was impossible. She had status reports in her duffel that she could go over. Sighing, she opened her duffel and pulled out a stack of reports, deciding that the best course of action would be to keep herself occupied. So, she read the reports, but didn't really find their contents interesting.

"We'll be arriving in Kentar in about three minutes. Have your transportation ducats ready," the pilot called over the transport's loudspeakers.

She put her reports back into her bag and looked back out the window. Kentar was one of the more beautiful cities on Jarada V. It was also one of the few cities that was not in the desert. Kentar was surrounded by a lush green forest, one of the few such areas on Jarada V. She sighed, a slight smile on her face as she looked at her home.

"Miss? Your ducat please?" the crewman assigned to her cabin asked. She handed him the ducat without looking at him. He smiled and said, "Thank you. Enjoy your stay in Kentar."

"I hope I will," she said, without thinking about what she was saying.

She watched the town grow as they got closer. As soon as the transport landed and they opened the doors, she was off the transport, taking a deep breath of the air she remembered so fondly from when she was growing up.

Without even thinking, she slowly walked straight to her parents' home. She looked around remembering her childhood. No one gave her a second look as she walked along the streets of Kentar. She stopped outside her parents' home. Suddenly, she was nervous about coming back. No one was looking out the window, so no one saw her as she stepped up the walk and stood in front of the door. The gate squeaked as it always had. She suspected someone had heard that at least.

She knocked, not expecting anyone to answer. *In fact,* she thought, her inner voice as glum as she felt. *It may be better if no one answers.*

"Coming!" a voice she recognized as her mother's called from somewhere inside the house. The door opened, and Cheria Ker'sal stood in the open doorway, a look of total shock on her face.

"Hello, Mother. May I come in?" Thala asked, her voice soft.

"Thala!" her mother cried, wrapping Thala up in a giant hug. "Of course you can, child. Welcome home. Your father will be so glad to see you. He should be home in a couple hours."

"It's... good to be home, Mother," Thala said as she entered the house she still considered home. As soon as the words came out of her mouth, she realized that it was the truth.

[184]

Cheria chuckled and smiled at her daughter as she closed the door behind them. She looked over the younger woman and sighed.

"You've lost weight, Thala. You need to eat more," Cheria shook her head.

"I needed to lose weight, Mother. I was getting fat," Thala sighed. "It was hindering my performance."

"Well, it's not healthy to be so thin," Cheria tsked. "And why are you wearing that uniform. You're obviously off duty."

"I don't have any clothes other than my uniform, Mother. I'll have to buy some at the market tomorrow," Thala sighed as she slumped in a chair. "How's Marron?"

"Your brother is fine. He'll be attending the Brohcal School of Music next year," Cheria smiled proudly as she set to tidying up. "I wish you had told us you were coming. We would have prepared a special welcome for you."

"I didn't know where I was going to be going until I found myself on Jarada V, Mother," Thala shrugged. "If I knew I was coming here, I would have called. It's been a very long week."

"You want to talk about it, Thala?" her mother asked, looking at Thala with pure concern in her eyes. "You know you can always talk to me if you have a problem."

"I know, Mother," Thala said. "I just don't want to talk about it."

"OK, Thala," Cheria nodded. "You don't have to. I just want to make sure you know that the option's open for you."

"I do, Mother," Thala said, smiling slightly.

They chit-chatted for a little while, then Cheria stepped into the kitchen to start preparing dinner. Thala sat in the living room, her eyes closed, trying not to think about him.

"THALA!" Marron thundered as he tore across the living room and wrapped her up in his arms. "Lords, I've missed you, sister! How are you? Did Mother tell you about my being accepted into the Brohcal School of Music? How long are you going to stay here?"

[185]

"Hello, Marron," Thala chuckled as she returned her brother's hug. "I've missed you, too. Yes, Mother told me about your being accepted. It's a fine school. You'll do well, I'm sure. To be honest, I don't know how long I'll be home, Marron."

"I wish you'd stay, Thala," Marron rumbled as he stood up straight. Suddenly, she realized how much her little brother had grown. Marron had clearly taken after their father. She had to look up at him now. Little brother, indeed! "We've spent so little time together. I'd like to get to know you a little more before I go off to school."

"I'd like that, Marron," Thala smiled, her first genuine smile in days. "I don't know how long I'm going to be away from the Star League Defense Force though. I'm on... a leave of absence." She sighed. "I've got... a lot on my mind these days, and I needed some time away."

"Well," Cheria said. "You're welcome here as long as you want to be here, Thala."

"Thank you, Mother," Thala smiled a sad little smile at her mother.

"Tobias was asking after you," Cheria said.

"Tobias?" Thala raised an eyebrow. "I haven't even thought about Tobias in years. He was really asking about me?"

"Yes," Cheria said. "Had I known you were coming home, I would have told him."

"I'll have to look him up while I'm home," Thala said thoughtfully.

"I'm sure he'd be happy to see you," Cheria said. "And I think it would be good for you, too."

"Maybe it will," Thala shrugged. "If you don't mind, I think I'd like to take a nap until Father gets home. I haven't really been sleeping well of late."

"All right, Thala," Cheria said. "Your room is just the way you left it."

"Thank you, Mother," Thala said, exhaustion showing in her voice.

Thala grabbed her duffel bag and headed off to her room.

"Mother, I think I'm worried about her," Marron said, looking after Thala. "I think there's something very wrong with her."

"I know, Marron," Cheria said. "And I agree that something is wrong. But we can't really do anything to help her until she's ready for us to."

Thala was floating. She had no idea where she was. All she knew was that she was cold.

"What in the name of the Lords of Jarada is going on?" she demanded.

"You are here because we have need of you," a sinister female voice said.

"Who are you?"

"That is not relevant. You will do as you are told," the voice said from all around her.

"I don't understand," she furrowed her brow.

"Understanding is not required," the voice hissed. "Only your compliance is. And you will comply."

"And if I don't?" Thala asked.

"Then there will be consequences," the voice said. "Such a lovely family you have. It would be a pity for something to happen to them."

"What do you want me to do?" Thala sighed, resigned to the fact that she was going to have to do whatever the voice wanted.

"You will know," the voice faded. "In time."

A black shape passed in front of her face, and she knew nothing more.

When she awoke the next morning, she remembered nothing of her dreams. She did feel refreshed though. It had been a long time since she had slept through the night like that.

"Good morning, Thala," Cheria greeted her as she walked out into the kitchen. "How did you sleep last night?"

"Like a rock," Thala smiled. "It was the best I'd slept in a long time, Mother."

"I'm glad." Cheria handed her a plate of eggs. "You looked a little haggard when you came in yesterday."

"I hadn't been sleeping well," Thala shrugged. She took the plate of eggs and took a bite. "And I've missed your cooking. I'm afraid I'm not much of a cook."

"Well, I'm sure in time, you'll learn how to cook," Cheria smiled.

"I was thinking I'd go to the temple today," Thala said thoughtfully.

"You might run into Tobias there. He's been there a lot lately since his sister was killed," Cheria sighed.

"Serin was killed?" Thala's jaw dropped.

"Yes. She was on the Grange when it was destroyed," Cheria looked down. "She didn't make it."

"Lords, I didn't know," Thala said softly, tears filling her eyes. "I didn't see her name on any of the casualty lists, Mother. If I had, I would have been home as soon as I had heard."

"I know, Thala," Cheria said. "So does Tobias. He still loves you."

"I don't really know how I feel about anyone anymore," Thala said in a distant voice.

"Well, maybe some time at the temple will help clear your head," Cheria touched her daughter's cheek tenderly.

"That's what I was hoping, Mother," Thala nodded.

Thala finished her eggs and headed out of the door. She looked around and took a deep breath. She smiled to herself. It was definitely good to be home.

She headed up the path to the temple. It was a long winding path up a hill that overlooked the town. She'd walked this walk many times, and she never got tired of the walk. The path was designed to clear the mind while the person walked up to the temple.

[188]

The temple itself was fairly small. No actual services were held in the temple. The people of Kentar came up to the temple to pray when they needed to pray. Most of the temples on Jarada V served the same purpose.

She walked into the temple, closing her eyes and remembering other times that she had gone into the temple, smiling to herself.

"Thala?" a tentative male voice said. "Thala Ker'sal?"

"Tobias," she said without opening her eyes. "I was told you might be here." She opened her eyes to see Tobias standing there looking at her. "It is good to see you again, old friend."

"I thought I'd never see you again, Thala. I've missed you a great deal." Tobias Jar'ra wrapped Thala up in his arms, holding her close as if trying to convince himself that she was real.

"Tobias, I heard about Serin. I'm so sorry," she said, genuinely concerned about the big man. "I didn't know until I had gotten home."

"It's OK, Thala," Tobias said, his features sad. "I know you would have been here had you known. I hear that the Star League is trying to make peace with the Brentax."

"Yes, they are," Thala said.

"I think it is a mistake. And I intend to do something about it. Are you with me?" Tobias asked, praying in his soul that she'd say yes.

"Yes," she said after a moment's pause. She leaned up and kissed him on the cheek. "I'm with you."

"I'll see you in town later?"

"Yes, Tobias. Now scoot, I need some time alone to sort some things out," she grinned.

"I'll see you later. I still love you, Thala. I've always loved you."

Tobias lumbered out of the temple, leaving Thala alone with her thoughts. She took her rank insignia off and examined it. Shaking her head, she placed the insignia on the altar and turned around and left the temple.

[189]

The Dawning of a New Age

She was never going to wear a rank in the Star League Defense Force again.

CHAPTER / 15

K'ALAN crept along the hall, his energy bow by his side. The bow was charged and humming softly, ready for him to draw and fire at a moment's notice. He kept telling himself that this was going to be easy. Of course, it didn't matter how many times he told himself, he still didn't believe it. He thought briefly of K'Itea and smiled a slight smile. She always did have that affect on him. He missed her, but he was more upset that she was back on the White Knight worrying about him.

He saw a couple of guards up ahead, and he ducked into a doorway. The guards looked down the hallway but didn't see him, and they moved on. K'Alan released his breath in a long sigh of relief, and, slowly, he started back down the corridor.

Idly, he wondered how Mario was doing as he made his way along the corridor. If he was right, the main computer control center was going to be on his right very shortly.

Very carefully, he made his way into the computer control center. It was empty.

Too easy, he thought to himself. *There should be at least one or two guards here.*

He looked around, and backed out of the room.

"Hold it right there," a guard said as he came around the corner.

K'Alan rolled his eyes and whipped around, firing a bolt from his energy bow as soon as he was facing the guard. The bolt struck the guard dead in his chest. The guard fell backward, stunned. K'Alan looked around to see if anyone had heard the scuffle. Not seeing anyone else around, K'Alan sighed and pulled the guard into the computer control center.

"Sorry, buddy," he said. "I can't have you waking up and following me."

He stunned the guard a second time and stuffed the body in a panel, hoping no one would come in and find the body anytime soon.

"The things I do for king and country," K'Alan muttered.

He made his way out of the computer center, his energy bow at the ready. He'd taken the guard's blaster rifle and had slung it over his back. The blaster rifle had been set on heavy stun, which was a comfort. He did not think the Brentax were expecting an assault. He made his way down the hallway towards M'Bek Tarmos's office.

Meanwhile, in another part of the complex, Mario was also making his way towards the office. He had drawn his sword before starting into the complex, hoping he wouldn't need it. He'd seen a couple guards, but he hadn't been seen. He counted himself lucky.

He thought about how K'Alan might be faring and pushed the thought out of his mind. No time for distraction behind enemy lines. He carefully picked his way along the corridor, keeping his sword in front of him. The sword danced in the light, and having it our made him feel a little more secure.

"Hold it right there," a guard said as he appeared suddenly.

"I'm sorry," Mario said. "I seem to be lost. Could you direct me to the casino?"

"Very funny," the guard said.

"Well, my mother said I should be a comedian," Mario said, flashing his winning smile.

The guard never saw the strike. All he knew was suddenly he was looking at his own feet... sideways. And that was a condition that didn't last long as, mercifully, his eyes stopped seeing anything.

"Well," Mario said to himself. "That was fun. It's so nice to know that I haven't lost my touch."

He shook his head and started down the corridor. Suddenly, he just didn't care about whether or not he and K'Alan were going to pull this off. He had the feeling that they were about to be in some very serious trouble.

He ran around the corner towards M'Bek Tarmos's office when he almost ran right into K"Alan.

"Fancy meeting you here," Mario smiled as he stood with his hand on his hip. "Going my way, big boy?"

"You're not exactly my type, Mario," K'Alan grinned. "Let's get this over with."

Mario kicked open the office door...

... and saw nothing.

The office was empty. The two friends looked at each other and bolted through the window just before the hallway and the office filled with tear gas.

The two Star League soldiers ran back to the Chancellor's house to regroup.

* * *

Kerrin Jameson had a stack of reports on her desk. That was nothing new and different. She always seemed to have a stack of reports on her desk these days. She chuckled as she imagined what it would be like to live in a totally paperless society. Well, it was an idea that had merit. She'd have to examine it closely.

Kerrin was in a good mood for a change. Lately, she dreaded going to work, because of the war. But today, she was in a good mood. She figured it was because she knew the war would be ending soon. And today would be the main reason behind the war's end.

There was a knock on the door. She looked up, surprised that someone would be knocking on her door this early.

"Come in," she called.

A white coated doctor walked in slowly. From the look on his face, Kerrin knew that it wasn't good news. She could feel her good mood fading away.

"Can I help you, Doctor...?" she trailed off.

"Doctor Mark Johnson, Madame President," the doctor said softly. "I'm afraid I have bad news."

"What is it, Doctor?" she asked. As soon as she asked, she knew that she did not want to know the answer.

"Perrin Hawks is dead, Madame President," the doctor lowered his eyes. "We did everything we could. We used all our capabilities. But we couldn't revive her. I'm sorry."

"Doctor," the president asked after a while. "What time did she die?"

"Four fifteen this morning, ma'am," the doctor said.

"Four fifteen..." she repeated. "Well, that explains it then."

"Ma'am?" the doctor looked at her with a puzzled look on his face.

"Never mind. Thank you for letting me know, Doctor Johnson," Kerrin dismissed him with a wave of her hand.

"I'm sorry we couldn't do more," he said, bowing. He left the office, but Kerrin never even noticed.

"Jane, I need to be booked on an immediate flight to Chicago. First available flight," she said into her desk intercom. "And all of my appointments today are to be cancelled. If anyone asks, I have personal business to attend to."

"Yes, ma'am," came Jane's voice immediately. "I can have you on a flight in twenty minutes."

"That'll do, Jane," Kerrin sighed. "That'll do."

2.7.2136
1012
Gamma Epsilon Station
Admiral John Bonetti's office.

"Admiral Bonetti," Sergeant Riggs called over his desk intercom. "The newest casualty report's here."

"Bring it in, Riggs," the admiral said, fighting the urge to sigh. All he really wanted to do was to run away until the war was over. He was getting tired of this daily routine.

Riggs came in with the casualty sheet. He handed it to Admiral Bonetti, and the admiral noted that there was a tear in Riggs's eye.

"Someone you knew on the list, Riggs?" John asked.

"My sister, sir," Riggs said, and John could tell that he was fighting to keep it together.

"I'm sorry, Sergeant," John shook his head. "Why don't you take the rest of the day off?"

"Thank you, sir," the sergeant nodded. "Would... would it be alright if I called my parents and let them know?"

"Normally, I'd say no," John sighed. "But under the circumstances, how can I? Give your parents my sincere condolences."

"I will," Riggs said softly. "Thank you, sir."

The admiral smiled at the young sergeant and watched him go. Then he looked at the list himself.

"Oh, Lord," he said when he saw Perrin Hawks name. "What do we do when our best gets taken out?"

2.7.2136
1113
SLS White Knight
The City

S'Era and K'Itea were sitting in the park watching the children play. Elam was practicing his pitching on a screen that K'Alan had set up before leaving on the mission. They watched as Elam threw pitch after pitch, only about a third hitting the red strike zone. Elam didn't get frustrated; he just kept throwing one pitch after another. Every so often, Elam would throw a near-perfect pitch. Whenever he did, he'd look over to see if his mother and aunt had been watching.

The two women watched Elam quietly. Each was lost in her own thoughts about the two men who were off the ship. They were each worried terribly, although K'Itea was convinced that S'Era was worried about her brother rather than Mario. It was true enough. S'Era was very worried about K'Alan. But she was in love with Mario. All she knew was that a piece of her would die inside if Mario didn't come back safely.

"I wish they'd just come back," S'Era said, breaking the silence by saying what they were both thinking.

"I know," K'Itea said. "I had to get sleeping pills to help me get to sleep last night. It's never been this hard to sleep without K'Alan before."

"Can I tell you something, Kit?" S'Era asked after a pause. "Something I'm not sure even K'Alan knows?"

"Of course, S'Era," K'Itea smiled. It was a warm and genuine smile. "You're my friend. You can tell me anything."

"I think I'm in love with Mario Bonetti," S'Era said.

K'Itea's jaw dropped. She was expecting her friend to say anything except that.

"Are you sure?" K'Itea finally managed to get out. "Does he know?"

"I think he does," S'Era nodded. "He's always been attracted to me for sure. I just don't really know what to say. I asked him if he wanted to go to dinner with me sometime. He had to think about it."

"He probably wanted to talk to K'Alan and make sure that he wouldn't be upset," K'Itea chuckled. "If I know my husband, he'll hem and haw, and make Mario feel lower than dirt, and then, when Mario's convinced that K'Alan's totally against you two dating, Kal will say something to the effect of, 'Well, if S'Era's got her heart set on you, then who am I to stand in the way?' and stay out of it." K'Itea smiled at S'Era. She had no doubt in her mind that what she had just said would be exactly how the conversation went. She had known her husband a very long time, and she knew his ways.

"I hope so," S'Era said. "I've never quite met anyone like Mario. He makes me feel all giddy inside. You know what I mean?"

"Yes, I do, S'Era," K'Itea grinned. "You just explained how your brother makes me feel."

They watched Elam throw the ball a few more times.

"You know, Kit," S'Era said. "The more I watch him, the more he reminds me of K'Alan."

"Oh? How so?"

"He's so damn stubborn."

The two girls shared a good long laugh.

2.7.2136
1123
Brentax III
Chancellor G'Kiron's home.

Mario and K'Alan had just gotten back to the chancellor's home from the Brentax Militia Headquarters.

They had taken a circuitous route so that they couldn't be followed. When they were sure they were safe, they had headed to the chancellor's home. It wasn't that they were worried about getting caught. They were pretty sure the Brentax Militia knew exactly what they had planned. They just didn't know how yet. But they were worried about getting Chancellor G'Kiron in trouble. He had, after all, been very helpful.

Mario knocked on the door. There was no response, so K'Alan pulled out his lock pick kit and picked the lock. It was an easy lock and didn't take long at all. K'Alan opened the door and looked around.

The place looked empty. The two Star League soldiers searched the entire house, from one end to the other. There was no sign of the chancellor.

"Mario, I think they may have our friend," K'Alan said.

"And I think we're in trouble," Mario added.

CHAPTER 16

ERRIN Jameson stepped off a transport and sighed. This was the least favorite part of her job. And it always would be. Occasionally, with certain casualties, she felt like she had to personally convey the news of the soldier's death to his or her family. This one however, was intensely personal. Seeing Perrin Hawks' family under these circumstances was not going to be easy. She walked slowly towards the el station, unconsciously dragging her heels.

Chicago, although most of the world had gone to hovercars and rail-less trains, still had ground transportation that ran on gas and wheels, and still had the el. The el had been a fixture in Chicago for decades. Even though the city had been pressured to modernize, the citizens had steadfastly refused, saying to make such

[199]

changes would remove the character from the city. And so the el remained.

Kerrin had always hated taking the el. Over the years, the ride had gotten rougher. It seemed like no one had paid attention to how the el ran, and it felt like there had been no maintenance in at least a decade, although she knew that there had been. She had always been afraid the el would come off the track, killing everyone on board and causing major destruction and panic. She had wanted to have the el taken down and replaced with a more modern rail-less train, but the decision was still up to the city government. She really didn't see the benefit of pushing the issue.

So she found herself waiting for the el, a mode of transportation she hated, to take her to a part of Chicago that she didn't want to be in to see some people she'd rather not be visiting under the current circumstances.

Yeah, she groaned to herself. *This is about a normal day for me.*

She watched the track silently, trying not to think about her friend. She'd talked to the doctors again before she had left for Chicago. They had assured her that Perrin died peacefully. There had been no suffering. For that, Kerrin had been grateful. Perrin was too good a friend to have a painful death. Besides, it would ease her family's pain to know that she'd died without pain.

Too bad nothing can ease my pain, Kerrin groused to herself. *This war's had too high a cost on me.*

The el clamored into the station, and Kerrin boarded without saying a word. She took a seat near a window and looked out over Chicago as the el started out over the city.

Maybe I'll retire here when my term is over, she thought. *Have my life end where it started. Keep the circle intact. Poetic justice that I spend the rest of my life in a city that's going to haunt me forever.*

She felt a tear roll down her face as she passed the apartment complex she grew up in. Her parents had long since passed away, having been killed in a hovercar accident when she was sixteen. She'd gone and lived with the Hawks right afterwards. They'd taken her in like their own daughter, happily. And she and Perrin had grown even closer.

When Perrin had decided to join the Star League Defense Force, Kerrin had laughed, but in the end she'd been supportive of Perrin's choice. It had turned out to be the right choice for her, and for that, Kerrin was even happier. She and Perrin had kept in close contact, and Kerrin had been present when Perrin was promoted to Captain.

Perrin couldn't have been prouder of Kerrin when she was elected President of the Star League. Perrin had always said that her friend was headed for greatness. She'd supported Kerrin during her bid for the presidency, and she was the first person that congratulated Kerrin on her victory.

And now Perrin was gone, and an ache had opened up in Kerrin's soul. She'd been tempted to call off the Gamma Strike mission and order a crushing blow on Brentax III, but something kept nagging at her that it wasn't the proper course of action. As rewarding as wiping the Brentax off the face of the galaxy, she knew that peace was the only option that made sense. The loss of life on both sides that would happen as a result of such a brutal assault was too prohibitive.

Kerrin sighed as the el pulled into her stop. She stood up, grabbed her briefcase and stepped off the el, nodding a thank you to the driver. She stepped on the platform and stopped to get her bearings. The Hawks' home was a ten minute walk from the el platform. She shook her head and started walking, trying not to think about what she was going to say.

When she got to the Hawks' house, she paused and looked at the driveway. Two hovercars and a ground car. She frowned, knowing that she couldn't put this off any longer. They were home. She had thought that maybe she might be able to get out of this because they were away.

[201]

Determined to get this over with, she walked up the driveway and up the walk to the front door. She rang the bell, hoping against hope that no one would answer. She waited a couple minutes before an older woman answered the door. Kerrin looked into the saddened eyes of Elizabeth Hawks, and almost started crying herself.

"Come in, Kerrin," Elizabeth said in a subdued voice.

Kerrin nodded and stepped into the house that had once been her home. She looked around and saw that the entire family was there. Perrin's mother, father and brother were all sitting in the living room.

They already know, Kerrin realized. *Of course, they know. Why else would I be here?*

"I came with bad news," Kerrin said, deciding it was best to just come out and give them the bad news. "Perrin's ship was heavily damaged this week in a brutal attack by the Brentax. She suffered severe internal injuries, and was brought back to Earth in a coma. She passed away this morning at four fifteen. I came as soon as I found out."

Elizabeth went over to her husband and put her arms around him. She buried her head in his shoulder and started crying. Kerrin's heart went out to the older woman.

"The doctors called us when they brought her into the Bethesda Naval Hospital," Gerald Hawks said, his voice breaking slightly. "They said then that her chances were slim. I was hoping they were wrong."

"I wish I were visiting with better news," Kerrin said, tears running down her own face. "You know how much Perrin meant to me. I just felt that I should be the one to tell you."

"Thank you, Kerrin," Gerald said. "Stay a little while. I know you're busy, but it's been a while since we've seen you. And you are our daughter."

She stayed most of the day.

CHAPTER 17

IT had no form currently. At least not a recognizable one. It was a mass of thought and matter, currently dormant. Once upon a time, though, it had ravaged across the galaxy. If it had not been for a small band of warriors, it would still be reigning terror on the various worlds in this part of the galaxy.

It had no clue of its true purpose in this state. While dormant, it had no idea of its own existence, let alone know what it would do when awoken.

No one knew about it, of course. The warriors that had driven it back to its nebula had thought they'd killed it. But the entity could not be killed. It could only be driven back into its dormant state. If they had known that they had not succeeded in killing the entity, it was unlikely they'd be able to do anything about finishing the job.

But it would make its presence known in time. Soon, it would start to coalesce into its true form. Soon, it would awaken from its slumber and begin a new reign of terror. The various people of the galaxy would once more tremble at the mention of its name.

The Dawning of a New Age

But for now it was content to be dormant in the Sheyada Nebula.

‹CHAPTER / 18›

K'ALAN sat in a chair in the sitting room contemplating the current situation. They'd gone over the entire house three times. There had been no sign of struggle, but there was also no sign of the Chancellor. K'Alan had been considering what to do for the past ten minutes. While he thought about the situation, Mario had decided to sweep the house one more time for recording or listening devices.

He wasn't sure what bothered him more, the fact that the Brentax knew about the assault and were ready for them or the fact that the Chancellor was gone when they got back. It was too much of a coincidence that the Chancellor was not at the house when they got back. K'Alan couldn't bring himself to believe that the Chancellor had deceived them.

"House is clear, Kal," Mario said as he came back into the room.

"Good," K'Alan nodded, looking out the window. The view was as drab as any other view on Brentax III. The Brentax architecture was as pleasing to the eye as the Brentax themselves were. Which is to say not at all. All the buildings were the same drab grey color. Even the sky was grey, as if the gods the Brentax believed in decided that they didn't need to bother making with color. Dark greys and light greys were all that met the eye. It was like looking at a black and white movie, only with less interesting contrasts.

"What are we going to do next, Kal?" Mario asked, interrupting K'Alan's thoughts. "We still need to get M'Bek Tarmos."

"I don't know, Mario," K'Alan shook his head. "I just don't know."

2.7.2136
1233
SLS White Knight
The Bridge

Erin Sykes strode onto the bridge. Her long brown hair was tied up in a bun. She looked refreshed, as if she'd just gotten up from a good night's sleep. She walked over to the command chair, looked at it, smiled, and then walked over to the executive officer station and sat down.

"I hate the command chair," she said when she saw Kath looking at her with a questioning look. "This one's more comfortable."

Kath laughed, a twinkle in her eye. She turned around and started monitoring her station again.

"Any word from the Captain or Mario?" Erin asked.

"None yet, no," Kath said, shaking her head.

"Kath, I was wondering if I could talk to you a moment," Erin said.

"Sure, Commander," Kath said, turning around in her chair. "What's on your mind?"

"Well, I've noticed that you've been a little distracted the last couple days. I was hoping I could talk to you about it," Erin said. She kept her voice soft so that the rest of the bridge wouldn't hear them. "Whatever it is, I'd like to hope that we can get it resolved before the Captain gets back."

"I don't think it's going to be quite that simple, Erin," Kath shook her head. "My life just turned completely upside down."

"What happened? If I may ask that is," Erin said, concern for the young lieutenant commander showing in her voice.

"Well, I just found out that I have a twin sister to start with," Kath sighed. "Plus there's a possibility that I may have empathic abilities. It's just been a lot to absorb at once."

"I can imagine," Erin said. "If you need time off to work it out, you can always take a few days."

"I don't think giving me free time to think about this is such a good idea," Kath shook her head, her curly hair gently swaying in front of her face. "I need to keep busy. I will work it out as best I can."

"The offer's open," Erin smiled. "And if you find you need the time, just tell me."

"Thanks, Erin," Kath said. "And as soon as I get word from K'Alan and Mario, I'll pass it on."

"Thanks, Katherine," Erin smiled.

2.7.2136
1238
SLS White Knight
The City

K'Itea Bryce was laughing. It had started so innocently. She and S'Era were in the park watching Elam pitch. She didn't know what in particular had set them off in peals of laughter this time, but she welcomed it. There was an old

Earth adage that she'd heard. "Laughter is the best medicine for whatever ails you." She knew at that moment that those words were true.

"Oh, S'Era," K'Itea said, between breaths. "I haven't laughed so hard in ages."

"Neither have I," S'Era chuckled. "But it felt so good."

"Didn't it?" K'Itea agreed. "Come on. Let's go get Elam and go have lunch."

"Sounds like a good idea to me," S'Era said, still laughing to herself.

2.7.2136
1242
Gamma Epsilon Station
Admiral John Bonetti's office.

John grumbled as he looked at his chrono again. Still four more hours before he should expect the White Knight to report in. But Lord was he impatient. He got up and started pacing.

"Admiral Bonetti," the sergeant who had replaced Riggs called over the intercom. What was her name again? Anne Riker. That was it.

"Yes, Sergeant Riker?" the Admiral said, exasperated.

"You have a priority one message from Captain Tom Keevan of the Creighton," the sergeant said.

"Patch it through," John said. A priority one message was almost never a good thing, and John was not sure he wanted to know what the captain of the Creighton wanted.

Captain Keevan's face suddenly appeared on his viewscreen, his face smiling even more than usual. *He seems especially happy,* John mused. *Wonder what's up?*

"Captain Keevan," John returned the man's smile. "What can I do for you?"

"Care for some good news for a change, John?" Captain Keevan asked.

"I could always use good news, Tom," John nodded. "What's on your mind?"

[208]

"The Creighton was just attacked by the Duhari class cruiser Dorania Toran," Captain Keevan said. "The Creighton suffered some very minor damage, but the Brentax vessel was completely surprised. The modifications we made to our proton torpedoes were extremely effective."

"That is good news," John smiled. "If this war does have to continue, we may have a chance."

"Has there been any word from Captain Bryce?" Tom asked, suddenly very serious.

"None," John sighed. "I'm expecting to hear from them in about four hours."

"I hope they succeeded. I could use a break."

"So could we all, Tom." John smiled a sad little smile. "So could we all.

2.7.2136
1302
Brentax III
Chancellor G'Kiron's home

"Are you sure you want to go back in there?" Mario asked. "We did almost get toasted the last time."

"Yes, but they won't expect us to go in there a second time, will they?"

"Kal, I wouldn't expect us to go in there a second time," Mario sighed. "It's suicide."

"Meet me there in an hour," K'Alan said. "There's something I need to check on before we leave."

"If you're not there in an hour, what do I do?" Mario asked.

"Assume I'm dead or captured and carry out the mission by yourself."

"But, Kal!" Mario protested.

"Don't worry about me. If I'm captured, I'll find a way out," K'Alan clapped Mario on the shoulder. "And if I'm dead, you can't help me anyway. The mission comes first above everything else."

"All right, but if you die, I'm not going to be the one to tell K'Itea," Mario grinned. "I like all my body parts where they are, and she'll probably rip my head off."

"Get going. I'll meet up with you outside the Militia Building," K'Alan chuckled.

2.7.2136
1310
Earth
Star League Headquarters

"This is outrageous!" Kieve Shala, the delegate form the Saluran system, bellowed. "I had an appointment to speak with the president! I demand to speak with her!"

"President Jameson is currently not in her office," Jane Swiftwind, the president's assistant, said as she looked up at the Saluran ambassador. "She left word that she had urgent personal business to attend to and that all of her appointments today were to be cancelled. If you'd like to reschedule, I'd be more than happy to accommodate you."

"What I'd like is to speak to the President," Kieve growled. "It is an outrage that she break her appointment like this."

"I'll be happy to pass along your unhappiness. I assure you that this was a sudden and unexpected trip," Jane said. "She had every intention of meeting with you today, Ambassador. President Jameson hates to break an appointment."

"I am most displeased," Kieve roared. "This outrage will be addressed at the next council meeting!"

"That is, of course, your right," Jane acknowledged. "But I think you should wait until you talk to President Jameson to put that on your schedule."

"Very well," Kieve sighed and rolled his eyes. The man could be overly dramatic when he did not get his way. "When can you reschedule me for?"

"Tomorrow morning?" Jane looked at him with a smile. "She has an opening at 9 AM. Will that suffice?"

"It'll do," Kieve growled.

Soran looked up from polishing the bar to see K'Itea, S'Era and Elam walk in. He smiled broadly and motioned for the three to come over to the bar. His smile grew even more broad when they accepted his invitation to sit down at the bar, Elam sitting protectively in between the two ladies.

"Let me guess," Soran chuckled. "You're here for lunch."

"Yes, we are," K'Itea smiled.

"Well, I have a new sandwich I'd like you three to try. On the house," Soran smiled. "I think you'll like it. It's called The Ballpark. It's a take on an old Earth sandwich called a hot dog. I am making it in honor of the Captain."

"Sounds good to me!" Elam piped up.

"I guess we'll all try that, Soran," K'Itea laughed at her son's excitement.

"Great! Three Ballparks coming up," Soran smiled as he started to prepare the sandwiches.

"So, Soran," S'Era grinned. "I need your help with something..."

K'Alan crouched outside the prison wall, looking in through a barred window at a cell. The older Brentax man that was in there was turned away from him, but he was certain it was Chancellor G'Kiron.

"Chancellor G'Kiron," he whispered. "It's Captain Bryce. Is that you?"

"K'Alan?" the old Brentax croaked. "Get away from here. If they see you here, they'll lock you up in here also. Go. Go do your job. I'll be OK."

"Not until I get you out of there," K'Alan said.

That was when he heard the footsteps. Before he could react, he felt a sharp pain in his side, then, mercifully, nothing more as the blackness washed over him.

CHAPTER 19

2.5.2143
2013
Jarada V

THALA Ker'sal was lying on her back on the roof of her parents' home watching the stars. She found that she didn't really miss being up amongst them so much as she thought she would. She had been among the stars for a long time. It was good to stop once in a while. She was content for the first time in a long time.

But she was also bitter. Bitter about the way her career had turned. Bitter about this last turn of events that had disrupted her life. But mostly bitter that K'Alan Bryce had spurned her again. She hated him for all she was worth. She wasn't sure how, but she would get back at him. Revenge against him consumed her.

It was a quiet evening, the three moons of Jarada V just rising over the skyline. The light from the two moons cast a pale orange glow over everything. The lush forest surrounding Kentar almost looked as if it were ablaze.

Thala had always liked spending time on her parents' roof. Ever since she was ten years old, she had spent time almost every night on the roof staring at the stars. It was almost a tradition with her.

She thought about the events of the day, a slight smile on her face. After she'd left the temple, she'd gone to the market and gotten some clothes to replace her Star League uniform. Her oldest friend, Tobias Jar'ra, had met her in the market with a smile and a hug. He'd given her a ring made of a lock of his hair, the traditional Jaradan engagement ring. She'd looked at him with shock at first, but smiled as she took it and wore it. It was almost fitting that she should fall in love with Tobias, considering the road she was thinking about traveling. When her mother saw the ring during dinner, she'd winked and smiled knowingly at Thala. Thala had simply shrugged. It was not a big deal to her.

Tobias would have his use. He just didn't know he was being used. In reality, he probably wouldn't care either. He was using her just as much as she was using him. Such was life amongst the Jaradan people.

Thala fell asleep on the roof that night, waking up the next morning somewhat stiff. She stretched and cricked her back, sighing at the stiffness. It was a good stiffness though. She felt more alive than she had in weeks.

She climbed back into the house and changed, selecting a subdued outfit. Thinking ahead, she packed the rest of her clothes in her duffel bag, leaving it on the floor next to her bed. She intended to leave that night, at least for a little while.

After she finished dressing, she headed down to the kitchen. Her mother greeted her with a smile.

"Did you stay on the roof all night long, Thala?" her mother asked.

"Yeah," Thala nodded. "I hadn't planned on it, but I fell asleep watching the stars."

"You used to do that sometimes," Cheria smiled. "Your father would sometimes go up there and carry you back in."

"I remember," Thala chuckled. She sighed before continuing. "Mother, Tobias and I are leaving today. I have to go to the Gamma Epsilon Station and resign from the

Defense Force. There's no place for me there. I should be home in four or five days."

"I understand," Cheria nodded. "You do what you think is best, child."

"This is for the best, Mother," Thala nodded. She smiled a sad smile, although she knew that her mother would not realize it was anything other than a smile. Her mother had never been able to read her true feelings. "And when we come back, Tobias and I will have a nice little wedding."

And I'll get one very sore chapter of my life behind me, Thala added to herself.

"That will be nice, Thala," Cheria smiled. "I'm glad you found someone."

Thala shrugged and grabbed a piece of ciuliwi for breakfast. She gave Cheria a hug and walked out of the house, chewing on the ciuliwi.

She headed down to the market, hoping to meet Tobias. As she'd hoped, he was there, buying provisions for a journey.

"You ready to go, Tobias?" she asked, putting her arms on his shoulders.

"Of course," he smiled at his love. "I've booked passage for us on a trade freighter that my cousin, Chular, owns. He was heading for the Gamma Epsilon station to pick up a shipment that he's been owed for a while. He was more than willing to bring us along. We leave in six hours."

"Good," Thala said, as she pulled Tobias close. "The sooner I get this over with, the happier I'll be."

Tobias nodded and hugged Thala. He smiled and turned back to his purchases. Thala looked around the market, but didn't see too much that she wanted. She kissed Tobias on the cheek, saying she'd meet him at the transport station in a few minutes.

She ran back to the house and grabbed her duffel bag. She avoided seeing anyone at the house. Indeed, it seemed as if no one was home. It was as if they knew she wouldn't want to see them before leaving. *Which,* she thought, *they probably did.* Sighing to herself, she headed back to the transport station and waited for Tobias. They boarded the transport together, and headed off to the spaceport, leaving Kentar behind.

⟨CHAPTER / 20⟩

OF the Watchers that had started watching the events of the past few days, only three of them currently stood watching the events unfold on the holosphere, two male and one female.

"They have failed," one of the males said.

"No, they have not," the female said. "But their way is much more difficult now. I believe they will still succeed. They must."

"He did not heed your warning, Kiara," the other male admonished. "His fate is written."

"I don't think so, John," the woman shook her head. "This one is more resilient and resourceful than we first gave him credit for. I believe he will survive."

"Yes, but will he be unhurt?" the first male said.

The Dawning of a New Age

CHAPTER / 21

2.7.2136
1328
Gamma Epsilon Station
Docking Bay Twelve

THE Jarada freighter, Sharash'di, slowly landed in the docking bay, its boxy bulk handling with better maneuverability than the dock handlers were expecting to see from the little freighter.

The hatch opened and three Jaradans stepped out, one of them wearing a Star League Defense Force uniform.

"Jaradan freighter Sharash'di," one of the dock workers said into the dock recorder. "Jaradan registry zero two two six three alpha. No cargo, one crew, two passengers. Logged."

The Jaradans walked through the customs area, letting the customs people check their Ids and baggage. When the customs officer saw that one of the Jaradans was a Star League Defense Force captain, he snapped to attention, saluting her. Thala returned the salute, motioning for the officer to be at ease.

[219]

"Captain Ker'sal, welcome back to the Gamma Epsilon station," the customs officer said. "You and your guests are cleared to enter the station, ma'am. Your quarters are in the habitat area level 4, rooms 433 and 434."

"Thank you," Thala said as she took her ID back from the customs officer.

"You're welcome." The customs officer smiled and turned to the computer to make an entry about the Jaradans and their baggage.

Thala lead the way down the corridor of the station, Tobias ever watchful at her side. The three Jaradans walked in silence, mindful of the other people on the station.

When they got to the assigned quarters, Chular looked at the other two and grimaced.

"I've got to go meet with my supplier," he said. "You to go take care of Thala's business, and I'll meet up with you later."

Without waiting for an answer, Chular headed off into the station. Thala and Tobias looked at each other and shrugged.

"You know where the office is," Tobias said. "Lean on." He gestured that Thala should leave the quarters first.

The walked down the corridor, hand in hand. Thala took some comfort from the touch. She was surprised at that at first. But as she thought about it for a few moments, she realized that she shouldn't be surprised. Tobias truly was one of her oldest friends. She doubted that, if K'Alan had ever given in to her wishes, she would ever have this level of comfort with him. It was a moot point, though. K'Alan would never have been hers. And Tobias was.

"I haven't met any humans," Tobias said, breaking her out of her thoughts. "I don't know really what to expect."

"They're a lot like us, Tobias." Thala shrugged. "They are an overly friendly people, though. In the end, you'll probably hate them."

"Why do you say that?" Tobias raised his eyebrows. "I like everyone."

"Humans are... unpredictable at best," Thala chuckled. In a way, she'd described herself too. Would anyone have expected her to resign from the Star League Defense Force over K'Alan Bryce, after all?

"How annoying," Tobias shook his head. "How thoroughly annoying. And these are the ones making the decision to end this war?"

"Yes, Tobias."

"How disgusting," Tobias grunted. "What are they thinking?"

"I don't know, my love." She shook her head. "I don't know. We're here. Now remember, let me do the talking."

"Yes, dear," he nodded, motioning her to lead the way into the office.

Thala and Tobias walked into Admiral Bonetti's outer office and stopped at the desk.

"Captain Thala Ker'sal, I am here to speak to Admiral Bonetti," the Jaradan woman announced.

"You'll have to take a seat," the sergeant behind the desk snapped. "He's busy."

Thala rolled her eyes and took a seat, crossing her arms. Tobias put his hand on Thala's leg to calm her. Thala closed her eyes and heaved a soft sigh, not wanting to be here, but knowing it was necessary. Tobias didn't understand her. He never had. He didn't understand what caused her to leave the Star League Defense Force, nor had she tried to explain the real reason. She wagered that had she, Tobias would never have agreed to aid her in her quest for revenge. She took only a little comfort in his presence, although she imagined her mother believed that she was far more comforted by her decision to marry Tobias than she actually had.

"Are you all right, Thala?" Tobias asked in a quiet voice.

"Yes, my love," Thala said, her voice equally as quiet. "Yes, I am."

"I worry when you get quiet like that, is all," the big man rumbled.

"There is no need for worry, Tobias," Thala smiled, gently placing her hand on his. "I will be fine."

"Admiral Bonetti will see you know, Captain Ker'sal," the sergeant behind the desk said.

Thala nodded and smiled, leading Tobias into the Admiral's office. The older man was sitting behind his desk. He rose with a smile as Thala entered.

"Thala," John beamed. "What can I do for you?"

"I don't think you'll be so happy when you hear what I have to say, Admiral," Thala said, her eyes blazing in the light of the office.

"Whether or not I'll be happy is irrelevant, Thala," John shrugged his shoulders. He motioned for the two Jaradans to take a seat across the desk from him. "You came to me for a reason. I'll do whatever I can to help you."

"Yes, I know, Admiral." Thala took one of the indicated seats, but Tobias remained standing. Thala looked at Tobias briefly before continuing. "I've done a lot of thinking in the past few weeks, John."

"Go on," the admiral nodded. In his eyes, Thala could see that he had an inkling of what was coming.

"I'm tired of war, John. Tired of fighting. When I left Gamma Strike, I went home. I hadn't been home in a long time. While I was home, I was reintroduced to my childhood friend, Tobias Jar'ra," she continued, indicating the man standing next to her.

"A pleasure to meet you, sir," John said, nodding to Tobias.

"Likewise, Admiral." Tobias nodded, giving a grim smile to the man behind the desk. "A pleasure."

"Tobias and I are getting married, John," Thala said as she removed the rank insignia from her uniform and slid it across the desk. "I realized when I returned to Jarada V that my place is there. Raising a family. I can't lie to myself anymore. This is hard for me, because I've been a soldier a lot of my life. But this is right for me."

[222]

John picked up the rank insignia and flipped it over in his hands before tossing it back to Thala.

"Keep it," he said. "Your resignation is accepted, but keep the uniform in case you change your mind. If you do, you're more than welcome to return. And if you return, you will be immediately reinstated to the rank of Captain."

"Thank you, Admiral," Thala said, reattaching the rank insignia to her uniform. She stood and saluted the Admiral. After he returned her salute, she slipped into a slightly less rigid posture. "Thank you for everything you've done for me."

"You're welcome, Thala," John said, standing. "And congratulations to the both of you. May your marriage be a long and happy one."

"Thank you, sir," Thala smiled. She took Tobias's hand and led him from the office.

"Dismissed," John said to their backs long after they'd left the office. He sat and started to go over his paperwork again.

Thala and Tobias returned to their quarters to find Chular waiting for them.

"All set?" Chular asked.

"Yes," Thala said. "Did you meet with your supplier?"

"Aye," Chular grinned. He raised a glass of fire wine in salute. "The shipment is being loaded onto the Sharash'di as we speak. We should be ready to raise ship within the hour."

"Good," Thala nodded. "I'll be glad to get off this station."

The Dawning of a New Age

CHAPTER / 22

MARIO Bonetti was crouched in a doorway across from the Brentax Militia Headquarters, keeping a careful watch on the building. He counted soldiers as they went in and out, many more entering the building than leaving. In slow quiet motions, he slid Wildfire from its scabbard. As he felt the comforting weight of Wildfire in his hand, he let his mind drift momentarily.

"This is some of the finest metal I've ever seen, sir," the smithy said in his thick Spanish accent. "It will be very easy to forge beautiful blades from this. Where did you say you got this?"

"Oddly enough," Mario said. "The metal was in a meteor that hit outside my house during my last furlough. I was told

you were one of the best at forging blades out of, shall we say, exotic material."

"I am indeed. And this will be a joy to work with. What would you like me to do with it?" The smithy sounded very excited to work with the metal.

"Two blades, one traditional Spanish blade, thirty inches long, with this hilt," Mario said pulling a drawing out of his jacket pocket. "The other a traditional Japanese katana."

"I think that can be arranged. The price will be quite high though, Colonel Bonetti," the smithy said, running his hands over the metal savoring its smooth qualities. "But it will be an enjoyable job for me."

"Price isn't a problem." Mario waved away the concern about money. Despite being just a morale officer, Mario had managed to sock away a great deal of money over the years. "How long will it take?"

"Give me a week, and they'll be done," the smithy said, never taking his eyes off the metal. "I think you will be pleased with the results."

This is nuts, he thought glumly as he snapped back to the present. *One person against the entire Brentax Militia Headquarters? What am I thinking? And just how the hell am I going to get to the shuttle with M'Bek Tarmos without Kal? Damn him to hell. Now I have to tell Kit he's missing.*

This is nuts, he concluded, smiling to himself. He knew that it was crazy to continue the mission without K'Alan. And he was just the madman to pull it off. *Ah, well. You only live once. I just hope S'Era knows I love her.*

Mario crept across the street and started making his way around the back of the building.

"You there! Stop!" came a voice from behind him in the alleyway.

Without even looking, Mario swept Wildfire behind him, cleaving the soldier's head from his shoulders.

"Oh, man!" Mario said to himself. "That's not a good sign for how this is going to go."

He hurried to the entrance that he'd used before and ducked inside the building. He entered a storage room near the entrance and peeked out through the door he left cracked open. There was a patrol heading his way, probably to check on the entrance. He eased the door closed and locked it. The young man stifled a sigh and looked around the room looking for something he could use.

The room was an empty storeroom.

So much for finding help, he thought glumly. *Why couldn't I have ducked into the armory? Well, maybe it's just as well I didn't. Probably crawling with guards.*

Mario crept to the door and cracked it open just enough to see out. Peering out, he saw the corridor was empty. The colonel nodded to himself and took a deep breath. When he was sure, he pulled the door open. Stepping out into the corridor, he looked both ways. No guards were in the vicinity.

Good, he thought. *It'll be quiet for a little bit then.*

He made his way down the hallway, his footsteps silent in the empty hall. He moved with purpose, keeping his back against the wall, and looking both the way he came and the way he was going. He was nearing an intersection he didn't recognize from the briefing maps.

Great, he thought dourly. *I'm lost.*

Thinking quickly, he ducked into what he hoped was an abandoned room. There was, however, a guard in the room with his back to the door.

This day just keeps getting better and better, Mario cursed to himself.

Quietly sliding Wildfire back in its scabbard, the young colonel crept up behind the Brentax guard and, in one quick motion, broke the guard's neck. He caught the body and gently laid it on the floor to make as little noise as possible. Mario picked up the man's blaster rifle and examined it. The setting was on kill.

I think they're expecting me, Mario thought. *I'll wager they're all set this way. Which just means I have to make sure I don't get shot.*

He checked the door. No patrols out in the hallway. Nodding to himself, he pulled out the mini holo-computer that all SLDF operatives carry on missions.

"Map," he ordered in a whisper.

In an instant, a small holographic representation of the compound appeared. The map rotated, orienting itself to show where he entered the compound. It showed the corridors he'd taken and where he currently was.

Mario groaned as he looked at where he was in relation to M'Bek Tarmos's office.

Ya gotta do things the hard way, don't you, Mario? he asked himself.

He looked at the map, memorizing his route. Closing up the holo-computer, Mario picked up the blaster rifle. Checking the charge on the rifle, Mario smiled to himself. He knew he was in for a fight at this point. Mario opened the door and peeked out.

A guard shouted and fired his blaster. Mario ducked just in time, as a blaster bolt hit the door frame right next to where his head had been just seconds before.

"Yikes!" Mario yelled as he fired back. The bolt from his blaster struck the guard in the center of his chest sending the Brentax man flying backwards. "They *are* all set on kill!"

Mario stuck his head back out and looked both ways. No more guards were in sight, so the young man crept out from the room and started towards his destination again.

He kept his back flat against the wall. Soon he neared a four way intersection of corridors, which, from the map, he remembered he needed to take the corridor straight ahead. He looked down both side corridors and saw no sign of guards

Mario's luck did not hold for long, though. As he started to cross the corridor, guards appeared in both of the side corridors.

"Hold intruder!" they ordered, raising their blaster rifles an preparing to fire.

Mario did the only thing he could think to do... He dove headfirst into the corridor across the way. The guards fired, missing Mario as he ducked and rolled into the corridor. Curious, the young man leaned back and poked his head back into the intersection to see what had happened. The blaster bolts that had missed him had hit the guards in the opposite corridors.

"Nice."

He shook his head and turned back down the hall he needed to take. Mario moved with a cautious grace, sliding across the side of the corridor, keeping the blaster rifle trained ahead of him as he constantly checked behind him. He worked is way deeper and deeper into the complex, taking out as many Brentax soldiers as he could along the way. Finally, after about half an hour of slinking around the complex, Mario saw the door to the Brentax Commander's office.

He grinned to himself and reset the blaster rifle to heavy stun. The colonel shook his head and started across to the closed door. He kicked it open and entered.

"Ah, you must be Colonel Bonetti," the Brentax behind the desk said. "Come in and have a drink. I must say, you've been a very interesting opponent."

The Dawning of a New Age

CHAPTER 23

COMMANDER Erin Sykes was bored. And she was nervous. It was a bad combination. She knew the Captain could take care of himself. She'd known him long enough to know that. She drummed her fingers on the armrest of her chair in absentminded thought.

"I figure it'll be another two or three hours, Commander," Kath shook her head. "No use worrying about them yet."

"I just have a bad feeling, Kath," Erin sighed. "Can't explain it."

"They'll be all right, Erin," Kath smiled. "Why don't you go grab some lunch. You've been on the bridge all day."

"Sounds like a good idea," Erin said, starting to rise out of the chair.

"Commander, incoming contact at high rate of speed," Masha called from the tactical station. "Cloak systems holding steady."

"Identify," Erin said, slumping back in her seat.

No rest for the wicked, she thought.

"Brentax heavy cruiser. It appears to be a Duhari class vessel. She's heading for the jumpgate at a very high rate of speed," Masha reported.

"Ease us away from the jumpgate. Bring up the tactical holo. And keep the damn cloaking screens up!" Erin barked.

Erin could feel the ship lurch just a little as the helm officer moved the massive ship away from the jumpgate. In the center area of the bridge, a 3-D tactical hologram of the situation fizzled into clarity. It showed the jumpgate, and the White Knight easing away from it. The Duhari class cruiser was shown streaking towards the jumpgate. As Masha had reported, they were moving at an extremely high rate of speed. The jumpgate flashed as the Brentax vessel entered it.

"They're in a hurry wherever they're going," Erin noted. "Track them through hyperspace as best you can."

"Acknowledged, Commander. Tracking now," Masha grinned as her fingers flew over her console. "Probable course is going to take them to the Khrinnus system. Only one SLDF ship is listed as being in that system, the Creighton."

"Kath, get me a tight-beam communication to the Gamma Epsilon station," Erin barked. "Admiral Bonetti will want to know this information."

"Acknowledged."

* * *

Rick Bentsen

2.7.2136
1441
Gamma Epsilon Station
Admiral John Bonetti's Office

John had just settled back down behind his desk after catching a quick meal. He'd not wanted to leave his office in case word came in from Gamma Strike, but Sergeant Riker had assured him that should word come in, she'd personally relay it to him. The more he thought about the mission, the more nervous he became. The nervous waiting was the part of the job he hated the most. He saw the casualty report still on his desk and amended that thought to be the thing he hated the second most.

"Admiral, there's a tight-beam communication coming in," Sergeant Riker's voice came over the comms. "It's from Commander Erin Sykes."

"Patch it through, Sergeant!" he exclaimed. *The waiting is over,* he added to himself with satisfaction.

"Patching it through now, Admiral," the sergeant nodded.

Immediately, Erin appeared on John's viewscreen. Her face was set in a look of grim determination.

"Admiral Bonetti," Erin acknowledged.

"Commander Sykes, report," the admiral stated.

"No word yet from the Captain's team, Admiral," Erin shook her head, clearly knowing that was what John wanted to know. Not that that was all that hard to guess. "But I do have other news to pass on to you."

"Go ahead," John sighed, unhappy that there was no news about K'Alan and his son. *Not what I wanted to hear,* he added to himself.

"Sir, we've been tracking a Duhari class heavy cruiser traveling at a high rate of speed through hyperspace," Erin reported. "They appear to be headed to the Khrinnus system."

"You're sure about where they're headed?" John asked.

[233]

"Fairly sure, sir," Erin sighed. "And they are in a big hurry."

"Probably out to ascertain what happened to the Dorania Toran," John smiled. "That ship met a somewhat grisly fate by underestimating the Creighton."

"Captain Keevan ok?" Erin asked.

"Yes," John nodded. "The Creighton sustained some very minor damage. They'll likely be fully repaired by the time this new vessel gets to them."

"This is good news!" A broad smile crossed Erin's face. "The Creighton took out a Duhari class vessel by itself?"

"Yes, they did. You needn't worry about Captain Keevan. I'll make sure he's got this warning. Thank you for reporting this." He paused. "I just wish you had had some report of the mission."

"Me too, Admiral," Erin sighed. "Me too. I'm a bit... nervous."

"As am I. Contact me as soon as you have something to report."

"I will, Admiral."

John cut the transmission and sighed. *No,* he thought. *The waiting is definitely not over.*

He flipped on the intercom to his aide.

"Sergeant Riker, get me Captain Keevan."

"Right away, Admiral."

2.7.2136
1501
SLS White Knight
Soran's Bar

"So K'Alan and I were sitting there as Mario just kinda dribbled through the drink she just poured over his head," Soran was saying "And all he could think to say was, "Is that a no?""

S'Era laughed. K'Itea just shook her head.

"Soran, how can I make him notice me?" S'Era asked.

[234]

"Well, you are S'Era Bryce, are you not?" Soran smiled. "He's told me many times, all of which were when your brother was not in hearing range of course, of your stunning beauty. His descriptions of which, by the way, do not compare to the real thing. He is quite enamored of you."

"But he's never said anything," S'Era pouted.

"S'Era," Soran smiled. "He's afraid your brother would not approve."

"You would think that after knowing my husband for 15 years, Mario'd know better," K'Itea chuckled. "Like I told S'Era. K'Alan is imminently concerned about his sister's happiness. If allowing Mario to date S'Era would make her happy, then, I would think he would whole-heartedly approve."

Soran laughed, a long hearty laugh. "And I'd wager that Mario and K'Alan talked about this on the long flight to Brentax III. It would be just like them to talk about something so totally unrelated to the mission at hand."

"Oh?" K'Itea asked. "How so?"

"See," Soran explained with a twinkle in his eye. "The way they think, they would rather joke around or deal with other things while preparing for a mission. It eases the stress. They feel that tends to make their missions go a whole lot smoother. From their track record, I'd say they're right. It's not a method I'd recommend for just anyone though. It doesn't always work. Unless you're K'Alan Bryce or Mario Bonetti, that is."

"Maybe it's just that they don't want to let us girls down," S'Era giggled. "After all, they know enough not to make us mad, don't they?"

* * *

The Khrinnus system was a small system, barely worth notice. There were four planets around a medium sized yellow star. Barely worth notice, yet it was one of the most hotly contested systems by the Brentax and the Star League. Oddly enough, even though it was so highly prized by both sides, the skirmish between the Creighton and the Dorania Toran was the first skirmish in the Khrinnus system.

Captain Tom Keevan of the Creighton did not expect the Brentax to forget. So he was less than surprised when Admiral Bonetti passed along Gamma Strike's report that another Duhari class heavy cruiser was headed to the Khrinnus sector. He was not surprised at all, in fact, to hear it. He believed that his easy destruction of the Dorania Toran would bring waves of Brentax ships to the attack against the Creighton.

Good, he thought. *Bring them on.*

"I understand, Admiral," the Creighton's captain said, snapping out of his thoughts to look at the admiral on the viewscreen. "We'll be ready for them. And thank Commander Sykes for passing along the info."

"Be careful, Tom," John cautioned. "We need all the good captains we can get."

"I'm always careful, you old warhorse," Tom chuckled. I'll let you know how we do. Creighton out."

The holo blinked out, and reports started coming in from his bridge crew.

"Cloaking system engaged and reading nominal."

"Weapons systems primed. Modified proton torpedoes in the tubes and locked."

"Scanners to full, reading only empty space."

"Communications chatter normal. No Brentax activity."

"Helm responding in nominal parameters."

[236]

"Engines showing one hundred seven percent efficiency."

Tom Keevan nodded to himself. They were ready. All they had to do was wait for the Brentax to show.

The Dawning of a New Age

CHAPTER 24

2.7.2136
1512
Brentax III
M'Bek Tarmos's Office

"WELL? Won't you come in and have a drink, Colonel?" M'Bek Tarmos asked.

"With you?" Mario chuckled. "I'd be drawn and quartered for even thinking of such a thing."

"Well, then," the Brentax Commander said. "What can I do for you, Colonel Bonetti?"

"I don't suppose you want to make it easy for me and just come with me to the shuttle," Mario raised an eyebrow.

M'Bek Tarmos laughed.

"I think not, Colonel. How would it look if I just turned myself over to you without a fight?"

"Just the same, you are coming with me," Mario said as he hefted the blaster rifle. "I'm afraid I can't take no for an answer."

[239]

"Such cocky creatures you humans are. You know, you'd never make it out of the building, let alone to the spaceport," the Brentax commander rasped. "It's best to just give yourself up now and save yourself the agony."

"Sure, I will," Mario chuckled. "I'll just go back to my boss and say, 'Sorry. I couldn't get him because there was no way I could get back to the spaceport without getting killed. Maybe next time.' That won't get me too far, Tarmos."

"I don't think you understand. If you try to take me from here by force, you will be dead before we leave the office," M'Bek Tarmos chuckled. "My guards will see to that."

"We'll see." Mario motioned with the blaster rifle. "If you'll get up, I'd rather not have to stun you. You're far too large to drag."

"How dare you insult me like that!" M'Bek howled.

"Hey, bubba. It's not like I'm the one who's obviously been packing away the super-sized meals. Seriously, you know you don't have to get the extra large fries with the burger." Mario chuckled at his own little joke. "Now. Stand up and away from the desk."

"I think not," M'Bek said His hand slowly traced across the bottom edge of the top of his desk. Before it got too far, his arm flopped limp, a knife sticking out of his bicep.

"I wouldn't try that again," Mario said. He waggled the rifle. "Next time, you'll get shot."

"Do you really think you're going to get away with this atrocity?" the Brentax commander snarled.

"How ironic that you should be complaining about atrocities, M'Bek Tarmos," Mario sighed. "You who are responsible for the deaths of millions of Duterians. That slaughter is an atrocity. This, well, this is just a friendly conversation."

"It will take much more than your flashy knife work to bring me in to your precious Star League, Colonel." M'Bek Tarmos cackled.

"There's a full squadron waiting for us at the landing pad," Mario lied.

"That's impossible. I know it was just you and one other that broke in here earlier." The Brentax shook his head. "And your partner has been disposed of."

"He's expendable," Mario shrugged, his face betraying no emotion whatsoever. "Now, if you please. I am in somewhat of a hurry to get out of Brentax space, if you know what I mean."

"You don't seem to get it," M'Bek sighed as he stood up behind his desk. "You're not going to make it out of Brentax space alive."

"You wanna lay odds on that?" Mario said. "I'm a betting man. I think your associates will be less inclined to shoot me down with you on board. That wouldn't look good on their resumes after all, being the one that shot down the Supreme Commander of the Brentax Militia. Not good for one's career at all." Mario clucked twice and hurried over to where M'Bek Tarmos was standing. He jabbed his blaster rifle in the man's back. "Now move!"

"Well, since you asked so nicely," the Brentax Commander smiled, showing off his sharp teeth. "Of course I'll go with you."

"And call off your guards as we go," Mario ordered.

"Why should I?"

"Because," Mario said as he jabbed the rifle further in the man's back. "This rifle's set on kill. And I don't think I'd miss from this range."

M'Bek Tarmos swallowed twice and started out of the office with Mario right behind him.

"You know," the Brentax commander said. "If you kill me, there's no way I can sign a peace treaty with your precious Star League. I assume that is the reason you're bringing me in to the Star League, isn't it?"

"Yes, it is," Mario admitted. "But if I don't return with you, the Star League will assume the mission failed and we're dead here. And if that happens, well, there's a full contingent of Star League battleships waiting for orders to destroy Brentax III. Me, personally, I'd like to see this war end peacefully."

There was a long pause while each man looked the other one over. Finally, M'Bek Tarmos looked away.

"Yes, well," the Brentax commander said quietly. "Perhaps the time has come for this war to end. I will go with you peacefully, Colonel. I have no desire to see my homeworld destroyed."

"Good. Now, please. Move."

The two men walked down the hall. They met minimal opposition, but the guards they did run into stepped aside at their leader's insistence.

It took them nearly an hour to make their way from the office, through the Brentax Militia Headquarters, and across Brentacchia to the Brentacchia Spaceport. Opposition continued to be light, and Mario began to worry slightly about the relative ease of their escape.

When they reached the shuttle, however, Mario breathed a small sigh of relief.

"I'm going to have to bind you until we get back to the White Knight," Mario said.

"I understand. I would do no less."

Mario set to work securing M'Bek Tarmos to his seat, then, once he was satisfied the Brentax commander wasn't going to be going anywhere, the Star League Colonel began preflight checks.

Without waiting for launch clearance, Mario punched the launch controls. The small shuttle shot out from the spaceport into the afternoon sky, achieving orbit quickly.

A few minutes into the trip back to the White Knight, the communications array began to beep loudly, startling both the colonel and the Brentax Militia Commander.

"Star League shuttle. This is T'Marik Kodan of the Brentax Duhari class vessel Torellia Corvax. You will stand down now and land your vessel at the Brentacchia Spaceport or you will be destroyed."

CHAPTER 25

"CAPTAIN!" the sensors officer called. "We have an incoming contact bearing 312."

"Can you identify it?" the capain asked as he turned in his chair to face his sensors officer.

"I believe so, sir," the woman nodded. "Silhouette confirms it a Duhari class heavy cruiser."

"Tactical holo!" Captain Keevan ordered.

Instantly, a holographic representation of the sector appeared in the communications holosphere. It showed the Duhari class cruiser entering the Khrinnus sector at high velocity.

"Captain, they're beginning a solon sweep," the woman at the sensor console reported. "I estimate three minutes before they penetrate the cloak."

"Damn. Helm, keep us ahead of the solon," the captain whipped around to the navigation station. "Use whatever evasive maneuvers you need. Give us as much time to launch the torpedoes as you can."

"Acknowledged," the helm officer said. "Beginning evasive pattern Alpha."

"Time until torpedoes are locked on target, Kara?" Tom Keevan asked his weapons officer impatiently.

"Four minutes," Kara replied, her attention never leaving her console.

"Evasive pattern Delta," the helmswoman announced.

"Solon sweep is holding," the sensors chief cursed. "They're steadily gaining on us, Captain. Computer estimates two minutes until cloak is pierced."

"Torps still need three minutes, Captain," Kara reported.

"Evasive pattern Omega," the helmswoman said through clenched teeth.

"We're pulling a little ahead of the solon sweep, Captain, but I don't think it'll last," the woman at the sensors reported. "One and one half minutes unttil cloak is pierced."

"Give me two minutes, Helmswoman," Kara grunted as she slammed some controls.

"Evasive pattern Phi," the helmswoman squeaked.

"Torps ready, Captain!" Kara yelled.

"FIRE!!" Tom Keevan yelled.

Kara slammed a control on the weapons panel, and two blue streaks of light lanced out from the forward launchers. On the tactical holo, two balls of phosphorescent blue light streaked across the holo towards the Brentax vessel.

Even on the tactical holo, the explosion was blinding.

"Get me Admiral Bonetti at the Gamma Epsilon Station!" Tom Keevan whooped.

⟨CHAPTER / 26⟩

2.7.2136
1622
Shuttle Kiarin

"WELL, this sucks," Mario sighed.

He was looking at the distinct sensor silhouette of a Duhari class heavy cruiser. And the sensors indicated that the ship with its gun ports open and trained on the shuttle. The identifying beacon indicated that the ship was the Torellia Corvax.

"Let me talk to him," M'Bek Tarmos said. "T'Marik is loyal to me. He will stand down."

"Do it," Mario nodded as he flicked on the communications array.

"T'Marik," the Brentax official croaked. "This is Brentax Supreme Commander M'Bek Tarmos. You will stand down immediately. That is an order."

"Supreme Commander, you know as well as I do that I cannot follow your orders while you are a prisoner," T'Marik intoned. He almost sounded sad. Almost.

"Fool!" M'Bek roared. "I went with him of my own volition. Do you really think that the Star League could truly hold me against my will should I so choose to leave?"

"As flawless as your logic is, and, as usual, it is flawless, Supreme Commander, you nevertheless are a prisoner of our enemy, and thus your order carries no weight," T'Marik's raspy voice came back. "If the Star League vessel does not stand down, I will order it shot down, Supreme Commander. Even with you on board."

"T'Marik, you are a short sighted fool." M'Bek slammed his hands on the console in front of him. Mario made a note to check the console for dents later. If you destroy this ship, the Star League will throw everything they have at us in a killer strike meant to wipe us out completely. They will do to us what we have done to so many others. Your wife and pouchling will not survive. Is that what you truly wish to happen, T'Marik?"

"No, of course not, Supreme Commander. But imperial mandates—"

"Imperial mandates be damned!" M'Bek Tarmos roared. "Who do you think truly runs the Empire? I do, as all Supreme Commanders before me have! Until my death or retirement, I am the Empire!"

"Supreme Commander, I cannot call off the attack. The Star League ship must not be allowed to leave Brentax space with you aboard. I have my orders."

"Your orders are countermanded!"

"You do not have the authority to do so while you are on that ship. I am sorry, Supreme Commander," T'Marik said. M'Bek almost believed he was sincere. "Star League officer, you have five standard minutes to surrender or be destroyed."

The communications system clicked off and Mario looked at the Brentax official.

"Loyal, eh? Got any other suggestions?" the colonel quipped.

"This shuttle. Does it have any weapons?"

"Not enough to take out a Duhari class vessel," Mario shook his head. "All we have is one proton torpedo."

"That will do," M'Bek Tarmos sighed. "I will show you where to target. You will take out external communications and weapons in one strike. It is the best we can hope for. They will need time to repair the weapons systems."

"Let's just hope it buys us enough time. I can cut down the trip back by about a day if the White Knight will meet us halfway." Mario flicked a switch on the console. "Weapons systems online, and Lord, I wish K'Alan were here to man them."

"Your shot must be precise." M'Bek Tarmos inclined his head at the silhouette of the Duhari class cruiser. "Near the engine intake is a small intake for the weapons. Your shot must hit the weapons intake exactly. If it does it will cause major damage to all the weapons systems and will cause collateral damage to the communications systems. External communications will be totally scrambled, and internal communications will be down for several hours. If you do not hit precisely, you will not get a second shot. Please, make your shot count."

"If ever there was a warning I didn't need," Mario smiled. "That was it, Commander."

"Your time is up, Star League vessel," the comms crackled. "What is your answer?"

The young colonel took a deep breath and lined up his shot. Praying to whoever would listen, he punched the fire controls. The proton torpedo leapt from the underbelly of the shuttle and streaked towards the Duhari class vessel. The torpedo impacted, and Mario slammed the thruster controls.

"So, can I take it since they're not firing back that I hit?" Mario raised his eyebrow.

"I think so, yes. But you'd best get us to your ship quickly. They will recover soon."

"You got it. Computer establish tightbeam communication with the White Knight."

[247]

The Dawning of a New Age

⟨CHAPTER / 27⟩

HE was cold. Not the numbing cold of space, but a dry spiritless cold that ate through to his soul. His eyes were closed. He felt little beyond the cold. Except for the steel, the cold, hard steel that bound his wrists and ankles. That he could feel. The steel pressed into his flesh, not enough for him to wince, but enough for him to know they were there.

He moaned softly, his cry quiet in the cold of the prison cell. There was no return sound... it appeared he was alone in the cell.

Great, he thought. *What am I doing here? I should never have gone to check on G'Kiron.*

The Star League officer slowly opened his eyes. The light that assailed his eyes, although not bright in reality, was too bright for him. He winced and turned his head away from the light.

[249]

After his eyes adjusted, he examined his cell. The walls were made of apparently solid granite. He was chained to the wall with large wrought iron chains. He tested each manacle, and found that they were quite solidly attached to the wall.

Damn, he cursed to himself.

Sighing, he looked down at himself. They hadn't beaten him too badly before chaining him. The biggest pain still came from the stun blast. Surprisingly, he still had his energy bow. He wondered how the Brentax had missed taking that. His sword was gone, as was his laser. He wondered how thorough a job the Brentax did searching him.

"K'Alan?" a weak voice from the cell across the corridor called. "You are finally awake?"

"Chancellor G'Kiron," K'Alan said, his voice no more than a rough rasp. "Are you all right, sir?"

"No," came the reply. "It is immaterial, however. What matters is that you must escape."

"Yes," K'Alan said, his voice slowly returning. "That is the first duty of a prisoner. Is escape from this prison possible?"

There was a very long pronounced pause before G'Kiron's answer.

"It is possible," the old Brentax croaked. "However, in the history of Brentacchia Prison, no escape attempt has ever been successful."

"Great," K'Alan sighed. "Escape from a prison that's never been escaped from. Well, there's supposedly a first time for everything."

"You must succeed. There is too much riding on you and young Colonel Bonetti for the two of you to fail."

"More than likely, Mario's continuing with the mission as we speak," K'Alan said. "I can only hope he's not stupid enough to try to rescue me before bringing M'Bek Tarmos to the Star League."

"He would leave you behind?" G'Kiron said, his voice sounding very surprised.

[250]

"Yes. He was so ordered. The mission is far more important than either his or my life singularly." K'Alan smiled wryly. "By myself, I'm expendable. If I were to die here, then my only regret is that I didn't get to know my son better."

"How old is your son? Why do you not know him? For a father to not know his son is inhuman."

"He was born about ten years ago," K'Alan said. He rolled his shoulders, trying to get some feeling back into his arms. "Because I was out among the stars, my wife and my sister decided that it would be best to not tell me until I was there to hear the news in person. So I didn't find out about my son until he was ten."

"I am sorry, K'Alan. A father should know his son."

"The worst part is that he resents me for not being a part of his life," he closed his eyes against the pain, this time emotional. "Gods know I wish I had been."

"There is nothing you can do to change the past, my friend," G'Kiron sighed. "However, you always have the future. Get out of this prison and go home to your family." There were sounds of heavy booted feet coming from far down the hallway. "Shhhh. Guards."

K'Alan nodded, even though he knew Chancellor G'Kiron couldn't see him from the angle he was at. The footsteps in the hall got closer. They stopped near what, K'Alan assumed, was G'Kiron's cell.

"Ah, G'Kiron," the sneering voice of the guard said. "I will look with joy on your execution."

"Execute me if you must, but let the Duterian go. He has done nothing," G'Kiron said.

"He is a war criminal. He too will be executed." The guard's voice got perhaps a little more of a sneer as he added, "After he is tortured of course."

"What would you have him do, D'Boran? The young man watched his homeworld be destroyed."

"Yes, and a glorious battle that was," the guard named D'Boran sneered. "I cheered as the pathetic Star League Defense Force futilely tried to repel us. Ah, yes. It was

[251]

glorious. My only regret is that I was not able to bed their ruler. I understand she is a beautiful specimen of her species. Of course, I would have slit her throat immediately afterwards."

A low growl began in K'Alan's throat. The captain charged suddenly, but the chains held him fast. The guard did a double take, startled by the fierce charge of the prisoner. He recovered quickly when he realized that the captive posed no threat. He laughed as he swaggered over to stand in from of K'Alan's cell.

"You know that woman?" the guard sneered at him, knowing there was nothing the prisoner could do. "Well, then. I really wish I had taken her to my bed. I would love to tell you how much she would have squealed, begged and pleaded with me as I had my way with her. It would be most satisfying."

"If you had had your way with her," K'Alan began, his voice soft and cold with danger. "I would have lead a massive assault on Brentax III. You would not be standing there having this pleasant conversation with me. I would have ripped out your heart and fed it to you."

"Such a pleasant thought," D'Boran sneered again. K'Alan began to think that the sneer was this guard's permanent expression. "I would love to continue this pleasant conversation, but I'm afraid I cannot. I have orders to bring you to... our torturer. I'm afraid I can't have you awake for the trip."

K'Alan barely had time to realize that a blaster rifle was being raised before he fell unconscious again.

◁CHAPTER/28▷

T
HE bridge was a bustle of nervous energy. Everyone was at their post, doing their best to look busy, although there was little more that could be done. There was nothing to do until the shuttle reported in.

Erin Sykes sat in the executive officer's chair, drumming her fingers on the armrest impatiently. She sighed to herself. She'd hoped to have heard from the Captain by now. The waiting was driving her crazy.

"Kath, any word?" the commander asked for the umpteenth time.

"Not yet. I'll let you know as soon as they call in," the pretty Angelian smiled.

"Masha, any indication of Brentax activity?"

"Not since that Duhari class cruiser went through, Commander."

[253]

"Good. Keep an eye on the—"

"Commander, incoming communication from the Shuttle Kiarin!" Kath shouted. "Audio only."

"Patch it through, Kath."

"Commander Sykes, this is Colonel Bonetti."

"Good to hear from you, Colonel," the commander sighed with relief. "Status report."

"Supreme Commander M'Bek Tarmos is sitting right next to me. We've got a Duhari class heavy cruiser on our tail. We'd appreciate it if you met us halfway to your location."

"Consider it done. Let me speak to Captain Bryce."

"I'm afraid he isn't here. He was captured. I'd like to bring Lancer squad back to Brentax III as soon as I land."

"I'm afraid that won't be possible, Colonel. We're under orders to make for the Gamma Epsilon station immediately upon your landing"

"But we can't just leave the Captain there, Commander!"

"We have no choice, Mario," Erin sighed. She didn't want to give the order any more than Mario wanted to hear it. "In the long run, he's expendable. Captain Bryce would tell you the exact same thing. As soon as we complete the mission, we'll see about mounting a rescue mission."

"Understood," Mario said, his voice bitter. "Better wait and let me tell Kit."

"Just get your tail back here in one piece, Colonel."

"I intend to," the morale officer said. "Colonel Bonetti out."

Erin sighed once more. It was going to be a long week.

2.7.2136
1742
SLS White Knight
The City

K'Itea and Elam were sitting in the park in the middle of the city. K'Itea wore a worried expression on her face, and Elam was leaning against her, his eyes closed. K'Itea was stroking his hair gently, the slow motions serving to calm the High Gentlewoman somewhat.

Where is K'Alan? she wondered to herself. *Is he OK? Will he be coming home soon?*

Her thoughts flew through her mind fast and furiously. She worried about her husband. She'd had trouble sleeping since he left on this mission. And she couldn't shake the feeling that he was in trouble. And she knew that there wasn't much she could do but sit and worry. S'Era was no comfort. She was too wrapped up in her own concerns about Mario.

The fact that the hot-headed Colonel Bonetti was with her husband gave K'Itea some comfort. She knew that Mario cared about K'Alan almost as much as she did. She knew that he'd keep her husband safe. *At least,* she told herself, *K'Alan had taken someone he could count on for backup.*

She pulled out of her thoughts with a start, realizing that her son was looking at her.

"You went away for a moment," Elam said. "I was just wondering if you were all right."

"Yes, Elam," K'Itea said. "I'm fine. I'm just worrying about your father."

"When will he be back?"

"He should be back in a couple days." K'Itea let a tear roll down her face. "Not soon enough," she added.

"I miss him," the young man said. It was a statement that K'Itea had not been expecting, but one that she found very welcome.

K'Itea looked down at her son and smiled. She hugged him close, ruffling his hair.

* * *

The view outside Admiral Bonetti's office window never changed. It was an unblemished view of the stars. The planet that the Gamma Epsilon station orbited was on the other side. John found the stars to be eternally, hauntingly beautiful.

John was watching a Star League starship prepare to dock with the station. For the umpteenth time, he wished he were still out there in command of a Star League ship.

"Admiral?" Anne Riker prodded as she entered the office.

"The problem with this view, Sergeant," John said, "is that the stars don't move. That's the problem with flying a desk instead of a ship. The stars stay constant, unmoving. It's disconcertingly still."

"Sir, there's a tight beam communication for you." The young sergeant smiled slightly. "It's from Commander Sykes."

"Patch it through, Sergeant," John said as he quickly returned to his desk.

"Right away, sir."

The young sergeant turned and left the office. Moments later, Erin Sykes appeared on the holo.

"Admiral Bonetti, we just received word from your son," Erin began without preamble.

"Yes, Commander?"

"They have successfully extracted M'Bek Tarmos. I'm ordering the White Knight into Brentax space to retrieve them. They picked up a tail." Erin smiled.

"Good! As soon as they land, make your best speed to the Gamma Epsilon station."

"Yes, sir. As soon as the shuttle lands, we'll make our best speed." She paused before continuing. "There is a problem, sir."

"Problem? What problem?"

"It seems that Captain Bryce is not on the shuttle. Mario has requested leading a rescue mission. I had no choice but to deny his request."

"Bad news indeed. You did the right thing. Until Captain Bryce can be returned, you have command of Gamma Strike. Commander."

"Understood, sir."

"And good work to your team, Commander."

"Thank you, Admiral."

The holo faded and John sighed to himself.

What else can go wrong? he thought.

2.7.2136
1802
SLS White Knight
Soran's Bar

S'Era Bryce had been drinking heavily for over two hours. Well, heavily for her at any rate. She was actually only on her third drink.

"Are you sure you're okay?" Soran asked as he continued to wipe down the bar. "I've never seen you drink so much before."

S'Era took a big gulp of her drink and sighed.

"I'm worried about him. I'm afraid he's gotten himself in some major trouble this time," the young woman said.

"Your brother?"

"No. K'Alan can take care of himself. It's that hot head Mario I'm worried about.

"You're worried about Mario," Soran laughed. Seeing the pained look in the young woman's eyes, Soran stopped laughing and looked down at the bar he was still polishing. "In the fifteen or so years I've known Mario, I've never known him to ever get into a situation where he was over his head. As difficult as this mission sounds, this was just a walk in the park to him."

"Still, I'm worried. I love him, Soran." A tear ran down her cheek. "I don't want to lose him."

"I know you do, S'Era." The bartender's voice was soft and tender. "The best thing you can do for yourself is to look after your sister-in-law and your nephew for your brother. He needs you to be there for them."

"You're right, of course," she sniffled. She looked at her glass with distaste. "I don't suppose you have something for the hangover I know I'm going to have tomorrow?"

"Coffee," Soran chuckled. "I start serving coffee at 0700."

⟨CHAPTER 29⟩

2.7.2136
2349
Brentax III
Brentacchia Prison

K'ALAN moaned in quiet pain. His wrists and ankles felt like they were bound with iron manacles, although he could not tell for sure. His head hurt too much for him to open his eyes. He felt a hard substance against his back, although he couldn't tell if it was wood or metal.

This must be the torture room, he thought to himself. *Well, I suppose torture it is.*

"Are you comfortable?" a voice next to his head asked. The voice was raspy and gravelly but quiet at the same time.

"Hardly. You know, I cold use a couple pillows to fall asleep properly," K'Alan quipped. "If I don't have a couple pillows under my head, I wake up all cranky with a massive headache."

"Ah, a lively victim," the voice laughed a raspy, hissing laugh. "Good. This will be so much more fun for me then."

K'Alan turned his head towards the voice and slowly, cautiously, opened his eyes. The face that greeted his gaze was not what he expected. Where he'd been expecting the green scaly visage of a Brentax officer, the face that greeted him was perhaps more menacing. The creature was an insectoid whose black carapace was tinted almost a dark bluish color. The face and hands were almost humanoid in appearance. Pale skin grew out of the carapace. The creature had no discernable nose, and his teeth were large and sharp. Large multi-faceted eyes dominated the creature's facial features. K'Alan could barely suppress a shudder at the creature's appearance.

"Ah, good," the creature's sibilant voice hissed. "I see my appearance startles you."

"Who and what are you?" K'Alan asked.

"I am Crovax. I am of the Cor'vat race."

"I'm not familiar with that race," K'Alan admitted, furrowing his eyebrows.

"It is not surprising, Duterian. The Brentax keep the Cor'vat as slaves," the Cor'vat spat in distaste. "The Brentax reveal little about their slaves."

"Slaves?" K'Alan spat. "Slavery is just one more atrocity the Brentax have committed. Why don't your people rebel."

"We would have by now, Duterian. But the Brentax are smart and keep us separated. There are very few of us in any one given place. For example, I am the only Cor'vat currently in Brentacchia."

"We were right then," K'Alan said, closing his eyes.

"What do you mean, Duterian? You were right about what?"

"We were right about the correct way to handle the Brentax situation."

"You speak in twisted words, Duterian. Speak plainly," Crovax snarled.

"Very simply, there have been different factions with different ideas about how to deal with the Brentax

[260]

situation. One side wanted to extract M'Bek Tarmos and force him to sign a treaty to end the war. The other side wanted to send a killer force and wipe the Brentax out once and for all," K'Alan opened his eyes and looked at Crovax. The Duterian's eyes were brimming with tears at the memories of his home world's destruction. "After the destruction of my home world, I was leaning towards retaliation and destruction of Brentax III. But I follow orders like a good soldier."

"They destroyed your home world?" Crovax hissed.

"Yes. Millions of my people were killed. They used heavy bombardments from orbit," K'Alan said bitterly. "There are just over fifteen thousand of my people left."

"That is intolerable!" Crovax roared. "War produces death, yes, but genocide is unnecessary. And your Star League did not react in kind." Crovax blinked several times, rubbing his chin in an almost human-like manner. "I must think on this in private. You have given me a great deal to thing about, Duterian."

Crovax slinked off, leaving K'Alan alone in the darkness wondering what had just happened.

The Dawning of a New Age

⟨CHAPTER / 30⟩

STAR League President Kerrin Jameson sighed as she waited for her transport. It had been a long day, and there was every indication that the next few days were going to be equally as long. Even if Gamma Strike had been successful in extracting M'Bek Tarmos, there would still be a great deal of negotiations in order for the peace treaty to be finalized. There was a great deal of work ahead of her and she did not relish it.

Shaking her head, she pulled out the treaty to look at one more time while she waited.

It had been written up two months ago. There had been some minor negotiations with a lesser Brentax dignitary, but the talks had fallen through. There were changes that would need to be made of course. She would seek compensation for the survivors of the Duterius Prime massacre. And the Star League would likely end up ceding

[263]

the Khrinnus system to the Brentax. She didn't see how that could be avoided now.

She read the treaty over thoroughly. Admiral Bonetti had written the treaty up. It was very well written, although the president wondered if the Brentax could live up to their end of the agreement.

"Now boarding at Gate 13. Local transport to Virginia. With stops in Richmond, Falls Church, and Norfolk," a male voice called over the station intercom.

Kerrin put the treaty back in her briefcase and headed towards Gate 13.

It would be good to get back to the office briefly before going home. She knew she'd made some of her people angry by going to Chicago for the day, but it had been necessary. The Hawks family needed her now more than ever, and, if she were going to be honest about things, she needed them just as much.

The transport from Chicago to Falls Church was a quick and uneventful one. Kerrin was left alone with her thoughts for just under an hour before the transport touched down.

The president stepped off the transport and headed out into the early morning air. Jane Swiftwind was there by a small hovercar.

"Hi, Jane," Kerrin said.

"How'd it go?" the president's aide asked as she opened the door to the hovercar for the president.

"It went as well as could be expected," Kerrin said, her voice strained.

The president of the Star League climbed into the hovercar and leaned her head against the headrest. She closed her eyes and moaned.

"Long day, Kerrin?" Jane asked, although it was a silly question.

Kerrin just nodded, her eyes staying closed. She slumped down in her seat and sighed before adding. "I don't suppose you have some good news for me."

"I do have good news, but there is some bad news attached to it," Jane reported. "The good news is that Gamma Strike has successfully extracted M'Bek Tarmos."

Kerrin allowed herself a moment's elation before opening one eye and looking at Jane. "And the bad news?"

"Captain K'Alan Bryce was captured during the mission, and is being held prisoner on Brentax III."

"Dammit!" Kerrin swore as she banged her fist on the side of the hovercar. "I won't accept that. As soon as you can, get me a tight beam communication to the White Knight. I want to speak with Colonel Bonetti. And get me the Creighton too."

"Understood, Kerrin. But the White Knight won't be in range until they get back to the Gamma Epsilon station in two days."

"I know. I just hope Captain Bryce can last that long."

The Dawning of a New Age

CHAPTER / 31

CAPTAIN Tom Keevan had just settled down in his bunk and was staring at the ceiling. It had been a long day with the various Brentax ships challenging the Creighton in the Khrinnus system. All he wanted now was a good night's sleep. And yet, as he lay in his bunk, he found he couldn't sleep. His mind kept running through the day's events over and over again.

He sighed deeply. When he'd called in to talk to Admiral Bonetti, he'd heard that there was no news yet about the Gamma Strike mission. He hoped that they had succeeded by now.

His thoughts drifted to the executive officer of Gamma Strike. He wondered what Erin was doing. Thinking about Erin centered him as it always did. He loved her. He knew she loved him in return. Not for the first time, he

[267]

considered proposing marriage to her. He was pretty sure she'd say yes, he just didn't have the nerve.

"Unreal," he chuckled to himself aloud. "I can face off against a Duhari class heavy cruiser without flinching, but put me up against my feelings for Erin and I wither like a flower that hasn't been watered in months."

He shook his head sadly and went back to staring at the ceiling. Sooner or later he'd have to come to grips with his feelings. He just hoped Erin was still there when he did.

He reached over to the table next to his bed and picked up the book he was reading. It was an old fantasy novel that Erin had suggested he read once upon a time. The book was over a hundred years old, having come out in the early 2010s.

He had just opened the book to start reading when the intercom sounded suddenly, startling him. He tapped his wristlink and sighed.

"Captain Keevan here," he said. "What is it?"

"Captain Keevan," the female voice on the other end said. "There's a priority one ultraviolet tight beam communication for you. It's from Earth."

"All right, Kim. Patch it through to my vid terminal. I'll take it here," he said.

Tom Keevan stood up, tossed the book back on the side table and threw a robe on before heading to his desk. He switched on his vid terminal.

"Accept incoming priority one ultraviolet transmission," he said to the computer. "Authorization Keevan delta gamma nine."

"Authorization accepted. Decoding message now," the computer's unemotional voice said.

The Star League Defense Force logo blinked off, to be replaced by the face of Star League President Kerrin Jameson.

"Madame President," Captain Keevan acknowledged. "To what do I owe the honor?"

"We have a problem, Tom."

"What's up, Kerrin?" There was concern in his voice. The president looked like she hadn't slept in days.

Come to think of it, Tom thought to himself. *She probably hasn't.*

"Gamma Strike was successful in extracting M'Bek Tarmos," Kerrin began.

"That's good news," Tom smiled.

"Yes, it is," she sighed. "Unfortunately, Captain Bryce is presumed captured."

"OK, that's not good," Tom grunted. "I assume Erin wants to go after him?"

"Commander Sykes is following orders and bringing M'Bek Tarmos back to the Gamma Epsilon station."

"But what about Captain Bryce?" Tom demanded.

"There will be a rescue mission. I'm afraid it's going to have to wait until Gamma Strike gets back to the Gamma Epsilon station in about two days."

"He could be dead by then," Tom closed his eyes.

"I know." Kerrin turned away for a moment, her face pained. She turned back to the vid and sighed. "The mission has to come first, Tom. You know that."

"What do you want from me, Kerrin?" The Creighton's captain crossed his arms. "Whatever it is, you got it."

"The Atlantia is on it's way to the Khrinnus system. As soon as it gets there, you are ordered to get your tail to the Gamma Epsilon station. Gamma Strike is going to stand down from active duty to become the honor guard for the peace conference after they get back. Colonel Bonetti will be joining you for the duration of the mission. You are going to take the Creighton into Brentax space and retrieve Captain Bryce. And Tom? Try to bring him back alive."

"I intend to, Madame President."

"Good. The Atlantia should arrive in about twenty two hours. And thanks, Tom."

"You can always count on me, Kerrin," Tom forced a smile.

"I know. Good luck, Captain Keevan." With that, the President of the Star League faded from Tom's vid terminal.

Tom slapped the controls on his console.

"Captain Keevan to all hands. We are now on battle readiness standby. All hands are to report to battle stations at 0800 hours tomorrow morning. Senior staff briefing at 0900 hours."

Tom sighed as he looked at his bed, shaking his head. He saw the book on the side table and shrugged. He wouldn't be getting any sleep tonight.

⟨CHAPTER / 32⟩

MARIO couldn't sleep. He didn't exactly trust M'Bek Tarmos not to try to escape. He wasn't sure the bindings would hold if the Brentax commander decided he wanted to be free. He eyed the Brentax official warily while still keeping an eye on the scanners.

"You haven't slept all night, Colonel. I give you my word that I won't try to escape," the Brentax said.

"Were K'Alan here, I might take a nap while he watched you, but I'd be remiss in my duties if I left you unattended." Mario turned and looked at the scanners more closely. "Even if you did save my life."

"I will not lie to you, Colonel," M'Bek Tarmos smiled. "That was as much to save my life as it was to save yours. If there were any other way, I would never have given you any information on how to disable my ship." The Brentax official's smile grew broader as he saw the shock on the

[271]

Colonel's face at that revelation. "Yes, the Torellia Corvax is my personal flagship."

Mario nodded, still staring at the scanners. The silhouette of the Torellia Corvax had dropped back, but it was still following them.

"She's still behind us," Mario noted.

"I'm not surprised. I figure it will still be another fifteen to twenty hours before they have weapons back," M'Bek Tarmos said.

"Great," Mario shook his head. "Let's just hope it's later instead of sooner. We can't pull that trick off a second time."

"Agreed."

The two men sat in silence for a time. Mario kept checking the readings on the scanners. He was hoping that the Torellia Corvax would drop back more, but it remained at a constant distance from the shuttle.

"So, Colonel," the Brentax Commander said after some time, breaking the monotonous silence. "What will you do when the war is over?"

"Dunno," Mario shrugged. "Kinda hope we go back to exploration. That, I think, would be exciting."

"I think I might retire as Supreme Commander. It is long past time I pick a mate. I have no pouchlings, and I think I might like to have some."

"Yeah," Mario sighed. "It'd be nice to find someone."

I just hope I didn't screw up everything with S'Era by losing her brother, the colonel thought to himself. *That's all I would need to make this week complete.*

"You have no mate either?" M'Bek Tarmos said, his eyes opened wide.

"Never found the right one," Mario shrugged.

Or have I? he wondered to himself.

"It is a shame. Life is something that you should share with someone. You may not believe it, but even we Brentax believe in love."

"Yes, Chancellor G'Kiron did mention that," Mario frowned and looked at the Brentax commander. "What will happen to him?"

"I will issue him a pardon from Star League space. I will also issue a pardon for your partner."

"Thank you," Mario smiled.

"He is your friend, I take it?"

"Yes," Mario nodded. "A very good friend. It irks me to be leaving him behind."

M'Bek Tarmos nodded and stared out at the stars quietly.

The Dawning of a New Age

⟨CHAPTER / 33⟩

2.8.2136
0519
Brentax III
Brentacchia Prison

UNABLE to sleep on the torture table, K'Alan fidgeted. He'd tried to reach the tools he needed to free himself, but he couldn't. He cursed himself for keeping his lock pick kit on his belt. He decided that, if he were to ever get out of this situation, he would find a way to stick a lock pick in the cuff of his uniform jacket when he went on a mission.

Just my luck, K'Alan thought. *I have the proper tools to get me out of my situation, and I can't even reach them.*

The Star League officer gently put his head back against the board he was lying on and sighed.

"OK, Lords," he called out to no one in particular. "If I get out of this, I promise to never go on a foolish mission like this again. Or at least to never get caught on another foolish mission like this again."

There was no response, although K'Alan wasn't expecting one. He closed his eyes and waited. Unsure of what information the Brentax wanted from him, the young Duterian could only wait for the torture to begin.

Crovax was an interesting puzzle for him. The Cor'vat obviously hated working for his Brentax masters. He wondered if he could use that to his advantage. *Probably not.* But K'Alan would be foolish to not look for any opportunity that might present itself along those lines.

Not for the first time, he wondered how Mario was doing. Did he follow orders and leave? And would he try to come back and rescue him? *No,* he decided. Erin Sykes would play it by the book and not let Mario come back. That was why he had wanted Erin for his XO. But the captain knew that he was on his own.

What did he have on his side? He still had his weapons, but he had no way to use them with his hands shackled like they currently were. He had one ally on this planet, but that man was also a prisoner slated for execution.

He felt a twinge of guilt as he thought about G'Kiron. The old chancellor had been arrested because he truly believed in a peace that may or may not ever exist. K'Alan was interested in the Great Thinkers that G'Kiron spoke of. What had he said? There was a great darkness on the horizon that the Brentax must ally itself with another power in the quadrant. What darkness? Could the Star League and the Brentax Empire push back whatever darkness it was together? Or was the old man just crazy? He didn't think G'Kiron was crazy, but he just wasn't sure what to make of the prophecies that the old chancellor kept referring to.

A slight breeze brought K'Alan to the present. His eyes snapped open, and he was instantly alert. The Star League officer looked around at the bare walls surrounding him. The wooden door was slightly ajar. He thought he could hear the sound of a chitinous material on stone clacking. Or was it just a figment of his imagination?

No, there it was again. The clacking sound was definitely getting closer. Whatever it was that was making the sound was definitely coming his way.

Perhaps, he thought. *Perhaps it's Crovax and it's time to start the torture. At least, I hope it's Crovax. Maybe I can get through to him and get him to set me free.*

The Star League officer waited patiently, watching the door to the room with interest. The clacking sound grew louder, and soon the door opened and Crovax slinked in. The Cor'vat was carrying a medium sized rectangular box. K'Alan wasn't sure he wanted to know what was in the box, but he assumed it was the tools of torture. K'Alan noted with interest that the Cor'vat's appearance wasn't as unsettling as it had been the first time.

Perhaps, he mused. *It's that I know what to expect this time. Last time, I was expecting a Brentax officer when I opened my eyes after all.*

"Good," Crovax smiled, his smile disarming at best. "You're awake. I have been instructed to begin the torture."

The Cor'vat moved behind the bench K'Alan was lying on and pulled a small table from under it. He moved the table to the side of the bench so K'Alan could see everything he did and placed the box on it. He opened the box and began pulling out implements of torture, many of which K'Alan had never seen the likes of before.

"I suppose I don't want to ask what you're going to do with those," K'Alan sighed. His mind was working double time to try to come up with a way to get the torturer to release him.

"Duterian, do not ask questions that you truly do not want the answers to," the Cor'vat said. "Before I begin the torture, I would like to have a conversation with you. You are, to say the least, an interesting person, and I would like the opportunity to speak with you one more time before your brain no longer will support such a tiresome task."

"Great," K'Alan groaned. "What would you like to talk about?"

[277]

"I'd like to talk about your Star League," the insectoid said. "There are some questions that I have based on our last conversation."

"All right," K'Alan shrugged. "I'll do my best to answer them but If you ask anything that would be considered classified, you know I'll have to decline answering."

"I won't ask anything classified, Duterian," Crovax said. "I am interested in learning more about the Star League. You said that you found slavery to be an atrocity. How does your Star League view slavery?"

"Much the same way as I feel about it. Any race that joins the Star League must not hold slaves. We believe very strongly in an individual's rights. Any individual has the right to be free," K'Alan explained.

"Would the Star League put that as part of a peace treaty?"

"They may," K'Alan said after a moment. "But only if they know about the slavery. They would require all slave races to be freed. The problem is that I don't think the Star League knows that the Brentax Empire holds slaves. You'll remember, I didn't know until you told me earlier."

"True." The Cor'vat sighed deeply as his antennae twitched. "Would you be willing to tell them if you were freed?"

"Crovax, I'd be willing to set up an appointment with one of the Admirals for you to tell them your story yourself."

Finally, he thought to himself. *An opening.*

"I could not do that while still a slave though," Crovax frowned.

"I can offer you political asylum, Crovax," K'Alan said, hope for his future blossoming. "You would be considered as if you were a citizen of the Star League."

"You would do this to me despite the atrocities I have committed to those of your kind?" Crovax asked, surprised.

"The torture you have inflicted on members of the Star League, you did under orders. You will not be held responsible for actions you committed while following orders.   Especially as you were a slave when you were following those orders."

"Then, I shall request asylum from you, Duterian.   I wish my people freed."

"I grant it, Crovax," K'Alan smiled.

"Good."

K'Alan barely flinched as Crovax broke the shackles that bound his hands.

"Before we leave Brentax III, there are two things I need to do," K'Alan said.

"I understand.   But hurry."

The Dawning of a New Age

CHAPTER / 34

COMMANDER Erin Sykes was early for the morning briefing. The briefing was scheduled for 0830, but the young commander was feeling restless, so she arrived in the conference room early. She noted that she was the first person there. Well that was fine. It gave her a few minutes to gather her thoughts. She made a point of going by the Captain's seat and sitting in her Executive Officer's seat. She had no doubt that her appointment as commander of Gamma Strike was a very temporary one. She hoped it would be a very short command.

The stars streaked by outside the conference room windows as the White Knight cruised along at maximum fusion drive. She could not imagine the stars not moving, it had been so long since she'd been on a planet for any length of time.

[281]

She smiled as the other members of the command staff started to file in one by one. They began to fill the seats at the conference table each one sitting at their own place, leaving two seats conspicuously empty. The captain's seat and Mario Bonetti's seat had been empty for days. One would be filled again tomorrow. The other...

She didn't want to think about how long it would be before K'Alan was back in command of Gamma Strike.

"We all here?" she asked, more to pull herself out of her dismal thoughts than anything else. There were nods of assent from around the table. "Great. Let's get started. Before we get to the sit rep, I want to go through and do department reports. Let's start with communications. Kath?"

Erin noted with interest that Katherine and Suela Yeuid refused to look at each other. She made a mental note to talk to the young communications chief about that at some point.

"Well," Kath started. "Comms are working good at this point. We've been receiving Shuttle Kiarin's telemetry beacon steadily."

"Weapons and scanners. Masha?" Erin continued.

"Weapons are ready. Scanners are on full screens. Our cloak is working perfectly. Not even any trace emissions. We are currently undetectable."

"Good. Sciences?" Erin looked at Suela Yeuid.

"I've been working on getting stellar cartography and astronavigation working properly. They're not a necessity during this mission as we know where we are and where we're going, but I estimate it'll be another month before those systems are online. The other sciences are ready to go when they're needed."

"Keep working on stellar cartography, Suela," Erin nodded. "Engineering?"

"Fusion drive's working better than I anticipated with a ship this size. I had expected problems, but we're consistently and safely surpassing my expectations as far as speeds and power conservation. I'm extremely pleased as to how the constant cloaking isn't causing the severe power losses I'd been fearing."

"Excellent. We'll be asking a lot of the engines the next couple days. Keep me appraised if there are any problems.

"Of course," Sarah chuckled. "My crew will be constantly monitoring the engines. Someone will be monitoring the situation at all times. You'll know if there's the slightest problem."

"Good," Erin smiled. "Medical?"

"Well, we've managed to clear out the last of the cases from the Duterius Prime massacre. We've been going fairly non stop since the massacre. We'd greatly appreciate a break. If you could avoid sending us casualties for a while, we'd greatly appreciate it."

"We'll do our best," Erin chuckled. She paused before continuing. "All right. As you know, we're en route to rendezvous with the Shuttle Kiarin. Colonel Bonetti is on board with Brentax Supreme Commander M'Bek Tarmos. Unfortunately, Captain Bryce is still on Brentax III, where he will remain until he can either get himself off the planet or a rescue mission can be sent after the peace conference starts."

"We can't just leave him there," Jewel said. "If nothing else, the Duterian people need him."

"I know. I had much the same conversation with Colonel Bonetti, Jewel. But as the captain himself would tell you, he is expendable for now. Don't worry. We're not going to forget him. Sooner or later we'll get the captain back. I'm voting for sooner myself. I don't want his chair after all."

"I told them they should have let me go with them," Masha grumbled.

"Be that as it may," Erin sighed, a headache beginning to form in her right temple. "As soon as the shuttle lands, we are to make our best speed for the Gamma Epsilon station. Gamma Strike will be standing down and attending the peace conference. As the honor guard."

[283]

"I don't like this, Commander," Masha sighed. "Do you really think the Brentax are just going to turn their war machine around and accept peace?"

"Let's just say I'm hopeful that they will, Masha. Now, I'm going to need everyone to give one hundred and fifty percent over the next week. I'm afraid we're going to have food and sleep as catch can for most of the next few days. We are, from this moment on, on full battle readiness. Dismissed."

She watched the other officers file out of the conference room and sighed.

Come on, K'Alan, she thought to herself. *Find your way back to the White Knight before we head back into Star League space. I hate your chair.*

2.8.2136
0922
SLS White Knight
The City

K'Itea Bryce walked along the streets of the city. It was amazing how her people had adapted to life on board the White Knight. Life was already returning to some semblance of normalcy. It was good to see.

She was due to be at the palace any minute, but she dreaded going into work. She decided today would be a stroll through the city day instead. It made her feel good to see how everyone was doing.

Her stroll took her past the park that her husband was going to turn into some form of a baseball field and smiled. She hoped that he would do so. She believed it would be good for morale. And it would give Elam and K'Alan something to do together. Elam had perked up so much when his father had began teaching him how to pitch. It was good to see her son and her husband bonding.

Chuckling softly to herself, she continued past the field and started down a narrow street. The temple was at the end of this street, and she found herself drawn to the peace that the temple always provided her.

The High Gentlewoman of the Duterian people smiled to herself as she headed towards the temple. She'd been trying to get her husband to spend more time at the temple. She believed that the priests could do much good for his soul. She worried about him.

The door to the temple swung open at her approach and she entered the temple, letting the warmth of the peace of the Lords of Duterius wash over her. It was a good feeling.

"High Gentlewoman, you honor us with your presence," one of the priests said.

"I came seeking peace," the young woman said. "This place, so much like the temple near my home in the Braga Valley, is the best place on the ship to find peace and hope."

"Peace and hope are best found inside a person," the priest smiled.

"How can one find peace when one is surrounded by war?" K'Itea sighed. "My husband is off on a mission to end this war, and I worry that he will not return."

The priest smiled and laid his hand on her shoulder.

"Fear not, child," the priest intoned. "Your husband will return. He walks a long and dangerous path however. Have faith. His love for you shall be his beacon home."

"His love for me?"

"His love for you is strong, child. I have seen it. It is stronger than the metal that holds this ship together. It is more durable than the engines of this vessel. And it will be his beacon home. You will see."

"I pray you are right," K'Itea smiled. "I do not know what I would do if he didn't return."

* * *

Suela Yeuid stood staring out at the stars as they streaked past the ship. Her tech crews were working on yet another problem in Stellar Cartography. Somehow the computers weren't registering new stellar data properly. She considered the idea of pulling out all the consoles and just starting from scratch, but she wouldn't have even known where to begin as to building the consoles. The ones that Sarah Hodge had made for Stellar Cartography should be sufficient...

If only she could get the damn things to work right!

There was a light footfall behind her. She didn't bother to turn around.

"Madeline, I told you to just put the new data on my desk," Suela sighed. "I'll get to it at some point."

"It's not Madeline," Kath said, a touch of anger in her voice. "It's Katherine."

"Well, Katherine," Suela said, rubbing her temples. "What is it? You haven't said one word to me in days."

"I don't know who or what you are, but I do not have a sister. Least not in the records I can find on me. Frankly I don't care who you are. All I want is to have us work together professionally. Is that clear?"

"Crystal, ma'am," the other woman said in a clipped tone. "But you don't have all the records. I can make the proper records available to you if you wish."

"Perhaps in time, I may wish to look at those records," Kath growled. "But for now, no. You are not my sister. That's the way it needs to be."

With that, the communications officer stormed out of the observation lounge, leaving a very confused Suela Yeuid shaking her head in disbelief.

* * *

Rick Bentsen

2.8.2136
1013
SLS White Knight
The Gym

Masha had the gym to herself. Mostly because when she stormed in everyone else had cleared out, knowing the look on the face of the security chief meant trouble. Masha was angry. And she was taking out her anger on the bag.

She'd warned Mario that she should have gone on the mission too. Now, with the Captain missing, she couldn't help but feel like screaming "I told you so!" at the top of her lungs.

Not that it would have done any good. Nothing seemed to do much good when all she could do is wait for the situation to resolve itself.

Meanwhile, she was angry.

Masha didn't wear gloves when she used the bags. She claimed the gloves cut off the circulation in her hands, which caused her to have ineffective punches. So she swung freely with her bare fists.

Masha continued to pound the bag, each time she hit it imagining she was wailing on a Brentax soldier that was responsible for the disappearance of the Captain. It did little to make her feel better.

She gave the bag one last vicious punch, tearing the bag in two and spreading its stuffing everywhere.

"I'll buy a new bag when we get to the Gamma Epsilon station," Masha snarled at the head trainer as she made her way out of the gym.

2.8.2136
1041
SLS White Knight
Main Engineering

Sarah Hodge settled into the leather chair behind the desk in her office and put her feet up on her desk. It had been a long morning. Since she left the briefing, she had had about a hundred minutiae adjustments to do on the engines. Nothing serious, but just little things that affected the smooth operation of the fusion drive. She was insufferably pleased with herself. Her engines were performing better than the engines on any other Star League vessel. And they had originally laughed at her designs.

"Root beer?" a voice from the door asked, pointing at the bottle on the engineer's desk..

"Sure is, Commander," the young engineer smiled. "You want anything to drink?"

"If you've got another root beer, I wouldn't mind," Erin chuckled. She took a seat and smiled before continuing. "How are the engines holding up?"

"Same as they were an hour and a half ago, Commander," Sarah chuckled. "Although I think I may have coaxed a little extra speed out of them. Maybe a half a percent. No more than that. You must be pretty bored to keep checking up on the engines."

"Bored out of my skull," Erin sighed as she opened the root beer. "Nothing for me to do. I don't know how K'Alan and other unit commanders handle this waiting."

"Pretty much the same way you are," Sarah smiled. "Captain Bryce kept checking with me about every twenty minutes while I was refitting the shuttle."

"God, I hope I never get that bad," Erin laughed.

"I just hope Mario's bringing my shuttle back in one piece. I put a lot of time into that thing," Sarah chuckled.

CHAPTER / 35

THE three of them had been watching the holosphere unceasingly for three days. Others had come and gone, but the three had remained constant, turning away only when sustenance was brought to them by one of the others. The three of them all felt that they needed to be there to see what happened. It did not matter how long it took for events to develop, they would be there to watch them.

"An interesting twist," Kiara said. "See? I told you he would find a way out."

"Yes," the one called Alan said. "You did. This is a factor I did not consider. The Cor'vat being freed is an unexpected happening."

"It changes nothing," the other male said. "That one is still the key. If he does not survive, then we are lost."

"He will survive, John." The one called Alan shook his head. "He is stronger than we believed."

The three fell silent as the scenes in the holosphere shifted yet again.

The Dawning of a New Age

⟨CHAPTER / 36⟩

2.8.2136
1214
Shuttle Kiarin

MARIO sat staring at the scanners. The Torellia Corvax was still following them at a bit of a distance.

The Brentax official was asleep in the chair next to him. It was quiet. It was, perhaps, the only time this ride had been truly quiet. Mario shrugged to himself and picked up a data pad. He began to slowly write a personal log entry into it, something he hadn't had a chance to do since they left the White Knight.

Personal Log: Mario Bonetti: 2.8.2136: I'm not really sure where to begin. A lot has happened since I left the comfort of the White Knight four days ago. And so much has happened since I had a chance to write my last log entry a couple weeks ago.

It was interesting to see my father again without the fights this time. It's so rare that we get a chance to spend

[291]

time together without arguing with each other. I just wish I could have seen all the rest of my family. It's been ages since I saw all of my sisters and brothers. And Mom's still upset that I didn't make it home for Christmas last year. You would think after having so many career military officers in the family as there are in ours, she would have gotten used to the fact that none of us ever make it home for holidays.

This mission I am on never really went right from the beginning. There were so many problems even during the long flight to Brentax III. Then there was the abortive first attempt to capture M'Bek Tarmos. And the disappearance of Chancellor G'Kiron. So I'm not at all surprised that this mission went south.

I'm on my way back to the White Knight. With the Brentax Supreme Commander, M'Bek Tarmos. Unfortunately, I'm returning to the White Knight without my friend and commanding officer, Captain K'Alan Bryce. He's stuck somewhere on Brentax III, and instead of going back and helping him, I'm ferrying this Brentax official back to Star League space. Given the option, I'd space him and go back and save Kal.

My thoughts keep going back to S'Era and Kit. God, how I don't want to tell them that Kal's missing. Kit'll probably deck me. And S'Era.

I don't know what S'Era will do. S'Era's been on my mind a lot lately. I definitely love her. I'm not sure when I realized this. Nor am I sure when I realized that she loved me too.

I always figured I'd never find someone to settle down with. Boy was I wrong. I'm glad Kal approves. I just hope I didn't mess up my chances with S'Era by losing her brother.

I don't even know if Kal is still alive down there. He went to check on Chancellor G'Kiron, and that's the last I saw of him.

Chancellor G'Kiron was, to say the least, an interesting individual. I wish I understood half of what he was talking about, but I get the feeling that Kal didn't really understand it either. That's the price of being a great thinker I suppose.

I hope someday someone doesn't understand what I say to them.

Mario sighed as he put the data pad down and looked over the scanners again. The Torellia Corvax was right there still constantly watching them.

The Dawning of a New Age

CHAPTER / 37

CAPTAIN Tom Keevan drummed his fingers on the armrest of his command chair impatiently. He wanted to be doing something other than just sitting there waiting for his ship's replacement in the Khrinnus system. He wanted to be out there trying to save Captain Bryce's butt. He owed K'Alan that much.

He had known K'Alan about as long as he'd known Erin Sykes. The three had served on the Endeavor together. Tom had been the Strike Leader and K'Alan and Erin had been two of his more hotshot pilots. They both made squad leader during that trip. He'd not been surprised when he found out that K'Alan had been given the XO position on the Gamma Strike unit. He was even less surprised when K'Alan was promoted to Captain and given the squad when Thala Ker'sal stepped down. And when K'Alan had selected Erin Sykes as the new XO, all Tom could do was chuckle.

[295]

He was curious about the circumstances surrounding the departure of Captain Ker'sal. He'd known Thala since the academy. He knew that the Jaradan was a hot head, but he couldn't think of what could possibly have prompted her to step down from a command position that most captains would kill for. There were rumors of course, but Tom Keevan had long since learned not to listen to rumors.

It was funny to Tom how situations kept working themselves out in such a way as to keep involving him. It did not seem to matter if he was involved from the beginning or not.

"Captain," Kim Ericson called from the communications station. "We're receiving a tight beam communication from the Atlantia."

"Holo," Tom barked.

Captain Laura Goldthorne was a fairly attractive woman, if you could get past the scars on her face. She had short cropped golden hair and deep blue eyes. There were scars running along each cheek and one across her forehead.

As the holo of Laura Goldthorne appeared in the holo viewer by Captain Keevan's chair, he was once again struck by her beauty. He had courted her once upon a time. The relationship had faltered, but they had remained good friends.

"Hi, Laura," Tom smiled. "Long time no see."

"I hear you've been whooping the Brentax good here in the Khrinnus system," the woman smiled.

"Took out two Duhari class heavy cruisers in the last two days," Tom nodded.

"Good work!" Laura smiled even broader. "President Jameson sends her greetings. We should be there in three or four hours."

"Yeah," Tom nodded again. "Soon as you guys get here, we have to jet. Bryce needs his arse pulled out of the fire again."

"You're always saving someone's butt," Laura laughed. The laughter died quickly though. "Bring him back alive, Tom."

"That would be my intention. I don't want to have to face down his wife if I don't."

"I've heard that the Duterian High Gentlewoman is actually quite reasonable," Laura raised an eyebrow. "I'm sure she'd understand. Just the same. Bring him back alive."

"I will do my best," Tom smiled.

"See ya 'round, Swamp Rat, Laura winked as the holo faded.

"Swamp Rat?" Kim chuckled, her eyebrows raised.

"Never mind," Tom groaned. "Helm, as soon as the Atlantia gets here, give me best speed back to the Gamma Epsilon Station. I want to be there before Gamma Strike."

"Acknowledged, Captain," the helm officer said.

The Dawning of a New Age

CHAPTER 38

"AND she just split the bag with one punch?" Erin asked, her face registering pure shock at the concept.

"I've not seen her so angry in a long time," the trainer shook his head. "And I've known her over ten years."

"This isn't good. All right," Erin sighed. "I'll have a talk with her."

"She did promise to replace the bag when we got to the Gamma Epsilon station, so don't be too hard on her."

"I'm more afraid of her being too hard on me," Erin chuckled.

The trainer shook his head and began picking up the pieces of the bag.

* * *

[299]

It was hard to get the security chief drunk. The Sandarian had one of the highest alcohol tolerances on board the White Knight. Yet she was just a little past tipsy, her words starting to slur just slightly.

"Ok, Masha," Soran said quietly. "I think you've had enough."

"Whazzat?" the security chief said. "Nozzo fazz with that had enough stuv, Zoran. I'makay."

"Sure you are. You want to talk about it while I get you some coffee?"

"Izza captain. He never jouda gone on that mizzion without a security type person."

"But he went with Mario," Soran nodded. "Shouldn't that have been enough to ease your fears, Masha?"

"Don't you understand, Zoran?" Masha shouted. "The captain'z mizzig."

"Missing?" Soran raised an eyebrow. "Perhaps we should talk about this in a less public place, Masha."

"No point talking public or private, Zoran. I'z juzz gonna get good and trazhed."

"How will that help the Captain though, Masha? And won't Commander Sykes need your expertise on the bridge?"

"Yeah, zhe prob- probably doez," Masha nodded. The security chief stood up from the barstool she was on—

And promptly fell right on her rump on the floor.

"Masha? You OK?"

"Juz peachy!" Masha looked up. "Got any detokz pillz, Zoran?"

* * *

2.8.2136
1432
SLS White Knight
Main Engineering

"Ensign, we have an energy spike," Jen Hutchins called from one of the engineering situation stations around the engines.

Sarah raced out from her office and headed over to the status monitor, a look of concern on her face.

"What's up?" she asked.

"Momentary energy spike in the cloaking systems," Jen noted. She ran the monitor data back to the spike. "See? Could have been enough for any nearby Brentax vessels to see us, but not for long."

"All right," Sarah nodded. "Run a diagnostic and keep an eye on it. I'll report it to the Commander. I'll be in her office and then monitoring from the bridge If anything more comes up, call me immediately."

"You got it boss," the engineer said.

Sarah scowled as she left Engineering.

2.8.2136
1445
SLS White Knight
Commander Erin Sykes' Office

The headache that had started as a gentle throbbing in Erin's temples had progressed to a full fledged migraine. She promised herself that she would go see Jewel about it, but she had too much to deal with before she could break away to go to the medbay.

She wasn't sure what to do with Masha. Between the incident in the gym and her getting drunk in Soran's bar, the security lieutenant was being a huge pain in the arse today. She wished one more time that K'Alan was there to deal with this instead of her.

Of course, she mused to herself. *If K'Alan were here, none of this would have happened in the first place.*

It was just these kinds of situations that made Erin not want to be promoted to Captain. She was happy to sit on the sidelines and help things run smoothly.

Command, she decided, was not all it was cracked up to be.

She looked across her desk at the security chief sitting across from her. Masha just sat there with her hands folded in her lap and her head bowed. Erin just shook her head and sighed as she looked at her.

"Masha," Erin sighed again. "Believe me, I don't want to have to deal with this any more than you do. But I have no choice. What did you think you were doing, destroying the gym bag like that?"

"I promised to buy a new one as soon as we got to the station," Masha said, looking up.

"I know. That's the only thing that's keeping me from ordering your pay docked for this." Erin closed her eyes and counted to ten. "But such displays of anger are not good, Masha."

"Commander, with all due respect, that's just bull." Masha shook her head as she glared Erin down. "Hear me out. My job is to make sure every member of this crew is safe. Especially the captain. By disregarding my recommendation the way he did and placing himself in imminent danger, he made my job impossible. How am I supposed to carry on and do my job to the best of my ability if the person I'm supposed to be protecting goes and gets himself in trouble?"

"There's no guarantee that had you been on the mission it would have gone any differently."

"There's also no way to know that he wouldn't have been captured if I were there, Commander," Masha yelled, making the commander wince.

"But getting angry about it then getting yourself drunk isn't going to make a difference, Masha. It'll just be counterproductive."

"I know. I'm sorry, Commander. It won't happen again," the lieutenant said sullenly.

A knock on the door caused both women to turn immediately to face the door.

"Enter," Erin called.

Sarah Hodge huffed into the room, having run all the way from Engineering.

"Next time I design a ship, I'm going to design a more direct route to the bridge from engineering," the young engineering chief muttered.

"What can I do for you, Sarah?" Erin sighed. *Is this day ever going to end?* she added to herself.

"Sorry to bother you, Commander. We had an energy spike in the cloaking systems. Not a long lasting one, but the cloaking system may have been compromised briefly. We're running a full diagnostic now on the systems, but you should be ready for any Brentax vessels that may have seen us."

"Great," Erin rolled her eyes. "Just great! Sarah, do your best to keep those cloaking systems online."

"Commander," Masha said. "With your permission, I'm going to head to the bridge and start prepping the weapons array. I'll also be able to give you a report on Brentax movements within ten minutes."

"Good. Go," Erin nodded.

After the two other officers left, Erin allowed herself a couple moments to bury her head in her hands and cry before wiping her eyes and leaving the office.

No, she thought bitterly. *Command is definitely not everything it's cracked up to be.*

The Dawning of a New Age

⟨CHAPTER / 39⟩

"**O**H, this is just swell," K'Alan rolled his eyes.

"You were the one that said he had a couple things he had to do before he left," Crovax reminded him.

"Yeah, I know," K'Alan growled.

K'Alan and Crovax were pinned down in a room in the prison. They'd been pinned there most of the day. The guards had found out about his escape and were trying to keep him from leaving.

"So, you got any bright ideas, Duterian?" Crovax asked.

"Please, Crovax. Call me K'Alan. That's my name," K'Alan said, closing his eyes. "As far as ideas, I'm fresh out."

"Then we will die here. I do not wish to die so close to freedom for my people, K'Alan," Crovax hissed.

[305]

"Believe me, I have no intention of dying," K'Alan smiled a grim smile. "But I won't leave this prison without rescuing Chancellor G'Kiron. He deserves better."

"Yes, he is much less ruthless than other Supreme Commanders have been. He was even considering releasing all the slaves prior to his retirement."

K'Alan nodded as a blaster bolt whizzed above his head.

"Ok, this is getting me seriously honked off!" he yelled.

K'Alan gripped his energy bow tighter. Crovax had made sure all of his stuff had been returned before they attempted to leave the prison. Seeing that the charge was nearly gone, he slipped a new charge cell in and grinned in satisfaction as the energy bow hummed to life, the twin blades of concentrated energy extending from the center grip.

The energy bow was invented by a Duterian over a hundred years ago. The energy bow was just that, a bow of pure energy. In standby mode, it's a simple small black box with a port for an energy cell. When activated though, the ends of the box open and concentrated energy forms the blades of the bow, which takes on the appearance of a recurve bow. Where the string would be is empty unless the archer is preparing to fire an arrow. When the archer wishes to fire an arrow, he simply grips where the string would be, and pulls back like he would any other bow. A string and an arrow made of pure energy appear, and releasing the string lets the energy arrow fly. Few Duterians actually mastered the art of accurately firing the energy bow. K'Alan Ilan Bryce was one of the best. K'Alan almost never missed what he was aiming for.

He did not miss this time either. He let fly with an energy arrow and one of the guards fell to the floor, a small hole burned into his chest where the arrow had hit. He fired a second arrow, then dropped back down behind the cover of the crates in front of them. He did not see where the second arrow hit, but he heard the curse as another guard went down.

"I've never seen a weapon like that," Crovax said.

"It's a Duterian energy bow," K'Alan said as he risked a peek around the crate. A blaster bolt almost took off his head as he ducked back behind the crate. "There are still six guards out there that I could see. And they're not getting spooked by their partners getting cut down."

"They wouldn't," Crovax shook his head. "They're more afraid of their bosses than they would be of you. Against you, they'll have a quick death. Their bosses will not be so merciful should they allow you to escape."

"Wonderful," K'Alan rolled his eyes. "This day just keeps getting better and better."

"Did you expect to just walk out of here?"

"I was kind of hoping it would be that easy." He watched as another blaster bolt left a black scorch mark on the wall next to him. "Then again..."

K'Alan cautiously rose to his knees over the safety of the crates. He let off two quick shots and ducked back down before the guards could pick him off. He watched Crovax lean around the side of the crate and pick off two guards with his blaster.

"Two left," Crovax said.

"Think they'd surrender if we asked them to?" K'Alan asked.

"There's your answer, K'Alan," Crovax said as two blaster bolts tore into the crate in front of them.

"Yeah. That's what I thought," K'Alan sighed.

Crovax shrugged and stuck the blaster out and fired, missing both guards. K'Alan, while Crovax was distracting the guards, brought his bow up to bear on them and fired twice, taking out both of them.

"Nice shooting, K'Alan," the Cor'vat said admiringly.

"Thanks. Now, let's go get Chancellor G'Kiron and get out of here.

"Agreed."

The Duterian and the Cor'vat crept from around the crates cautiously, still expecting more guards to show up. When no more guards did, they breathed a sigh of relief and slowly made their way back to the A cell block where K'Alan had been prisoner just a few short hours ago. Crovax proved to be an excellent guide, and they soon found themselves in front of G'Kiron's cell.

"G'Kiron, wake up," K'Alan said.

"K'Alan? What's going on?"

"No time for questions, Chancellor," K'Alan smiled. "Get away from the door."

K'Alan raised the energy bow, and G'Kiron raced back to the back of the cell. Energy lanced from the bow to the locking mechanism, and the door swung free on it's hinges, creaking slightly as it did so.

"Thank you, my boy!" the old chancellor croaked as he rushed out of the cell.

K'Alan smiled at the old chancellor then led the way back out of the cell block. There was a guard post just outside the cell block that they had to go past. K'Alan motioned for the other two to stop and be quiet. The three men hurriedly hid themselves in a supply closet near the guard post.

"How many guards would be in the guard post, Crovax?" K'Alan whispered.

"No more than six," Crovax hissed quietly.

"Six?" K'Alan chuckled. "That's it? Ok. I think I can get most of them to leave, but we'll likely still have a couple left to deal with."

"We will be ready, K'Alan," Crovax assured the Star League captain.

"Ok. You'll hear some explosions," K'Alan warned the other two. "Don't let it surprise you. It's just me."

"Thanks for the warning," Crovax mumbled. "Just don't get killed, all right?"

"I don't intend to," K'Alan smiled. "I have a baseball game to play in a couple days."

K'Alan slid out of the supply closet leaving Crovax and Chancellor G'Kiron looking at each other and shaking their heads in classic "he's lost it" fashion.

The captain pulled the energy bow back off his belt and checked the settings.

Good, he thought. *This should make some interesting sounding explosions.*

Checking the guard post quickly, he noted that the door was closed. That was a condition that wouldn't last long if what K'Alan had in mind worked. K'Alan wordlessly activated the energy bow and fired five energy arrows in rapid succession. Before the first one hit, he dove back into the supply closet and left the door slightly ajar. He kept an eye glued to the open crack of the door and waited. The explosions came seconds later. As he expected, the five explosions caught the attention of the guards. Five guards rushed out of the guard post in the other direction to check on the source of the explosion.

K'Alan put his energy bow back on his belt and drew Shatterstar, the blade that Mario had given him. Wordlessly, he opened the door to the supply closet and nodded to the other two. They'd watch his back, he knew. He kicked the door of the guard post open to see one remaining guard.

The guard, upon seeing a free and armed prisoner, began to move his hand over to the alarm button—

Only to find his hand severed from his wrist by an angry Duterian.

"I wouldn't do that if I were you," K'Alan said simply.

The Brentax guard just looked at him with a blank expression on his face.

"You won't get away from this prison, you know," the guard, whom K'Alan recognized as D'Boran, said.

"Care to lay odds on that?" K'Alan chuckled. "I think I have a better than average chance of making it."

"You will be a hunted man, Duterian," D'Boran croaked. "Nothing can save you from the gibbet."

"I beg to differ, D'Boran isn't it?" The guard nodded. "Not only am I going to leave this prison, I'm going to leave Brentax III unharmed."

The sounds of blaster fire punctuated his statement.

"K'Alan," Chancellor G'Kiron called. "The guards are returning. We're taking care of them, but we must hurry."

"Well, that sounds like my cue to leave," K'Alan smiled. He started to turn away from D'Boran, then turned back and placed the tip of Shatterstar against the guard's neck. "Oh, and by the way. The High Gentlewoman that you spoke of in such disgusting terms happens to be my wife."

The last word was clipped and punctuated with the thrust of the sword. D'Boran's lifeless body slid off the point of K'Alan's blade, the guard's face freezing in an expression of total shock.

"Come on," K'Alan growled as he exited the guard post. "Let's get out of here."

CHAPTER 40

2.8.2136
1602
SLS Creighton
The Bridge

CAPTAIN Tom Keevan leaned forward in his chair, willing the Atlantia to go faster. Itching to beat the White Knight to the Gamma Epsilon Station, he was slowly going wacko because of the inactivity caused by the time it was taking for the Atlantia to arrive in the Khrinnus system.

"Helm, ETA of the Atlantia?" he asked for the thousandth time.

"They are entering the Khrinnus system now, Captain Keevan," the helmsman replied.

"Good. Prepare to take us out of the Khrinnus system. Prepare to get to the Gamma Epsilon Station at best possible speed," Tom ordered.

"Acknowledged," the helmsman nodded and turned back to his console.

"Captain Goldthorne on the line for you, Captain," Kim Ericson said.

"Holo," Tom ordered.

"Hello, Swamp Rat," Laura said.

"Laura," Tom said, blushing slightly and shaking his head. "The Khrinnus system is all yours."

"Great. Now go bail Captain Bryce's arse out."

"That's the plan, Laura," Tom smiled. He couldn't believe how Laura Goldthorne still set him on edge.

"Good. I expect to hear that the mission was a success in a couple days, Swamp Rat." The blonde woman smiled. That smile had always been a little bit disarming to Tom.

"Expect no less," Tom chuckled. "Captain Keevan out."

The holo flicked out, and Tom couldn't help but notice that his communications officer was snickering at her post.

"So, why does she call you Swamp Rat, Captain?" Kim asked innocently.

"That's a very long story that if you get me very drunk some day I might tell," he shook his head at Kim. "Helm, get me to the Gamma Epsilon Station as fast as you can." He turned back to Kim. "You will have to get me very very drunk."

⟨CHAPTER / 41⟩

2.8.2136
1622
SLS White Knight
Medbay

COMMANDER Erin Sykes strode into the medbay rubbing her temples. Jewel came running up to her, a look of concern on her face.

"Commander? Can I help you?" the doctor asked.

"Yeah," Erin nodded. "You got anything for a migraine?"

"I can give you a shot of polypropezene, Commander," Jewel shrugged. "Only thing is you're going to want a nap after a while."

"I have news for you, Doctor," Erin smiled a weak smile. "I already want a nap."

Jewel chuckled as she prepared the syringe. She rolled up the commander's sleeve and swabbed an area of her forearm with an alcohol wipe. Carefully and quickly, she stuck the commander with the needle.

[313]

"There," Jewel smiled. "You should feel better in no time."

"Thank you, Doctor," Erin took a deep breath. "It's just been one of those days, you know?"

The doctor's only response was a small nod and a faint smile. Erin wondered how much sleep the doctor had gotten since the Duterius Prime massacre.

"Commander Sykes to the bridge," Kath's voice called over the shipcall. Erin rolled her eyes at the loudspeaker and sighed loudly.

"No rest for the wicked," the commander said on her way out of the medbay.

2.8.2136
1631
SLS White Knight
The Bridge

The bridge was a bustle of activity when Commander Sykes strode on the bridge and over to her station. Her face was an expressionless mask as she sat at her station.

"Report," she barked.

"Commander, we have the Shuttle Kiarin on short range scanners," Masha reported. "They are being closed on by a Duhari class heavy cruiser."

"Damn!" Erin swore. "Drop cloak and put us between the cruiser and the shuttle. And open all gun ports. Bring all weapons to bear on that cruiser."

"Acknowledged," Masha said as her fingers flew over her tactical panel.

"Commander, the Brentax vessel is hailing us," Kath said.

"Holo," Erin sighed.

"This is Subcommander T'Marik Kodan," the particularly ugly specimen of a Brentax officer that appeared in the holo said. "You are in violation of Brentax space. You will either turn your ship around immediately or surrender. If you do not, you will be destroyed."

"This is Commander Erin Sykes of the Star League Defense Force," Erin said, absent-mindedly tugging on the bottom of her uniform tunic. "We're leaving Brentax space soon enough. But we're not leaving without our shuttle."

"The shuttle stays," T'Marik growled. "It contains war criminals. They are to be brought back to Brentax III for trial and execution."

"Sorry. I can't allow that to happen. Soon as the shuttle docks, we'll be on our way, but not a moment before," Erin smiled.

"You have been warned," T'Marik roared.

"Have a nice day," Erin said sweetly as the holo faded.

"Masha, as soon as the shuttle is on board, I want all the cloaking systems back on. Helm, as soon as the cloaks are activated, turn back to the jump gate and give me better than the speed that we got here with. Sarah, keep a close eye on those engines. I want to know immediately if something goes wrong."

"Understood," all three officers said in unison.

Seconds felt like hours as the White Knight sped to position herself between the Brentax vessel and the shuttle. As soon as the shuttle was safely behind the protection of the White Knight, Erin let out the breath she hadn't realized she'd been holding.

"Commander, the Brentax ship has weapons lock on us," Masha reported coolly. "Her weapons are hot."

"Damn," Erin swore under her breath. Louder, she added, "Full defense screens!"

"Defense screens are full," Masha acknowledged.

"Commander, Colonel Bonetti is on the line for you," Kath reported.

"Holo!" the commander barked.

Mario's face appeared in the opening in the center of the bridge, his smile plastered on his face.

"Excellent timing, Commander," Mario said. "Few more seconds there and it would have been bye bye Mario."

"It's good to see you too, Colonel," the commander said. Erin gripped the armrests of her chair as the White Knight shuddered under a direct hit from the Brentax vessel. "While I'd love to talk longer, Mario, get your tail on board. Now!"

"Don't have to tell me twice, sweetheart," Mario chuckled.

The holo faded with that smile Erin found so damn irritating still plastered on Mario's face.

"Do you think K'Alan would mind if I hurt him just a little?" Erin whispered to Kath.

"Not sure, Commander," Kath chuckled. "If he asked me, I would tell him that it was justified though."

"Damage report," Erin barked getting back to the business at hand.

"Defense screens holding," Masha reported. "No structural damage. Screens are holding steady at eighty seven percent."

"Excellent. What's the status of the shuttle?"

The bridge rocked as they were hit again.

"Screens down to seventy eight percent," Masha reported. "Shuttle is entering defensive screens now. Five minutes before they're docked."

"Understood," Erin sighed.

"Shall we return fire?" Masha asked.

"Fire all weapons on low settings. I want to distract and disable them not destroy them."

"You got it, Commander," Masha nodded as she started the firing sequence.

The bridge officers watched as pricks of light danced across the space from the White Knight to the Brentax vessel. The beams impacted against the Brentax ship, most reflecting harmlessly off the ship's defensive screens. A couple shots, however, penetrated the screens. The blasts impacted upon the hull of the Brentax vessel, causing small fires to flare momentarily before being extinguished in the cold vacuum of space.

"Minor damage to their outer hull, Commander," Masha reported. "They're still coming at us."

Erin cursed under her breath as the bridge rocked with another hit. The lights on the bridge flickered off for just a moment.

"We can't take too much more of this," Erin sighed. "Masha, keep firing. And let me know as soon as the shuttle is on board."

"Aye, Commander," the security chief nodded as she continued to implement the fire orders. The ship rocked again as they were hit solidly. "Shields down to fifty seven percent, Commander. The shuttle has just landed."

"Commander, reading a minor hull breach in section 7," Sarah reported from her engineering station. "Emergency bulkheads are in place. I am sending repair and rescue crews now."

"Good," Erin sighed. "Cloaking systems on now!"

"Cloaking systems engaged," Masha reported.

"Helm, take us back to the jump gate. Full fusion drive!" Erin ordered. "And get Mario and his guest to the conference room."

"Acknowledged, Commander!

2.8.2136
1702
SLS White Knight
The City

Inside the palace, K'Itea Bryce had felt the ship shudder under the impact of the Brentax weaponry. Having talked to the commander about the possibility of a Brentax attack while retrieving the shuttle, she was well aware what the shaking of the ship meant. Her priority over the last half hour had been to try to alleviate panic amongst her people. She was about to address them in fact. S'Era was waiting at the podium to announce her. The address would be broadcast throughout the city. It was an important address. She knew how many of her people felt about the Brentax, and she had to word everything just right. There were many amongst her people that would not welcome peace with the Brentax, although she believed that it was necessary.

She only hoped K'Alan was all right.

S'Era motioned for her to go to the podium, and the High Gentlewoman composed herself, putting on her mask of authority, and headed to the podium. She looked out at the assembled Duterians and smiled at them. Her people meant a great deal to her

"My fellow Duterians," she began. "I come before you today to speak of history. I come before you to speak of hope. And I come before you to speak of peace.

"Our prophets referred to a coming time that will be known as the Trial of Fire. It is said that this Trial of Fire will reshape not only our future, but the future of the entire quadrant. I cannot tell you for sure that this is true. I can only tell you that I believe that the Trial of Fire is upon us.

"The prophecies say that the Trial of Fire will begin with the deaths of many of our people by an alien race. The prophets went on to say that we would have to put aside our differences with that same alien race and form an alliance. The prophets believed that if the Duterian people made it through the Trial of Fire, they would be stronger, more unbreakable.

"I believe this is so. Much of what we do is based upon our prophets' words. Our beliefs and our faith is what makes us unique amongst the cosmos. Despite our small numbers, we are one of the cornerstone races in the Star League. Even now, President Jameson of the Star League rallies around our cause.

"The Brentax Empire and the Star League are in the process of beginning negotiations of a peace treaty for the purpose of alliance." She had to wait several minutes before she could be heard over the crowd again. "I repeat. The Star League is beginning negotiations with the Brentax Empire for the purpose of alliance.

"I believe that this is necessary for all of our futures. Were it not, I would have asked for a retaliatory strike against Brentax III for what they did to us!" K'Itea again had to wait for the noise of the crowd to die down; this time, though, it was loud cheering that she waited for to die down.

"There will be no such strike, however. The future of our people hinges upon the accord that the Star League and the Brentax Empire will reach. We must reach past our hatred and rally behind this new peace accord.

"Even now, this vessel that we are on is transferring the Brentax delegate to the Gamma Epsilon Space Station to begin the peace process. My husband, the captain of this vessel, whom many of you have gotten to know over the past week, was on the team sent to bring the delegate in."

There was a momentary pause and a flash of panic on her face. She composed the mask she wore back quickly, though, and she doubted anyone other than S'Era had actually caught the change in her demeanor.

"This ship is currently in Brentax space. The shuttle that was bringing in the Brentax delegate was under attack from a Duhari class vessel. This ship intercepted the Duhari class vessel and allowed the shuttle to dock. The shaking we all felt a short time ago were energy hits upon our ship. I have been informed that there is no major damage to the vessel and that we were able to get away undetected.

"This peace accord has the blessing of the Star League's top officials as well as, so I am told, the Emperor of the Brentax Empire himself.

"I only pray that this peace accord comes about not too late to be of help to the quadrant." She looked over the assembled Duterians again. "Peace is worth fighting for, I believe. But in this case, peace is worth living for.

"Thank you for listening, my fellow Duterians."

The High Gentlewoman stepped away from the podium and wiped her brow. S'Era looked at her with concern.

"Are you all right, K'Itea?" S'Era asked.

"I had a vision when I was speaking, S'Era," K'Itea said, her voice a strained whisper. "I do not think K'Alan was on the shuttle."

Erin fidgeted in her seat at the conference table. She had some reports in front of her that she had no interest in looking at. She was waiting, somewhat impatiently, for Mario and the Brentax delegate to arrive. Those two individuals were of much more interest than any reports.

"Commander," a sergeant said opening the door to the conference room. "Colonel Bonetti and Supreme Commander Tarmos are here."

"Show them in, Sergeant," Erin nodded. She closed her eyes and waited as the two people she'd been waiting to talk to came in. Without opening her eyes, she said, "Have a seat, gentleman."

She opened her eyes to see the Brentax officer sitting a few seats down on the opposite side of the table. Mario stood directly across from her, refusing to sit.

"I want to go back and get the Captain," Mario said without preamble.

"I'm afraid that won't be possible, Colonel," Erin sighed. "We have orders to get back to the Gamma Epsilon Station immediately. We don't have the time to prep a shuttle for combat conditions."

"With all due respect, Commander," Mario growled. "Those orders suck!"

"I agree, Colonel," Erin closed her eyes again, her migraine coming back in force. "But orders are orders."

There was a deafening CRACK as a small table near the door was reduced to splinters.

"Well," Mario sighed, looking from the wreckage of the table he'd just destroyed to the Commander. "In that case, I have to go tell the High Gentlewoman that her husband is stuck on Brentax III."

[320]

"Mario," Erin said quietly. "If it counts for anything, I want to go back and get him as much as you do."

"It counts, Commander," Mario said as he turned towards the door. "But not for much."

"At least try to be tactful, Colonel," Erin rubbed her temples. The polypropezene had worn off and her migraine was back in full force.

"I'll be gentle as a kitten, Commander," Mario flashed his winning smile. "I just hope she goes easy on me is all."

With that, the Colonel stormed out of the conference room.

"If I were in his position," M'Bek Tarmos spoke for the first time. "I would be reacting much the same way, Commander. I understand that he and his partner are very close friends."

"They are. It's eating him up inside, I know." Erin shook his head. "I imagine your people aren't too happy with you right now. It must look to them like you're selling out."

"Except that I have the support of the Emperor to negotiate a peace treaty," M'Bek sighed, looking suddenly very tired. "Despite being under martial law, our Emperor still retains quite a bit of power. He wants this peace for personal reasons.. He is, however, keeping those reasons, whatever they may be, to himself. It is the right of imperial privilege to keep such thoughts to himself. Nonetheless, he desires peace with the Star League. Therefore, I am empowered to negotiate such a treaty. I could not tell anyone on Brentax III, as that would betray an imperial confidence." M'Bek shrugged. "It is time for us to lay down our guns as we have laid down our lives."

"I agree. Admiral Bonetti and President Jameson will be very happy to hear that you are so willing to seek peace," Erin smiled.

* * *

[321]

K'Itea and S'Era were sitting in the palace in silence, each one lost in her own thoughts. Since her statement to S'Era about where she believed K'Alan was, K'Itea had all but completely withdrawn into herself out of fear of losing him.

S'Era, meanwhile, had begun to cry, her concern for her brother showing in each tear that rolled down her face.

Neither woman looked up when the door opened. Mario Bonetti slowly walked in.

"The guard told me you were both here," he broke the silence.

"K'Alan did not return with you from Brentax III," K'Itea said without turning. "I already know, Mario."

"I'm sorry, Kit," Mario heaved a deep sigh. "I want to go back and get him, but the Commander won't authorize it."

"The peace initiative is more important," K'Itea turned to Mario, tears streaming down her face. "This I understand. It is even more important than my husband. I believe he will be returned to us when the time is right."

"Still, I want to go back and get him back," Mario gritted his teeth. "I hated leaving him behind."

"I know, my friend," K'Itea placed her hand on Mario's shoulder. "You did everything you could. Come, sit with us a while, Mario. It will do us all good."

CHAPTER / 42

2.9.2136
0805
SLS Creighton
Rec Room

"OK, Jack. Let's try this again."

Tom Keevan had landed on his rump. Again. It had been no less than the sixth time in the past hour.

"Tom, why don't you just give up now?" Jack chuckled. "Or do you just enjoy falling on your arse this much?"

"Oh, hush, Jack," Tom snarled. "And that's an order."

Tom and his security chief, Jack Benton, had been sparring for just over an hour. Jack, the better boxer with a much longer reach, had been knocking his captain around.

"OK, Swamp Rat," Jack grinned wickedly.

"You know, it's bad enough Laura still calls me that, Jack," Tom put his hand to his head. "You calling me that is just downright embarrassing."

"Aw, you love the nickname and you know it," Jack said as he ducked a clumsy punch from the captain.

"I've hated that nickname since you and Laura conspired to start calling me that."

"Captain Keevan," his wristlink sounded. "You have a priority message from Admiral Bonetti at the Gamma Epsilon station."

"Patch it through to the rec room," Tom sighed as he pulled off his gloves.

The small holo emitter in the rec room flared to life as a very angry Admiral John Bonetti appeared with his arms crossed and glaring at the captain from the holo.

"Captain Keevan," the admiral began without preamble. "Would you care to explain to me why you are leaving the Khrinnus system?"

"I'm under orders to report to the Gamma Epsilon station, Admiral," the captain said.

"Oh, very funny, Captain," John glowered. "I issued no such orders."

"I did not say the orders came from your office, sir," Tom closed his eyes. "The orders came from President Jameson herself. Sets of sealed orders should be arriving before I do that will explain everything."

"Meanwhile the Khrinnus system is unprotected, I assume."

"No, sir. President Jameson sent the Atlantia to the Khrinnus system to continue patrolling," Tom reported. "We were under orders to remain in the system until our replacement arrived. The Atlantia had arrived before the Creighton left, sir."

"I am not happy about this turn of events, but if the President ordered it, who am I to say anything. Carry on, Captain. I am sure we will speak more of this when you arrive,"

The holo fizzed out, and Tom Keevan sighed deeply, rubbing his forehead.

"This is going to be a very long week, Jack," the captain sighed deeply a second time. "It's going to be a very long week indeed."

The Dawning of a New Age

⟨CHAPTER / 43⟩

2.9.2136
1522
Gamma Epsilon Station
Admiral Bonetti's office.

SERGEANT Anne Riker had to duck the brandy bottle that went flying across the room crashing into the door right about where her head was.

"Admiral?" she asked concerned. "Are you all right?"

"No, I am not, Sergeant," Admiral Bonetti scowled. He tossed a datapad on his desk. "That woman is going to ruin this peace initiative before it begins!"

"Who are you talking about sir?" the sergeant asked.

"President Jameson ordered a retrieval mission to bring Captain Bryce back. Does she know the effect this will have on the peace process?"

"I'm sure she does, Admiral," Riker nodded. "I'm sure she's weighed out her options and has decided that this is a worthwhile mission."

"It's a fool's errand!" Admiral Bonetti roared. "It'll cause the peace process to fail as well as cause the deaths of many of our people."

"I believe the president knows what she's doing, Admiral." The sergeant laid a comforting hand on her commanding officer's shoulder. "It'll be all right."

"Maybe you're right, Sergeant," John smiled weakly.

"Thorrin Jade and President Jameson are waiting out in the outer offices for you," Anne smiled.

"Send them in," he said as he sat behind his desk. He watched the sergeant turn to leave before adding, "And, Sergeant?"

"Yes, Admiral?" the young woman turned back to face him.

"Sorry about the brandy bottle."

"Don't worry about it, Admiral," Anne chuckled. "I'll get someone in here to clean it up for you."

"Thank you, Sergeant. Now, go send them in, please."

2.9.2136
1601
Gamma Epsilon Station
A corridor

The two Jaradans were nervous. They were standing and looking over a little niche in the corridor. The two Jaradans were dressed in the brown sack cloth of the Jaradan priesthood. They knew that no one would give two Jaradan priests on a Star League space stations a second glance.

"You are sure the procession will pass by this position, Toran?"

"Yes, Joval," the one called Toran said. "I have been given the plans for the peace initiative, including the path of the procession the Brentax delegation will take from the White Knight to the conference room. They will pass by this point."

"Then here is where it shall happen," Joval said.

[328]

"Then let us prepare."

The two Jaradan priests looked at the niche one more time then made their way back to the quarters that they had been assigned.

"And this is where the conference itself will be," Admiral Bonetti was explaining. "The Brentax delegation will sit here. Thorrin Jade will sit on this side between the two parties, and President Jameson and myself will sit on this side."

"I have read the treaty you had written previously, Admiral Bonetti," Thorrin Jade said in his quiet voice. "It is a good beginning, however it needs to be built on."

"I'm a soldier, Thorrin," John smiled. "Not a diplomat."

"I understand, Admiral," Thorrin returned the smile. "That is why I am here."

"How soon until the White Knight arrives with the Brentax delegation?" Kerrin asked.

"They should be here sometime tomorrow, Madame President," John sighed. He knew he was asking for trouble, but he had to broach the topic. "President Jameson, is it really a good idea to be sending a retrieval team in to get Captain Bryce back? I'm just afraid that such a mission will ruin the peace process."

"The Brentax would expect no less of us, Admiral," Thorrin interrupted. "It may work to our advantage that we send the team. Besides, the actual risk is low."

"Define low, Thorrin," Admiral Bonetti sighed deeply. "We're sending another ship into what is currently enemy space to pick up someone we're hoping is a prisoner of war and not dead in the first place. And the Brentax won't be happy to see that particular ship as it's taken out two of their Duhari class cruisers in the past week. I have the

[329]

utmost faith in Captain Keevan's abilities, but this is a suicide mission."

"It is the very fact that the Creighton knows how to handle the Duhari class vessels that prompted me to send them instead of another ship, Admiral," Kerrin said. "And we're sending someone with them that knows the lay of the land so they can go in and out."

"Are you so sure that Mario knows where Captain Bryce is being held?" John asked.

"It stands to reason that he would be the most likely person to, John," Thorrin said. "After all, he has been on Brentax III. How many of your other Star League officers can you say that of?"

"All right," John conceded. "I just want it noted that I am officially protesting this mission, President Jameson."

"Noted, Admiral," Kerrin sighed wearily. "But they must succeed. We cannot allow Captain Bryce to remain a prisoner on Brentax III."

⟨CHAPTER 44⟩

C APTAIN Tom Keevan was not a happy man. His command staff had not been able to give him a lot of information about Brentax III or the city of Brentacchia.

"So basically," Tom sighed. "We can't even plan this mission until we get Colonel Bonetti from Gamma Strike. That's what you all are telling me?"

"Tom, you know we'd give you more info if we could," Jack Benton said. "You've got all the information we have about Brentacchia."

"Which isn't much," Tom noted. "All right, folks. We'll be at the Gamma Epsilon Station early tomorrow. I want some preliminary plans in place. At least come up with something about how we're going to get to Brentax III and contingency plans for attacks by Brentax vessels. There

[331]

will be another staff meeting tomorrow at 0730. Dismissed."

Most of his senior staff got up and left. Most, but not all.

"Coming down a little hard on us, don't you think, Tom?" Jack said.

"Jack, there's nothing I'd like better than to waltz into Brentax III with guns blazing," Tom smiled. "But in this case, I want a plan of attack. You guys aren't being really helpful in coming up with such a plan of attack. There's a man out there stuck on Brentax III that's depending on us. So yeah, I'm coming down hard on you. I have to."

"Tom, when have we ever failed you?" Jack asked seriously.

"Never," Tom admitted.

"Why would we start now?" Jack smiled. "Is there something else that's bothering you?"

"Yeah, there is," Tom said, taking a small square box from his uniform pocket and handing it to Jack.

"Why, Tom!" Jack squealed. "I didn't know you cared!"

"It's not for you, moron," Tom chuckled. "It's for Erin. I just don't know how she'll respond."

"I've seen how she looks at you, Swamp Rat. She'll say yes."

"I hope so."

⟨CHAPTER 45⟩

K'ALAN, G'Kiron, and Crovax had holed up in the Chancellor's home. They felt that it would be the best place to hide from the Brentax militia.

"K'Alan," Crovax said. "I hope you have a plan. Just sitting here, we're going to get caught sooner or later."

"I know," K'Alan sighed. "Crovax, do you know where we might be able to borrow a ship?"

"Borrow? Surely you don't mean to come back and return it?" Crovax said with horror.

"Poor choice of words." K'Alan frowned. "How about acquire? Do you know where we might acquire a ship?"

"About the best I could suggest would be get a roid skimmer. They're not great for deep space, K'Alan, but you can hide on one of the asteroids until a rescue party arrives."

[333]

"I'm not sure a rescue party will come, Crovax," K'Alan said quietly. "I left Mario with orders not to bother with me, but to make sure the mission succeeded. Stubborn as he is, he'll follow orders."

"You underestimate your worth, K'Alan," Chancellor G'Kiron said. "Yes, Mario will follow orders. But I'll wager that as soon as M'Bek Tarmos has been delivered to the Star League, Mario will be back to pick you up."

"Well, I hope you're right, Chancellor," K'Alan said. "I miss my wife and son." He turned back to Crovax. "Can you get that roid skimmer, Crovax?"

"Of course I can," Crovax snorted. "It may take some time though. Wait here. I'll be back as soon as I have the ship."

Without waiting for a response, Crovax quietly crept from the house into the city. K'Alan busied himself the best he could while the Cor'vat was out picking up the ship.

It was very late at night when Crovax slipped back into the house.

"Come quickly," the Cor'vat hissed. "But be very quiet. There are guards about."

Crovax led K'Alan and G'Kiron out on a winding journey into the city. There were many twists and turns. K'Alan had to refrain several times from asking Crovax if he knew where he was going.

Eventually, K'Alan found himself looking at one of the ugliest ships he'd ever seen.

"She's not much to look at, but she'll get us where we're going," Crovax assured him. "It's the best I can do, K'Alan."

"Then it'll be good enough," K'Alan smiled. "Thanks, Crovax. For everything."

With that, K'Alan entered the little ship.

⟨CHAPTER / 46⟩

2.10.2136
0712
SLS Creighton
Main Conference Room

TOM Keevan sat quietly in his chair in the empty conference room, waiting for the rest of the command staff to show up. He hadn't slept well the previous night; visions of Erin Sykes kept going through his head. He was very afraid of how she'd respond when he proposed marriage to her. He was more nervous about that than he was about the rescue mission.

Rescue missions I can plan in my sleep, he reasoned to himself. *This is different.*

To keep his mind off Erin, he'd gone over his own notes about the Brentax and Brentax space.

He knew his ship and crew could handle any ship that was unlucky enough to try and stop them from picking up Captain Bryce. He also knew that overconfidence had led to the deaths of many a captain. Although he never said it aloud, he thought that may have been part of what

[335]

happened with the Grange. Good as she was, Perrin Hawkes had gotten overconfident.

What I'd like more than anything is a simple in and out, Tom thought to himself. *It's not likely to happen though. We better plan for the worst.*

"Morning, Tom," Jack called as he walked into the conference room and sat down. "Sleep OK?"

"Kept thinking about her," Tom admitted. "I couldn't sleep."

"Thought so," Jack shook his head. "Listen, I was thinking about the Brentax problem. At least about the problem about our likely attracting every ship they have in Brentax space."

"Yeah," Tom said. "I've been thinking about that too. We've proven we can take out their Duhari class cruisers."

"Thing is, Tom, we're not going to have the chance to pull the same trick we've been pulling," Jack said. "The only reason that trick worked was that we had the time to sit back and plan the shots. We won't be given that time when we're on the attack."

"What have you got in mind, Jack?" Tom asked.

"Well, first of all, when we get to the Gamma Epsilon Station, I want to get a triple load of torpedoes."

"All right, I'll requisition them," Tom nodded.

"I'm going to modify the forward torpedo bays so I can set them to do an automatic rapid fire," Jack said. "That way, we don't have to be as precise. We'll get, oh, six or seven hits in the time it would take us to line up and fire once."

"That's crazy, Jack!" Tom exploded in a way that he hoped Jack's crazy torpedo set up would not. "Suppose one torpedo jams? The rest would likely go boom."

"I thought about that too. I'm going to wire in some safety measures. Should a torpedo jam, the bay will shut down and disarm the remaining torpedoes, including the jammed one."

"I still think it's crazy," Tom said. "Sounds like a plan though. We'll go with it."

[336]

The rest of the command staff started filing in. They had no sooner sat down when Tom's wristlink sounded.

"Captain Keevan, we're on approach to the Gamma Epsilon Station," Kim Ericson said. "Admiral Bonetti wants to talk to you."

"Patch him through to the conference room."

"Acknowledged, Captain. Patching him through now."

The wall viewer sprang to life, and Admiral Bonetti appeared, sitting behind his desk.

"Captain Keevan," Admiral Bonetti said.

"Admiral Bonetti," Tom smiled. "What can I do for you this fine morning?"

"I notice you're on final approach to the station, Captain. When you dock, I'd like you to join me in the commissary for breakfast."

"I'd be delighted to, Admiral. We should be docked in about an hour," Tom said.

"Then I'll expect you around 0900 hours in the commissary, Captain. Admiral Bonetti out."

The viewscreen faded to black, and Tom turned back to the table and his senior staff.

"All right people. Here's what Jack came up with."

2.10.2136
0857
Gamma Epsilon Station
The Commissary

"Glad you could make it, Tom," Admiral Bonetti said. He wasn't smiling when he led Tom Keevan to a table.

"How could I refuse, John?" Tom said sitting. "You have real eggs here."

"True enough," John chuckled. He sighed before continuing. "I was against this mission, Tom. I think it will cause problems with the peace process. But the President thinks it's necessary, so I'm letting it go through. What can I do to make sure this mission is successful?"

"You should be receiving a requisition list, John," Tom said, buttering a piece of toast. "If I can get everything on that list, we should be all right."

"All right. I'll see what I can do. You'll leave as soon as the White Knight arrives and Colonel Bonetti can get his temporary transfer order." John took a bite of egg. "And Tom? Try not to leave anyone behind."

"I don't intend to, John."

⟨CHAPTER 47⟩

KITEA Bryce hadn't been able to sleep all night. Even though she knew that K'Alan was safe, it didn't help. She was still worried about him. All she wanted was for him to be back with her on board the White Knight. Even Elam had been little comfort the past two days. She watched him sleeping peacefully and sighed.

When will you be home, my love? She thought to herself. *When will you return to me?*

She sighed again and slowly dressed. Unwilling to stay cooped up in her quarters any longer, she stepped out into the city.

* * *

Commander Erin Sykes stared out at the stars streaking by. The White Knight would be back at the Gamma Epsilon Station late this evening. Sarah had poured everything she safely could into the engines to coax a bit of extra speed. It looked like she'd knock the time of the journey down by half. Which, in Erin's opinion, was just fine. The sooner she dropped off the Brentax Commander, the happier she'd be. She wasn't too thrilled about honor guard and security duty for the peace conference, but she figured that would be a piece of cake compared to dealing with the events of the past week.

She'd had Masha draw up security and honor guard duty details and a security plan using all available crew members. What Masha came up with was an incredibly complex set of plans that looked quite good. There were few, if any, security leaks in the entire plan. Erin was pleased with the plan, especially when Masha volunteered to be the coordinator, thereby allowing Erin to just take a security shift.

Let Masha do the hard work on that plan for a change, Erin had thought to herself.

It made sense. Masha was first and foremost a security officer. Erin was a soldier. A career pilot before she was promoted to Commander, Erin felt much more comfortable in the cockpit of a Starfire than stuck on the bridge. K'Alan's only response when she mentioned that was to shrug and say that she'd adapt.

Adapt, she thought bitterly. *Hell, I should be the one out there lost on Brentax III instead of K'Alan. I can't believe he left me here on the White Knight while he risked his neck on a fool mission. And I'm the one who's supposed to adapt? I'm going to wring his neck when he gets back.*

With that pleasant thought in her mind, she tapped her wristlink.

"ETA to Gamma Epsilon Station?" she asked the bridge officer on duty.

"ETA to Gamma Epsilon Station is about 2330 hours, Commander," the voice of Mara Silvermaine responded. "I don't think we can push the engines any more than we already are. I'd like to get there in one piece personally."

"Understood," Erin sighed. "I'll be taking the third duty shift tonight, Ms. Silvermaine. I expect primary crew to be on duty then. Get some sleep as soon as you get off shift."

"Aye, ma'am."

Erin nodded at her wristlink and flicked it off. She stared out the viewport some more, scowling to herself.

2.10.2136
1311
SLS White Knight
Soran's Bar.

Colonel Mario Bonetti sat by himself in a corner of the bar. He'd been spending a lot of time by himself over the past two days, trying not to think about K'Alan, and trying to avoid talking to too many people about what had happened on Brentax III. He was trying to avoid S'Era too. He felt extremely guilty about leaving her brother behind, even though he was following his orders. And every time he looked at her, he could see how upset she was about K'Alan being missing.

He wondered idly if she'd ever forgive him for leaving K'Alan behind.

"Feeling sorry for yourself won't change anything," a familiar voice said from nearby.

"I'm not feeling sorry for myself," Mario muttered.

"Mind if I sit?" the voice asked again. Mario nodded, not looking up. Soran sat across the table from him and smiled. "Sure you are. Mario. See, I know how you're feeling right now. I've been there."

[341]

"Soran, no offense, but you can't possibly know how I'm feeling right now."

"You think I was a barman all my life, Mario?" Soran chuckled as he slid a large flat box across the table. "Open it and look inside."

Mario opened the box and his eyebrows shot up.

"The Platinum Star?" Mario said, surprised. "I didn't know you were in the Defense Force, Soran."

"I was. About fifty years ago. I made Captain before I resigned my commission."

"Why'd you resign?" Mario was truly curious.

"Maybe I'll tell you sometime. It's not relevant to your problem. You say I don't know how you feel. Well, let me tell you a little story. About sixty years ago, I was a Commander. I was Strike Leader in my unit. I was cocky.

"I was in love with this sparky Lieutenant Commander that was one of the squad leaders. She was a lot like your S'Era. She was kind, caring, and full of life. Her name was K'Aria Danare. She and I were inseparable. We did everything on the ship together. I made it so we had the same duty shifts.

"We went on a ground mission. In those days, more often than not the pilots were also ground pounders. K'Aria and I got separated from the rest of our detachment. I don't know what happened. We were under attack. K'Aria was shot in the stomach. I patched her up the best I could.

"The rest of the mission is still a blur. I wish I knew how it happened. All I remember is that when we got back to our dropships, K'Aria wasn't there. I led a rescue mission to find her that day, but it was no use. She was gone.

"I never married. I always felt it would be a betrayal of her love. I've been reliving that day for a long time, Mario. So, yes, I know how you feel."

Soran was looking away from Mario, and the young colonel felt a little ashamed.

"I'm sorry, Soran," Mario said quietly.

"It's all right, Mario," Soran smiled. "I just wanted you to know that if you needed to talk, there was someone here who knows what you're going through."

"Good to know," Mario said. He knocked back the rest of his drink and smiled. "I have to go, Soran. There's some things I need to get done."

"Stop by any time, Mario," the barman smiled. "I'm always here."

"I will," Mario smiled and headed out of the lounge.

The Dawning of a New Age

⟨CHAPTER / 48⟩

2.10.2136
2310
Gamma Epsilon Station
Admiral Bonetti's Quarters

JOHN was lying in bed trying to fall asleep. He was tossing and turning, unable to get comfortable.

"Admiral Bonetti," the admiral's wristlink squawked. "There is a Star League ship on fast approach to the Gamma Epsilon Station. Markings indicate that it's the White Knight."

"I'm on my way," John said as he tapped his wristlink. He got dressed and hurried out of his quarters.

2.10.2136
2329
Gamma Epsilon Station
Command and Control.

John Bonetti strode into Command and Control, fidgeting nervously as he took the command seat. It was rare that the station commander actually was in command and control, but this was a special case.

"ETA of the White Knight?" he asked.

"They just requested docking clearance. They should complete docking in about half an hour," a station tech said, swiveling in his chair.

"Grant clearance for Docking Bay 12. And have Colonel Bonetti and Commander Sykes report to my office as soon as they dock," John ordered."

"Understood, Admiral," the tech said.

2.11.2136
0004
Gamma Epsilon Station
Admiral Bonetti's office.

John paced his office as he waited for Commander Sykes and his son to arrive. He'd been hoping to put this moment off a bit longer, but now that it was here, he had no choice but to go through with it. As soon as the door chime sounded, he straightened his uniform and sat behind his desk.

"Enter," he called.

The door slid open and Erin and Mario stepped through into the office.

"Commander Erin Sykes and Colonel Mario Bonetti reporting as ordered, Admiral," Erin said, snapping to attention. Mario followed suit and stood at attention, although a bit slower than Erin had done.

"At ease," John said. "Sit, the both of you. We have a couple situations that need to be worked out."

"Situations?" Erin asked.

"Yes, Commander. First of all, do you have the security plans drawn up for the peace conference?"

"Yes, Admiral."

Erin passed over a data pad with the security plan on it. John took it and looked it over.

"It looks good. Except that there is one small problem."

"Problem?" Erin asked, furrowing her brow.

"Yes. You're going to have to reassign some of these duty assignments. Colonel Bonetti will not be staying on the station."

"I won't?" Mario asked.

"No, Colonel, you won't." John sighed. "You have orders directly from President Jameson, Colonel. You are being temporarily reassigned to the Creighton."

"That's Tom Keevan's ship, isn't it, Admiral?" Erin asked.

"Yes, it is. The Creighton is being sent to Brentax III. It seems the president is most anxious to have a certain package that was left on the planet returned to Star League space."

The light that seemed to go on in Mario's eyes told Admiral Bonetti that the young colonel was more than happy to get the change in orders.

"Why send the Creighton and not the White Knight?" Erin asked.

"I would think that it's because the Creighton has a much more extensive battle record against Duhari class heavy cruisers, Commander," Mario said. "It makes sense. Send the ship you know can handle the situation the best."

"That's right, Colonel," John nodded. "Since the Creighton has taken out two Duhari class cruisers this week alone, that makes them the best ship to handle the mission."

"Mario," Erin said. "Make sure you keep an eye on Tom. Don't let him do anything stupid, OK?"

"I promise, Commander," Mario said. "I will do everything I can to keep Captain Keevan safe." The colonel looked at Admiral Bonetti. "If I may be dismissed, I need to go get ready. I have some, ah, supplies I need to get from my quarters."

"The Creighton's docked at Bay 3. Dismissed," John nodded.

Mario stood and hustled out of the room. John turned to Erin and smiled weakly.

[347]

"Don't worry about the peace conference security, Admiral," Erin said. "I have my best people on it."

"I know you do, Commander," John smiled. "I just have a bad feeling about it is all. Let's go over the procedures involved anyway."

2.11.2136
0055
Gamma Epsilon Station
Docking Bay 3

Mario huffed into the docking bay, two rucksacks in his hands. Jack Benton was in the docking bay waiting for him.

"Colonel Bonetti, Captain Keevan's waiting for you," Jack said. The big security chief broke into a broad smile when he saw the two rucksacks. "I see you brought some supplies with you. Good. I like to see someone who's prepared."

Jack led the way on board the Creighton, smiling at Mario.

"Just a couple things I thought I might need. Some, ah, extra firepower," Mario grinned.

"I've heard about your extra firepower. You're the envy of half the security chiefs in the Defense Force," Jack winked. "myself included."

"Well, I do have a way with weapons," Mario snarled. "And this is personal."

"I know. That's why you're going to be planning the rescue mission itself."

"Captain Keevan trusts me that much, eh?" Mario said.

"Well, you've been on Brentax III. You know where Captain Bryce is likely to be. You're the best person for the job."

"Thanks, I think."

Jack and Mario arrived on the Creighton's bridge, and headed right over to Captain Keevan's chair in the center of the bridge.

"Colonel Mario Bonetti reporting as ordered, Captain," Mario saluted.

"At ease, Colonel. Briefing's at 0900 hours tomorrow morning. Jack will show you to your bunk." Captain Keevan looked Mario over. "I hope you're as good as everyone thinks you are, Colonel. Dismissed."

Mario nodded and slung one of the rucksacks over his shoulder. Jack led him off the bridge.

> *2.11.2136*
> *0115*
> *Gamma Epsilon Station*
> *Guest Quarters 2335-A*

Commander Erin Sykes was dead tired by the time she got to the quarters she had been assigned on the Gamma Epsilon Station. She flopped on the bed and laid back.

First K'Alan and now Tom, Erin sighed. All the people I care about are going into danger.

She stared at the ceiling for a few minutes before pulling her boots and socks off. She padded over to the food dispenser, her bare feet sinking into the deep plush carpeting.

Out of the corner of her eye, she saw something on the desk. Furrowing her brow, she went over and picked it up. It was a small box, about five inches to the side.

"A holocube," she chuckled. "Now who could have sent me this?"

She placed the holocube on the floor and hit the button on the side with her foot.

"Hello, Erin," the life size hologram of Tom Keevan said as soon as it appeared. "I'm sorry I'm not here to talk to you in person. But Admiral Bonetti was shipping us out to bring your captain back as soon as you guys arrived.

"I'm pretty nervous about this, even just recording this hologram. I've come to care about you a great deal.

"Inside the holocube, you'll find a ring. I've scrimped and saved. Even a captain's salary isn't that much these days. But I hope you find the ring satisfactory." The hologram knelt down in front of Erin. "The next time you see me, you can give me your answer to this. But what I want to ask you is will you marry me?"

CHAPTER / 49

"T HESE controls are crazy," K'Alan sighed. "I suppose I shouldn't complain, but nothing's where it should be."

"Can you fly it?" Crovax asked, his sibilant voice anxious.

"Oh, I can fly it, but I'll need help. Crovax, can you handle the scanners?"

"Yes, I can, K'Alan," the Cor'vat said.

"G'Kiron, I need you to work the communications and weapons arrays," K'Alan said.

"Um, K'Alan?" G'Kiron said. "This may not be the best time to mention this, but roid skimmers aren't armed."

"Not armed?" K'Alan raised his eyebrow. "All right. I suppose we will just have to pray we don't run into any trouble then. Man the communications array at any rate. I'll need to concentrate on piloting. Crovax, make sure I know about any Brentax contacts."

The Dawning of a New Age

"You will know, K'Alan," the Cor'vat assured him.

"Let's see what this thing can do."

K'Alan took a deep breath and pushed the control stick forward, launching the roid skimmer spaceward.

❰ CHAPTER / 50 ❱

THE president of the Star League had woken early. Eager to get the peace talks underway, she hadn't been able to sleep. She got up and padded over to her desk.

Kerrin knew something needed to be done to prevent something like this lengthy war from happening again. She wanted to be remembered for ending this war, it was true. But she wanted even more to be remembered for quick thinking and for preventing such atrocities from happening again.

Out of the corner of her eye, she caught sight of a memo from Admiral Bonetti. The memo had been on her desk for some time, but she had not given it more than a cursory glance before now. She picked it up and read it over thoroughly, smiling to herself.

[353]

The Dawning of a New Age

⟨CHAPTER / 51⟩

2.11.2136
0855
SLS Creighton
Main Briefing Room

MARIO was standing at the viewscreen looking over a street map of Brentacchia when Tom Keevan walked in, leading the rest of the senior staff.

"That's Brentacchia, Colonel?" the captain asked.

"Yes," Mario nodded. "Although this map's not the best, it'll be good enough to plan our assault."

"You have a plan in mind then, Colonel?" Jack asked.

"Yes," Mario smiled. "I'm planning a full out frontal assault. I brought some extra supplies that I think we might need."

Mario took the two rucksacks he brought on board with him and began to empty them on the conference room table. Weapons and equipment of all kinds were soon piled on the table.

"Some extra supplies my arse," Tom chuckled. "You brought an arsenal."

"You get me to Brentax III and give me five good men, and I'll get the captain out, Captain," Mario smiled. "I promise you that."

"Good," Tom said. "Jack, pick four more men to go with yourself and Colonel Bonetti. Colonel, you are in command of the ground mission."

"Understood," Jack and Mario said in unison.

"Captain, we're nearing the jump gate," a bridge officer called over the captain's wristlink.

"Good. As soon as we get to the jump gate, engage jump engines."

"Acknowledged."

⟨CHAPTER / 52⟩

"**S**O do you have a plan?" Crovax asked for what felt like the hundredth time. K'Alan thought the Cor'vat was even more impatient to leave Brentax space than K'Alan was.

"Yes," K'Alan said. "We're going to hide and hope someone comes to get us."

"Good plan," Crovax grunted. "I--" The Cor'vat stopped and looked at the scanners. "K'Alan, we've got trouble."

"What?"

"Three Duhari class cruisers are headed our way," Crovax reported.

"Great," K'Alan grumbled. "All right. There's not much we can do about that. Find me a good asteroid to land on."

"Working on it," Crovax said. After a few minutes, the Cor'vat said, "I have one. You should have the coordinates on your console now."

[357]

"I got them. G'Kiron, can that communications array send a low frequency coded transmission?" K'Alan asked.

"Yes, but it would have to be very short. No more than one or two words," G'Kiron nodded. "You'd have to be very specific with the message, K'Alan."

"Leave the text of the message to me," K'Alan said. "You just be ready to send that message at a moment's notice."

"I will be."

K'Alan guided the small craft to a surprisingly gentle landing on the surface of the asteroid.

"All right," K'Alan said. "I'm going to cut power except for life support and minimal scanners. We'll be harder to see that way."

The other two nodded and K'Alan flipped the switch, cutting the power. The lights dropped to almost nothing. Crovax monitored the scanners, and all three held their collective breaths as if that would help the Brentax from finding them.

"They're heading this way, K'Alan. Slowly, but they are," Crovax reported. "They're checking each and every asteroid in the belt."

CHAPTER 53

"THE Brentax delegation should be here shortly, Admiral," Kerrin smiled. "They have to go through the propriety of getting to the conference room for the first day. It is symbolism at its best."

"I know," John Bonetti growled, checking his chrono again. "Worried about the Creighton is all."

"I figure they should be getting to the jump gate any minute if they haven't already," Kerrin noted. "They were supposed to be doing some engine modifications. I'm not sure how well the new modifications will take though. From the jump gate, it's about twenty hours in hyperspace then another twelve hours to Brentax III. Give them about six hours to retrieve Captain Bryce, then they have to fly back. God willing, they'll be back in less than four days."

[359]

"And hopefully there will still be a peace initiative going when they get back," John scowled.

"Admiral, do you really think I would jeopardize the peace process on purpose?" Kerrin asked. "I've been looking forward to the end of this war for as long as you have. I've been looking forward to an end of the war even more so after Perrin died."

"I keep forgetting we've all lost people we care about in this war, Kerrin," John said quietly. "In light of the fact that my son keeps managing to land himself in danger, there are days when I wonder how I haven't lost a child in this war."

"You have been fortunate then, Admiral," Thorrin Jade said as he entered the conference room. "I see the Brentax delegation has not yet arrived."

"They're on their way, Thorrin," Kerrin said. "They should be here in a little under a half an hour."

"Good. I cannot wait to get these talks underway."

2.11.2136
1049
Gamma Epsilon Station
A Corridor

The two Jaradan monks stood in a niche in a corridor of the Gamma Epsilon Station. Word of the peace conference had spread throughout the station, and the corridors were lined with people who wanted to get a glimpse of the Brentax delegation. The two Jaradans were able to blend in with everyone else.

Way down the corridor the procession of security and the Brentax delegate had slowly started coming down the corridor. The security officers were doing their best to keep people away from the Brentax official. One onlooker was dragged away after trying to rush over and club the Brentax delegate.

"Security is tighter than you said it would be, Toran," one of the monks said.

"Yes," Toran said. "It is an unexpected problem, Joval. We shall not fail though. She is counting on us."

Toran slowly pulled the small throwing dagger he had secreted in his robes. Joval followed suit, and both monks checked to ensure that the poison had been carefully applied to the blades.

The procession neared, and the two monks tensed for action.

As the procession started by, the two monks let fly with their daggers before the security officers could react. Neither dagger hit the Brentax official, but each one hit one of the officers in the security detail. The two human security officers crumpled to the floor almost immediately, and the two monks rushed out and fell on top of the fallen security officers. Each monk pressed his ring against one of the fallen guards' forehead, leaving a small mark, no more than an inch wide. It was a circle with a fancy T inset in it.

Other members of the security detail hauled the two monks off their fallen comrades and led them away.

2.11.2136
1102
Gamma Epsilon Station
Main Conference Room

Commander Erin Sykes led the procession into the conference room, a grim look on her face. She smiled weakly at everyone else in the room and shot a look at Admiral Bonetti that said "I need to talk to you right now."

John took the hint and headed over to the corner of the room, and Erin followed.

"We have a problem, Admiral," Erin said without preamble.

"What happened?"

"There was an assassination attempt," Erin sighed. "Two Jaradan monks threw poisoned throwing daggers. They hit Ensigns Dalton and Kelleher. They're dead."

[361]

"I assume the Jaradans responsible have been detained?"

"They're in lockup waiting to be interrogated. I thought you might want to be there when they are."

"You're damn right I do," John growled. "Let me just go explain my absence to the president and Mr. Jade. Then we can go interrogate your prisoners."

John stormed over to the president and Thorrin Jade and sighed.

"What's going on, Admiral?" Kerrin asked.

"Assassination attempt on Commander Tarmos," John fumed. "I'm going to talk to the would-be assassins."

"Assassins. What else could go wrong?" Kerrin sighed. "Go. We'll deal with it."

2.11.2136
1134
Gamma Epsilon Station
Security Visitation Room 3

The two Jaradan monks were sitting in chairs in the security visitation room. They were chained, and they were both staring straight ahead.

"They almost look proud of what they did," John snarled. "Two good security officers dead."

"Let me do this, Admiral," Masha growled. "Dalton was one of my brightest security officers."

"Go ahead, Lieutenant," John said.

"Thank you." Masha smiled as she walked over to the two monks. "I want some answers."

"We'll tell you very little," one of the monks said.

"What poison did you use on those knives?" Masha asked. "It didn't register on the stations medscanners."

"Wouldn't you like to know?" the same monk said.

"What was that symbol you two burned on the foreheads of the security officers?"

"All I will tell you is this, Lieutenant," the other monk said. "It has begun."

Both monks bit down on something at the same time, and their eyes glazed over. Masha reached over and felt for a pulse.

"They're dead. I would say they've poisoned themselves," Masha announced.

"What has begun?" Erin wondered aloud.

The Dawning of a New Age

CHAPTER 54

"ALL right, guys," Mario said. "We need to make sure you all know how to use this equipment before we reach the insertion point."

"I hate to ask this," a young ensign said. "But aren't we bringing too much stuff?"

"No such thing, Ensign," Jack smiled. "Tell you what. What would you do if you ran out of charges for your plasma rifle and you had a bunch of Brentax officers still coming at you?"

"I'm not sure, sir," the ensign admitted. There was a decidedly sheepish look on the young man's face.

"That's why I bring the extra equipment along, Ensign," Mario said. "Now everyone will be fitted with the same stuff, so let's go over what you'll get."

Mario started pulling equipment out of the rucksacks and laying them out in piles of identical items. As he pointed to the different piles, Jack explained what they would be using.

"First, we have the regular plasma rifles you'll be assigned. Each person will receive two refill charges for their rifle. You'll also receive two rechargeable shock grenades. These shock grenades can be used up to three times each before their charges are expended. In addition, each person will receive a regulation sword and three throwing daggers. We'll also be assigning regulation shock troop outfits for the mission fitted with adamantine linings. Our battle helmets have been refitted with IR and UV scanners. Each person will also receive a mini-computer that will be preprogrammed with as much information about Brentacchia and the Brentacchia Prison complex as we have."

"Over the next seven hours, we will go over how to use each piece of the equipment," Mario said. "By the time we reach Brentax III, you will all be well acquainted with all of the equipment, and will be able to more than competently use it."

2.12.2136
0902
SLS Creighton
The Bridge

"Captain," the helm officer said. "We've reached the Brentax jump gate."

"Initiate jump to normal space," Tom ordered.

"Jumping to normal space now," the helm officer said.

"Soon as we're clear of the jump gate, I want best speed to Brentax III," Tom said.

"Yes, sir," the helm officer said.

"Shall I put up the cloaking screens?" the person replacing Jack at the tactical station asked.

"No," Tom shook his head. "Transfer all power from the cloaking systems to the engines. I want all available power to boost the output of the engines."

"Understood."

Tom nodded and smiled to himself. His crew would get them there in one piece. Then it was up to Mario.

2.12.2136
1215
SLS Creighton
The Gym

"All right," Mario said. "The shock grenade is a special weapon. It will incapacitate several enemies at once, but it can incapacitate yourself as well, so you need to be careful. Before you activate the grenade make sure your auditory and visual sensors on your battle helmets are dampened. Otherwise you'll be as stunned as your enemies."

"What does the grenade do?" Ensign Hawthorne, who was the ensign that had criticized the amount of equipment earlier, asked.

Mario nodded at the Ensign, thinking it was a good thing the Ensign was asking questions rather than keeping his attitude about the extra stuff.

"Basically," the colonel said. "The shock grenade emits a loud auditory pulse as well as an extremely bright light. The light causes temporary blindness, and the sound can cause hearing to fail temporarily. The end result is that the people affected are stunned and unable to act for a period of time. They have been very effective against the Brentax in the past."

"Great," Hawthorne said. "So we have to make sure it doesn't stun us too. Good to know."

"Ensign, I've used them before," Jack sighed, exasperated. "They're kind of fun."

"Fun?" Mario chuckled. "You're sounding more and more like Masha all the time."

"Yes, but would she have thought of making the proton torpedo tubes do an auto rapid-fire?" Jack asked.

"She probably would, but I bet the Captain nixes it," Mario laughed. "Anyway, back to practice, gentlemen."

2.12.2136
2037
SLS Creighton
The Bridge

"Captain, we're entering the Brentax system," the officer at the helm station announced. "We should arrive at Brentax III in under an hour and a half."

"Good," Tom said. "Let me know as soon as we make orbit."

"Understood."

CHAPTER 55

"K'ALAN, look!" Crovax called from where he was monitoring the scanners. "The Brentax vessels are pulling away."

"Let me see!" K'Alan said. He looked closely at the scanners. "There's another ship out there. Can you get me more information about that new ship?"

"Looks like a Star League vessel. Pegasus class," Crovax said. "I'm getting a fix on the registry now. SL-2166."

"That's the Creighton!" K'Alan exclaimed. "G'Kiron, prepare to send that message as soon as the Creighton's in range."

"Have you figured out what you want to say in the message, K'Alan?" G'Kiron asked.

"Endeavor," K'Alan said. "Captain Keevan will know what it means."

[369]

"I hope so," G'Kiron nodded as he began to prepare the message.

"It's the first ship we served on together," K'Alan explained. "He'll know that it means I'm here and he'll know I know who's out there."

"The message has been sent, K'Alan," G'Kiron said as he finished tapping out a series of commands on his console.

"Now we wait."

CHAPTER / 56

"CAPTAIN, three Duhari class cruisers coming up fast," Jack reported. "They have their weapons primed."

"Our weapons are hot, Captain," Mario added from tactical station 2. "Ready to sweep targets on your orders."

"Steady, Colonel," Tom said. "Give me full defensive screens and a tactical holo."

"Defense screens full, Captain," Mario said.

"Tactical holo up now, Captain," Kim called from the comms station. "Captain! We're receiving a low frequency communication. It's in code."

"Decode," Tom said. "Where's it coming from?"

"From a small ship on the asteroid the Duhari class vessels came from, Captain," Kim said. "Decoding message, now." After a moment, she looked up and exclaimed.

"Captain, it's an automatic computer message. The message is just one word. Endeavor."

"That's Captain Bryce!" Tom shouted excitedly. "Helm, put us between the Duhari class vessels and that asteroid. Kim open a channel to that vessel. Mario, start targeting the Brentax ships. Engines and weapons only please."

"You got it, Captain!" Mario said as he began to track the three vessels. "They won't know what hit 'em."

⟨CHAPTER / 57⟩

"K'ALAN, we're receiving a communication from the Star League ship," G'Kiron said.

"Are we able to do a holo on this ship?" K'Alan asked.

"No. Audio only," G'Kiron said.

"All right," K'Alan said. "Let me hear it."

"Patching it through now, K'Alan," G'Kiron nodded.

"This is the Star League vessel Creighton," Tom Keevan's voice came over the speakers. "To the ship on the asteroid, if Captain Bryce is on that ship please respond."

"This is Captain Bryce," K'Alan said. "Good to hear your voice, Tom."

"Good to hear yours too, K'Alan. President Jameson sent me to pull your arse out of the fire. Seems like that's what I do a lot, buddy."

"And I appreciate it, Tom," K'Alan laughed. "President Jameson sent you herself, eh? I didn't know I rated so

[373]

highly. Anyway, can you keep those Brentax off our backs while we launch?"

"Sure," Tom said, chuckling. "We brought a few surprises for them. Head straight for the landing bay. We'll lower the screens when you get here long enough for you to land."

"Much obliged," K'Alan said.

"Hey, I'm not doing this for you," Tom laughed. "I expect a big kiss from your exec when I get back."

"See you on the deck shortly, Tom," K'Alan laughed. "Captain Bryce out."

"I hate to remind you that there are three Duhari class starships out there," G'Kiron said.

"I know," K'Alan said as he buckled his seat restraints. "You both might want to buckle in. This is likely to be a rough ride."

K'Alan's hands flew over the control panel and the roid skimmer's engines flared loudly to life. He grabbed the control stick and nudged the ship spaceward. The first fifteen minutes of the flight were uneventful, but K'Alan knew that such easy flying would not last long.

"Fighters!" Crovax called.

"Great. I see them," K'Alan said as he began to initiate some evasive maneuvers.

He watched in horror as two Brentax fighters started to bear down on the roid skimmer. The next second the two fighters had become a ball of flame as several proton torpedoes arced from the distant Creighton and plowed into the unsuspecting fighters, turning them into small fireballs.

"What the..?" Crovax started.

"Whoever's manning the weapons on that ship is a madman," K'Alan said simply as he straightened course towards the Creighton.

With interest, K'Alan noted that the Creighton managed to hold off any attackers from getting to the roid skimmer while still keeping themselves from being pulverized by the Duhari class vessels. K'Alan knew they wouldn't be able to last long and tried to coax a little more speed out of the old vessel.

Soon, though, the roid skimmer reached the Creighton.

"The defense screens are down," Crovax called as they approached the Creighton.

"Good. Let me get us in quickly then," K'Alan said as he concentrated on getting the roid skimmer landed.

As soon as the roid skimmer touched down on the Creighton's landing bay, K'Alan closed his eyes and let out a huge sigh of relief.

The Dawning of a New Age

CHAPTER / 58

2.12.2136
2202
Gamma Epsilon Staiton
Admiral Bonetti's Office

"YOU wanted to see me, Madam President?" John said as he indicated the seat across from his desk for her to sit.

"Yes, I did, John." Kerrin sat in the offered seat. "I have a proposition."

"I'm listening," John nodded.

"You sent me a memo some time ago outlining a proposal on how to use the White Knight. Especially about how to use the City as it is now being called."

"I remember," John nodded. "What do you have in mind?"

"After this peace conference is over, I'd like to form an advisory council," Kerrin explained. "I'd like all six core races of the Star League as well as the Brentax Empire to all have seats on this council. Hopefully, by being able to mediate disputes through such a forum, we'll be able to keep something like this from happening again."

"Agreed," John nodded. "And you'd like to use the White Knight for this?"

"Well that was the original purpose of The City before the Duterius Prime incident," Kerrin nodded.

"I will request that proper support ships be permanently assigned to the White Knight in the case of some kind of emergency, Kerrin," John said.

"That's reasonable," Kerrin nodded. "Have Captain Bryce select two ships when he returns."

"Of course," John nodded, deciding not to pursue that particular issue. "I have a feeling I know one of the ships will be the Creighton."

"A good choice," Kerrin smiled. "I will see you at the conference session tomorrow.

The President of the Star League smiled and strode out of his office, leaving John shaking his head at her back.

⟨CHAPTER 59⟩

2.12.2136
2237
SLS Creighton
The Bridge

"**T**HEY'VE landed, Captain," Jack said.

"Screens up!" Tom ordered.

"Screens are full," Mario announced.

"Strafe those Duhari class cruisers, Colonel," Tom said.

"Aye, Captain. I am beginning a strafing run now."

As Mario's hands flew across the tactical board, torpedo after torpedo shot out of the Creighton and impacted against the Duhari class cruisers inflicting minor hull damage to each.

"I think that got their attention, Captain," Jack said. "And I think they're mad."

"Helm, get us the hell out of here," Tom ordered, leaping to his feet.

"Initiating getting the hell out of here maneuver," the helm officer said.

[379]

"Best speed back to the jump gate," Tom said. The only response from the helm officer was a grunt and a nod.

Minutes ticked by as the tactical holo showed the Brentax ships slowly falling further and further behind.

"We're losing them, Captain," Jack announced.

K'Alan stepped on the bridge at that point. Tom saw him and smiled.

"Welcome aboard, Captain Bryce," the Creighton's skipper chuckled. "You look a little the worse for wear."

"I could be a lot worse. Thanks, Tom," K'Alan smiled.

"You had us all worried, Kal," Mario said.

"Mario? What the hell are you doing here?" K'Alan laughed.

"Who do you think the President sent to bail your arse out?" Tom shrugged. "Join me for supper, Captain. There's much I want to talk to you about."

"Sure," K'Alan laughed.

"You should take a shower first, Kal," Mario said as he sniffed the air. "You smell like a Brentax."

2.12.2136
2357
SLS Creighton
The Mess Hall

Some time later, K'Alan emerged in the mess hall, having cleaned up and put on a fresh uniform.

"I'm afraid the food here isn't that great, K'Alan," Tom said as he, Mario and K'Alan sat at a table in the corner of the mess hall.

"Tom, I've been living on Brentax K rations for the last five days. This is going to be a feast."

"I can imagine," Tom sighed. "It couldn't have been easy for you on Brentacchia."

"If it weren't for G'Kiron and Crovax, I wouldn't have made it," K'Alan kept his voice soft. "I hope your crew is treating them with respect."

"They are," Tom nodded. "Crovax told us how he helped you escape the prison. A little thing like that tends to get people to treat him a bit better."

"How's Gamma Strike holding up, Mario?" K'Alan asked.

The colonel had been sitting in silence since he sat down at the table. Now he looked at K'Alan and smiled a slight little smile.

"I think it's safe to say a lot of us are mad at you for getting caught," Mario said simply. "Masha, uh, kind of got drunk and wrecked a punching bag."

"Oh, Lords," K'Alan rolled his eyes. "Erin must have had a fit."

"She's probably the person most mad at you," Mario smiled wryly. "I don't think she likes command."

"Oh, joy," K'Alan slumped in his chair and sighed. He took a bite of the chicken and shook his head. "I can just hear her when I get back. I told you not to go. I told you it was a suicide mission. Don't ever leave me in command of this unit again."

"I imagine it will go something like that," Tom said. He was distracted, but K'Alan did not immediately pick up on it.

"How did Kit take my disappearance, Mario?" K'Alan asked quietly.

"Well, she already knew you weren't on the shuttle." Mario put his knife and fork down. "It probably has to do with the bond you have. But she took it better than I did. She'll be very happy to have you back."

"I owe Elam a baseball game," K'Alan smiled.

The Dawning of a New Age

CHAPTER 60

"I demand the Star League cede the Khrinnus system to the Brentax Empire!" M'Bek Tarmos thundered.

"The Khrinnus system has been inhabited by the peoples of the Star League for fifty years!" John Bonetti roared. "It belongs to the Star League!"

"Nevertheless, I demand that it be ceded to the Brentax Empire," M'Bek Tarmos stood. "This is a point we will not waver over, Madame President. If we do not receive the Khrinnus system, then this peace conference will not work and I will walk out that door."

"Ladies and gentleman," Thorrin Jade spoke suddenly, his quiet voice cutting through all of the discussion. "We need to stop fighting and stop threatening to walk from this table—"

[383]

"Admiral Bonetti," John's wristlink sounded, interrupting Thorrin's words.

"Admiral Bonetti here," John said, tapping his wristlink.

"Sir, the Creighton has just docked in bay 18," the woman on the other end reported.

"Understood. I'll be with you shortly. Bonetti out." John tapped his wristlink and the comm line closed. "Ladies and gentleman, I must take a brief recess."

"This conference shall recess until 1330 hours," Thorrin Jade announced. "At which time, we will discuss the Khrinnus system situation."

Without waiting for further conversation, John stood and bolted from the conference room.

2.13.2136
1148
Gamma Epsilon Station
Docking Bay 18

John Bonetti rushed into the docking bay as K'Alan Bryce, Mario Bonetti, and Tom Keevan were leading a few other people out of the airlock.

"I see you were successful, Captain Keevan," John smiled. "Good work." He turned to face K'Alan. "Welcome home, Captain Bryce."

"Good to be back, Admiral," K'Alan smiled. "Admiral, would it be possible to go speak in your office? There's an urgent matter that I must bring up in regards to the peace conference."

"Absolutely," John nodded. "Meet me in my office in half an hour, Captain."

"Yes, sir."

* * *

Rick Bentsen

Tom Keevan fidgeted outside the door to the quarters that had been assigned to Erin Sykes. Extremely nervous about seeing her, the captain of the Creighton took a couple deep breaths and knocked on the door.

There was no response to his knock, and Tom knocked a little louder.

"Erin?" he called when his knocking still received no response.

"Oh, she's not here, Captain," a passing officer said. "Last I saw she was heading towards the White Knight."

"Thank you, Ensign," the captain said.

He wasn't sure if it was relief or dread that we was feeling.

John was sitting by his desk when K'Alan came in escorting G'Kiron and Crovax. He stood and gave K'Alan a quizzical look.

"Admiral, may I introduce two of the people responsible for my escape from Brentacchia Prison?" K'Alan said.

"By all means," John said, sitting behind his desk.

"This is Chancellor G'Kiron," K'Alan said, indicating the Brentax official. "He was the person Mario and I went to meet on Brentax III. He was instrumental in planning our mission. If it weren't for his help, we never would have succeeded. He had been arrested by the Brentax Militia. I couldn't leave him there, so I went to find him and release him. That's when I was captured."

[385]

"I tried to tell K'Alan I was fine and that he needed to take care of the mission he came to Brentax for," G'Kiron said. "But K'Alan proved to be more stubborn than many Brentax officers I've worked with. He would not leave without me. Even when he was making his escape, he refused to leave without setting me free first."

"I don't leave friends behind when I can at all help it, G'Kiron," K'Alan said. G'Kiron simply nodded. Pointing to Crovax, K'Alan continued. "This is Crovax. He has some information that I think you need to hear before the peace initiative goes any further."

"I'm not familiar with your race, sir," John said, looking Crovax over.

Crovax looked at K'Alan before answering.

"My race is called the Cor'vat," Crovax said. "You've said much the same thing that K'Alan said when he first met me. And I shall tell you the same thing I told him. It is no surprise that you have not heard of my race. The Brentax does not let much out about their slaves."

"Slaves?" John asked. "They keep slaves?"

"Yes," Crovax said, his voice subdued. "My entire race is enslaved. We are kept separated from each other so that we do not revolt. We do some of the most revolting jobs for the Brentax. Many of us are janitors and the like. I, myself, was the torturer at the Brentacchia Prison. It is a job I disliked. The Cor'vat are essentially peace loving, Admiral. When I met K'Alan, I found myself given an opportunity to not only get out of the job I despised, but also an opportunity to help my people free themselves from the oppressive rule of the Brentax Empire. I come to you now asking you to help my people by requesting that the Brentax Empire free all of their slaves."

"This is not news that can be taken lightly," John said gravely. "Crovax, I would ask that you come to the next session of the peace conference. I would like you to tell your story to all present."

"I would be glad to, Admiral," Crovax nodded. "And thank you for taking me seriously."

"You've already proven yourself to us, Crovax," John smiled. "What you did for Captain Bryce will be remembered by many of us."

"That was what the officers on the Creighton told me," Crovax smiled.

2.13.2136
1248
SLS White Knight
The Bridge

Commander Erin Sykes was sitting at the commanding officer's station. The bridge was nearly deserted and she found herself enjoying the peace and quiet that came with the light duty crews.

She'd been thinking about Tom Keevan's proposal of late. She hadn't decided whether to say yes or no. She tried the ring on, and felt a little weird having it on without making a decision, so she had taken it off again.

It did look good though, she thought to herself. She shook her head. *Not something I'm going to decide quickly.*

"So, can I have my station back?" a voice from behind her asked.

Erin, startled, stood and turned.

"K'Alan!" she shouted and ran over to him. When she got to him, she wound up and slugged him on the arm.

"Ow! What was that for?"

"That was for making me worry about you,' she snapped. "And for leaving me with that damn chair for so long!'"

2.13.2136
1330
Gamma Epsilon Station
Main Conference Room

Admiral Bonetti took his seat just as Thorrin Jade stepped to the table.

"This peace conference will now resume," Thorrin said. "We will discuss the Khrinnus system now."

"The Star League cedes the Khrinnus system," President Jameson said. "The Brenteax Empire was kind enough to pay reparations in excess of what we asked for in relation to the Duterius Prime tragedy. We feel it only proper. I have already sent orders to the Atlantia that was patrolling the Khrinnus system. They have pulled out and should arrive at this station sometime in the next couple of hours."

"Well, that is settled then. Is there any other business with regards to the peace treaty?" Thorrin asked.

"Yes," John said quietly. "There is someone waiting outside the conference room who wishes to address the assembly."

"Have the person brought in then," Thorrin nodded.

"Send them in," John said into his wristlink.

The door to the conference room opened and K'Alan walked in leading Crovax and G'Kiron. Upon seeing Crovax, M'Bek Tarmos shot to his feet and started to protest, but was cut off by Thorrin Jade.

"Captain Bryce, it is good to see you again," Thorrin said.

"And it is good to see you, Ambassador," K'Alan bowed. He indicated Crovax. "This man saved my life. His name is Crovax, and he wishes to speak. What he has to say I think you all should hear. I hope it affects you the same way it affected me."

"You have the floor, Crovax," Thorrin Jade said. "You may speak your piece."

Crovax stood and bowed to Thorrin Jade.

"Thank you," Crovax hissed. "I have heard much about the Star League from K'Alan Bryce. It is because of him that I am here. K'Alan faced the possibility of torture at my hands, and yet he reached out with his heart and agreed to help me in return for his release.

"He told me that he would bring me here and I could tell my story to the people that may be able to change things.

"My race, the Cor'vat, are one of several races that the Brentax holds as slaves."

"Lies!" M'Bek Tarmos shouted. "He lies. We have no slaves."

"Oh?" Crovax said. "Well then, tell me this, Commander. Where is my mate?" M'Bek sat down, shaking his head. "That's right. You don't want them to know that, do you? Well, I'll tell them. My mate, along with all females and children of my race, are kept apart from the men. They are kept in a place that we can't get to so that we will stay subservient."

"Is this true, M'Bek?" Thorrin asked with a look of horror. M'Bek could only nod.

"I ask you to consider making the emancipation of my people a part of your treaty," Crovax added.

"It will be done," M'Bek said weakly. "The Brentax will release all of its slaves."

"Thank you," Crovax bowed. He turned to K'Alan and smiled. "Thank you, K'Alan. Thank you for keeping your word to me that you would give me a chance to free my people."

"Is there anything—"

"Admiral, four Brentax Duhari class cruisers are on fast approach with their weapons ports open," a voice sounded over John's wristlink.

"Those idiots!" M'Bek roared. "We were on the verge of peace!"

"Captain Bryce, recall your bridge crew," John said. The Creighton and the White Knight will handle this."

"Understood," K'Alan said. He tapped his wristlink. "All White Knight bridge, engineering, fighter crews, pilots, and weapons officers are hereby immediately recalled to the White Knight. I want you all on board within fifteen minutes. This is not a drill."

[389]

The Dawning of a New Age

⟨CHAPTER / 61⟩

2.13.2136
1400
SLS White Knight
The Bridge

K'ALAN settled in his command chair and nodded to himself. He looked over the two levels of the bridge and made sure everyone was at their station and ready.

"Launch," he ordered.

He felt the floor throb as the engines started and the powerful ship undocked from the station.

"Captain, we have four Duhari class heavy cruisers on long range scanners," Masha reported.

"The Creighton has launched," Kath reported. "Captain Keevan on the line for you."

"Patch him through, audio only," K'Alan said.

"Audio only," Kath acknowledged.

"What's your plan, K'Alan?" Tom asked.

"We're gonna sandwich them, Tom. I want you to flank them one hundred eighty degrees," K'Alan said.

"I can do that," Tom acknowledged. "We'll catch them in between. Good sound tactic."

"Keep this line open, Tom. Audio only. We'll coordinate this way."

"Understood."

"When you're in position, launch all your fighters," K'Alan said. "The Brentax will likely send out theirs too. Our pilots will be badly outnumbered, but their job is to distract the fighters while we take on the base ships."

"Understood."

"Commander Sykes," K'Alan said. He turned to look at his executive officer. He knew she was going to be happy with what he was about to say. He knew a lot of other people would be happy about it as well. "You're in command of the fighter detachment. I want all fighters ready to launch in ten minutes. As of this moment, you are Gamma Strike's strike leader."

"Yes, sir," Erin nodded. She flicked a switch on her console. "All fighter pilots report to the flight bay in full flight gear immediately. We hit space in ten minutes."

Erin ran off the bridge towards the flight bay. K'Alan watched the activity on the bridge with pride.

"Tactical holo," he ordered.

Masha nodded, and the tactical holo appeared in the center area of the bridge showing the four Duhari class cruisers accelerating towards the Gamma Epsilon Station.

"Helm, keep us between those cruisers and the station," K'Alan ordered. "Masha, give me full defensive screens."

"Screens up," Masha said.

"Start targeting the lead ship, Masha. Weapons and engines, please," K'Alan said.

"You got it, K'Alan."

"How's the Creighton doing?" K'Alan asked.

"They're nearing position," Kath reported.

"Let's just hope they get there quickly."

* * *

"Barnes, Danang, bear hard right, you've got raiders on your tail," Erin barked into her ships commlink. "Jenkins, Tags, engage those raiders."

"Commander," Ensign Jennifer Harrison called from the other cockpit. "We've lost Lancers 4 and 7."

"Damn," Erin swore. "All right, guys. Everyone watch your six. We're getting pummeled. Where the hell are the Creighton's fighters?"

Erin put the Starhawk through its paces weaving in and out of the attacking fighters and taking out a number of them. More than once, she had to pull a slick maneuver to avoid being shot down herself, and she watched with frustration as some damn fine pilots bought it at the hands of the Brentax.

"Commander, this is Jenkins," a high-pitched male voice called over the comms. "One of those bastards just shot my right high engine. I can't keep a constant thrust."

"Pack it in, Jenkins. Land on the White Knight as soon as you can," Erin called while blasting a raider.

"Aye, Commander," Jenkins replied. "I'll see..."

There was a loud explosion on the line and then silence. Silently, Erin cursed as yet another promising young pilot died in battle.

"Captain, our fighters are taking heavy casualties. We've lost fifteen fighters already," Masha reported."

"Damn. Keep firing on that base ship, Masha."

The Dawning of a New Age

⟨CHAPTER / 62⟩

2.13.2136
1423
SLS Creighton
The Bridge

"CAPTAIN, we're in position," the helm officer said.

"Good. Launch all fighters," Tom ordered.

"Aye, sir," Jack said. "Fighters are launching. Captain, they're badly outnumbered."

"I know," Tom nodded. "Let's see what we can do to help them. Jack, start firing on the closest base ship. Target their weapons, engines, and fighter bays."

"Aye, sir. Proton torpedoes locked on target."

Five proton torpedoes arced from the Creighton and slammed into the closest Duhari class vessel. The torpedoes impacted on the vessel's shields.

"Sir, the White Knight has taken some damage," Jack reported.

"Nothing we can do about that, Jack," Tom said. "Just keep firing on that ship."

"Captain, there's another ship coming in fast," Jack reported.

"Can you get a read on what it is, Jack?"

"Trying, Captain," Jack said as his fingers flew across his console. "It looks like the Atlantia, sir."

"K'Alan, do you see that?"

"Yeah, Tom. Great timing for her to show up," K'Alan responded.

"This a boys' night out or can anyone join in?" Laura Goldthorne cut in on the comms channel.

"Come on in," Tom called. "We could use the extra firepower."

"I should have known that you'd be sitting here on your arse, Swamp Rat," Laura chuckled. "I'll launch all our fighters as soon as we arrive. Let's take it to them."

The battle raged on, fighters from both sides turning into clouds of ash and metal debris. When the Atlantia arrived and launched her fighters, though, the tide seemed to turn to the Star League's favor.

"They're running!" Erin called from her Starhawk. "Shall we pursue?"

"Negative," K'Alan called over the chan. "All fighters return to your respective ships. Let's pack it in and see if they can salvage the peace conference after this."

⟨CHAPTER / 63⟩

"WITH the opposition from the last vestiges of the old Brentax Empire quashed," M'Bek Tarmos began. "I would like to take this moment to welcome a new era of peace in this quadrant."

With that statement, M'Bek Tarmos signed the peace accord between the Brentax Empire and the Star League. There was great applause as President Jameson also signed the treaty.

"Captain Bryce, may Admiral Bonetti and I have a word with you?" the president asked as she walked over to where K'Alan was standing with Captain Keevan and Captain Goldthorne.

"Yes, of course, Madame President," K'Alan said, bowing slightly in respect to the president.

'You'll have a full briefing on this by the time you return to the White Knight," Admiral Bonetti began. "But we need to talk to you about it. The White Knight will be carrying the Star League Advisory Council as it was originally supposed to. We need to assign two permanent support ships to the White Knight in case of emergency."

"We'd like you to request two ships," Kerrin finished.

"Well," K'Alan thought for a second before continuing. "I can't think of two better ships than the Atlantia and the Creighton."

"Done," John nodded. They'll be reassigned within the hour. You will have full command of the fleet with a promotion to Commodore. Congratulations."

"Er, thanks. I think," K'Alan stammered.

"You've earned it," John smiled, clapping K'Alan on the shoulder. "Your rank insignia will be waiting for you in your office on the White Knight."

"Have you talked to the Duterians about who their representative will be?" K'Alan wondered aloud.

"No," John said. "But I think I can imagine who it will be."

K'Alan nodded and smiled.

"Well, I should get back to the White Knight," K'Alan said. "Tom, Laura, we're going to need to have a meeting to talk about the new assignments. But not tonight. Tonight, we have a party."

"Sounds good to me," Tom smiled.

CHAPTER 64

"COMMODORE, the President is about to speak," Kath said.

"Holo," K'Alan said as he settled into his chair. He briefly looked around the bridge, noting all his officers were where they belonged and he smiled to himself. It was good to be back on board the White Knight.

President Kerrin Jameson and Brentax Supreme Commander M'Bek Tarmos appeared in the holoprojector in the center of the bridge. They were standing next to each other, and both were smiling. President Jameson stepped forward and began to speak.

"Today, the Star League signed a peace treaty with the Brentax Empire. A copy of the treaty will be made available to all Star League citizens. This is a historic accord that will be spoken of for years to come.

[399]

"As we enter a new era of peace with our Brentax neighbors, we must look forward towards a new future. And now we know that it will be a future marked by a lasting peace in this quadrant of space.

"To this end, I announce the formation of the Star League Advisory Council. The six core races of the Star League and the Brentax Empire will all send representatives to the Star League Advisory Council. This council will meet to oversee disputes between Star League races. It is our hope that this council will prevent conflicts like the long war with the Brentax Empire that we have just ended.

"We have all faced great losses in the past several years, and we now have time to mourn. And mourn we all will. But now we also have a chance to shape a future that all of our children will grow strong in."

The smiling president took a step back and the holo faded. K'Alan flipped a switch on his chair.

"Good work all," K'Alan said over the shipcall. "It's time we all celebrated. There will be a party in Soran's Bar this evening at 2100 hours. All crew members not on duty are invited to attend."

Mario stood up and headed up to the second level of the bridge from where he'd been sitting at the damage control station.

"Kal, I'll see you at the party. There's something I need to do before I head to Soran's Bar," Mario said, a twinkle in his eye.

Without waiting for a response, Mario strode off the bridge, whistling quietly as he went.

"Commander, you have the bridge," K'Alan called to Erin. "I have a baseball game to play."

* * *

All of the tables had been cleared out of the bar, and it was festively decorated, with gold and silver decorations on all the walls. Despite the size of the room, and it was one of the largest single rooms on the ship, there were quite a few people pressed together in the bar. Crewmembers from all three ships, the White Knight, the Creighton, and the Atlantia, were all having fun celebrating the new peace with the Brentax Empire.

Soran was making the rounds and making sure everyone had the drinks they wanted. He glided over to where Masha was talking with Jack Benton.

"Masha, can I get you something to drink?" he asked, noting that Jack already had one.

"Yeah, Soran. Maybe a soda?" the security chief winked.

"A soda it is then," Soran chuckled and went to pour one. Masha turned back to Jack as the barman swept away.

"So tell me the truth. Did you really rig the torpedo launchers to do an automatic rapid fire?"

"Yes, and you should have seen Captain Bryce's face when he came on board. He was white as a sheet. You see, we were shooting at a bunch of fighters close by him at one point."

"He must have had a fit."

"Yeah," Mario said breaking into the conversation. "He told me later that if he ever found out who was shooting like that, that he would personally kick that person's arse. I didn't have the heart to tell him it was me."

"You were manning the weapons console?" Masha snorted. "I would have loved to have seen that!"

"It was great," Mario grinned. "The modified torpedoes worked perfectly."

K'Alan and K'Itea walked in. Soran swept over to them, happy to see his long-time friend and his wife.

"Captain Bryce," he smiled, then corrected himself when he saw the rank insignia on K'Alan's dress uniform. "Commodore Bryce. Welcome back. This is the first chance I've had to welcome you back. Planning for this party's been taking up much of the past couple days."

"I understand, Soran," K'Alan smiled. "And it's good to be back where I belong!"

"Yes, I'm sure it is."

Soran smiled and swept over to another group of officers that had just entered.

"You and Elam looked like you were having fun in the park tonight, K'Alan," K'Itea said.

"Yes, I think he likes baseball," K'Alan chuckled. "I think he may end up being a better pitcher than his old man."

K'Itea laughed. She looked around at all of the people in the room.

"Mario," she called. "Come over here please."

"Anything for the High Gentlewoman," the colonel smiled, bowing. S'Era was at his side, looking dazzling.

"S'Era, you look marvelous tonight," K'Alan said.

"Thank you, brother. I borrowed the dress from K'Itea," S'Era said, twirling so they could get the full effect of the dress.

"Mario, I have to ask," K'Alan said. "Where did you go when you left the bridge this evening?"

"I had to go make sure someone came to the party tonight."

"Oh? Who?" K'Alan asked, very curious.

"You'll see. Surprise for Soran."

K'Alan raised his eyebrow.

Captain Tom Keevan of the Creighton walked over at that moment.

"K'Alan, good to see you not covered in muck," Tom chuckled.

"Thanks again for coming to get me, Tom," K'Alan smiled. "Have you seen Erin yet? I think she was looking for you earlier."

"She was?" Tom swallowed. "Did she say anything to you about me?"

"No, actually, she was too busy giving me hell over going and doing something dangerous. And she punched me in the arm." He furrowed his brows. "She said something about never wanting my chair again."

"That sounds about right," Tom laughed.

"There you are, Swamp Rat," Captain Laura Goldthorne called, walking over to the small group.

"Hi, Laura," Tom blushed.

"So, Swamp Rat," Laura smiled. "Commander Sykes was looking for you earlier. She said she better see you at the party. I haven't seen her here yet."

"Er," Tom said, looking rather uncomfortable. "Do you happen to know if she was happy about wanting to see me?"

"I don't know, Swamp Rat," Laura said. "Never was able to read her well."

"Great," Tom sighed, fidgeting. "Just great."

"Something you want to share with the rest of the class, Tom?" K'Alan said, a twinkle in his eye.

"Not really, K'Alan, but I suspect you'll know soon enough anyway."

The door opened and a female Duterian that K'Alan didn't recognize walked in.

"Well, I'll be back in a bit, kiddies," Mario said. "Don't do anything I wouldn't do. And if Tom spills about what's going on, make sure you tell me later, Kal."

"Of course," K'Alan chuckled. "Whatever it is, is bound to be good gossip over our next poker game, Mario."

"Boys," S'Era groaned, rolling her eyes.

Mario gave S'Era a playful swat on the rump then headed over to the Duterian that K'Alan didn't know.

"This spot taken?" Erin asked from behind Tom.

[403]

"Er, hi," Tom said, blushing. "K'Alan and Laura said you wanted to see me?"

Erin nodded. She held up her hand and smiled. Tom let out a huge sigh of relief when he saw the ring on her finger.

"Congratulations, Swamp Rat," Laura laughed. "And it's about time, if you ask me."

"I thought she was going to say no!" Tom gasped.

"Why you—" Erin never finished the sentence as Tom leaned over and kissed her.

Soran had finished circulating and was standing at the bar, pouring a Duterian Sunmist for K'Alan when Mario stepped up to him.

"Hey, Soran," Mario said. "Got a minute?"

"Sure, Mario," Soran said as he turned. "I—"

Soran dropped the glass he was pouring the drink in.

"Hello, Soran," the Duterian woman standing next to Mario said. "It's been a long time. I see you remember me. I thought I'd never see you again."

"K'Aria?" Soran asked. "K'Aria Danare? Is it really you?"

"Yes," K'Aria smiled. "It is."

Knees shaking, Soran sat on the nearest stool. Mario left the two alone, unnoticed by the barman.

"I tried to bring you back to the ship, K'Aria. I went looking for you. I never wanted to—"

"I forgave you a long time ago, Soran," K'Aria smiled. "And I never forgot you. Colonel Bonetti remembered seeing my name amongst the survivors, and came to find me. He told me you were on board, and my heart rejoiced. I had no idea what had happened to you."

Soran was at a loss for words. Turning back to the bar, he made her a drink, a Tomarian Moondance, just the way she liked it.

"I remember making this for you a long time ago," Soran said quietly. "I've never made one since I thought I'd lost you."

The two old friends continued talking, and Mario, smiling, headed back to K'Alan.

"May I have your attention please?" K'Alan called loudly. All conversation in the bar slowly ended, and everyone looked towards the captain. "I wish to propose a toast. This crew's been through a lot in the past month, and you have all done far better than anyone could have hoped for. You are all the best crew a captain could ask for. To Gamma Strike and to peace!"

There were choruses of "Hear! Hear!" around him, and K'Alan raised his glass in salute to the crew.

His crew.

The Dawning of a New Age

EPILOGUE

THE picture in the holosphere faded and the four grey-robed figures stepped away from it. Each of them had their own thoughts about what they had seen.

The leader of the Watchers pulled back the hood on his robes and grimaced as he watched the static in the holosphere fade to nothing.

"Things have gone in an unpredictable direction," Alan said. "The way this alliance came about is completely unexpected."

"Yes," Kiara smiled. "But I believe that things have gone in a direction that can be used to our benefit."

"Time will tell, Kiara," John said. "Let us see if this alliance can stand. If it can, then perhaps…"

John trailed off as he turned from the holosphere and walked into the shadows once more.

"It is as Ugatu foresaw," Kiara's soft voice came from the shadows. "The time of the great war he spoke of is upon us."

"Not just yet," Samantha spoke for the first time in days. "Michael would know better than I, but there is much to come still before the war Ugatu spoke of comes."

[407]

The Dawning of a New Age

"This alliance indeed has many challenges yet to face together," Alan nodded. *He took Samantha by the arm and led her out of the Central Chamber.*

"The time is upon us," Kiara repeated to the empty chamber. *"Preparations need to be made."*

With that, Kiara, too, left the Central Chamber, heading off to start her own preparations for what was to come.

To be continued...

Join the crew of Gamma Strike for their next exciting adventure....

THE WINDS OF CHANGE

Coming soon from Steel Drake Press

THE WEDDING

The Wedding

THE WEDDING

A Gamma Strike Short Story

ARE we online?" Kiara asked quietly as she entered the imaging chamber.

"Not yet," Martin sighed. "The damn holoprojector is on the fritz again."

"Can it be repaired?" she asked. "Events are about to take place that we must bear witness to."

"I'm doing my best, Commander Westlake," Martin sighed. "This whole system needs to be rebuilt eventually."

"Do what you can, Chief," Kiara nodded. "Let me know the moment the holomatrix has been established."

"Yes, Commander," Martin said, turning back to the control panel.

"Don't you think you were a little hard on him, Kiara?" Samantha asked from behind her. "The poor man's doing the best he can under the circumstances. I don't think even Alan understands all the modifications that have been made to the holoprojector, and he designed it originally."

"That may be, Sam," Kiara sighed, "But I believe we are missing events surrounding the one we have been searching for."

[411]

"Yelling at Martin won't change that," Sam smiled. "Besides. Why are you so sure we're about to find the one we've been searching for? We've been searching for over a hundred years so far."

"Call it an instinct," Kiara chuckled. "You used to trust my instincts, once upon a time."

"Only because Alan did," Samantha reminded the other woman. "I would have thrown you out had he not."

"I've never been your enemy, Samantha," Kiara said softly.

"You've never been my friend either."

"That may be, but when have I ever given you reason to mistrust me?"

"Some questions are better left unanswered," Samantha said as she laid her hand on Kiara's shoulder. "This is one of those questions. Now go. Get the others. We shall watch this together."

"Yes, Captain," Kiara said sharply, snapping off a sharp salute before turning on her heel and leaving the imaging chamber, her grey robes rustling as she moves quickly.

"You were hard on her, Sam," Alan said quietly as he put his arms around her. "She is one of us."

"I don't trust her, my love," Sam said quietly. "And I never have."

"I know," Alan nodded. "I'm not really saying you should, but at least try to be nicer to her."

"I will try, my love. For you and for the cause," Samantha nodded. "But I still don't trust her."

"I can live with that," Alan smiled at her. "Now. Let's see what Martin has come up with, shall we?"

The two walked over to where Martin was lying with his head and shoulders buried deep in the panel housing the holoprojector controls.

"Before you two ask, I've just about got this thing fixed," Martin called from inside the panel.

"Good," Alan nodded. "Let us know when it is fixed, Martin."

"I will," Martin grunted. "It'll go a lot quicker if everyone doesn't keep asking me how it's going."

"Point taken," Alan chuckled.

Kiara walked into the imaging room just then, leading the eight other Watchers. Sam and Alan walked over to the rest of the group.

'It's just about time, my friends," Alan said, indicating with a wave the twelve lighted spots around the holosphere.

Each of the twelve, minus Martin who was still working on the holoprojector, took their usual spot, waiting impassively in their grey robes.

"I have it," Martin called from inside the panel. "You should be seeing haze right now, but the picture will clear in a couple of seconds.

The picture indeed began to clear as Martin took his own spot around the holosphere. As the haze cleared, a picture began to focus within the holosphere.

5.26.2125
0855
Duterius Prime
Braga Valley Great Hall

K'Itea Bryce sat on her throne in the Great Hall of Braga Valley. It was the first thing in the morning, and she was waiting for her daily dose of supplicants to begin arriving. She loved what she did, and she loved helping people, but sometimes she really hated dealing with the trivialities that were brought before her.

As the morning supplicants were shown in, K'Itea looked them over. Many of them she knew, others would be appearing before her before her for the first time.

But it was one of the new supplicants that caught her attention. He was a tall Duterian male with long black hair and piercing blue eyes. He had chiseled features and he appeared to be quite muscular. He wore the uniform of the Braga Valley militia, wearing the rank of Lieutenant. But what caught her attention the most was the fact that,

[413]

unlike the other supplicants, he was not bowing in her presence. Instead, he was gazing straight at her, an almost perceptible sneer on his features.

"J'Anai, bring the first supplicant before me," K'Itea said in a soft voice to her aide.

The old man nodded and walked towards the supplicants. He scanned the group, and his eyes locked with the strange military officer. Furrowing his brow, J'Anai headed over to the stranger and the two exchanged some whispers.

J'Anai turned on his heel and headed back to where K'Itea was sitting.

"I do not trust that man," he whispered to her. "I suggest you deal with his supplication first and get it over with quickly so that he can leave quickly."

"As in all things, J'Anai," K'Itea whispered with a touch of amusement. "I trust your judgment. Send him forward."

"Very well, Gentlewoman." J'Anai stood, and his voice boomed out. "The Gentlewoman will now hear your supplications. K'Orin Thamur, please step forward and present your petition."

The strange lieutenant strode forward with measured strides. He stood at attention before K'Itea and took a small breath before beginning.

"I thank the Gentlewoman for agreeing to hear my petition," he began. K'Itea nodded, waving him on. "I understand that the Gentlewoman is to be married in short order. I submit that she has the wrong groom picked, however, and I humbly submit myself for consideration for her husband." He dropped to one knee as he said this, and his petition brought gasps from the assorted petitioners.

"You know not of my intended, Lieutenant Thamur," K'Itea said quietly after the commotion died down. "I do not think that you would believe the bonding to be wrong if you did."

"I know that he does not stay on Duterius as he should," K'Orin shot back. "Nor does he stay to honor his

Gentlewoman and his intended as he rightfully should. I would do this."

"It is immaterial whether you would or not," K'Itea said, her voice firm. "The match has the blessings of the gods. It cannot be undone."

"Even so, it shall be," K'Orin growled, his voice dropping in volume to barely above a whisper. "One way or the other, this wedding will not proceed unless I am the groom."

"I think not," K'Itea smiled. "Your petition is denied, Lieutenant. The guards will show you out."

As if on cue, two burly members of the royal guard appeared on either side of the lieutenant and took him by the elbows.

"This is not over," he shouted as he was escorted out of the Great Hall. "You will be mine, Gentlewoman. One way or the other, you will be mine."

K'Itea watched him all the way out as he was thrown out of the Great Hall.

She stood and motioned for all the supplicants to come forward.

"I will listen to all of your supplications today, my people," she began, spreading her hands. "However, I must ask for a few minutes to myself after that first supplicant. The guards will show you to waiting rooms. I promise to hear every one of you before I leave the Great Hall today, though."

The people nodded in understanding and began to file out to the appropriate waiting rooms. She turned to J'Anai, and the old man stepped forward.

"Has there been any word from K'Alan, J'Anai?" she asked.

"No, K'Itea, there has not," J'Anai said in a pained voice. "The Quintanilla is currently engaged in battle and has been off and on for the past two weeks, and the ship is on communications blackout. I have been able to confirm for you that, as of this morning, he is still quite alive though."

"I hope he does make it, J'Anai. I do not wish any more events such as this morning's petition."

"I understand. If you wish, I will have Lieutenant Thamur barred from the Great Hall."

"Please, J'Anai. And have him watched," K'Itea sighed as she sat back in her throne. "I do not believe we've heard the last of him."

"Neither do I, my lady."

5.30.2125
1047
SLS Quintanilla
Captain Starlos's Office

Captain Thane Starlos had had a long day. Commodore John Bonetti had been riding all of the ships in the attack wing pretty hard the last few weeks, and Thane had not had a chance to do all his paperwork and performance evaluations.

But now, there was a lull in the action, and Thane was taking this opportunity to catch up with his paperwork. Not a task he overly relished, but it needed to be done nonetheless.

So when there was a knock on his office door, Thane sighed a sigh of great relief.

"Come in," he called.

Ensign K'Alan Ilan Bryce walked into Thane's office slowly, a bit hesitant with making the request he had to make.

"Captain, I was wondering if I could have a moment of your time?" the young ensign asked.

"You can have as long as you want, K'Alan," Thane chuckled. He motioned for K'Alan to take a seat in the chair across from his desk. "I'd much rather talk to you than do these reports."

"I can understand that," K'Alan nodded as he took the offered seat. "Commander Westphalen has been shuffling a lot of her paperwork on me of late."

"I hope that's not a criticism of the Commander, Ensign," Thane sounded amused. "I'm not sure how that would be taken." It was a joke, and both men knew it.

"I would never think of criticizing a superior officer, sir!" K'Alan barked in mock seriousness.

"I would hope not!" Thane laughed. "Now, what can I do for you, Ensign? You obviously came here for something more than making me laugh."

"Sir, I need to ask for a small furlough," K'Alan said. "I have some personal matters to attend to on my home world."

"Business on Duterius Prime?" Thane leaned back in his chair, resting his hands on his stomach. "And what, pray tell, is so important on Duterius Prime that it is taking one of my brightest and most promising crew members away from my ship?"

"It's..." K'Alan started and trailed off, starting to fidget nervously.

"It's what, Ensign?" The captain looked his pilot over with an upraised eyebrow.

"It's her," K'Alan said quietly as he slid a datapad with a woman's picture on it. "I'm to marry her in a little over a week. With how busy we've been lately, I was afraid I would miss my sealing ceremony, but with things so quiet at the moment, I really would like to go."

Thane took the datapad and looked K'Alan's intended over. His other eyebrow raised in appreciation. "She's beautiful, Ensign," Thane said.

"Yes, she is," K'Alan said, a broad smile crossing his face.

"I don't see how I can say no to your request, K'Alan. I would not want to make such a woman angry with me," Thane returned the smile. "There is a condition attached to it though."

"A... condition, Captain?" It was K'Alan's turn to quirk an eyebrow.

"You and the other Duterians I've served with have always spoken of the great beauty of your home world. I

[417]

The Wedding

would like to see it. The Quintanilla will take you to your
home world. And I will go down to the planet with you."

"Thank you, Captain," K'Alan smiled. "I'd be honored to
have you along."

6.2.2125
0849
Duterius Prime
An Antechamber in the Braga Valley Capitol Building

The two Star League officers fidgeted in the
antechamber waiting. K'Alan held his flight helmet in his
hands, turning it over and over again.

"You know if you wear that, you'll have a bad case of
helmet hair when you get to see her, K'Alan," Thane
chuckled.

"You are no help, Thane," K'Alan grumbled. He could
not stay angry at his friend for long, though.

"Can I help you two gentleman?" a voice from behind
them called. "I assume you are here for an audience with
Gentlewoman Bilso?"

"I know that voice," K'Alan said without turning. "I
know that voice very well."

"And I know that voice," the voice continued. "It
belongs to a young upstart that had to go and join the Star
League Defense Force, leaving the Gentlewoman a very
lonely person. How inconsiderate of him to do so."

"J'Anai Sirrus," K'Alan said as he turned and gave his
old mentor a hug. "It is good to see you again."

"And it is good to see you too, K'Alan Bryce," the old
man smiled a warm smile. "I am pleased that you were able
to come for your sealing with Gentlewoman Bilso. She was
afraid that with the war you would not be able to make it."

"I wasn't sure until recently that I'd be here, J'Anai,"
K'Alan sighed. "This war has been rough. But I'm here,
and I can't wait to see Kit."

"You will find that she's only gotten more beautiful than
the last time you were here," J'Anai said.

[418]

"I find that hard to believe, J'Anai," K'Alan chuckled as he placed his flight helmet back on his head.. "I find it hard to believe that she could ever be more beautiful than I've ever seen her, as she's the most beautiful woman I've ever seen."

"Do you intend to wear that helmet in the Gentlewoman's presence, K'Alan?" J'Anai asked, looking slightly shocked. "You are aware of the level of offense she will take."

"I think she'll forgive me," K'Alan smiled. "I just want to surprise her."

"Oh, she will be surprised, all right," J'Anai laughed. "She has no idea whether you are coming or not. I will go announce that two Star League officers wish an audience."

With that, he bowed and headed into the Great Hall.

6.2.2125
0853
Duterius Prime
Braga Valley Great Hall

The Great Hall of Braga Valley was full of light from the large windows overlooking the gardens. The newly ascended Gentlewoman, K'Itea Alana Bilso, sat on the throne with a bored expression on her face.

"Your Excellency, there are two representatives from the Star League Defense Force here to see you," J'Anai Sirrus said as he entered the main chamber.

"Show them in, J'Anai," she whispered.

"At once, Excellency," he bowed and left.

Moments later, he returned leading two men in uniform. One was wearing a flight helmet, the other, a man wearing the rank insignia of Captain, was not.

"Ensign, I must ask you to remove your flight helmet," K'Itea said. "It is a measure of disrespect for the court to hide one's face in my presence."

"I'm sorry, Kit," K'Alan said as he removed his helmet. "I did not mean to offend. I did mean to surprise you though."

"Kal!" she shrieked as she bolted across the room into his arms. "It's so good to see you!"

"K'Itea Bilso, may I introduce Captain Thane Starlos, my commanding officer. He refused to let me take leave unless he came with me."

"I've always wanted to see Duterius Prime," the captain bowed. "I've heard time and again of its endless beauty, and I've wanted to see for myself if what I have heard is true."

"And what do you think, Captain?" K'Itea asked, a light smile playing across her face.

"I think that what certain people have told me about how beautiful this planet is can't come close to the reality of its beauty," Starlos smiled. "It rivals my home planet of Earth as the most beautiful planet I've seen."

"Well, I'm glad you approve," K'Itea smiled. "There is a dinner tonight. I would like you to join us. As a guest of K'Alan, you will be accorded the utmost respect."

"I understand that you two are to be married," Starlos said. "I wish you both the best."

"You are, of course, welcome to attend the wedding," K'Itea smiled. "A friend of K'Alan's is a friend of mine."

"Thank you, good lady. I am honored."

"I think I will take the rest of the day off. J'Anai, see that Captain Starlos is given the best accommodations available. When they have settled in, I think we four shall go on a picnic."

"Would the Gentlewoman allow me the honor of a kiss?" K'Alan said formally, trying hard not to grin.

"Would the Ensign like a boot in the butt for being so formal with me?" K'Itea grinned.

K'Alan smiled and took Kit in his arms. He held her tight and kissed her gently.

"I've missed you so much, Kit," he whispered.

[420]

"And I've missed you. Now go get settled. I want to go on a picnic!"

6.2.2125
1127
Duterius Prime
K'Alan Bryce's quarters

The quarters that K'Alan had been assigned to during his stay on Duterius Prime were quite spacious, far larger than he was used to from being in the Star League. As far as he could tell, the closet was bigger than his entire allotted space, storage and sleeping, on the Quintanilla.

He dropped his rucksack on the bed and went over to the window. He gazed out over the city he grew up in, sighing contentedly.

"I forgot how much I loved this city," he said quietly. "It's amazing how something as simple as the beauty of one's home can make you feel."

"Perhaps you should be home more often then," a male voice from behind him sneered. "If you had been, then perhaps things might have gone differently than they are about to."

K'Alan whirled around to find himself looking at a lieutenant in the Duterian militia. But what caught his eye immediately was the laser being held in the man's right hand. K'Alan cursed himself for packing his energy bow instead of carrying it on his belt, but people don't generally walk into the Great Hall armed.

Besides. How many Star League Defense Force ensigns actually carry such a weapon? It would have been a dead giveaway.

"Who are you?" K'Alan asked to buy himself a little time. "And what do you want?"

"My name is K'Orin Thamur," the lieutenant sneered. "And what do I want? That's simple. I want you out of the way so that I can have your intended for my own. You should not have come back."

"Well, that's interesting, Mr. Thamur," K'Alan said, slowly edging himself towards the bed. "Because I want much the same thing. I want you to go away so I can enjoy the time I'm about to spend with my intended. She's not for you to take from me."

"And that's where you're wrong," K'Orin snarled. "She is mine. And you will not stand in my way."

K'Alan noticed the lieutenant's trigger finger twitch, and tried to jump out of the way, but the other man's aim was true, and K'Alan fell unconscious.

6.2.2125
1227
Duterius Prime
An open field outside the Braga Valley Capitol

Thane Starlos and K'Itea Bryce were out in the fields surrounding the Great Hall, a blanket spread out on the ground, and sweet smelling foods lay out on the blanket.

"It's not like Kal to be late," K'Itea frowned.

"Especially considering how much he's been looking forward to coming to see you," Thane nodded. "He talked of you often on the way here, my lady. He loves you, you know."

"Yes, I know. We have loved each other a long time, Captain Starlos," K'Itea smiled. "Even before we were promised to each other, I think."

"Your marriage was arranged?" Thane asked, his eyebrow quirking upwards.

"Most members of our caste have their marriages arranged, yes," she nodded. "We were fortunate that our parents agreed to promise us to each other. I have loved Kal since I was five years old. And I truly believe he has loved me since then too."

"Judging by the way he talks about you, I think I can believe that," Thane chuckled. "I've never heard anyone talk about the person they love in quite such glowing terms."

K'Itea chuckled then looked at her chrono and frowned.

"I'm starting to get worried, Captain Starlos," she said. "This is very much unlike Kal."

"I agree," Thane nodded. He tapped the contact on his wristlink. "Captain Starlos to Ensign Bryce, come in please."

Static was all that answered the Captain's call. K'Itea and Thane both frowned.

"Maybe he doesn't have it with him?" she asked, a hopeful note in her voice.

"Star League regulations during wartime specifically state that all officers must wear their wristlinks at all times, even when on shore leave," he smiled sadly at K'Itea. "I'm afraid he'll even have to wear it during your wedding."

"I expected as much," she nodded. She looked at her chrono again. "I think we should return to the Great Hall, Captain Starlos. Perhaps we can discover what happened to Kal there."

"I agree," the captain nodded.

6.2.2125
1239
Duterius Prime
A warehouse

K'Alan slowly woke up with a groan. His chest hurt from where he was hit with the stun blast. Looking around, he noticed that he was chained by his wrists to a wall, his ankles unbound, in what appeared to be a large and empty warehouse. Out of the corner of his eye, he saw movement, and he moved his head to the side enough to see that it was Lieutenant Thamur heading towards him.

"You're awake," the lieutenant said. "No matter. There's nothing you can do to stop what's happening. At least not chained up like the dog you are."

"Why do you hate me like this?" K'Alan asked. "Is it just because Kit loves me and not you?"

[423]

"That's exactly it," K'Orin sneered. "Why should she love a popinjay like you when she could have a real military officer like me?"

"In case you hadn't noticed, the Star League Defense Force is fighting a war," K'Alan growled. "It is a war that I happen to be right in the middle of. And I put my life on the line every second of every day. And what does the Duterian militia do? March around on maneuvers, playing at being soldiers. I think I'm the real soldier, Lieutenant." The last word was laced with sarcasm and disdain.

"This war you speak of does not affect us here," K'Orin said. "Why should I care about it?"

"The Brentax want to conquer and enslave all of the Star League," K'Alan snarled, testing his chains. "Last time I checked, that includes Duterius Prime. That is, unless I missed a memo. But then, I think Kit would have let me know of such a change."

His last comment had the desired affect. K'Orin charged at the supposedly helpless K'Alan. At the last second, K'Alan brought his legs up, kicking hard at K'Orin's stomach, doubling the other man over. He kicked at K'Orin's head, knocking him over on his backside.

"You can hang there and rot for all I care," K'Orin roared after he caught his breath. "K'Itea is mine now. And nothing you can do will stop that from happening."

K'Orin stood on shaky legs, and he ran out of the warehouse. K'Alan watched him go then closed his eyes, concentrating on the bond that he shared with K'Itea. He focused all of his energy to opening a mental connection with her.

Kit, he sent. *Kit, we're both in trouble.*

* * *

"No, Gentlewoman, we've not seen him," the guard she was talking to said. "We've not seen him at all since we dropped him off at his quarters."

"I understand," K'Itea nodded. "Thank you, guards. If you see him, please send him to me."

"Of course, Gentlewoman," the guard bowed. "By your leave."

"Go," she nodded. She turned to J'Anai and Thane before continuing. "No one has seen him."

"Unfortunately, that about sums up our results as well," Thane grimaced. "It's like he just vanished off the face of the planet."

Kit, K'Itea heard in her head just then. *Kit, we're both in trouble.*

"Kal?" she asked aloud, eliciting odd looks from both J'Anai and Thane. She turned to J'Anai. "Is it possible that Kal could send thoughts to me before the bonding takes place?"

"Theoretically, if the match is pure and true, it is possible, but it's relatively unheard of," J'Anai nodded. "Why?"

"I think he just did," she said, her voice shaky.

"Close your eyes and concentrate on the bond you two share," J'Anai instructed. "Picture him in your mind, then simply think your reply. If, in fact, he is able to send thoughts, then you will be able to as well."

"I'll try," K'Itea nodded. She closed her eyes and focused on K'Alan and her love for him. *Kal?* she thought back. *Is that you?*

Yes, he replied. *I'm not sure how long I'll be able to keep this up, but I needed to tell you we're in trouble. K'Orin Thamur is responsible for my not making it to the picnic. He was waiting in my quarters, and stunned me. I'm in some*

[425]

kind of warehouse chained to a wall. I don't know where I'm located, but Captain Starlos should be able to provide you with a location using the Quintanilla's scanners.

Are you sure it was K'Orin Thamur? K'Itea sent. If so, I know what he wants. He wants me, and will stop at nothing, or so he said, to get me.

That is the name he gave me, K'Alan sent back. Personally, I don't like him. Stay with Captain Starlos and J'Anai, Kit. And get a group of guards together and meet me wherever I am. Also, please get my energy bow from my rucksack. I wish I'd had the presence of forethought to wear it instead of packing it.

We'll be there as soon as we can, Kal, K'Itea sent, a smile on her face. I'm just glad you're all right.

I'm glad you're all right too, Kit, K'Alan sent back. I'll do whatever I can to make sure K'Orin Thamur doesn't bother you again. Count on it.

"He's all right," K'Itea said. "Captain Starlos, would the Quintanilla's scanners be able to pinpoint his location?"

"We should be able to," Thane nodded. "All Star League officers have a subcutaneous location transponder on their person somewhere for just this instance. I should have thought of it sooner, honestly. I'll have them scan the area right away and get a location."

"Thank you, Captain," K'Itea smiled.

6.2.2125
1455
Duterius Prime
A warehouse

K'Alan was alert when he noticed movement at the far end of the warehouse. A large group of people headed towards him, the unmistakably recognizable forms of K'Itea Bilso and Thane Starlos leading the group. A broad smile spread across his face when he saw them.

"And here comes the cavalry!" he called.

[426]

K'Itea came running across the warehouse and wrapped her arms around him. She kissed him tenderly as Thane picked the locks on the manacles that were holding his wrists fast.

"I was worried about you," she said.

"I was worried about me too," K'Alan quipped. "But it's all right. I'm all right. You're all right. And K'Orin Thamur is about to find out what it's like to be on my bad side."

"Here's your energy bow, Kal," K'Itea said as she pressed the small black box into his hand.

"So," K'Alan grinned as he checked the charge on his energy bow. He slammed the extra cartridges onto his belt. "Who wants to go hunting with me?"

6.2.2125
1927
Duterius Prime
A dead end alley

K'Orin Thamur was cornered, and he knew it. He didn't know how the Star League officer had gotten free, but it was obvious to K'Orin that that was who was chasing him. And what was worse, was that the Star League officer had managed to corner him. K'Orin didn't like this turn of events. No, he didn't like this at all.

"K'Orin Thamur," called the voice of that damned officer. "You are surrounded. There is no escape. Come out and no harm will come to you. You will have to atone for your actions, but you will be afforded every courtesy."

"And if I don't come out?" K'Orin shouted back.

"Then we will come in and get you," K'Alan shot back. "And we've been authorized by the Gentlewoman of the Braga Valley province to use whatever force is necessary to bring you out. You will come out willingly, or we will be forced to open fire."

"Fat chance," K'Orin yelled. "I still haven't gotten what I wanted. I can't lose now."

"You're not going to get what you want either," K'Alan shouted. "What K'Itea and I have is a true bond. That's something you could never offer her."

"She will still come to love me in time, once I've removed you," K'Orin snorted.

The only response was a lance of energy from an energy bow that slammed into the wall just over K'Orin's head.

"That was a warning shot, K'Orin," K'Alan called. "We will give you five minutes before we come in. I don't think you can take all of us out before you are taken down."

"We'll see," K'Orin sneered. "We'll see just how good you really are, soldier boy. And your little trinket there doesn't really frighten me. I've never really understood the fascination some hold with the energy bow. I think it's overrated, personally."

In response, a bolt from the energy bow slammed into the wall. The bolt exploded against the wall, creating a good sized hole in the wall, and sending chips of stone and brick everywhere. K'Orin paled slightly as he looked at the damage the bolt had done.

"That wasn't even the highest setting, K'Orin," K'Alan admonished. "Imagine what that would do to your head though."

"I'm still not impressed," K'Orin snickered. "Besides. How would your precious K'Itea feel about you killing someone in cold blood?"

"She probably wouldn't like it," K'Alan said. "But she'll forgive me for it if it comes to that. Personally, I'd rather take you back alive to face a trial."

"I'm sure you would," K'Orin said dryly.

"Your time's up, K'Orin," K'Alan called. "Are you coming out or not?"

"I'm thinking.... Not," K'Orin announced as he fired out towards the area where K'Alan was talking. He could tell by the sounds outside that he'd missed everybody.

A squadron of royal guards, led by K'Alan, headed into the alley, lining up shots as the picked places of cover. K'Orin shot at some of the guards, felling several of them.

[428]

Rick Bentsen

While K'Orin was firing at the guards, K'Alan lined up a shot with his energy bow.

"Drop the laser, K'Orin. It's over," K'Alan called.

"Not yet it isn't," K'Orin bellowed as he brought his laser to bear on K'Alan.

It would have taken a very fast draw to line up and take a shot when his opponent already had a bead on him. K'Orin wasn't nearly fast enough though, and K'Alan fired his energy bow long before K'Orin had a shot on K'Alan lined up. The bolt hit K'Orin square in the chest, and the lieutenant was dead before he hit the ground.

Swearing to himself, K'Alan stood and headed back towards the street where K'Itea was waiting with J'Anai and Thane.

"I'm sorry, Kit," K'Alan sighed. "I was forced to fire on K'Orin. He's dead."

"That's all right, Kal," K'Itea said softly, touching his cheek. "You gave him every opportunity. I saw the whole thing. I'm just glad that it's over."

"Yes," K'Alan nodded, smiling slightly. "It's over. Let's go back to the Great Hall and get ready to finally go on that picnic."

6.4.2125
1258
Duterius Prime
Braga Valley Great Hall

The Great Hall was decorated with all manners of colors and banners. Crowds of well wishers lined both sides of the main aisle and smiled as the two officers walked down the aisle in full dress uniform.

"I've never been to a Duterian wedding before," Captain Starlos noted.

"They're not too much different from an Earth wedding. Well, there are some minor differences, of course. But it's not too different."

"Fair enough."

The two officers stood before the priest. The priest wore long, elegant white robes. He was very plain, his pale skin almost as white as his robes.

"Which one of you is the intended?" he intoned.

"I have that honor," K'Alan said boldly.

"Have you proven yourself?" the priest asked.

"I have walked through fire and flood. I have breathed where no air exists. Through it all, my love remains. I have conquered great giants. I have helped the simple lion. Through it all, my love remains," K'Alan recited the words, a feeling of calmness and peace flowing through him.

"Then walk where there is light, my child. Take comfort in the one you shall share your life with. Become one with her."

"This I would gladly do," K'Alan bowed.

"I see. Where is this man's betrothed?"

"I am here," K'Itea called from the end of the aisle.

K'Alan turned slightly so that he could see K'Itea. He bit his cheeks to keep from dropping his jaw in awe. As beautiful as he had always found her, K'Alan had never seen her looking so beautiful as she was this day. Her golden ringlets of hair were swept back and held in place by a circlet of gold. Inset in the center of the circlet was a dazzling green gemstone, the same shade of green as her eyes. It was a haunting effect that gave her the appearance of having a third eye.

With the way they had spoken to each other with their minds, the idea of K'Itea having a third eye was even more intriguing. *In a way,* he mused. *That is what the bonding is truly about. It gives each of us that innate sense of the other.*

"And has he proven himself to you?"

"He has won my heart with kind words and with fierce battles. He has roped the moon for my chariot and the stars for my steeds. He has built my castle and torn down the mountains that upset my view."

"Then join him here and take comfort in he whom you shall share your life with."

K'Itea walked down the aisle and stood next to K'Alan. She did not look at him. She looked straight at the priest and stood straight, her hands clasped in front of her.

"These two come before the gods of Duterius to be bonded for life and beyond. They have proven their worth to each other and to the gods. They are about to embark on a journey that only they can go on. Should anyone disapprove of this bonding, speak now or forever hold your peace." The priest waited a few minutes before continuing. "K'Alan Ilan Bryce, will you honor and protect this woman? Will you walk through fire for her? Will you walk through darkness for her? Will you stay with her through all time?"

"I will," K'Alan said, looking at the woman he loved.

"K'Itea Alana Bilso, will you honor and obey this man? Will you follow him though fire? Will you follow him through darkness? Will you stay with him through all time?"

"I will," K'Itea smiled at the man she was bonded to already.

"Take each other's hand." He waited until they had complied. He took a blue and red scarf from the altar and began to slowly bind their hands together

"Through all time, these two shall be bonded. They shall be able to feel each other across the vastnesses of space and time. They shall be together for all time. This is witnessed by the gods. Let their love be a beacon for all Duterians for years to come. This ceremony is concluded. Go in peace."

The priest turned around and walked out. K'Alan and K'Itea started towards their quarters.

* * *

K'Itea lay snuggled up next to K'Alan, her head on his chest. She sighed a contented little sigh and looked up at K'Alan.

"Thank you for being able to be here, my love," she said. "I really didn't want to wait for this moment."

"Neither did I, Kit," K'Alan chuckled. "And this night was definitely worth the wait."

"I'm glad you agree," K'Itea chuckled as she snuggled closer. She gently ran her fingers over his chest. "You have no idea how happy I am at the moment."

"Probably no happier than I am," K'Alan smiled at her. Just at that precise moment, his wristlink beeped from the small table beside the bed, eliciting a groan from K'Alan. "Why couldn't I have disobeyed orders and left the damn thing on the ship?" he muttered.

"They certainly seem to know when it's the worst time to use it," K'Itea sighed. The wristlink continued to beep insistently. "You better answer them, Kal. I don't think they're going to go away whoever they are."

"Ensign Bryce, go," he sighed as he tapped the contact on the wristlink. "And this really had better be important. I'm on vacation."

"I'm sorry, Ensign," Thane Starlos said on the wristlink. "I really hate to do this to you, but I'm afraid I need to recall you to active duty. The fleet was just recalled. You need to be back on board as soon as possible."

"I don't suppose you could just offload my fighter and I could catch up to you?" K'Alan groaned.

"I'm afraid not, Ensign," Thane saidy. "I'm not happy about this either, K'Alan. I'd like nothing more than to give you two the time to enjoy yourselves. The best I can do is promise to get you back to Duterius Prime as soon as possible. Tell the Gentlewoman that I am sorry for taking you away from her."

"That's all right, Captain," K'Itea said. "I understand that this is the way things will be for us."

"I wish my wife was as understanding sometimes, my lady," Thane chuckled.

"Captain, how long do I have until the shuttle comes to retrieve me?" K'Alan asked.

"Most I can give you is two hours, Ensign. I hope that will be enough time to say good bye appropriately." There was a touch of amusement in the Captain's tone. "Enjoy your slight reprieve. I'll see you on deck when you arrive."

"Thank you, sir," K'Alan grinned slightly as he cut the connection. He turned to K'Itea. "It seems I still have a couple hours to spend here..."

7.7.2125
1158
Duterius Prime
Courtyard in the Braga Valley Capitol Building

It had been a month since K'Alan had left Duterius Prime after the wedding. He'd called a few times, but it didn't look good that he'd get a chance to come back home anytime soon. The Quintanilla had been hit hard in the battle that had ensued after they left Duterius, and Captain Thane Starlos had been killed. K'Alan had been devastated when he told K'Itea the news about his friend's death.

And now, K'Itea was worried about her husband. He was able to call once a week or so, so she knew he was all right, but it didn't alleviate her worry.

So she sat on this particularly sunny day watching the birds in her courtyard, silently thinking about her husband.

"You've been very quiet lately, K'Itea," S'Era Bryce said as she soundlessly walked into the courtyard behind K'Itea.

The Wedding

"I've been worried about your brother, S'Era," K'Itea responded without turning. "I hope he comes back to me safely."

"I do too, of course," S'Era said, gently placing her hands on K'Itea's shoulders. "He is my brother after all."

"I know." K'Itea turned to face S'Era before continuing. "Which makes what I'm about to ask you that much harder. I must have your word that you will not tell K'Alan what I am about to tell you unless I tell you to. He'd give up his career if he were to find out, and I can't do that to him."

"You have my word, K'Itea. You know that," S'Era nodded. "But it must be quite a secret if you're that worried about his reaction."

"I'm with child, S'Era."

"An unexpected turn of events," Kiara said as the holosphere faded to black. "A child complicates things a bit."

"It will be a son," Michael said, his eyes closed in deep meditation. "And he will not know his father. Yes, this child will complicate things, but it will also make some things easier for K'Alan."

"Is he the one we seek, Commander Roberts?" Kiara asked. "Is he the one that is spoken of in the words of Ugata?"

"It is difficult to see, Kiara," Michael intoned. "But yes, K'Alan is the one spoken of. Things have begun to be set into motion..."

To be continued...

BLITZKRIEG

Blitzkrieg

BLITZKRIEG

A Gamma Strike Short Story

6.5.2125
0815
SLS Quintanilla
Main Conference Room

K'ALAN Bryce strode into the briefing room, wondering why he was being called into the senior staff meeting. He took a seat at the far end of the table and waited patiently.

"Now that we're all here," Captain Thane Starlos grinned at K'Alan. "Let's begin. In two days, the Argus will be leading an attack wing to try to liberate the Corathi system from the Brentax. We've been assigned to the attack wing. It's important that we get this system back because of how close in proximity it is to several key systems in the Star League, including the Duterius system."

K'Alan started at the mention of his home world which he had just left. He locked eyes with his Captain as if to say that he'd do anything to keep his home world from harm.

[437]

"What kind of force are we dealing with here, Captain?" Commander Stephanie Westphalen, the second in command on the Quintanilla, asked.

"All we know is that a large body of Brentax forces is currently holding the Corathi system," Captain Starlos said softly. "We don't even know the nature of the ships holding the system. Every ship we send to do reconnaissance doesn't come back."

"This doesn't sound like a good tactical situation for our side," K'Alan pointed out. "I'm guessing that Commodore Bonetti is counting on the element of surprise?"

"Yes," the captain nodded. "But from what I gather surprise won't be easy to achieve."

"So what is our assignment in this glorious battle?" Colonel John Jameson, the ship's tactical officer asked. "Is there a specific quadrant we're supposed to be attacking?"

"Our specific battle orders will be coming in soon. For now, we just need to be prepared for anything." Captain Starlos turned to K'Alan before continuing. "You will not be going out in a fighter this time, Ensign. As part of your training, I want you on the bridge. You'll act as my second-in-command during this battle."

"Sir?" K'Alan asked, surprise evident in his voice. "Are you sure?"

"Yes, Ensign. The command staff has discussed this and it was felt that you should get the experience," Thane smiled. "Of course, you'll need a promotion to go with it. Can't have an Ensign acting as my executive officer, can I? No, I'd think you'd need to be a Lieutenant at the very least."

K'Alan wasn't sure how to react to this. Certainly it was the last thing he was expecting when he walked into the briefing room. He looked around at the rest of the officers in the room. Each one was smiling at him.

"Are you sure, sir?" K'Alan asked, trying to grasp why this was suddenly happening. "I'm not overly sure I've earned this."

"I'm quite sure. Your performance evaluations have been exemplary, and I have to take what happened on your shore leave into account."

"I'm not sure you should, sir," K'Alan frowned. "I did kill a man down there."

"Yes, but it was in the line of duty," Thane smiled. "I'd consider saving a prominent member of your government as being in the line of duty. Besides, everyone at this table is of one mind about this. Face it. You're being promoted whether you want it or not."

"Yes, sir!" K'Alan grinned. "I just hope I won't disappoint you."

"You wouldn't be getting this promotion if I thought you'd disappoint me, Lieutenant Bryce," Thane grinned. "Your main duties during the battle will be coordinating the fighter squadrons. After the briefing, coordinate with Commander Westphalen about the squadrons."

"Yes, sir," K'Alan nodded.

"If no one has anything else, then this briefing is concluded. We'll meet again when we have more concise orders regarding our involvement in the coming battle."

The other officers nodded and started to shuffle out, smiling and offering their congratulations to K'Alan as they walked out.

6.5.2125
1127
SLS Quintanilla
Captain Thane Starlos's Office

"Something on your mind, K'Alan?" Thane asked as he looked at the man standing at the opposite side of his desk. "You don't seem as happy about this promotion as I thought you'd be."

"I know you gave your answers to why you promoted me in the briefing, Captain," K'Alan started. "I just don't feel that I've earned it."

[439]

"I didn't tell you all my reasons, Kal,' Thane smiled. "There was one reason I purposefully omitted, but I'll tell you now. You have the makings of a great command officer. I want to start grooming you for that."

"Command?" K'Alan's eyebrow shot up. "Are you sure? All I really want to be is a fighter pilot."

"Power is never given to those who seek it, Kal," Thane said. "Remember that. It goes to those who have earned it."

"I think I understand," K'Alan nodded. "It's just that it's so unexpected."

"Do you really think Commander Westphalen would have been delegating so much of her paperwork to you if it weren't at my instigation for you to learn it?" Thane winked. "Thing is, Steph loves her paperwork. She didn't want to pass it off to you until I made it an order."

K'Alan chuckled.

"Somehow, I have no trouble believing that," K'Alan said, still chuckling. "My only concern is making a mistake."

"We all make mistakes, Kal. It's what we do when we make a mistake that make us the people we are," Thane said as he leaned back in his chair. "I think we'll find that, when you make mistakes, and you will, make no mistake about that, we'll find out the man you truly are."

"I wish I had your confidence, Captain," K'Alan frowned.

"That will come with time," Thane said softly. "Do you think I was this confident when I was given my first taste of command?"

"Probably not," K'Alan admitted. Then he winked. "But then we all know that was hundreds of years ago."

"I'm not even going to dignify that with a retort, Lieutenant," Captain Starlos glared. "Now, you should probably go get some sleep. Tomorrow will be a long day of preparations."

"Yes, sir!"

* * *

K'Alan frowned as he looked at the tactical display. The senior staff was discussing the fighter deployment for the battle. He brought up a specific quadrant on his personal monitor and frowned deeper.

"I'm not sure this is the best tactical configuration to use," he said. His sudden outburst silenced the rest of the senior staff. "We're leaving delta quadrant open to attack."

"We are?" Thane asked, startled at the sudden comment from K'Alan who'd been silent most of the briefing. He brought up the quadrant on his monitor and frowned as deeply as K'Alan was. "So we are. Well, that's not good. The Brentax could easily slip in and attack the Quintanilla directly. What would you suggest then?"

"If we shift the squadrons slightly like this," K'Alan said as he tapped some commands on his terminal. A new fighter configuration appeared on the main tactical display. "We'll have more complete fighter coverage on all quadrants. We'll also be able to both attack and defend with all squadrons."

"Very good, Lieutenant," Commander Westphalen nodded. "Apparently your tactics classes have been paying off."

"I'd like to think so," K'Alan grinned. "I've been learning from the best."

"But as you've just noted, even the best can make mistakes, Lieutenant," Colonel Jameson chuckled. "None of us noticed what you pointed out until you mentioned it."

"True enough," K'Alan chuckled. "Perhaps I should take that to heart."

"Perhaps you should indeed," Captain Starlos nodded. "And therein ends the unintended lesson. Now, let's get back to the business at hand. The Brentax have four

Duhari class heavy cruisers and two Kovat class light cruisers defending the system."

"That's a *lot* of firepower for one system," K'Alan noted. "Other than being a good jumping off point for attacking the Duterius system, what strategic importance does the Corathi system have?"

"Not much," Colonel Jameson said, bringing up a statistical display of the system. "There are some important mineral and metal deposits within the system, but nothing that can't be found elsewhere. The only real tactical significance of this system is the proximity to your home world, Lieutenant. I'm afraid the only conclusion that can be drawn is that the Brentax are planning on attacking Duterius Prime."

"That is the Commodore's assessment as well," Thane nodded. "And that is why it's so important for us to drive the Brentax off."

"Captain, I have a personal interest in making sure that we succeed," K'Alan said, his voice strangled with emotion.

"Yes, and I'm sure your wife will be appreciative of your very best efforts, Lieutenant," Thane grinned. "But keep your mind on the battle. Distractions can only hurt you."

"I understand,' K'Alan nodded. "The Quintanilla would have no problems with the Kovat class ships, but I'm not sure we could take out a Duhari class cruiser."

"Which is why our assignment is to take on the Kovat class cruisers," Thane said, a twinkle in his eye. "Our specific job is to take on the two Kovat cruisers and make sure they don't join in the battle amongst the larger ships."

The officers looked at each other, knowing that it would be a tough battle and knowing they'd be depending on each other immensely the next little while.

"That concludes this briefing," Thane said softly. "Lieutenant Bryce, you should go familiarize yourself with your new station."

"Yes, sir," the young Duterian nodded. He headed out towards the bridge, leaving the rest of the senior staff.

"Well?" Thane asked the rest of his staff. "How do you think he'll do?"

"He's got a gift," Stephanie Westphalen said. "You saw how he caught the flaw in the tactical deployment."

"Yes, I did," Thane nodded. "That flaw shouldn't have been there to begin with though."

"That would be my fault, Captain," Colonel Jameson sighed. "Commander Westphalen asked me to draw up tactical scenarios for the battle. I never caught the fact that we would be leaving the delta quadrant open for attack."

"Well then," Thane grinned. "We should be glad that young Lieutenant Bryce has been paying attention to your tactics classes, John."

"He's an excellent student, Thane," John nodded. "I'll be honest. With a little seasoning, he'd be an officer I'd be proud to serve under."

"I agree," Stephanie added. "He's shown all the qualities of an excellent leader. He even has the respect and loyalty of all the pilots."

"That's a good sign," Thane nodded. "I think he'll do well, also. Steph, why don't you go show him the ins and outs of his new station."

"Certainly," the dark-haired second in command nodded, smiling.

6.6.2125
1515
SLS Quintanilla
The Bridge

"And this is the tactical holo controls," Stephanie Westphalen was saying. "They work exactly like the tactical holos in fighters work, only there are two different systems. One is the main tactical holo, which the entire bridge sees. The second is the mini tactical holo for your station only. I recommend you use that second system as you coordinate the fighters in the battle as you can zoom in on specific sectors without interfering with the general working of the bridge crew."

K'Alan nodded then pointed to another bank of controls. "I recognize this. This would be a communications array so I can coordinate with each individual fighter if I need to. It looks pretty similar to my Starfire's comms array."

"It should. It's exactly the same," Westphalen grinned. "Colonel Jameson was right. You are a good student. You'll do fine. Just remember one thing. If something happens to Captain Starlos, you're to let me know immediately."

"I understand. Believe me. I don't want *his* job," K'Alan grinned.

"Who are you kidding, Kal?" Westphalen chuckled. "You don't even want *my* job."

"True enough. But just answer me one question, Commander," K'Alan said with a gleam in his eye. "Since I do have your job for now, do I get to pawn off my paperwork too?"

6.6.2125
2100
SLS Quintanilla
K'Alan Bryce's Quarters

K'Alan tried to sleep, but sleep was a hard time coming. Sighing, he stood and headed over to his desk.

"Computer, prepare to record a message for delivery to Duterius Prime," he said softly.

"Recording..." the computer announced in its feminine monotone voice.

"Kit, I don't know when you'll actually get this message. I might actually be able to talk to you first before this gets to you."

"I'm about to go into battle. And this one scares me. There's such a high price of failure on this one. If we fail, then Duterius Prime itself might be the next target.

[444]

"Normally, I have no trouble sleeping before a battle, but I can't help thinking about you and what will happen to you if I fail. If we fail, I mean.

"I fear for you and for my sister. You will be directly in the line of fire if we do not succeed. I will do everything in my power to ensure your safety. But then, you already knew that.

"I hope I can come to see you soon, but I don't know when I will be able to. I think about you all the time, and can't wait to see you again.

"I think I'm going to try to go to sleep now. I'll send this off as soon as I'm able. Computer, end recording and save."

K'Alan rubbed his eyes and headed back to bed.

6.7.2125
0900
SLS Quintanilla
The Bridge

The mood on the bridge was one of quiet desperation and apprehension when K'Alan walked onto the bridge to take what would be his station for the upcoming battle. K'Alan checked over the systems on his console before nodding to the captain that he was ready for what was to come.

"All systems ready, Captain," Colonel Jameson noted to Thane Starlos.

"Good," Thane nodded. "Kim, signal the Argus that we're ready to proceed."

"Aye, sir," the communications tech nodded and proceeded to relay the message.

"Lieutenant, signal the alert to the pilots to prepare to launch," Thane said as he turned to face K'Alan.

"Aye, sir," K'Alan nodded. He flicked a switch on his console. "All pilots report to your fighters immediately. Repeat. All pilots report to your fighters immediately. Be ready to launch on my signal."

"Response coming in from Commodore Bonetti, Captain," Kim Ericson announced.

"Holo," Thane ordered.

"Aye, sir."

"Captain Starlos," Commodore Bonetti said as he appeared on the small holopad by the Captain's chair. "Is the Quintanilla ready for your part of this battle?"

"Yes, Commodore," Thane nodded. "We're ready."

"Good," Bonetti smiled. "The Argus, Haphaestus, and Arden Lake II will head in first and start attacking the Duhari class heavy cruisers, leaving you and your fighters to take on the Kovat class light cruisers."

"Understood," Thane acknowledged. "When do we begin the battle?"

"Soon," Bonetti said. "The Haphaestus has some last minute repairs they need to finish then we'll go in. Perhaps an hour."

"Good. We'll be waiting for the launch order."

"Good," Bonetti nodded. "Commodore Bonetti out."

The bridge continued its pre-battle preparations. Bridge officers hunkered over their stations checking settings and making sure everything is in readiness.

"Nervous, Lieutenant?" Thane asked quietly.

"Shouldn't I be?" K'Alan countered. "It's a bit different being on this side of the battle instead of out there in my fighter."

"Yes, I know," Thane nodded. "I once felt the same way that you do now."

"I bet all fighter pilots that turn into command personnel feel the same way," K'Alan chuckled.

"Yes," Thane grinned. "It's that way with all fighter pilots. Every one I know that came up through the ranks of the fighter pilots felt the same way. It's normal."

"I also feel like I'm abandoning my squad mates," K'Alan sighed.

"I can understand that too," Thane nodded again. "But you're not abandoning them. You're simply with them in a different way now."

"Honestly, I'd rather be out there protecting them in my own Starfire," K'Alan chuckled.

"I'm sure," Thane winked. "Just keep your mind on your task at hand."

"I will," K'Alan said as he gently laid a picture of K'Itea on the top of his console where he could see it but it wouldn't interfere with his normal duties.

"Good," Thane nodded. "We're all counting on you, Lieutenant. As the acting XO, you're a key figure in this battle."

"I know, sir," K'Alan said, before turning back to his console and running one last system check on the station.

"Captain," Ensign Ericson announced. "Commodore Bonetti just signaled to proceed into the Corathi system."

"Acknowledged," Thane nodded. "Helm, flank speed ahead."

6.7.2125
0935
SLS Quintanilla
Alpha Launch Bay

"OK, folks, it's the real deal," Stephanie Westphalen said to the rest of the assembled pilots. "We just got the word that we're going in. Mount up and be ready to launch in five minutes!"

There were assorted cheers as the pilots grabbed their helmets and climbed into their fighters. Stephanie, chuckling softly to herself at their enthusiasm, jumped into her own cockpit and sealed herself in. She signaled to the bridge that she and the rest of her squadrons were ready to launch at a moment's notice.

"Commander Westphalen to Lieutenant Bryce," she called over her commlink. "How are things up on the bridge?"

"All things considered, ma'am, I'd rather be going out there with you," K'Alan chuckled over the comms. "This is gonna be rough on me."

[447]

"You'll get used to it. And you'll do fine, Lieutenant," Stephanie laughed.

"That seems to be the message of the day, today," K'Alan pointed out. "And while I'm glad I have all of your faith in me, I still don't want this job."

"Do you think I did the first time I was given that job, Kal?" Stephanie asked, a touch of almost motherly tenderness in her voice.

"Not really, Steph," K'Alan said. She could almost hear the smile in his voice. "But as they say, a soldier has to do what he or she is ordered to."

"This is true," Stephanie nodded. "At any rate, we're all ready to launch on your order. Remember, let me know immediately if anything happens to Captain Starlos."

"Acknowledged," K'Alan said. "Bridge out."

6.7.2125
0937
Draxus Porida
Main Bridge

On the bridge of the Draxus Porida, Commander M'Tak Jolan drummed his fingers on his chair in complete boredom. His ship was the flagship of the fleet currently in the Corathi system. It had been a very easy victory taking the Corathi system, but now the fleet's commander was bored.

If only the orders would come down to attack the Duterius system, he snarled to himself. That would indeed be a welcome change to this boredom.

"Commander," the sensor tech called. "I'm reading Star League vessels on fast approach to us."

"Well, then," the commander smiled. "Perhaps the boredom will end quickly. Hail the rest of the fleet. Prepare for an attack!"

* * *

6.7.2125
0942
SLS Quintanilla
The Bridge

"Entering the Corathi system now, Captain," the helmsman said. "Five minutes to contact with Brentax forces."

"Understood," Thane nodded then turned to Colonel Jameson. "Colonel, target the two Kovat class light cruisers. Begin with weapons, shield generators and engines."

"Yes, sir!" the Colonel barked. His fingers flew across his console and he acquired several target locks on each ship. "Targets acquired, Captain. Ready to fire on your command."

"Hold fire until the order is given, Colonel," Thane said.

"This is Commodore Bonetti to all ships in the Argus fleet," the voice of the Commodore drifted in the stillness of the bridge as he addressed the fleet on fleet wide communication. "Find and acquire your targets and commence operation. Launch all fighters and attack!"

"That's our cue, people," Thane grinned. "Colonel, start firing on those two Kovat class cruisers. Lieutenant Bryce, issue the launch order to our squadrons."

"Aye sir!" K'Alan and Colonel Jameson said in unison.

"All fighters, launch when ready," K'Alan said as he flicked a switch on his console. "Prepare to engage enemy fighters when they launch from the Brentax vessels."

They could all feel slight shudders as all of the fighters on the ship rocketed down the launch tubes into the coldness of space.

"Fighters away, Captain," K'Alan announced.

"Good," Thane nodded. "Colonel Jameson, concentrate your fire on the right hand Kovat class cruiser. Target engines only."

"Aye, sir," Jameson said, nodding slightly. "All weapons firing now."

[449]

"Now, let's see what damage we can do," Thane grinned.

6.7.2125
1001
Draxus Porida
Main Bridge

"Commander, the Brecos is starting to take serious damage from the SLS Quintanilla," the sensor tech reported.

"Fire a series of cluster bombs at the Quintanilla then turn our attention back to the Argus," Commander M'Tak Jolan ordered.

"Aye, sir!"

6.7.2125
1012
Commander Stephanie Westphalen's Fighter

Commander Westphalen ducked her fighter under the fire of two Brentax fighters and swooped around over them, firing her lasers as she came around. The laser blast lanced through one fighter, and the ensuing fireball took out the second."

"Two for one meal deal!" she shouted into the comms. "God, I love my job sometimes."

"Commander, you've got a Brentax on your tail," Ensign Mark Roderick cautioned. "I'm in persuit."

"Thanks, Mark!" she called as Roderick's fighter destroyed the Brentax that was tailing her. "I was feeling a bit closed in there. Men never give you the space you need."

"I think I resent that comment, Commander," Roderick snickered.

"I think you resemble that comment, Mark Roderick," Sergeant Kelly Winters cut in.

"Yadda yadda yadda," Mark retorted.

"Clam it you guys," Stephanie admonished. "Let's just concentrate on these fighters."

"Commander, the Quintanilla just took a bad hit," Roderick reported. "Looks like it hit near the bridge."

"There's not a lot we can do for them, Mark," Stephanie said, frowning. "We've lost communication with the Quintanilla. I just tried. Let's just keep the fighters off her back for now."

"Yes, ma'am!"

6.7.2125
1019
SLS Quintanilla
The Bridge

The smoke was very thick on the Quintanilla's bridge. Support beams had crashed into the center of the bridge, causing dust and sharp shards of metal to be thrown into the air, making breathing even more dangerous.

"Damage report," K'Alan ordered through the dust.

"Structural damage to decks 3 and 4, Lieutenant," Jameson coughed. "Repair teams are already working on it."

"Casualties?" K'Alan asked, forrowing his brow.

"Casualties report coming in now, sir," Kim Ericson announced. "Looks like mostly bumps and bruises.

It was then that K'Alan noticed the Captain's chair had been thrown off its moorings.

"Someone check on the captain," he ordered, doing his best to maintain control of the situation.

Kim knelt beside the Captain, who'd been thrown near her console. She felt his neck for a pulse and frowned.

"There's no pulse, sir," she said softly. "He's dead."

"Lieutenant, we've lost communications, sensors and weapons," Jameson frowned. "We have minimal shields, and we've got full maneuverability, but we're in trouble."

"Kim, start working on the communications array. I want to be able to talk to our fighters," K'Alan began issuing rapid-fire orders. "Colonel, get to work on the weapons, and have a team start working on the sensors."

"Aye, sir!" Ensign Ericson and Colonel Jameson said in unison.

"We're in trouble, Kit," K'Alan said in a soft voice as he gently touched the picture on his console.

6.7.2125
1028
SLS Argus
The Bridge

"Commodore, the Quintanilla's in trouble," Tom Nichols noted from his tactical station. "We can't raise her, but she took a direct hit."

"Captain Starlos can take care of himself," Commodore Bonetti said with measured tones. "Keep an eye on her, but we need to focus on these Duhari class cruisers. Report if there's any change in communications status with the Quintanilla."

"Aye, sir."

6.7.2125
1038
Commander Stephanie Westphalen's Fighter

"Commander, I'm in trouble!" Kelly Winters called over the comms. "I seem to have three suitors."

"You're too young to have that many men interested in you at once, Kelly," Stephanie chuckled. "Let me cut in."

She swung her fighter around in an arc so that she was pointing at the three Brentax fighters following Kelly Winters.

"Hurry! I can't shake them!" Kelly whimpered.

"Don't worry, I've got them dead to rights," Stephanie grimaced as she lined up the shots. In quick succession she fired off three volleys, each one connecting with a different Brentax fighter. "Now I just have them dead."

"Thank you, Commander!"

"Anyti—"

Stephanie didn't have time to finish her statement as a Brentax fighter, damaged in battle, rammed into her Starfire from out of nowhere.

6.7.2125
1046
SLS Quintanilla
The Bridge

"We're losing a lot of fighters, Lieutenant," Colonel Jameson frowned. "I can't make out who's been shot down and who hasn't yet."

"Work on the weapons, John," K'Alan ordered gently. "There'll be time to count the dead later."

"Aye, sir," Jameson nodded.

K'Alan brought up the tactical holo and focused on the two Kovat class cruisers. He started to hum slightly to himself then headed over to the helmsman.

"Do we have full engines?" he asked.

"Yes," the helmsman nodded. "It's about the only system that's not shot to hell."

"Good. Here's what I want to do..."

6.7.2125
1053
SLS Argus
The Bridge

"Commodore, the Quintanilla has no weapons," Tom Nichols fired. "They're also reading as having no sensors or communications."

"Send a squadron of fighters over to help them out," Bonetti ordered.

"Aye, sir. Sending Red Squadron."

* * *

"Lieutenant, it looks like Commodore Bonetti is sending us another squadron of fighters," Jameson reported. "That should even out the fighter battle."

"Good," K'Alan nodded. "If my plan works, the Brentax fighters won't have a base ship to land on. At least, they won't have the Kovats."

"No offense, Lieutenant," Jameson chuckled. "But I'm not wild about your plan. You're taking a big risk."

"And right now we're sitting here with a big target on us, Colonel," K'Alan sighed. "We need to do something. If you have a better idea, I'm more than willing to consider it."

"Unfortunately, I don't have a better plan," Jameson shook his head. "I just hope yours works."

"Me too, Colonel," K'Alan muttered. "Me too."

6.7.2125
1101
Draxus Porida
Main Bridge

"Commander, the SLS Quintanilla has sustained major damage," the sensor tech reported. "They are no longer firing on our Kovat class cruisers."

"Good," M'Tak Jolan said. "Tell the Kovar and the Brecos to concentrate their fire on the Quintanilla's engines. As soon as we dispatch the Argus and the Haphaestus, we'll help destroy the Quintanilla."

"Yes, sir."

* * *

6.7.2125
1113
SLS Quintanilla
The Bridge

"All right," K'Alan said, crossing his fingers. "Take us in, nice and slowly. Put us between the Kovat class cruisers."

"Aye, sir," the helmsman said, heading right to work on getting the ship where it needed to be.

"Colonel, how much punishment can our shields take at the moment?" K'Alan asked.

"Shields are at sixty percent, Lieutenant," Jameson reported. "We can take several direct hits."

"Good," K'Alan nodded. "We're going to have to if this is going to work. This is going to be very hard on this ship."

"Yes, sir," Jameson nodded. "It will be. She's a tough little ship though."

"Let me know when we're in position, helmsman," K'Alan ordered as he began to prepare for phase two of his plan.

"Aye, sir."

6.7.2125
1118
SLS Argus
The Bridge

"Commodore, this telemetry for the Quintanilla is confusing," Tom Nichols frowned. "It looks like she's positioning herself between the two Kovat class cruisers."

"What?" Bonetti jumped up to look at the telemetry for himself. "What the hell do they think they're doing?"

"Unknown, sir," Tom frowned again. "This makes no sense."

"Any success in raising the Quintanilla?" the commodore asked.

"None, sir. They're unable to respond," Tom sighed softly.

"I sure hope they know what they're doing over there, then," Bonetti shook his head.

6.7.2125
1121
Ensign Mark Roderick's Fighter

"What the...?" Mark Roderick pondered on the comms. "Where is the Quintanilla going?"

"Looks like she's headed for the Kovat cruisers, Mark," Kelly Winters responded, a note of worry in her voice. "What's the Captain up to?"

"I don't know," Roderick admitted. "But it's not like we can really do anything to help out at this point. I think we've got enough to worry about."

"Yeah," Winters added. "Like the Brentax fighter I just shot off your tail. You are so going to owe me when we get back aboard the Quintanilla."

"Keep yappin', Sergeant," Roderick grumbled.

6.7.2125
1128
SLS Quintanilla
The Bridge

"Lieutenant, we're in position," the helmsman reported. "The two Kovat class cruisers are moving into our position."

"Colonel, are the antimatter pods ready?" K'Alan asked as the ship shuddered with the impact of a direct hit.

"Ready to drop on your mark," Jameson confirmed.

"Helm, as soon as we drop the pods, we need to be going full fusion drive," K'Alan ordered.

"Aye, sir. Full fusion drive ready on your mark," the helmsman nodded.

[456]

"Good," K'Alan nodded. He took a deep breath, looking at K'Itea's picture before giving the command. "Drop pods and engage fusion drive now!"

K'Alan gripped the armrests on his chair as he was thrown back in the chair due to the rapid acceleration.

"The pods cleared the Quintanilla's field before we accelerated, Lieutenant," Jameson reported. "They're now homing on the two Kovat cruisers."

"Holo," K'Alan ordered.

In the center of the bridge, a holographic image of the two Kovat cruisers loomed, two bright white pods nearing the two ships, gradually getting closer. After a few seconds, the pods collided with the Kovat cruisers, resulting in two giant fireballs in space.

"Now that was effective," Jameson smiled.

"Was there any damage to us in the maneuver, Colonel?" K'Alan asked.

"Shields down to thirty percent, but otherwise no damage," Jameson reported.

"Status on repairs?" K'Alan demanded.

"Communications should be back online in five minutes," Kim reported. "Sensors and weapons should both be back online now."

"Good," K'Alan grinned. "Let's go see if the Commodore needs a hand then."

6.7.2125
1135
SLS Argus
The Bridge

"I don't believe it!" Tom Nichols gasped. "The Quintanilla has just destroyed two Kovat class cruisers without having weapons online."

"Captain Starlos is a brilliant tactician," Bonetti chuckled. "I'd have been surprised if he couldn't destroy the two Kovats."

"Commodore," the communications tech called. "I have the Quintanilla online. Audio only. It's Lieutenant Bryce."

"Lieutenant Bryce?" Bonetti asked, raising an eyebrow. "Where's Captain Starlos?"

"Captain Starlos was killed early on in the battle, Commodore," K'Alan reported. "I've been in command during most of the battle."

"So you're the one responsible for that rather unorthodox move?" Bonetti chuckled.

"What can I say?" K'Alan snickered. "I never was one to conform to the norm. We've finally got our weapons back online. We're coming to assist you guys in whatever way we can."

"Good," Bonetti nodded. "We could use a little help."

"We'll be there momentarily," K'Alan said, a slight grin in his voice. "Quintanilla out."

"Well, how about that," Bonetti marveled.

6.7.2125
1249
SLS Quintanilla
The Bridge

"That's the last of them, Lieutenant," Jameson reported. "All Brentax fighters have been destroyed."

"Good," K'Alan nodded. "Recall all our fighters and start preparing damage reports and casualties lists, please."

"Recall order issued, Lieutenant," Kim acknowledged. "Lieutenant, Silvers 1, 3, and 7 and Golds 2, 3, 5, 6, and 9 were all destroyed. I'm afraid Commander Westphalen was shot down."

"Stephanie too? Damn," K'Alan swore. "I was hoping I could relinquish command to her."

"I think you did well in command, Lieutenant," Colonel Jameson winked. "You certainly managed to keep a cooler head than I would have been able to."

"Thanks, Colonel. That means a lot."

"I'll have the damage reports and the casualties lists for you shortly, Lieutenant," Jameson smiled.

"Commodore Bonetti on the comms for you, Lieutenant," Kim announced.

"Holo," K'Alan barked.

"Lieutenant Bryce," Commodore Bonetti nodded in greeting. "You did well today."

"Thank you, Commodore," K'Alan nodded, smiling sadly. "We lost some good people today though."

"Yes, I know," Bonetti sighed. "It is the price of war."

"I think the cost is too high, Commodore," K'Alan bit off.

"I'd have to agree."

6.7.2125
2002
SLS Quintanilla
K'Alan Bryce's Quarters

Lieutenant K'Alan Bryce sat staring at his desk, unable to focus. Now that he was alone, he let the tears flow, tears that he'd been holding ever since his friends were lost in battle.

He flicked a switch on his computer and sighed softly, composing himself.

Personal Log: K'Alan Bryce: 6.7.2125: The battle is over. We won.

It doesn't feel like we won, but we did.

We lost a lot of good men and women during this battle, including Captain Starlos and Commander Westphalen. I hurt from the loss of these two friends like I've never hurt before. I don't ever want to feel like this again.

On the bright side, Kit is safe. The Brentax have lost their foothold on this sector of space and therefore they can't attack my home world easily. I shall have to keep an eye on developments in this sector from now on.

I miss Kit. I miss her a lot. I think that my being in the Star League Defense Force is going to be tougher now that we're married. The long time between visits is going to be rough. I only hope I can visit her soon. I doubt I will though. Duty is keeping me here for now.

I truly wish I hadn't been here for this battle, although I fear the outcome may have been different had I not been.

K'Alan flicked the log recorder off and leaned back in his chair, rubbing his eyes.

"Lieutenant Bryce," the voice of Ensign Kim Ericson, the communications tech on duty, called over the intercom. "Commodore Bonetti requested your presence on board the *Argus.*"

"Understood, Ensign," K'Alan sighed, wondering what else could happen today. "Tell him I'll be there presently."

"Aye, sir."

K'Alan groaned softly and headed off towards the shuttle bay.

6.7.2125
2117
SLS Argus
Commodore John Bonetti's Office

K'Alan Bryce sighed softly and fidgeted as he stood in front of Commodore Bonetti's desk. He waited, somewhat impatiently, for the Commodore to notice him.

"You wanted to see me, sir?" he asked after another minute had passed without the Commodore looking up from his paperwork.

"Yes, Lieutenant," Bonetti said, looking up. He indicated the chair on the opposite side of the desk. "Have a seat."

"Thank you, sir," K'Alan nodded as he sat in the offered chair.

"Well, Lieutenant," the Commodore began. "You've had quite a day."

"You could say that, sir," K'Alan said, still a bit subdued about the day's events.

"Captain Starlos was a good man. I understand your feelings of anger and sadness," Bonnetti nodded. "But you handled the situation well."

"Both Captain Starlos and Commander Westphalen were good friends," K'Alan nodded. "They were the first people that I cared about that died in this war. I'll be damned if I let them die in vain."

"And they didn't," the Commodore smiled. "With your help, we were able to drive the Brentax out of the Corathi system."

"Good. They can't attack Duterius Prime then," K'Alan smiled sadly.

"At least not yet," the Commodore sighed. "I believe that it is still something they intend to do eventually, but we've set their plans back for quite some time at any rate."

"I see," K'Alan frowned. "You know I'll do whatever I can to prevent my home world from being destroyed by the Brentax."

"Yes," Bonetti nodded. "I saw that during the battle today. I also saw that the reports sent to me regarding you were accurate. You'll be a fine commanding officer someday. You handled you ship and your crew admirably today."

"Thank you, Commodore," K'Alan nodded.

"I'd like you to retain command of the Quintanilla until I can find a suitable replacement," Bonetti added. "I'm not sure how long the search will take, but you might be in command for a few weeks. At least while the Quintanilla is in dry dock."

"I understand," K'Alan nodded. "I assume this means the request for time off to finish my honeymoon is going to be declined."

"Unfortunately, Lieutenant," Commodore Bonetti nodded. "I'm sorry we had to take you away from that, but at the moment, I can't spare you. Welcome to the ranks of the unexpendable."

"Thanks, I think," K'Alan said, slightly bitterly.

[461]

"I have something else for you, Lieutenant," the Commodore said. "Something else you've earned." John took a box from the drawer of his desk and slid it across the desk to K'Alan. "A Golden Palm. You've earned it."

"Thank you, sir," K'Alan smiled, his first true smile since the battle ended.

"Now go. You've got a lot of work ahead of you. I want a complete damage report on my desk by the time we reach the Gamma Epsilon Station."

"Yes, sir!"

6.10.2125
0915
SLS Quintanilla
K'Alan Bryce's Quarters

K'Alan sat at his desk, staring at the blank monitor screen. He'd put off this call a while because he didn't want to tell her everything. Mostly he didn't want to admit just how hard he was taking the loss of his friends. To her or to anyone else.

He flicked the switch next to the monitor activating the comm circuit.

"Kim, patch me through to Duterius Prime, Braga Valley Great Hall, please," K'Alan said softly.

"Right away, sir," the comm tech said.

The monitor flared to life with the emblem of the Braga Valley Great Seal. Moments ticked by as he waited for Kit to appear. Finally, she did, looking as lovely as ever.

"Kal!" she grinned.

"Hi, Kit," he said with a lot less enthusiasm than Kit.

"OK. That was less enthusiastic than I'd have expected," Kit frowned. "What's up?"

"We just finished a rather long battle to retake the Corathi system," K'Alan started. "It was a tough battle."

"Are you all right?" Kit asked, a bit concerned.

"Physically? Not a scratch. Emotionally...?" he trailed off.

[462]

"Not so good I take it?"

"Kit, Thane's dead," K'Alan said, a tear rolling down his cheek.

"Oh, Lords, Kal. I'm sorry," Kit said. "I know he was a good friend."

"It gets worse," K'Alan sighed, closing his eyes. "Commander Westphalen was also killed in the battle. I'm the interim commanding officer until Commodore Bonetti can assign a new CO and XO."

"Kal, I wish there was something I could do for you," K'itea said sadly.

"I know you do, beloved," K'Alan smiled, but there was a great sadness in the smile. "But right now there's not much that anyone can do. Certainly there's no way to change what's happened."

"When will you be back, my husband? I miss you greatly."

"I don't know," K'Alan said quietly. "I doubt I'll get any time off anytime soon. Not while we're in drydock at any rate. And certainly not until the new CO is assigned."

"I understand," K'Itea nodded. "I love you."

"I love you, too," K'Alan smiled. "But now, I need to go. Commodore Bonetti needs a full report of our battle damage."

"Please keep in touch, Kal," K'Itea said softly. "I worry about you."

"I will."

As K'Alan closed the link, a tear rolled down his cheek.

To be continued...

Blitzkrieg

About the Author

Rick Bentsen released his first novel in 2001. It was a simple science fiction story that was somewhat well received. Although it never sold very well, the people that read his first novel enjoyed it immensely. From that first moment, Rick was hooked.

Rick has long loved science fiction and fantasy books and movies and that love has turned into a writing passion. He has recently added a mystery/thriller series to his normal science fiction and fantasy series as projects to complete.

Rick lives in southeastern Massachusetts which he believes is the most beautiful place in the world. Fall in New England, he finds to be the most inspirational time of the year with all the colors.

Rick can be reached through his facebook page (www.facebook.com/RickBentsenAuthor) or through his webpage at rickbentsen.com

www.ingramcontent.com/pod-product-compliance
Lightning Source LLC
Chambersburg PA
CBHW020922020726
47495CB00002B/300